With trembling hands, Runnolf untied the laces of Rowena's gown. Ignoring her weak, sleepy protests, he slipped it over her head and dropped it with her other clothes in a heap on the floor. At last she lay in unguarded innocence across his lap, no part of her denied to his gaze.

Cradling her in his arms, he knelt beside the tub and carefully lowered her into the warm water.

Rowena languidly opened her eyes and then closed them, relaxing into the wonderful sensations. Only a dream . . . except this time it was better, she could feel his presence. Her face lifted; her lips parted softly.

It was too much! Runnolf pulled her closer and kissed her deeply, then with ragged breath broke free. If he did not stop now, he would take her and the damage would be irreparable. But Rowena had desires of her own.

"Please, my lord, do not leave me," she whispered. "Please, do not let the dream end."

PASSIONS OF THE REALM

JOAN BALSER

PAGEANT BOOKS

Publisher's Note: This is a work of fiction. The charac-
ters, incidents, and dialogues are products of the au-
thor's imagination and are not to be construed as real.
Any resemblance to actual events or persons, living or
dead, is entirely coincidental.

PAGEANT BOOKS
225 Park Avenue South
New York, New York 10003

PAGEANT and colophon are trademarks of the publisher

Cover artwork by Sharon Spiak

Printed in the U.S.A.

First Pageant Books printing: August, 1988

10 9 8 7 6 5 4 3 2 1

To my parents,
who started it all.

To Roberta Gellis,
who encouraged me.

To my husband, Larry,
who supported me in every way.

To my family,
who gave me the space I needed to do my thing.

To my friends,
who never laughed at my efforts.

Author's Note

◆◆◆◆◆

HENRY, DUKE OF ANJOU, *pursued his inheritance of the English throne on several occasions. His final and winning thrust came at Wallingford during a very bitter winter night when he forced King Stephen to offer truce. All of the terms are not known, but Stephen of Blois was allowed to withdraw to safety. The following year, in November of 1153, at Winchester, Stephen formally recognized Duke Henry's hereditary right to the kingdom of England. For such acknowledgment, Duke Henry conceded that Stephen should hold the kingdom for the rest of his life, on the condition that all the magnates bind themselves by oath to Henry's peaceful succession. And, all castles erected without permission since the death of King Henry I, Duke Henry's grandfather, would be destroyed.*

Duke Henry returned to the Continent before Easter of 1154, to undertake the control of his unruly vassals in Normandy. He was besieging the castle of Torigny when he received the news of King Stephen's death. On December 7, 1154, Henry of Anjou and his wife, Eleanor of Aquitaine, crossed the channel from Barfleur to England. On December 19 at Westminster Abbey, Henry of Anjou was crowned King of All the English by the Archbishop of Canterbury.

The first year of King Henry's reign was extremely busy and important. He selected his three most important councillors: to head the royal administration, Richard de Lucy; as cojusticiar, Robert de Beaumont, Earl of Leicester; and as chancellor, Thomas à Becket. With his administrators chosen, Henry was ready to restore order to the land, which had suffered nineteen years of anarchy under his predecessor. His first order of business was to destroy the adulterine castles that had been erected. To accomplish this formidable task of destruction, the new king sent out the trusted knights of his household.

Runnolf le Geant and his men, and Rowena, her family, and keep are all fictitious, woven into a tapestry of history.

Prologue
✦✦✦✦

As was her custom, Rowena, daughter of Hugh fitz Giles, rushed out to meet her father on his return from the monastery market. Each time her father left, she anticipated the rejoicing among their people that accompanied his home-coming and the presents he would bring her. But as her father rode into the keep, she knew this trip had been like no other. Despite his ef-forts to deceive her with false gaiety, she sensed the despair beneath his words and noticed the tired lines etched into her beloved father's face, and she would not allow him to humor her. Now that she was a woman grown, she would not be treated as a child.

But it was not until they were sitting snug in their solar that evening that Sir Hugh finally told her all that he had heard.

"You know the story of our coming to the Marches," he began in a whisper.

Rowena nodded. Although her mother was dead, she remembered her parents telling of their fight to win their holdings. She knew the story well.

"What you do not know," Sir Hugh continued, "is that we hold no royal charter for the land. In truth, we do not need it, but . . ." He slumped deeper into his hard wooden chair as the weight of his troubles washed over him afresh. "The new king, Henry fitz Empress, has decreed that all must be as it was in the days of his grandfather, the old King Henry."

"But this land belonged to the Welsh," Rowena protested.

"Yea, the Welsh." He sighed heavily. "This land belonged to them only because the Earl of Chester and his sons could not wrest it from them."

"But you succeeded where they failed," she responded proudly.

"Yea . . . but I hold no charter! Therefore I have no right to the land! The new king has claimed all land not under charter from his grandfather."

"But—"

"But me no buts," Sir Hugh retorted, now more in control. "The king has spoken."

"What will happen?"

"The king will send his seneschal to disseise us," he answered, his voice now so heavy with fatigue that Rowena could barely hear him.

"The monks say the seneschal is a great

knight," Sir Hugh continued. "And that he fought beside Henry against King Louis and was with him at Lisieux and at Wallingford. He is almost a legend." He half smiled at her, trying to lighten his words. "Everyone speaks of his immense size and great strength. But no man save a giant could be as powerful and strong as they say he is."

Chapter One

✦✦✦✦

ROWENA'S DEEP, FATIGUE-INDUCED sleep lightened as the recurring dream began to take shape. Wisps of gray smoke drifted down the valley to curl menacingly around her home. She tossed restlessly as the smoke became heavier and small, insidious tongues of flame began to appear about the wooden palisades. *Fire!*

The flames became larger and fiercer, engulfing the people crowded in the bailey. She whimpered despairingly. Her father's people, who had assembled to help him stand against the king, were trapped. Their faces swam before her as the flames consumed them.

Soon the flames crawled up the earthen foundation to the keep itself, and everything was afire. Panicked now, Rowena climbed the unending stairs from bailey to keep, not quite one step ahead of the encroaching inferno. Yet even inside, she did not feel safe. She continued to climb, reaching for the sanctuary of the solar.

Trumpets invaded her dream, bringing a new element to the familiar nightmare. She thrashed the bed linens in her effort to escape. Frantically she struggled to awaken, to be free until another night.

And then the loud noise was repeated. Rowena sat upright in bed, disoriented and drenched in sweat. Her stomach heaved involuntarily as she struggled to calm herself, to sort out the real world from her dream world.

The trumpets blared again. Trumpets! They were not part of her dream. They were real! The king's seneschal had finally arrived. The fate she dreaded in her dreams was now at the gate.

With leaden heart, Rowena realized that her father must be captured, or else the king's knights and trumpeters would not now be outside. Hugh fitz Giles had been gone for almost a sennight. But there was no time for worry. Rowena jumped from her bed, hurriedly straightening the clothes she had slept in. She donned soft leather shoes while trying to hold the hair out of her eyes. Her heart beat in fear as she raced down the long flight of stairs from the keep, across the bailey, and up the wooden steps to the palisade.

Her clothing was rumpled, and the signs of her restless night's sleep were still heavy upon her. Her long blond hair flew loose about her in the morning breeze like cobwebs painted gold. Yet in spite of her disordered appearance, no one who saw her proud carriage would have a moment's doubt that Rowena was The Lady of the keep.

Norbert, the steward, scowled at her as she entered. Her presence momentarily distracted him and the nearest of the castle guard from the scene beyond the gates.

"Get out of sight," he ordered, quickly recovering his aplomb, to again become her guardian and steward. "You will ruin our plans if they see you."

A protest rose to Rowena's lips but after the argument with Norbert the night before, she had resigned herself to the necessity of a charade. Everything they feared had come to pass. The king's seneschal was at the gate, and now she must disguise herself as a servant.

"Rowena, now!" Norbert bellowed in frustration. If she did not leave immediately, all their plans would be for naught.

"Find Elaiva and Owain," Norbert shouted at her retreating back. "Remember our plans! They know to stay with you!"

Rowena's heart thudded in her breast as she rushed back downstairs to follow his orders.

"Elaiva! Norbert said we are to stay together," she panted to a gray-haired woman stuffing food into a canvas sack in the kitchen. Elaiva's normally round, cheerful face was now ashen and drawn from the strain of impending catastrophe.

"Oh, my lady! We had prayed this would never happen," the woman wailed, rushing to her mistress and embracing her fiercely.

Rowena returned the woman's embrace and then stepped back. "Norbert said . . . the plans . . ."

"Yea, plans," Elaiva said, remembering the necessity of the moment. "Fetch your belongings and meet me here," she instructed. "I will finish collecting the food."

Spurred on by fear, Rowena ran to the solar and hurriedly changed into her blue work bliaud, its hem heavy with the money and jewels she had sewn in them the night before. Carrying Elaiva's brown one, she returned to the kitchen shed.

"Here, put the brown over the blue," the older woman directed, helping Rowena to straighten the bulk and tying the sides loosely. "Now, this over them both," she instructed, handing Rowena a brown dress of her own. "This will hide your body and leave your hands free to help carry food."

The disguise would have been ludicrous if the situation had not been so dire. Elaiva was a little taller and much heavier than Rowena, and her bliaud dragged the floor by many inches. She handed Rowena her corded belt. "Wrap it around as many times as necessary. Now, let the top cover the belt . . . that's it."

Looking down at herself, Rowena had to agree that she no longer resembled the daughter of Hugh fitz Giles. Although she was trim and rounded, she now looked lumpy and squat. As Rowena studied herself, Elaiva tightly braided her mistress's hair and then looped the braids about her head.

"Now, cover your hair with the coif, and remember to keep your hair hidden and your head down at all times. Keep your hands in your sleeves lest someone notice their whiteness. And let Owain or me do all of the talking when necessary."

When Elaiva had inspected Rowena and pronounced her ready, they moved to the bailey to mingle with the rest of Sir Hugh's people. Rowena strained every fiber of her being to hear over the heavy thudding of her heart.

"I am Runnolf, seneschal of Henry, King of the English. Who speaks for this keep?" The king's knight spoke in their language, heavily mispronouncing several words, which in no way lessened the power of his voice.

Rowena's imagination was fired as she listened to the authority in the seneschal's voice. It was in no way diminished as it traveled through the thickness of the palisade walls and hovered over the people crowded into the close confines of the bailey. Rowena shivered. If his voice was any indication of his size, he must surely be every bit as gigantic as his reputation implied.

Rowena heard Norbert reply from his position on the ramparts near the gate. Hearing his firm but less powerful answer only intensified Rowena's first impression of the seneschal's power and size.

"I am Norbert, vassal of Hugh fitz Giles and steward of his keep," the young man answered.

"Your lord, where is he?"

"He rode to the assistance of his neighbor, Rolf de Witt." It was almost but not quite a lie.

Runnolf waved his hand and a knight rode forward, carrying another shield beside his own.

"Do you recognize this?" the deep voice inquired.

Norbert's throat constricted. He thought he recognized the battered shield of his lord. It was old and well used, the snarling head of a wolf barely discernible. It could have been duplicated by anyone who knew fitz Giles, but the king's seneschal did not.

"I see a shield," Norbert stammered, hoping it was a subterfuge.

"We did battle two days past, the owner of this shield and I," Runnolf said to those listening on the walls. "He acquitted himself well but he is dead."

The silence of the bailey was broken by the low moans of many people.

"Lady . . . child . . . we are sorry for your loss," Elaiva whispered, placing her arm consolingly about her mistress's shoulder. Tears welled in Rowena's eyes and a sob choked off her reply.

"I command you to open these gates in the name of Henry, your king," Runnolf called above the growing din.

"Sir knight, how do I know this is not some trap?" Norbert asked resolutely. "I know you not. And the shield is . . ." He let the sentence trail into nothingness.

If Runnolf was offended by Norbert's unfinished sentence, he gave no sign of it. He returned the level scrutiny of Norbert's gaze, measuring the man as opponent and ally.

What he saw was a man a few years younger than himself who was fair muscled, indicating a knowledge of arms but also showing that warfare was not his primary occupation. And like so many others defending the walls, his body was protected only with a gambeson.

"Priest!" Runnolf shouted without rancor.

A small gray-haired man, stooped with years, was set on the ground from his seat behind one of the knights. He limped forward.

"Do you recognize this man?" Runnolf demanded. Runnolf's question was directed at Norbert, but he indicated them all as his eyes traveled along the faces looking over the palisade.

"Yea, Sir Knight. It is Father Dominic," Norbert answered, and a murmur of assent followed. "He is of this keep."

"Does he lie?"

"Nay! He is a priest!" Norbert exclaimed.

"Then listen to his words."

Father Dominic limped closer to the walls and began his narrative. "Two days past, I was with Sir Hugh and Rolf de Witt . . . when they did battle with this knight. The fighting was fierce and bloody . . . Sir Hugh . . ." The priest's voice cracked and he hung his head for a moment before continuing. "Sir Hugh fought long and well!" he avowed, and he delivered this eulogy with great pride, but then he finished in sorrow. "With a heavy heart . . . I buried him at dusk."

"The others?" Norbert's voice choked and the priest guessed the question more than heard it.

"The men of this keep . . . none survive," he answered.

"De Witt?"

"He fled when our lord was unhorsed," the priest said, with bitterness.

Norbert, rocked by one devastating piece of news after another, clenched and unclenched his hands, longing to grab a pike and fling it at the king's knight, yet fighting to control his emotions lest he jeopardize the people's chance for survival.

"Return the priest to the injured, where he can be of service," Runnolf ordered. "He is no longer needed here."

Hastily Father Dominic was remounted and carried back through the rows of men.

"Your lord is dead," Runnolf repeated after giving the defenders time to absorb the priest's story. "Yield to the king!"

"What of the people here?" Norbert persisted.

"For those trained in arms, pledge allegiance to the king through me and I will offer a place with my men. Otherwise, you may fight to the death."

"And the others?"

Runnolf shrugged. "Of the serfs, when the time is right, they will be allowed to seek new masters. Until then, they will serve me and my men while we recuperate from battle and await word from the king."

"There are no serfs here," Norbert answered

proudly. "Sir Hugh took service only from freemen."

Runnolf's surprise was reflected momentarily in the prancing of his great black destrier.

"I will grant them the same status," he answered firmly.

Runnolf noticed an almost imperceptible relaxation in the stiffness of Norbert's neck and shoulders.

"No harm will come to you or those in your care," Runnolf reiterated. "My word I pledge in the king's name."

Norbert hesitated only a moment longer and then gave the order to open the gates.

Rowena's heart pounded. Blood raced past her eardrums, drowning out the creak of saddle leather and the clink of armor as half of Runnolf's troop moved within the bailey, the other half stopping in the archway of the gate. Rowena staggered as mounted knights pressed into the small space before the keep. Her senses swaying, she tried to count them as they stationed themselves about the walls. She lost count at twenty.

A knight of immense proportions rode ahead of the pack. Their leader was truly the largest man Rowena had ever seen, and his horse was near twice the size of normal animals.

"Steward of this keep, surrender your arms to Sir Guy," Runnolf commanded as one of his men rode forward. "And have your men do the same."

"Clever, this one," Owain the forester whispered from behind Rowena. She had not been conscious of him in the milling crowd, and his unexpected presence startled her. "See how well trained they are. He has not given them one order that would call attention to his treachery and yet they obey."

Rowena was too frightened to speak.

"Surrender our weapons?" Norbert sputtered. "But you offered us a place with your men! We have offered you no hostility!"

"I do not know you," Runnolf answered. "This may be a trap." His words were spoken without rancor or mockery.

Norbert purposefully studied the knights who surrounded them, reaffirming that resistance would be futile.

"When you have proven your loyalty, you will be accepted," Runnolf added.

His face ashen, Norbert slowly descended the wooden stairs to the bailey. With heavy heart, he unbuckled his sword and gave it to the knight who came forward. Then, dejectedly, he moved to stand before the seneschal.

Not until the last of fitz Giles's men had handed over their weapons did Runnolf dismount, dropping the reins of his destrier. He was dressed in a suit of mail that covered his arms to his fingertips. The hauberk had skirts that fell below the knee and was split, back and front, so that he might ride in comfort.

Rowena's wildest imaginings could not conceive the weight the king's knight wore so easily. Her father's hauberk had short sleeves and a skirt that fell only above his knees. And he was shorter than this knight, yet it was all she could do to carry its weight when she armed or un-armed him.

She watched in fascinated horror as the king's knight removed his helm for the first time, revealing his face. It was almost an anticlimactic gesture. She did not know what she expected, but what she saw was not the face of Satan but the face of a very hot and tired man. Fighting her inclination to feel sympathy for his discomfort, she reminded herself that he was the one responsible for her father's death and the loss of her home.

The cool of the morning had turned exceptionally warm, yet Runnolf paid no attention to the rivulets of sweat that ran down his face to disappear into the neck of his hauberk. His shoulder-length hair was dirty and matted, and he had a growth of beard several days old.

He let his gaze drift from man to man as they stood silently, and a bit rebelliously, in front of him. His gray eyes were steady as he addressed them, waiting for an answer.

With Norbert and the seneschal standing next to each other, Rowena was able to judge the true size of the king's knight. Runnolf was at least a head taller than the young steward, and twice as broad in the chest. The rest of him was hard to judge while he wore his hauberk, but she was sure that he was equally well proportioned.

"Now, show me all," Runnolf commanded.

Meticulously the two men moved through the outbuildings of the bailey, the kitchen, the smithy, the dairy, and even the small cottages of the servants. Runnolf said nothing, but his quick glance did not miss the supplies and the sharpened tools stacked everywhere, and he appeared especially interested in the stables.

"Your keep is well fortified," he remarked as he neared the steps leading to the keep itself.

"My lord provisioned it before he went to do battle," Norbert answered proudly.

"It seems your lord did many things well," Runnolf continued. "For whom did he prepare the defense? A wife? A son?"

Norbert's face lost all color and then turned crimson. "His wife is dead," he managed to stammer through a closed throat. "He had no son living."

For the first time since their meeting, Norbert did not look Runnolf in the eye. He shifted nervously from one foot to the other, keeping his gaze focused on the ground. He did not like to lie—in fact, he was not a good liar—but he felt compelled to offer Rowena every protection by keeping her identity secret until she reached safety.

Runnolf noticed Norbert's sudden change in behavior, and the small hairs on the back of his neck rose slightly, giving him a sense of unease but not of imminent danger.

"No son?" Runnolf persisted.

"No sons living," Norbert answered truthfully.

Runnolf looked at him closely, but did not ask again. "We will remain here and rest while I make my reports to the king. As you can see, Sir Lyle has already posted the men on the battlements and the horses are being stabled."

Surprisingly, this news did not seem to further distress Norbert. In fact it seemed to settle him, and Runnolf's unease began to disappear.

"Do you wish to inspect the keep?" Norbert asked, steering the conversation safely away from Rowena.

Runnolf glanced casually over Norbert's shoulder and received a nod from his man, who stood at the upper entrance to the keep.

"No, I believe the keep to be in the same splendid order as the bailey," he answered. "Dismiss your people to their homes. I will sleep awhile. Wake me when the meal is served."

Rowena watched Runnolf climb the timbered stairs to the keep two at a time and disappear within, before settling her attention on Norbert.

"There is no doubt that Sir Hugh is dead," Norbert began, addressing the assembly. His voice was shaky, but he did not allow his personal grief to overcome his responsibility to the people before him, who were still loyal to their dead lord. "Sir Runnolf has pledged his word for our safety. In return, he asks that we serve him and his men while they rest and await orders from the king.

"Go about your duties . . . as you would if Sir Hugh were still . . ." He tried to continue, but his voice was cracking. "All will be well as long as we offer no hostilities."

Chapter Two

✦✦✦✦

As Sir Hugh's people began to disperse, Runnolf sighed heavily. He had given the main hall a cursory inspection before mounting the stairs to the solar. Now, he settled himself on a low stool, his head bowed upon his chest, his forearms resting upon his thighs.

His body ached from the fierce battle fought with Sir Hugh. It had been one of the most honorable, well-fought battles he'd had since beginning his mission: reclaiming the unlicensed castles in the king's name. There had been other battles, some fought with treachery, others in which he had lost men, but there had never been one as hard fought or so dearly won.

The strangeness of the past day swirled about him like an impenetrable fog. It was easy to see that the people of the keep were genuinely grieved by their lord's death; their allegiance to him was unmistakable. The keep had been fully manned and was fairly well equipped. So why hadn't they fought?

What was it that changed their minds? he mused. Fitz Giles's death was certainly a factor, but still there must be something more that he was too tired to see. As a warrior, he had learned to be careful.

Runnolf sat on the stool, waiting for his squire to attend him, and then realizing, swore bitterly. Odo had died in the battle with fitz

18

Giles. Odo had been an extremely loyal squire, and had been defending Runnolf's back when he was killed. There were many truly fine things Runnolf could write Odo's grieving father about his son's valor. They would give him pride but would not fill the void of a dead son.

The battle had been well fought and so dearly won! Runnolf cursed again. He had lost almost half his men to death or injury. Fitz Giles's men, combined with de Witt's, had been of equal number to Runnolf's own, although under-armed; it had been de Witt's treachery that had caused fitz Giles's defeat.

If the rest of these men are as well trained as the others, Runnolf consoled himself, I will have my replacements and will not have to send to the king for more men. I only hope their loyalty to me will be as great.

Interrupting Runnolf's musings, Roger of Devonshire appeared in the stairwell. "Leben has been stabled," he said as he entered the solar. Roger had served Runnolf for some years and was attuned to his master's moods and needs. Although already a knight, he did not hesitate to divest Runnolf of his hauberk. He carried it to the corner of the room, laid it down carefully, and returned to remove the gambeson worn underneath.

During the process, Runnolf nodded only once and then remained silent. When Roger left, he stood up stiffly and wandered over to the coffer supporting the washbowl and pitcher. Absently he noticed that the pitcher was full of clean water, and he poured a generous amount into the basin. Several times he splashed water on his face, letting it run through his sprouting beard and onto his massive chest, reveling in its refreshing coolness. Not bothering to dry himself, he trudged to the large bed. He did not remove the coverlid but threw himself across it and was instantly asleep.

Down in the bailey, Rowena stood resolutely as the crowd began to thin. "Come to the kitchen," Elaiva whispered. "The best place to hide is the most obvious. For you, it will be under his very nose."

Exhausted from her efforts to control her emotions, Rowena did not at first comprehend the older woman's strategy.

"The kitchen is the busiest place in the keep," Elaiva explained to the young woman. "You can work there with the rest of us, in plain sight. And perhaps soon Runnolf will bring his own servers, and we will be free to travel with you to the monastery, where you will be safe."

Rowena gripped her servant's hand in gratitude. Words were still too difficult for her.

"You have a fine hand for pastry," Elaiva continued, slightly unsettled by the tears glittering in her mistress's eyes. "Settle yourself at the table on the far side. It will keep you from sight. For those who work in the kitchens, things will be as always, only they will see more of you than usual."

"Remember," Owain warned as the three of

them walked toward the kitchen, "keep your hair covered and your head down."

Because Runnolf had arrived at dawn and negotiations had lasted the entire morning, the side of meat for the noon meal would not be ready until nightfall. In fact, it had not even begun to cook, and was still hanging in the butcher shed.

"Elaiva, the meals must be reversed," Rowena said, forcing herself to think practically to keep her sadness from overwhelming her. "Collect food for the table. Cheeses, fruits, broken meats," she continued, concentrating on her responsibilities as chatelaine of the keep.

"Send word to Sir . . ." She paused, her rebellion smoldering. She would not give him his proper title. She would never obey him; he was nothing, an inconvenience for a time, someone she could eventually trick into revealing his weakness, and then . . . "Send word to That One. Tell him that the meals will be reversed and a light supper is all we have to offer now. The full meal will be served at dark."

Lost in her duties, Rowena was more fortunate than the rest of the servants. In half a day, the population of the small keep had doubled, causing great confusion. In the past, they had to deal only with Sir Hugh, Lady Margaret, and Lady Rowena. Now they encountered nobility every time they turned from one chore to another. Eventually the majority gave up trying to show proper courtesy to the multitude of knights, who ignored their efforts anyway.

Though Rowena was no stranger to hard work, she had never been restricted to one task for overlong or to the physical confinement of a coif. Her hair, knotted and piled on her head, caused her head to ache and reinforced her new semi-imprisoned status. She preferred to wear her hair loosely braided as her mother had; it was so simple a thing and yet, in so doing, she gave her father great pleasure. He had often complimented her on its fine golden color, and teased her for its thickness and weight. It was one of the few outward traits she had inherited from him.

But she had inherited her temperament from her father too. Buried but nonetheless present was a stubbornness that was slowly beginning to surface.

"I could not find the giant," Elaiva told her mistress as she returned to the kitchen. "But I found one other who also speaks our language," she chuckled. "At least he tries and is understandable."

"Well?" Rowena demanded.

"The young one, Sir Roger," she began, "said the knights would wait for the great meal at sundown if they could but eat a light meal now." In fact, Roger of Devonshire had told Elaiva that it would be better that way, as they had many things to do.

Rowena nodded and sighed audibly, somewhat relieved that she would not have to face the king's seneschal anytime soon.

The rest of the day passed in a blur of activity, ending at last when the fires were banked and the servants departed to find their rest.

"You will share with us," Elaiva said softly. "You cannot return to the solar with the king's knights in residence."

"What of the servants?" she inquired tiredly.

"They cannot remain there either."

"They have found shelter where they could," Elaiva answered as she led her young mistress over the sleeping forms scattered about the bailey.

Rowena had been inside Elaiva and Owain's thatched cottage many times, but she had never slept there before. Inside, the fire had not been lit and there were no candles to illuminate the extra people sleeping in the shadows. She stumbled over an inert form and then bumped heavily into the plank trestle-table. The strain of the day caused her to sob softly in frustration from the slight injury.

"You will feel better after a night's sleep," Elaiva promised as she patted the girl's shoulder. She woke Owain, asleep on a straw pallet in the corner, and told him to sleep on the floor. Then she gestured for Rowena to lie down.

"Oh, Elaiva, you are too kind. I can sleep on the floor." But Elaiva would not listen.

"It will not be the first time Owain and I have shared space without a pallet," she said lightly as she smoothed the coarse woolen rug cover and patted it invitingly. "We have often shared the rushes on the floor as well as the grass in the meadow," she teased as Rowena slumped down onto the mattress. She was asleep as soon as her head settled.

The night ended swiftly for Rowena. In order for the knights to break their fast at first light, the servants were awakened when the watch called the hour before dawn. Kitchen fires had to be built, porridge made, and the bread baked. And before the last knight had eaten, the kitchen was astir with preparations for the noon meal. Food was also in constant demand by knights going out on patrol, and more was needed when they returned hungry. Rowena had never seen so much consumed in so short a time.

Following a day behind the knights and Sir Runnolf were their personal servants, their grooms, extra horses, lightly armed foot soldiers for scouting, other foot troops with swords, and archers equipped with crossbows, all of whom were needed in case of a siege.

By the end of the third day the keep was overflowing with men, and so was the bailey. Some of the cottages had been turned into extra stables, and Rowena was forced to send displaced people outside the gates to seek accommodations with their neighbors.

But worse than the housing crisis was the food shortage. The dairy cows the keep maintained could not produce enough whey to satisfy the needs of the table. Her supply of honey, the only sweetener she knew, was quickly exhausted, and she was forced to send the children into the forest seeking wild bees for a new supply.

The small dovecote maintained by Sir Hugh was sorely depleted, and Rowena was afraid she would have to resort to butchering mated pairs to augment the heavier meals. The demesne could not support this number of men indefinitely, and Rowena was numb from the amount of food these men consumed and the amount of work involved in its preparation.

In desperation, she secretly sent word to the villains that they were not to butcher their own stock for their meals but should hide the best cattle across the mountains in preparation for the day when they would be set free. For now, they would eat leftovers. She allowed nothing to go to waste; nothing was left to spoil and no one went without.

Rowena labored from sunup to sunset, and the days seemed to blend together. The sharp pain of her father's death was still with her, but for the most part she was too busy to notice the other inhabitants of the castle as they went about their own chores. Yet whenever Runnolf was about, his presence drew her from her lethargy.

On one occasion, Rowena found herself watching Runnolf as he split wood for the forge in the blacksmith shop. He was clothed only in his braies and chausses, his magnificent body exposed to the sun. Rowena could see, through the fine pelt of hair covering his body, that his shoulders were slightly sunburned. She stood transfixed in the safety of the kitchen yet she could feel his physical power emanating from across the bailey.

His size and strength awed her while he swung the ax as if it were a sword and he was in battle. His movements were steady, methodical, and portended danger. She tried to shrug aside the strange shivers of emotion and fear that trickled down her spine as she watched him. Her mind's eye envisioned each piece of wood as his enemy. The power of his body, the determination of his movements, the graceful elegance of his killing ability both attracted and frightened her.

She watched, fascinated, as his muscles rippled with the rise and fall of the deadly weapon that seemed an extension of himself, and she hated him for being so expert a warrior. Hated him for besting her father. Yet the man was a contradiction; his strength also had a gentler side to it. When it was necessary for the farrier to shoe the more difficult destriers, Runnolf calmed the fiercest of the giant warhorses, telling them there was no danger if they submitted to his will.

Rowena also couldn't deny his calm authority or the loyalty he inspired in his men. He gave himself no airs. In the mornings he helped to groom the horses, trained his own men, and moved fitz Giles's men here and there into the vacancies within his troops. In the afternoons, when he was not writing dispatches to the king, he inventoried the confiscated goods that arrived daily. He shared all meals with his men and accompanied them when they rode patrol, familiarizing himself with the countryside.

In the evenings, after the lighter meal, the knights found time for relaxation, and Runnolf often joined them. Some threw dice, or diligently studied the chessboard, trying to beat their leader. From the gossip brought back to the kitchen, Runnolf was as formidable an adversary at the game as he was on the battlefield. In fact, the servants who had come in direct contact with him and his knights seemed to believe that he was an honest man. One who was superior in power, strategy, and fairness. One who was almost as good as their former lord.

Rowena was surprised that the man Runnolf seemed fair, not a murderous beast. To her heart, no one would ever replace her father in strength, in wisdom, in concern and care for his people. And yet, she recognized that the king's seneschal was also concerned for the well-being of his men as her father had been. His fairness she also could not deny: none of the servants or villains were ever abused. And sometimes she wondered if her father might not even admire this man.

Chapter Three

✦✦✦✦✦

RUNNOLF SAT IN the solar, shortly after the main meal, working at a large table. A sennight had passed since his arrival, and he was trying to finish his maps of the area for King Henry. It was at this time that the priest, who had not been in the area since that first day, entered unannounced.

"I ask a boon, Sir Knight," the priest interrupted without preamble. "A boon to give peace to your soul and to others in need."

"What boon?" Runnolf demanded, looking up in annoyance. Report writing and map making were not his favorite occupations, but he took meticulous care to do them properly and he hated interruptions.

"The Lady Rowena. I would pray with her for her father's soul."

"I do not know of her," was Runnolf's terse reply.

"Surely you jest, Sir Knight," Father Dominic protested vehemently. "Rowena! Daughter of Hugh fitz Giles! Where have you sent her? I would go to her and offer what comfort I might."

Runnolf stared long and hard at the priest, but the man returned the steady appraisal with a stare of his own.

"So Hugh fitz Giles had a daughter," Runnolf hissed.

"Surely you knew," the priest insisted. "He

left her here when he set out to do combat for these lands. He could not afford to divide his garrison to provide her escort to the monastery."

"What does she look like?"

"She is small, with hair the color of ripe wheat. And eyes large and soft, innocent, the mirror of her soul," the priest replied, allowing his devotion to the young girl to enhance his description. "Her skin is—"

"Cease your flowering phrases and tell me!" Runnolf commanded between clenched teeth.

"She is not too young, but not yet past marriageable age . . . born before Sir Hugh claimed these lands—"

"Tell me!" Runnolf shouted, standing up abruptly and slapping his hand upon the table, upsetting the inkwell over the scattered parchments.

"She is small," the priest stuttered, intimidated by Runnolf's rage. "Light hair . . . brown eyes . . . delicate of bone but of sturdy build."

"Did you not see her in the bailey?"

"I did not look for her there. I assumed—"

Runnolf brushed past the trembling priest and thundered down the steps to the hall, ordering his men to sound the alarm.

At the sound of the trumpets, the villains rushed from their fields for the safety of the bailey. Once they were all inside, the gates were shut and barred.

Rowena stood in the shade of the kitchen waiting to hear what the next calamity would be. She was instinctively aware of the strangeness of the situation. Something was wrong, drastically wrong, more menacing than a threat from without. She looked about her. Maybe it was the silence, when there should have been much noise if the men were preparing for a siege. Why were the knights on the palisades facing inward instead of out? And why were they not battle-ready?

A shiver of apprehension swept over Rowena as she looked toward Runnolf, who was standing on the steps of the keep, just above the heads of the people. He wore a short, unadorned tunic which hung to his thighs. On his feet were a pair of soft leather shoes. Rowena's gaze was drawn to his powerful hands and the ink-stained fingers that rested quietly at his sides. He had not shaved since arriving, and his thick new beard needed trimming. His hair fell in a mass over his deeply furrowed brow, and the muscles in his neck stood out like corded rope.

A movement at the door of the keep drew her attention. Her breath locked in her throat as she saw Father Dominic emerge. Sweat ran down between her breasts and under her arms. Even the tiny breeze of the morning had stilled as if waiting to hear Runnolf's words.

Runnolf studied the crowd assembled in the bailey. The hairs on the nape of his neck were on edge, but he did not feel threatened by his prisoners. And prisoners they would be, until the matter of fitz Giles's daughter was settled to his satisfaction. Until now he had treated them as simple country folk, incapable of subtlety or subterfuge. Apparently he had been mistaken. They had lied to him, and now they would be punished.

He waited, using the heat, the silence, the menacing presence of all his men to unnerve the assembly.

He was angry at Norbert for lying but moreso at himself for not following his original instincts. He had known that Norbert's explanation for the elaborate provisions in the keep was a lie. And he had been lax in his observations. He had casually looked through the coffers in the solar and had seen women's clothing, but had attributed it to fitz Giles's dead wife. Now, much to his chagrin, he knew differently.

"Norbert, vassal of Hugh fitz Giles, come forward!" Runnolf called in a booming voice.

With a sinking heart Norbert came forward, frantically racking his memory for some offense that would call attention to himself in such fashion. But he could think of nothing, save the matter of Rowena, that would have put such a cold edge of steel in the seneschal's voice.

From where she stood, Rowena could barely see Norbert over the heads of the people. Slowly, so as not to draw attention to herself, she pulled a stool over behind the roof support and climbed atop it. Now, from the protection of the posts, she could see everything.

"Rowena, daughter of Hugh fitz Giles, come forward!" The cold voice of authority called over the crowd.

The entire bailey was stunned into a deep
silence. Mothers enfolded children in their
skirts so they could not give the secret away.
No one looked about. All eyes remained focused on Runnolf. The whole group acted as
one, shielding Rowena's identity. These people
had truly loved Sir Hugh, and now they came
together to protect his daughter.

"Rowena, daughter of Hugh fitz Giles, come
forward!" Runnolf repeated.

The authority in his voice almost broke Rowena's immobility. She began to step down from
her vantage point on the stool, but Owain
blocked her way.

"Norbert!"

"Yea, Sir Knight," Norbert answered, his
mouth dry with fear.

"Where is she?"

Norbert controlled the urge to turn his head
and look for Rowena. Perspiration stood out on
his brow, but his lips, drained of all color, were
drawn in a tight line of defiance.

"What, no more lies?" Runnolf demanded
while grudgingly acknowledging the man's control in the face of his obvious fear.

When Norbert refused to·answer his jape,
Runnolf motioned for three knights to come forward. Without further word, two grasped Norbert by the arms while a third ripped off his
shirt, exposing his bare back. He struggled, momentarily surprised, then became still.

A ripple of apprehension ran through the silent crowd. The only sound was a slight distur-

bance in the kitchen as Rowena tried to push past Owain to answer the summons.

"Norbert, vassal of Hugh fitz Giles, you lied to me about this keep. For that you will receive ten lashes."

Rowena stiffened in shock as she heard the sentence.

"Norbert, vassal of Hugh fitz Giles, you have refused to answer a question lawfully put to you. For that, you will receive another ten lashes."

The people in the bailey moved restlessly in concern. There were very few men within the confines of the bailey who had not, at one time or another, felt the sting of the lash before coming to fitz Giles's service. It was a universal punishment but one that Sir Hugh rarely needed. His forceful personality, impartiality when sitting in judgment, and fair tenancy of the land were enough to bind his people to him.

Human nature being what it is, he had, on occasion, resorted to corporal punishment. On such occasions, Rowena had been witness. Then she had understood the need for discipline, the need to set an example, but Norbert's case was different. Norbert was obeying his lord. He must not be punished for obedience!

"Who helped you to hide her?" Runnolf demanded.

Norbert's only response was to look straight ahead, over the palisade, holding his lip firmly with his teeth. But if Norbert did not answer, there was an answer of sorts from the villains who shifted about, almost as one entity. Runnolf's instinct was affirmed. There was not a person there who was unaware of Rowena's hiding place.

"Ten strokes more," Runnolf intoned dispassionately, although he was having trouble keeping his anger in check. These people and their conspiracy of silence! "One time more will I ask. Where is the Lady Rowena?"

Norbert, more visibly shaken than before, still refused to answer.

Rowena held back a scream as a burly teamster answered Runnolf's summons and unfurled a long whip.

"Lady, hush," Owain pleaded. "Norbert understands the necessity of silence." Distressed that he must forcibly put hands on his mistress, he covered her mouth so she could not cry out, holding her against his body so she could not pull away. "Norbert will—" But he did not get the chance to finish as Rowena's teeth bit into his hand. In pain and surprise, he let her go.

"Hold!" she cried as the teamster drew back his arm. "Hold, I say!" she commanded, now more in control of her voice.

Her demand was enough to halt the teamster's motion. He turned to Runnolf, then looked out at the assembly, then back to Runnolf. A barely perceptible nod from his lord told him to relax his stance.

"I am Rowena, daughter of Hugh fitz Giles," she affirmed as she moved forward, removing the coif from her hair and using it to wipe the sweat and flour from her face. Now that the time for hiding was over, the need for deceit past, Rowena could be herself and face her enemy openly. Her step was almost light as she moved out of the shadows.

"Lady, nay!" Norbert shouted in despair. "For God's sake, nay!" He shouted, struggling against his captors, but it was of no use. He was held fast.

Runnolf watched her approach, matching her against the words of the priest. He could see that her voice was familiar to the villains, for they made way for her without having to see her. She held herself with assurance, moving lightly and gracefully as one used to the out-of-doors.

"Where have you been hiding?" Runnolf demanded, noting the dark circles under her eyes and her drawn, fatigued face.

"I have not been hiding," she answered firmly, though barely disguising her fear of him. "I have been working in the kitchen, preparing your meals."

Runnolf's brows drew together as he studied her for a moment. "Do not play word games," he snarled, although her grease- and flour-stained clothes attested to the honesty of her answer. "Why were you hiding in the kitchen instead of taking your place in the keep as befits the daughter of Hugh fitz Giles?"

"It was by my command!" Norbert answered for her. "We had to keep her safe!"

"*Your* command?" Runnolf asked incredulously. "When does a steward command?"

"We did not know your intentions!" Norbert insisted. "Our duty was to protect her!"

"What makes you think the daughter of a knight would be in danger from the king's seneschal?" Runnolf demanded, in a cold and deadly tone.

"You killed my father," Rowena answered for herself, her voice ragged with unshed tears. "What should we have expected from you?"

"Your father challenged the king, openly and in defiance of the law. We met honorably on the battlefield, where he asked no quarter and was granted none. And for this I honor him," Runnolf stated firmly and without hint of guile. "Your father possessed courage and honor. You shame him by hiding and pretending to be what you are not."

As he spoke, his gray eyes held her prisoner. She felt her cheeks burn. It was as though he looked into her very soul and could see the fear she fought to keep hidden.

"Since you have chosen the servant's life, then so be it," he concluded, seeking a way to punish her for her deceit. "I have need for a varlet. You will have to do," he said, dismissing her.

Rowena had never disobeyed any authority, be it her mother, her father, or even Norbert. But she knew she must challenge the king's seneschal and prove to him she was not a coward.

Runnolf read the signs of her inner conflict; her eyes were dilated as she fought to hide her fear. The calmness she had hoped to show her father's people was betrayed by her squinting and her tightly convulsed jaw. But Runnolf still did not expect rebellion from the girl.

"I know not the responsibilities of a varlet," she answered firmly. "You will have to find another."

There was a sharp intake of breath from the knights at her refusal. Runnolf's back stiffened.

"I will hear no naysay!" he snapped. "There is no one here who has not participated in the lie to hide you. Therefore, no one here, including you, is free of punishment."

"You would not dare to punish them for obeying their lord!" she countered indignantly.

"The king is their lord. I am the representative of the king. They have lied to the king through me!"

The power in him compelled her to do his will. White with terror, she searched frantically for a way to save her father's people.

"And if I agree to be your varlet . . ."

Runnolf shrugged his massive shoulders in answer.

"I will hear your words," Rowena demanded.

"The villains will go unpunished."

Rowena let her shoulders slump slightly and nodded her head in agreement.

"Go you inside, and I will tell you what is expected."

In a daze Rowena trudged up the endless steps. Her only consolation was the knowledge that she had saved her father's people from an unmerited punishment. Her trancelike state was shattered by the crack of the whip and Norbert's piercing scream.

Spinning about, Rowena felt her stomach lurch sickeningly as Norbert spasmodically took the pain but did not cry aloud again.

"Hold! You cannot do this," she cried, darting back down the steps and attempting to pass Runnolf. "You have no right! He has done no wrong! You swore!"

But Runnolf's reflexes were too quick for her. He scooped her up under his arm, ignominiously holding her there while the punishment continued. He held her thus even after her struggles had turned into racking sobs of grief.

"All here present, hear me!" Runnolf commanded when it was over. "No man, or woman, lies to me without punishment. Take this man to his people and have your herb woman tend his wounds."

Turning on his heel, Runnolf carried the sobbing Rowena up the steps and into the keep, where he dropped her unceremoniously on the rush-covered floor.

"Varlets have not the time for tears," he stated unfeelingly. "Get you up!"

"You are not lord here," Rowena shouted from her seat on the floor, her anger allowing her to forget the danger of defying him. "And I am not your body servant, nor will I be! I am the chatelaine of this keep!"

"I am lord here by the king's word," he responded coldly. "You are varlet here by your choice. As lord, you, varlet, will obey me!"

"You are a treacherous liar! I honor not a promise made to a liar!"

Runnolf grabbed Rowena by the front of her bliauds and hauled her off the floor, leaving her feet dangling. His short, rasping breath was in her face, and she could see the individual hairs of his beard. It was the closest to death she had ever come and she knew it. Death and freedom became synonymous to her in that moment as she threw all caution to the wind.

"You are a liar!" she repeated recklessly. "You pledged your word that no harm would come to us if we surrendered and offered you hospitality. You lied! You pledged no one would be punished for protecting me. Again you lied!"

Runnolf trembled from head to foot, fighting to control himself. He wanted to shake her, like a hound would a rabbit, until the pieces of her body flew into a thousand different directions. But he could not. She was only a woman, and women did not understand honor, obedience, and discipline.

"Norbert lied to me and was punished," he snarled, his face so close to hers that she had trouble hearing him. Soft and deadly, he continued. "I promised that no villain would be punished for hiding you. Norbert is not a villain. He was your father's steward! I did not lie to you then, nor do I lie to you now! I tell you: the next person . . . to lie to me, freeman or no, will be punished . . . punished so severely that he will pray for death."

Runnolf released her. She fell to the floor, staring in disbelief at his retreating back. Danger was a heady experience and an exhilarating one, but with it came a price. As soon as Runnolf was out of sight, Rowena began to tremble. In the heat of the afternoon, she suddenly turned cold.

Chapter Four

✦ ✦ ✦ ✦

ROWENA'S STOMACH REBELLED and her head spun. She was nearly faint and definitely ill, when Elaiva found her.

"Are you hurt?" the servant whispered as she looked around apprehensively.

"Only sick," Rowena replied shakily.

" 'Tis to be expected," Elaiva consoled as she helped her mistress to her feet. "Norbert's punishment was unpleasant."

"Norbert! Where is Norbert?"

"Owain is taking him to our cottage. I will tend his injuries."

"I must go to him," Rowena gasped as she started toward the door. Her legs were unsteady, and she was forced to lean heavily on Elaiva as they descended the stairs to the bailey.

"What of That One?" Elaiva demanded, nodding her head toward the solar.

"I do not know the responsibilities of a body servant, nor has he yet told me," Rowena answered, taking a deep breath and trying to steady herself. "I am sure he will tell me when the time comes."

They entered the cottage to find Norbert lying on his stomach on her pallet. Rowena rushed to the unconscious form and for the first time saw the marks.

Why did such a thing have to happen to her father's loyal steward? she wailed silently. Kneeling beside him, she let her anguished tears flow unchecked. In her heart she was afraid that his young life was to be sacrificed for her, and she could hardly bear the responsibility of such a sacrilege. She was too young to remember his coming to the keep, but his story was as dearly known to her as her parents' own story. The memories of her father and mother and Norbert were intertwined and inseparable.

Norbert had come to Hugh fitz Giles's service as an eager, green lad, seeking knowledge and a place to pledge his heart. He had found both with Sir Hugh and his family. And with him, Norbert brought a quick mind and a devotion to be given freely and without bounds.

As a child, Rowena had tagged along in adoring obedience as Sir Hugh taught Norbert the duties of stewardship. Lady Margaret had taught Norbert as well when she instructed her own daughter in good manners and the social graces. And Norbert in turn, under the ever-watchful eye of Sir Hugh, had been allowed to teach Rowena to hunt small game with the longbow and to recognize the tracks of the animals in the forest.

The avid student became a virile young man

and a trusted steward. Fiercely loyal, Norbert accepted his new position with great seriousness. When Lady Margaret died, the three became even more tightly knit.

During the crises, Sir Hugh delegated Norbert master-at-arms for the keep. Having been trained foremost as a steward, Norbert found the added responsibility almost overwhelming. Now the safety of all the inhabitants of the keep was in his hands.

"Oh, Norbert, why did he do such a thing to you?" Rowena sobbed uncontrollably. "You only obeyed Father and tried to protect me."

"He was punished for lying," Owain answered sullenly. "Not for protecting you."

"But it is the same!" she protested vehemently.

"You placed . . . yourself . . . in jeopardy," Norbert gasped, barely conscious yet aware of her presence. "You did . . . that . . . for me."

His words made Rowena uneasy and she recalled her last real conversation with him the night before the seneschal's arrival. They had been arguing about the need for a disguise.

"I am the daughter of Hugh fitz Giles, not a servant!" she had cried in rebellion. "I am not ashamed—"

"You are naive," Norbert had scolded, grasping her by her upper arms. "Your father is in open rebellion to the crown. When they meet on the battlefield, there will be only one victor!" He said no more, allowing her imagination to make his point for him.

"Nor do we know the honor of this knight, only his fighting ability. We do not know what

his intentions would be if he saw your beauty."
Unconsciously Norbert pulled Rowena closer.
His face softened, and there was a strange light
in his eyes she had never seen before. He had
started out offering her comfort in her distress,
but something changed. Then, her embarrassment at his touch had conveyed itself to him and
he had immediately released her.

Rowena's face flushed anew at the memory,
and she remained silent.

"I will brew him a sleeping draught," Elaiva
said, bringing Rowena out of her reverie. Her
hand softly caressed Norbert's head. "We will
take advantage of nature's way and allow him to
sleep for a day. While he is unconscious, I will
smear his wounds with salve that will draw the
pain and speed the healing."

"While I care for him, go you to the kitchen,"
Elaiva continued, practically. "The others need
to be assured that all is well, and the knights will
want to eat."

"How can I reassure them of what I do not
believe?" Rowena protested.

"You must believe it or someone else will be
injured," Owain answered. "If it had not been
for the armed knights there might have been real
trouble when he laid hands on you."

In the flickering shadows of the cottage fire,
Rowena could not see Owain clearly, yet she
thought she detected a twinge of guilt in his
voice. She was not sure, but he too had put
hands upon her, though there was a difference:
he had been trying to protect her. She paused at
his stool on her way to the door.

"Owain, ever have you done what you thought was right for me," she said as she placed her hand on his slumped shoulder. "Never have you been wrong in your heart's decisions."

Moved by her forgiveness, Owain took her hand and kissed the back of it in homage. "Lady . . ."

"I will always trust you with my life," she whispered.

Reluctantly she withdrew her hand from Owain's comforting grasp and left the cottage.

"Greetings, my child," Father Dominic said from the shadows.

"Did you tell him of my presence?" she demanded, before the priest could greet her.

"I came to pray with you for your father's soul," he intoned solemnly, ignoring her rudeness. "Will you accompany me to a quiet place?"

"My father has no need for your prayers," Rowena answered briskly, a loving child convinced of the perfection of her parent. "Why did you tell him of me?" she persisted. "Do you see the damage you have caused?"

"My child, your grief has control of your tongue," the priest cautioned her. "Come, we will pray for the repose of your father's soul."

"If you want to pray, then pray for Norbert. His needs are greater."

"The soul should be considered first," he preached. "When the soul is cared for properly, the body will care for itself as God wills it."

"I do not have time for prayers," she replied bitterly. "I must needs see that no one else suffers because of me. If you are so concerned for my father's soul, then see to the spiritual needs of his people. Then will his soul be at peace."

Rowena brushed past the stunned priest and returned to the kitchen, where she finished baking meat and vegetable pies. She was ashamed of her behavior with Father Dominic, but only partially so. She did not believe that her father could commit a sin so great as to prevent his entering heaven. The priest had given their secret away to Runnolf. For the first time in her life, she could not give Father Dominic credit for doing his duty.

As the day wore on, Rowena saw that Elaiva had been correct. Her presence in the kitchen had a calming effect on the servants as well as on herself. The work kept her hands busy and her mind occupied so that she could not dwell on her own miseries, nor on Norbert, nor on her anger toward the priest. Before she was aware of it, it was dusk and she was summoned to Runnolf's presence.

Reluctantly she washed the flour and gravy from her hands and slowly climbed the stairs. Resigned but not despondent, she calmly walked into the hall, her glance darting here and there, noting that the firepit was cleaned of old ash and plenty of wood was at hand. The tables were clean, the benches also, and the rushes on the floor had been cleared of any discarded foodstuffs. She must remember to tell the servants of her pleasure.

"Sir Knight?" Rowena addressed him as she approached, deliberately denying him the title of lord.

"There is no cloth," he stated flatly as he ran his hands across the table, feeling the smoothness of the wood from years of wear.

"Cloth is for Easter and Christmas," Rowena answered civilly. "It is too precious to waste during the rest of the year."

Runnolf studied her for a moment, noting the proud lift of her chin. He had the feeling she was trying to challenge him but did not quite know how. However, if she were, he would not accept challenge over something so logical.

"Very commendable. Nothing which is precious should ever be wasted," he answered softly, and then continued more loudly, intent on continuing her punishment. "It is time to begin your first lesson as varlet. Bring the basin that I may wash my hands before eating."

"My father and his men always washed before coming to table," Rowena quipped, pointing to the table by the entrance which held the basin, pitcher, and napkins.

Again Runnolf felt slightly irked, this time from the comparison between himself and her father.

"Did your father have a varlet?" he asked, in an impersonal tone.

"Nay."

"Well, I do," he explained patiently. "Usually the squire brings the basin, napkin, and pitcher to his lord so that his lord may wash his hands.

Since I have no squire, you will also perform his functions. Now, bring them to me."

Rowena stood indecisively for a moment and then walked to the large table. She picked up the pitcher, which was fashioned in the likeness of a sitting dog, and placed it into the basin. She placed the napkin in the empty bowl as well and carried them back.

"A squire kneels beside his lord, holding the basin, the napkin over his arm, and pours from the pitcher," Runnolf explained as he draped the napkin over Rowena's arm and settled himself on the bench beside the table.

Rowena stood still. Her father had never displayed such outlandish behavior toward his servants, and she could not decide if Runnolf was making sport of her.

"Come over here," he commanded her. "Kneel down so I can reach the basin."

Deciding that he was indeed serious, Rowena did his bidding. There was a presence about Runnolf that commanded her. She poured the water over his fingers as he washed. Her heart skipped at the power of his huge hands. And yet there was a masculine beauty which the scars of battle could not destroy. Even his nails were clean.

As Rowena felt the magic of the man, she fiercely reminded herself that she must not find anything good about the king's seneschal. She studied his hands minutely, even the hairs on the back of them, and remembered how quietly they had rested at his side in the bailey this afternoon as he pronounced sentence on Norbert. She fought an inner battle of rebellion. He was her enemy and she should avenge her father's death. How? When? Now, of course! But how?

Runnolf made a show of deliberately drying his hands as he watched Rowena's eyes squint slightly and her jaw muscles tighten. Just before she stood up, she spilled the basin of water into his lap.

Calmly Runnolf used the napkin to wipe the water from his clothes. "Your balance seems a little unsteady," he remarked coldly. "But it will improve with practice."

Whatever mischief Rowena had intended, went unserved. Yet, it was a victory in the inner battle to resist her impulse to obey.

"Now, put away the basin and begin to serve my meal."

"I do not know how to serve your meal," Rowena hissed at him. "Father always served himself, then me."

"This keep has been thoroughly cared for, and I am sure you have been trained properly," Runnolf answered, again using a bland tone. "Serve the meal as if your father were sitting here, and stop embarrassing his memory."

Rowena was stung by his words and had to fight the tears that threatened. "I have been trained as chatelaine, not as varlet," she retorted, squaring her shoulders and glaring at him.

"Then order the meal served."

Rowena nodded to the servants, and they began to bring in the trays of food that had been prepared in the kitchen and carried up the long flight of steps from the bailey to the keep.

She did as she would have done with her father, combining those actions he would have performed with her own, and managed to get through the meal.

Not for the first time Runnolf noticed the simplicity of the offering and yet its adequacy. This keep would be a jewel in any man's possession. Indeed, Sir Hugh had been a good landlord, and it was a shame he had set himself against the king.

Since the first day, Runnolf could not help but notice the attention given to every building, the precision with which the land was managed, and the obedience of the servants and villains. They gave ground before his knights yet they did so with dignity. They were well clothed in russet wool, not rags. Nor were they stupid with fear or weak from hunger. Because of their manner, Runnolf had ordered that they were not to be abused and no woman was to be taken against her will.

Runnolf's mind roamed, remembering the different keeps he had destroyed since becoming the king's seneschal. He thought of the serfs' poverty, and abject fear, in dynamic contrast to the arrogance of the barons and their riches. He even compared the overabundance of the king's court to the simplicity and plenty of this marcher demesne. The maslin bread here, made from rye and beans, was filling and much better tasting than the burned bread at the king's table. At court, the meats were either undercooked or burned to cinders, while the seasoning was uneven. The common ale here was better than the vinegary wines served at the lesser tables of those eating with the king.

Of course there was a vast difference between what was served to the king and what was served to lesser dignitaries and knights. But that system was not in evidence here. Runnolf noted that all of his men, no matter what their rank, had been served the same food.

What Runnolf did not know was that Rowena had ordered no special dishes for him as she would have for her father. Nor did she serve the best wines. That was another of her secret rebellions.

Rowena watched Runnolf's eyes grow soft as he absently ate his meal. He was far away from the present, and his inattention made her first tasks as varlet easier. Whenever his full scrutiny was upon her, it left her feeling powerless, devoid of her own will. It was only with intense concentration that she was able to withstand him.

"Did the priest find you?" Runnolf asked her unexpectedly. "He came to help you pray for your father."

"Yea, I saw him," she answered, trying to forget her rudeness and discourtesy. Hastily she murmured a prayer begging God's understanding and forgiveness.

"Your father was a brave man," Runnolf said.

"He should never have set himself against the king."

"My father did not set himself against the king. He stole not from the king nor from any of his barons. He took land unoccupied, unfarmed, and uninhabited except for the Welsh. The land was his by conquest. The king set himself against my father."

Runnolf shrugged his massive shoulders. What use was there to argue with a stubborn female?

When the meal was over, Rowena was again directed to bring the basin, pitcher, and napkin so that Runnolf might wash his hands. This time she dared not spill the water but sought some new irritant. But before she had thought of one, Runnolf had walked away to join his knights.

After that, Rowena was too busy to notice him. The tables had to be scrubbed, then stacked away for the night, and the last of the food distributed to her father's people. In the kitchen she and Elaiva banked the kitchen fires, then they walked to the cottage.

"Norbert is still sleeping," Owain reported as they entered the darkened cottage.

"That is well," Elaiva replied, and began putting fresh salve on his back.

Rowena offered to help but Elaiva would not allow it.

"Lady, rest now while you may. Tomorrow will be another long day, and you do not know what chores That One will assign you."

"I have brought another pallet." Owain nodded to the darkest corner of the cottage. "The straw is fresh and full. It will give you a good night's rest."

"Whom did you deprive that I might sleep so well?" asked Rowena quietly.

"His horse's bedding is a little thinner tonight but he will not mind," Owain answered gleefully. "No one goes near that devil so no one will notice."

"Then how . . . ?"

"While he was in the stableyard, being groomed by Lord . . . er . . . him." Owain corrected himself.

"My thanks," Rowena said, chuckling softly. "I will be sure to tell him how well I slept."

But a sound night's sleep was not to be.

Chapter Five
✦✦✦✦

RUNNOLF KICKED OPEN the cottage door and entered carrying a torch.

"Rowena!"

"Yea, I am here." Startled into wakefulness, she hurriedly scrambled up from her pallet and stood uncertainly in the middle of the floor.

"You do not belong here," he said in the impersonal tone he had decided to use when speaking to her. "As my body servant you belong within range of my voice. Never let me find you this far again."

"I have told you," she retorted after a moment of shock, "I know nothing of being a varlet!"

"Nor did you ask," he countered. "Now come!"

Rowena hurried along behind him. It was impossible to keep up with his long strides without running. In utter disbelief she heard the watch call the hour before sunrise, yet it seemed as if she had just gone to sleep. As they entered the hall, she saw a score of knights already up and armed.

"Sir Roger has armed me, since you were not available," Runnolf explained matter-of-factly. "We will be back before dark. While I am gone, attend to your duties."

"How many times must you be told—" Rowena began in exasperation, only to be cut short.

"A varlet keeps his lord's clothes clean and mended. He cleans his lord's chambers daily as well as serving his meals," Runnolf replied in what Rowena was beginning to recognize as his teaching voice. Then he added more forcefully, "While I am away, see to the things that are your responsibility."

It was too early for the normal patrol to be riding out. A subtle urgency about them all stopped the thought of rebellion that half formed in Rowena's mind. Something was afoot that might threaten the safety of the keep and her father's people.

"Will you break your fast before you ride out?"

Rowena asked, wondering if the fires had been yet kindled and the porridge made.

"Bring some cheese and fruit to the stables," Runnolf commanded. "But first fetch my helm and sword from the table in the solar."

Unconsciously responding to authority, Rowena hurried to do his bidding. The sword was almost as tall as she, and very heavy. Carrying it, she felt exceedingly clumsy. She wrapped the belt about the hilt haphazardly in her haste, but it insisted upon coming unwrapped. In exasperation she let it hang, picked up the helm, and hurried down the stairs. Rushing, she paid scant attention to the circling stairs and her voluminous skirts. Her feet tangled in the hems of her many bliauds and she fell into the hall, sprawling at the feet of Sir Roger. Disgusted, he picked up the scabbard and sword but left her lying on the floor.

"These country oafs will never learn properly," he swore under his breath in Norman French as he buckled the weapon about Runnolf's waist. Once satisfied that it was on properly, he retrieved the helm from where it had slid across the floor.

"It is a shame you cannot remember how it was for you those first days," Runnolf chided him softly, also speaking in French. "Firmness is necessary but never discourtesy," he continued as he reached down and lifted Rowena to her feet. "You were older when you came to my service and long used to handling weapons. But here, fitz Giles would not have had—"

"My father did for himself," Rowena interrupted, acutely embarrassed but angry that they were speaking as if she were not present, and worse, that her father was made to sound a knight of little or no worth. "He dressed himself and armed himself! He was a man grown, not a child to be cosseted!" She continued in English. She was too disturbed to think of the proper French words.

Runnolf stared at her as if seeing her for the first time, stunned that she was speaking his native tongue. "More lies and secrets?" He did not wait for her to answer before stalking out of the hall.

"Do not forget the cheese and fruit," an older knight reminded Rowena kindly, and patted the shaking girl gently on the shoulder as he passed by on the way out. Rowena followed him down the stairs and hurried to the kitchen to begin assembling the food Runnolf had ordered.

"Willa, cut the cheese into large hunks." Rowena loaded her skirts with apples. "And help me carry these things to the stables. Grab a pitcher of ale," she called as she herself picked up the largest pitcher.

Runnolf's mount stood outside the stable area while he was in discussion with some of the men who would stay behind.

The knights helped themselves to the cheese and apples, and drank from the communal pitchers. Few offered a courteous "thank you" except for the older knight who had spoken to Rowena earlier.

"How are you called so that I may address you properly?" She dropped him a short curtsy of respect.

"I am Sir Lyle," he answered and moved on to make room for another.

All had broken their fasts except Runnolf. Rowena waited outside the stables for him. She took pity on Willa, who was uncomfortable around the large horses and unusually taciturn knights, and allowed her to return to the kitchen with the leftovers.

With the noise in the bailey Rowena was not aware of Runnolf's destrier until he was behind her and snorting loudly. Startled, she squealed and spun about, finding herself staring up into the face of the huge black stallion. The bailey was instantly silent, except for the creak of leather as the other horses pulled on their reins, anxious to be away from the black.

"Rowena," Runnolf called softly from the depth of the stables. "Be as still as you possibly can. I will be with you in a trice." He approached her slowly.

"Do you think me lack-witted simply because I do not know how to be a varlet?" Irritated by his instruction, Rowena turned her attention back to the destrier. The enormous war-horse snorted again, this time pawing the ground and dropping his head as if to butt her.

"Are you hungry too?" she crooned softly to the giant beast, opening her apron for his inspection. "There is not much left. Would you like an apple?"

The horse seemed to understand her words

and raised his head, once again looking at her from his lofty height.

"I am sorry there is not more." She held her ground and did not back away in fear.

He snorted and stamped his hoof into the dirt, then dipped his head into her open skirt and helped himself to the three remaining apples.

"Your master will not like you eating all of his food," she whispered conspiratorially. "If you are not careful, you will find yourself his varlet as well as his horse." She giggled, and gently rubbed his velvety nose.

The destrier had a reputation for viciousness and rarely allowed anyone besides Runnolf near him. There was a deep bond of respect and love between the two, that even the best grooms could not equal. Yet here stood a young woman, unafraid and apparently accepted.

"Father would have loved to own so fine a destrier as you," Rowena half whispered, as she looked into the large brown eyes. Her own eyes had a softness to them that overcame the fatigue in her face and made it quite lovely.

"Where do you go?" Rowena asked Runnolf, bringing herself back to the present as he moved cautiously to the destrier's side and picked up the trailing reins.

"Tell the villains to watch for raiders." He ignored her question, then said offhandedly, "There is a possibility that the Welsh are raiding in the area." He led Leben away from Rowena before mounting, and galloped through the gates.

Rowena froze at the news. Runnolf must have

discovered some of the stock missing, and now was blaming the Welsh for her orders.

"Oh, well." She chortled to herself as she started back to the kitchen. The Welsh were only seen when they wanted to be seen. And even if they were blamed for the missing stock, it was unlikely they would be found or punished.

Rowena had respected the Welsh and their strange ways of fighting from an early age, when she listened to her father drill his men on the best methods of combating them. Now, after many years of skirmishes and raiding, there was a peace of sorts, and Rowena was sure there would be no danger from them. She even planned to approach the Welsh in case she needed assistance after the keep was destroyed. That is, if she could find them. For the most part, they moved about like wisps of smoke, phantoms and shadows.

With Runnolf gone, the garrison dispensed with the formality of eating in the hall and arrived in the kitchen to break their fast, and Rowena was busy throughout the morning. She asked Elaiva to reverse the order of the meals, planning the main meal to coincide with Runnolf's return at dark.

When all was in order in the kitchen, she decided it would be a good time to go to the solar. She needed to make peace with the room, now that her father was gone. Slowly she climbed the stairs. It was a wonderful home, such a haven of love; what a shame it would soon be destroyed by the whim of the king. She stopped on the top step and looked into the room. It was the same and yet different. Runnolf's presence was everywhere, his soft shoes beside the unmade bed, his clothes strewn across it as though he had hurriedly dressed. His personal travel basket was beside her father's coffer. . . .

Instinctively Rowena raced to the coffer and lifted the lid. Her father's belongings were ruffled but nothing seemed to be missing. She dug deeper, looking for her mother's things, and found them also intact. Then she shut the lid firmly, embarrassed that she had silently accused Runnolf of theft.

The knight's papers were scattered across the large table. Cautiously Rowena rummaged through them, not truly spying, she told herself, just looking for the sake of looking. There was a half-finished report to someone about the contours of the countryside, but ink spilled over most of it made it illegible. Several scraps of maps were scattered about but they too had ink on them and were unrecognizable. Guiltily she left them alone.

Rowena was still not sure what the responsibilities of a varlet were, but she did know her duties as chatelaine of the keep. She began to clean the solar, knowing that whatever she left undone would be brought to her attention. She stripped the bed of dirty linen, then fluffed the bolster and feather mattress, removed fresh linens from the coffer, and deftly remade the bed.

Then she carried the soiled linen downstairs. Standing in the deep shadows, she wondered if the laundry would ever be clean again. Or would it burn to ash along with everything else? In anguish, she thought of the loving care her father had put into their home over the years. The ladders between the floors had been replaced with steep circular stairways. The firepit in the main hall had been hooded with a device that directed the smoke outside, and the solar had braziers for heat. Open windows, which offered no protection, had been fitted with grids for defense during siege and with stretched hides in winter to protect against the cold. But it would all be gone soon, and there was little she could do about it.

Shrugging away her sadness, Rowena returned to the solar. She ignored Runnolf's travel basket as she moved about the room, straightening the light coverlid on the bed, moving the candle from the bedside coffer to the larger table and then back again. Finally she decided she could pass by his personal belongings no longer. The only garments Rowena had ever handled were hers and her father's, and she felt as if she were probing the seneschal's most secret identity. Cautiously she opened the lid to the travel basket. There were not many things but they were all in need of a thorough washing and some needed mending. Her cheeks stained with embarrassment, Rowena hastily shut the lid and walked away.

She stood at the window, staring out over the fields and cottages and finally looking to the orchard at the foot of the mountains. A small stream bubbled forth from a spring in the mountains that separated their land from the Welsh. It had been dug out to form a deep, quiet pool. It waited for her now, if only she dared.

Runnolf's words of last evening ran through her mind. "Stop embarrassing his memory!" It had been like a slap in the face.

She would no longer be a coward! She would behave as the daughter of Hugh fitz Giles!

The later summer heat had continued mercilessly, and Rowena had not bathed since the coming of the king's knights. And his clothes were in need of washing. Without another thought, she dashed to her own coffer, withdrew a bliaud and summer kirtle, then grabbed Runnolf's basket of clothes. Cautioning herself to be calm, lest she be stopped by one of the knights on guard, Rowena descended to the bailey and stopped at the kitchen to get a batyldoure.

"Willa, tell Elaiva that I have gone to the stream to do laundry," Rowena said as she started across the bailey and out the gates.

Rowena was more fortunate than most women in that she lived far away from the harsh restrictions of society and the rigid behavioral limitations imposed on women. She was in the habit of coming and going as she pleased, within the confines set for her by her loving father. And surely Runnolf would not learn of her brief outing.

The freedom of walking down the road was exhilarating; she was so excited to be away from the bailey she hardly felt the weight of the basket or the intense heat. Nor did she feel in any danger. She was on her own land, surrounded and protected by the king's knights and at peace with the Welsh. Her step was light, almost a skip that wanted to be a run, but she forced herself to walk. As she neared the orchard, the smell of ripening fruit, the sheltering shade, and the cool water urged her to hurry, but again she forced herself to walk so as not to draw undue attention.

At last, entering the shade, she let restraint fall away and ran toward the pool at the heart of the orchard. Tossing the basket aside, she kicked off her shoes, waded into the pool, and knelt in the refreshing water. She let its clear coldness wash over her, removing the dirt from her skin as well as some of the tension that had possessed her. Happily she stripped away many layers of clothing down to her kirtle and began to beat them clean with the batyldoure. She sang, she hummed short melodies, skipping from refrain to refrain, never finishing one before she was sliding into another.

When she had finished her own clothes and hung them to dry, she emptied Runnolf's clothes into the pool. She washed them also, but this time she used the batyldoure with a vengeance, pretending that she was giving the huge knight the beating of his life. She repeated every name she had ever heard her father or his men call one another even though she did not know the meaning of some of them. But the fierce mood only lasted a short while, and she soon was back to singing as she worked.

Chapter Six

❖ ❖ ❖ ❖

RUNNOLF RETURNED TO the keep in a foul mood. They had found no sign of the Welsh, only a few broken twigs along an almost impassable trail where several sheep had been driven.

Entering the solar, he saw that the bed had been made and that his travel basket was missing. He assumed that Rowena was somewhere in the bailey doing laundry, so he called Sir Roger to help him disarm and then went to the windows hoping for a breath of air. The weather was too warm for comfort, making him edgy and short tempered.

Looking out over the meadows and farmlands, Runnolf saw in the distance a lone figure who seemed to be carrying an awkward object. The figure was just entering the orchard. A serf after ripening fruit he supposed, and then corrected himself: a villain. The people here were free.

Fitz Giles, Runnolf murmured to himself, studying the landscape. You had a miraculous touch for the land. Why, oh why, did you set yourself against your king?

Runnolf's gaze drifted to the cottages along both sides of the road leading to the keep. Without having been in any of them except the forester's, Runnolf knew that they were of the finest. The roofs were thatched with straw and reeds, making them tight and warm. There was no doubt in Runnolf's mind that they were still as clean now as when newly constructed. As clean as the outbuildings in the bailey. Fitz Giles would have had it no other way.

Runnolf shook his head sadly. Fitz Giles had lost so much, and now his daughter had lost it also. But what one man lost, another would find. He would write Henry and suggest that this keep be claimed by the crown instead of being destroyed. His mind made up, Runnolf scratched a hasty letter to the king and went in search of a messenger.

Then he decided he needed a bath, clean clothes, and a shave. Maybe there would be some dry already. In this heat, everything should be dry in seconds; everything, that is, except perspiring humans. Anticipating a temporary relief from the heat, Runnolf went directly to the kitchen to look for Rowena.

"She took the batyldoure," Willa stated simply as if that explained things.

"Where did she go?" Runnolf demanded, irritated by the vague answer.

"To the stream to wash, my lord," Willa replied quickly, becoming alarmed.

"To what stream?" The icy edge of anger replaced the irritability in his voice, leaving Willa trembling and barely able to answer him coherently.

"In the orchard," she stammered, now totally frightened. Why weren't her answers satisfying him? With a shaky hand she pointed in the general direction of the orchard beyond the bailey walls.

"She did not have my permission to leave

the keep!" Runnolf thundered in disbelief.

"Is she a prisoner here, my lord?" Elaiva asked, drawn to the conversation by Runnolf's angry tone. "You left word this morn that you would return by dark. Lady Rowena postponed the main meal until the evening. She will be back in time to serve you but now she obeys you by doing your laundry." There was no lack of courtesy in Elaiva's explanation, nor did she fear to speak openly.

"That addle-brained daughter of fitz Giles's is going to get herself killed," Runnolf swore under his breath as he turned and headed toward the stable. If that happened, he certainly would have an uprising on his hands. He was not afraid of the villains, but it would be a shame to be forced to kill them because of a slack-witted woman.

On his way to the stables, Runnolf stopped only long enough to disarm one of the sentries coming off watch. He buckled the belt and then slung it over his shoulder, knowing full well it would not fit him around the waist. Disregarding either saddle or armor, he led Leben out of the stables. There was no doubt in his mind that the lone figure he had absently watched earlier was Rowena.

Leben was as tired and hot as Runnolf, but he knew his master's moods. He offered only token protest when Runnolf mounted.

Entering the orchard, Runnolf paused to listen. Far ahead, he could hear the constant slapping of something against water. Quietly he withdrew his borrowed sword, hefted it to judge

its balance, and then urged Leben toward the
sound.

Ears pricked, the beast moved deeper into the
orchard. The closer they came, the more Runnolf
was sure that he also could hear talking. Did he
hear only one voice? No one seemed to be answering.

They stopped at the edge of a small glade.
Runnolf stared in disbelief at the golden
woman in the shaded pool. It was Rowena, but
Rowena as he had never seen her before. Now
there were no bulky clothes to conceal her full
figure. The sweat and dirt that had hidden the
lustrous gold of her hair had been washed
away, and the lines of fatigue in her face had
disappeared. Only the smudges under her eyes
remained.

She stood knee-deep in a pool of clear water.
Her wet kirtle clung to her as skin. Her wet hair
glistened as it fell loose, cloaking her in fine
gold. There was color in her cheeks from the
cold water, and she was utterly unaware of her
surroundings as she happily beat upon his
clothes with the batyldoure.

His anger at her treachery caused him to ignore
her beauty. Another lie! Not a lie, he corrected
himself, but certainly not the truth, either. She
had hidden her beauty with the dirt and grime of
her labors. Runnolf cursed himself yet again and
urged Leben forward into the clearing.

"By what form of woman's devilment do you
transform yourself?"

Squealing in fright, Rowena dove into the
deep center of the pool. She held her breath until

her ears thudded with the effort. When she could hold it no longer, she surfaced slowly.

"It is you!" she gasped when she saw that there was no danger. "You should not sneak up on people and scare them."

"Your carelessness will get you killed," Runnolf snarled, trying to control his anger. "Come out of there and I will escort you back to the keep."

"There is no danger here," she protested. "You have your patrols out, more than my father ever had. And the villains would not harm me. How am I to be killed unless it is you, scaring me and causing me to drown?"

"The danger is in your stupidity," Runnolf answered coldly. He gave this woman very little credit for her intelligence, but a great deal for treachery. He was now convinced that not only was Rowena a liar, she lacked even common sense. "If one of my patrols had come upon you, you would have been dishonored and I would then have been forced to punish them because of you." He spoke very precisely, hoping to impress upon her the danger.

"Did you not forbid your men from taking any woman against her will?" she demanded angrily. "And do your men not obey you? Therefore, there is no danger."

Runnolf stared at her. Her ignorance was appalling! "Men obey when the eyes of authority are watching," he tried to explain. "When the eyes of authority are elsewhere, things happen. Even more, there are reports of Welsh raiders in the area. I told you that this morn."

"The Welsh!" Rowena almost shrieked in derision. "If the Prince of Gwynedd or his brother Cadwaladr were about and wanted to do us ill, we would never know it until it was too late. They are excellent woodsmen."

"And I suppose you are not afraid of the Welsh," he sneered.

"I have no reason to fear the Prince," Rowena retorted. "My father was at peace with him!"

"And Cadwaladr?"

Rowena recognized the trap he had led her into and nearly bit off her tongue in consternation. She had said too much. She stood with the water gently lapping under her chin, glaring at him through slitted eyes.

"Father fought them on their own terms and won," she replied, carefully measuring each word. "They respected him and made peace."

Runnolf could imagine such an agreement. After all, had he not himself defeated fitz Giles, though still holding him in the highest esteem?

"And Cadwaladr?" he repeated.

Rowena refused to say more.

Runnolf misunderstood her silence, assuming it to be arrogance. He wanted to shake her as he had yesterday. It had been the only time since his first encounter with the inhabitants of this keep that he had felt in total control. But that momentary control had been at the price of his own self-restraint. And that price was too high.

"I will tell you again," he said, forcing himself to patience. "Come out of there and I will escort you to the keep."

"Sir Knight," Rowena began placatingly. "You have allowed your destrier to undo an afternoon's work. If I may retrieve those muddied clothes, I will rewash them and hang them to dry."

Runnolf barely looked to where Leben was standing but backed him away from the clothes scattered about the ground. Other than that, he refused to move farther away.

"I ordered the meals to be reversed," Rowena continued, encouraged by his cooperation, "so that when you returned tonight, you would be fed unbroken meats." Rowena moved closer to the shore, her knees now resting on the shallow bed of the stream. She could come no farther without exposing herself to his hostile gaze. "I will return to the hall in time to serve at your table."

"You cannot remain here alone. Finish your chores. I will wait."

"You do not expect me to come out with you watching!" she exclaimed in indignation. "Have you no sense of propriety?"

"And have you no sense of honesty, daughter of Hugh fitz Giles? I have found more treachery in this keep than in all of Henry's court!" he thundered in return.

"The villains are honorable people who have pledged their word to my father to guard and protect me! There is no treachery in holding to their given word!"

"The villains, aye. They are with honor. But what of you? I would have thought that this far from the intrigues of court, women might hold to the truth. All of you must be born with treachery as your true nature. Even your father's blood could not prevent it in you."

Rowena was stunned. For a few minutes she had thought that she was winning her way, but clearly she had been mistaken. She opened her mouth to protest but was curtly interrupted.

"Be done with your deceitful prattle! Finish your washing!"

After long minutes of waiting for Runnolf to turn at least his head, Rowena began to shiver. Stubbornness grew to anger as she realized that he had no intention of giving her the privacy she demanded. Enraged, she stood and splashed out of the pool to retrieve the dirtied garments. A flush of embarrassment, mingled with the heat of anger, rose to her cheeks and her ears burned as she suffered his scrutiny. This was altogether improper! She violently beat the muddied clothes before tossing them across low-hanging branches.

She was still consumed with fury when she was finished with the clothes. Defiantly she glared at him, hoping he would feel her anger and now, at least, have the good sense to turn away. But he remained impassive, oblivious to her.

But Runnolf himself felt anything but aloof. He tried hard to maintain the fury he had felt earlier, but her femininity was easily penetrating his reserve. He was aware of her every attribute. Her full breasts jiggled with each movement. Her nipples, sensitive to the cold, boldly thrust themselves against the wet, finely woven kirtle.

As a mocking charade to modesty, her hair fell about her shoulders like a cloak of fine golden threads. He wanted to brush it from her face, to run his hands through the long silken strands, to use it to hold her to him.

Runnolf had had few dealings with women, and those were purely from the need to satisfy his body. Most he treated with scant civility, never warmth or interest. He did not believe Rowena herself deserved respect, but he would give it to her in her father's name. Sitting uncomfortably on Leben, he felt his clothes constricting his body. He was aware that his animosity had been replaced by a growing desire that needed to be eased. But he would not allow himself to harm her.

Rowena quickly waded out of the water and picked up her dry clothes. She was almost to the large apple tree when her courage deserted her, and she darted behind its scant branches, but they had not the screening effect she believed.

If Runnolf had not been in such dire need himself, he would have laughed outright at her predicament. Her efforts to maintain her modesty and dignity and to remain hidden were strangely provocative. As she wrestled to replace her wet kirtle with her dry one, his problems became more acute. She was causing more havoc than if she had brazenly stripped and stood naked before him! He imagined the feel of her body, his hands moving over the roundness of her hips and buttocks, the sweetness of her cool skin.

Long golden strands of her wet hair dripped

over her dry kirtle, setting fire to Runnolf's imagination. Instead of outlining her every curve and valley as the wet one had, the dry kirtle was now a mixture of textures to tantalize him. In exasperation Rowena bent over, pulling her hair free and wringing it out much as she had done the clothes earlier. Runnolf groaned as he viewed her buttocks through the soft material.

Rowena had been complimented on her beauty, being the only Lady of the keep, but she had no way of knowing how truly lovely she was. All her life she had listened to her father sing praise to the beauty of her mother, and she had never considered that someone would accord her the same adulation.

Keeping her back to the knight on horseback, she hung out the rest of the clothes. She was determined not to return until they were dry. Seeking a space in the filtered sunlight, she settled herself to wait, combing her hair with her fingers. She had felt Runnolf's intense gaze upon her ever since his arrival, and she could cope with it no longer. She glanced over her shoulder and saw such a strange expression on his face that for a moment she was concerned for his health. There was a glitter, a deep intensity in his look that was settled entirely on her. Her fingers, tangled in her long hair, became weak and unresponsive to her will.

Chapter Seven

✦✦✦✦✦

INSIDIOUSLY THE POOL beckoned to Runnolf as it had to Rowena, and he felt an urgent need to submerge himself in the cold water. Rowena's presence, the heat of the past days, the fruitless search for the raiders, and the knowledge that his patrols were out ensuring their safety, all combined to entice him to recklessness. He glanced around quickly for intruders.

Rowena watched over her shoulder as Runnolf sat astride his giant destrier as immobile as a statue, his sword still lying unsheathed across his knees. It was hard for her to believe that two such large beings had been able to enter the orchard and come upon her so silently. Only the Welsh were that quiet. But then, she reminded herself, she had been beating the laundry and singing loudly. She herself had made it possible for them to approach her unnoticed.

Rowena watched as Runnolf fought with his own wish to bathe in the cold stream while mistrusting the unknown countryside. He looked around, apparently satisfying himself that all was well. He sheathed the sword and slipped quickly to the ground. Again he searched the immediate vicinity, then glanced at Leben, who had moved unconcernedly to the edge of the stream and was quietly cropping grass and eating fallen apples. The only sound in the orchard was the tinkling stream, Leben's teeth sharply clicking together as he cut the clover short and clean, and the buzz of flies.

Hastily Rowena averted her glance as Runnolf began stripping off his tunic, boots, and chausses. She felt a searing pain in the center of her being that set the blood racing to her face and her heart beating wildly. It was not the first time such pain had struck her unexpectedly, but this was the most severe and awe-inspiring. It had happened several times in the past week, each time when Runnolf was near.

With the pain came a strange sensation. And when it was gone, she was left feeling weak and listless, with an emptiness inside, a wanting for more. But more of what, she did not yet know. Heat radiated from her body, and she was short of breath as if she had been running. Yet the only running she had done was in her mind as she tried to flee the temptation that swept over her. She wanted to see what he looked like without his clothes. But she accepted the pain as an intuitive warning. Such sights were unworthy of a woman, married or no.

Rowena heard the water splash as Runnolf entered the pool. Then all was quiet again. She knew that if she dared, she could see right through the crystal-clear water, but she fought the temptation. Snatches of Father Dominic's sermons against the sins of the flesh filled her mind. Deliberately Rowena forced herself to look at him, to see if he had guessed at her sins of immodesty. Then she held her breath as she let her gaze steal down his body to the pale pink of his buttocks before swiftly forcing herself back to less dangerous thoughts.

Gazing at him so shyly, she became intrigued by the illusion of light that filtered through the leaves and played upon his body. He stood motionless, the slight current massaging his skin. Even in the deepest part of the pool, his head and shoulders were still out of the water, reminding her again of his immense height.

Runnolf turned and laid his head back, letting his hair float, to be rinsed of grime and sweat. The cold spring water had momentarily eased his fatigue. She could hardly believe the difference in him. Were her eyes playing tricks on her? His features seemed softer now, more relaxed. His eyes and mouth had a brilliance about them that was almost inviting.

In spite of her earlier anger, Rowena was relentlessly drawn to this giant of a man. Her fingers ached to touch him, and she desired to be as near him as physically possible. She had never felt so for any man, and it threatened her plans for rebellion and eventual freedom.

Without realizing when she had moved, Rowena found herself sitting on the side of the stream with Runnolf's level gaze upon her. She searched his face and found nothing to welcome her or encourage her to openness, but she could not be silent for long. Her natural friendliness, her stubborn nonacceptance of gloom, overcame her reticence.

"My father dug it," she told him, her voice still husky with desire, her eyes soft and dreamlike as she boasted of her father's accomplishment.

"Your father may have done many things," Runnolf answered, "but he did not dig this stream."

"Not the stream," Rowena corrected him, almost laughing at his obtuseness. "Only the pool. At first it was for the newly planted trees, but then he had the center dug deeper. After that it became a cooling spot on hot summer days."

"If your father had spent half as much time teaching you responsibility and caution, as he did making the keep run so smoothly, you would not find yourself a servant to another," he reminded her before shutting his eyes, trying to dismiss her presence from his mind.

The censure in his voice against herself and her father hurt Rowena immensely. She wanted this knight to respect her, but above all she needed him to respect her father as much as she did, and to recognize once and for all his right to the land.

"If I had met you at the gates as Hugh fitz Giles's daughter and allowed you entrance," she asked softly, "what then would have happened?"

"You would have been allowed your jewels, your wardrobe, and your freedom," he answered without hesitation.

"It is all the same," she sighed. "You will burn the keep, and I will still have my freedom."

"Without your jewels and your wardrobe," he corrected her without opening his eyes. "You forfeit them with your pretense. But I will give you escort to your relatives to honor your father."

"My father had no dealings with his family during his lifetime," she answered firmly. "I will honor his choice after his death."

Runnolf studied her between slitted eyes. He detected no slyness or deceit, but he could not entirely trust her innocence. After all, he had trusted these people before and had been played false.

He watched as she listlessly pulled her hair over her shoulder and braided it loosely. In one easy motion she stood up and slipped on a clean peach-colored bliaud of fustian. Quickly she moved to the old blue one hanging nearby and shook it out. She was saddened to have to cover the peach, because it was one of her best, but . . .

"Deceit is no longer necessary once you have been found out," Runnolf said coldly.

Startled, Rowena froze as still as a fawn in the forest. She had thought his eyes were closed, that he was ignoring her. She looked at him in bewilderment, blushing scarlet to the roots of her hair and thinking guiltily of the small treasure sewn into the hem of her gowns. Did he know of it also?

"The bliauds," he said indifferently. "One is all that is necessary. You have been found out."

Rowena's embarrassment intensified. Should I tell him? she wondered silently to herself. He already believes me without honor, so what purpose would it serve to reinforce his view? she argued with herself. Better another time, when he is not so cold and distant. Carefully she folded the bliaud and set it aside.

"Are any of my clothes dry yet?" he asked, forcing himself to briskness. For one as large as himself to be completely submerged was pure luxury. Mentally he made note to return here when there would be no distractions and he could enjoy the tranquillity of the place alone.

Rowena inspected the clothes that were hanging from every available tree limb, collecting the dry ones and moving the still damp ones farther into the fading sunlight. Her heart was heavy at the distance that Runnolf kept between them, even though she knew she was somewhat to blame.

"There is a pair of chausses dry and a tunic," she answered, laying them out for him. "And all these fine white garments. I do not know what they are called."

"Hold it up and let me see what you are talking about."

Rowena dutifully held up a large white garment with long sleeves and wide cuffs. The skirt of the garment was slit in four places.

"That is a sherte," he explained, his voice dropping into its neutral tone.

"The material is the finest I have ever seen." Rowena was genuinely awed as she studied the fine weave of the linen.

"The material is from Anjou. It is called chainsil. I had several made for me, but they were never properly finished."

"I did not see any cut cloth in your travel basket. If you will give them to me, I will finish sewing them for you. I can use these as a guide."

"They are finished enough to wear," Runnolf

answered offhandedly. "What is not finished is the fancy needlework at the neck, cuffs, and hem. But needlework of that kind is not counted in the duties of a varlet."

Rowena's eyes clouded with tears. What had she done to be rebuffed so? Yet surely he was only reminding her that she had given up her status as pampered daughter of the lord and now was merely chatelaine and untrained body servant. Carefully she folded the shertes and placed them in the bottom of the basket. The rest of his clothes were almost dry, and she folded them into the basket also. She would hang them about the solar and they would be dry by morning.

As she worked, Rowena saw Runnolf out of the corner of her eye. He rubbed himself briskly and then began to wade out of the pool. She deliberately kept her back to him, giving him as he dressed the privacy of which he had deprived her.

"Give the basket to me," Runnolf commanded, when he saw her lift it and balance it on her hip.

Rowena almost protested, but fought the urge. It was a long, hot walk back to the keep, and the basket of damp clothes would become very heavy, very soon.

Runnolf walked over to his war-horse and mounted, then watched closely to see that Leben did not become agitated and was only mildly surprised when the giant allowed Rowena to approach unchallenged. She handed the basket up to him as he directed and then began to lead the way out of the orchard.

"Rowena, when we get to the road, I want you to ride pillion. But be quick to step aside if Leben offers any resistance. He has never allowed any to ride so before, but for some reason he tolerates you. I will see how much."

Runnolf realized that if he had to dismount and walk the destrier to the keep, pacing himself to Rowena, he would lose what benefit he had gained from his bath. And besides, it would be interesting to see how Leben behaved with Rowena on his back.

"Well, if he tolerates me so well, maybe I should be his groom instead of your varlet," she quipped. "At least, I know about grooming horses and—"

"I do not have need for a groom," Runnolf answered levelly, "only a varlet."

"If he will tolerate so few, then who grooms him?" Rowena asked, becoming more interested in the beautiful destrier.

"Sometimes Sir Roger. But I do as much as possible," he answered.

They were on the road now. Runnolf shifted the basket to his hip to prepare for lifting Rowena, but she ignored him.

"What happens when you are at court?" she asked.

"What happens to what?" he countered in exasperation.

"What happens to Leben? Who grooms him when you must be with your king?"

"I do all that is necessary. Now come." He held out his hand to her.

Rowena stood still in the middle of the dirt road.

"What is the matter with you?" Runnolf demanded.

"I do not know how to ride 'pillion'. I do not know the word you use."

Runnolf studied her carefully. Her eyes were clear and looked straight into his. He knew she was not lying.

"Pillion is when someone rides behind," he began. "You sit sideways with both feet to one side."

"That is a silly position. Why would someone ride like that?"

"Some women prefer it. And very young pages are sometimes too short to ride a palfrey astride."

Rowena nodded her head slightly, considering his answer. "I can understand young pages," she replied slowly. "But what woman would want to ride pillion? She could not hunt in such a position."

"Some women are very spoiled and cosseted," he answered briskly. "Now come, I wish to test Leben."

Rowena approached the giant destrier and Runnolf's offered hand. He had her slightly off the ground when Leben began to prance sideways, forcing him to release her immediately.

"I do not blame you," Rowena coaxed as she cautiously stroked the giant's head. "If I were a fine destrier like you, I would be insulted to have someone riding me who did not know how."

"Can you ride astride?" Runnolf demanded.

"Verily," she retorted. "How else would I hunt?"

Surprised, but not displeased, Runnolf held out his foot for her to step upon and hefted her into position behind him.

Rowena could feel the tension in the giant and knew that he was bunching the muscles in his hind legs to pitch her off, and Runnolf also, if he could not hold on without a saddle. Without waiting to be told, she dismounted ungracefully.

"Now what?"

"You will have to walk," Runnolf snapped, for once irritated at Leben's behavior. "And we will have to walk with you."

"I could ride in front of you," Rowena challenged, enjoying the discomfort the destrier's antics were causing his master. "It is the only place, except where you are, that we have not yet tried."

Runnolf's jaw clenched shut against a sharp retort. He stuck out his foot again and lifted her up in front of him. Leben pranced a few steps and then stopped, laying his ears back along his head.

Rowena lay over his neck, gently stroking him. "You are very beautiful," she crooned softly. She could feel the quivering tension build again. "And you are so very strong. Surely I am not too heavy for you?" As she moved forward, stretching out ever so gently, her legs brushed against Runnolf's. She could feel the tension in him also as he tightened in anticipation of trouble.

"You must get down," Runnolf commanded quietly. "As soon as your feet hit the ground, run for cover."

Rowena ignored him. It was too late. The destrier started to prance sideways again. Her heart missed its regular beat as Leben swung his head back and snapped menacingly at her bare leg. She heard the teeth snap shut and waited for the pain. When there was none, she breathed a prayer of thanksgiving that he had not bitten her. Leben rolled his eyes at them both and pawed the ground.

Rowena entwined her hand tightly in his long black mane as he dropped his massive head down between his front legs. She never once stopped talking, trying to reason with the giant as if he were a person. "If you throw me off," she gently crooned, "I will be bruised and all the clean clothes will be dirty."

Unexpectedly, Leben threw his head into the air, his front hooves coming off the ground only slightly, then stomped forward and gave a short buck with his rear legs.

Rowena squealed delightedly. For all of Leben's immense size, he was taking little bucking steps, enough to unseat a poor rider, but not a good one. He was playing with them, testing them, challenging them!

Within a few minutes, Rowena could feel Runnolf relaxing his grip about her waist, and for the first time she was aware that he had been holding her, trying to protect her against being thrown and injured.

"You have won Leben to you," he said quietly. "A talent with animals is very special and very rare."

"Thank you," Rowena whispered, ecstatically happy. It was the first compliment Runnolf had ever given her. But she did not have time to dwell on its uniqueness, because Leben was not yet finished playing. Together they matched their movements to Leben's as he strutted and pranced, paraded and kicked, constantly changing his gait whenever his riders became too complacent. The mighty horse held his head high, his eyes alight and his nostrils flaring, issuing an occasional shrill neigh to announce his pleasure to the world.

The heat of the sun gave Rowena's skin a glow. Her eyes sparkled. She was invigorated from the refreshing bath and delighted at the cavorting charger. For a short time, she was able to banish the sadness of her life, to forget tomorrow and the unknown that faced her. She reveled in the great destrier's beautiful movements and the heady exuberance of his spirit.

Nor was Runnolf immune to their infectious happiness. The joys of his life had always been through simple things—the warmth of a campfire, dry clothes in wet weather, a good, faithful horse to carry him into combat. His lips twitched in an unusual smile at Rowena's squeals and Leben's antics.

At first, amazed that Leben had accepted Rowena, Runnolf had felt a twinge of jealousy. For years, the great horse would not allow anyone else to share their comradeship. He tried to reason away the feeling and discovered a slight similarity among the three of them. They were each alone, each with nothing to call their own, each having only the other. His resentment faded further when he saw that Rowena was able to put aside her grief as she laughed.

As private as Rowena believed her world to be, her ride to the keep and entrance into the bailey did not go unnoticed nor uncommented upon. The servants and villains greeted her quietly, touching their hands to their foreheads, seemingly not surprised by her lack of disguise or her presence astride the destrier. Not so the knights in Runnolf's retinue. They stared in openmouthed amazement; first, that anyone would be riding with Runnolf, and second, that the lumpy varlet had metamorphosed into a lovely woman.

Their stunned amazement lasted only until Runnolf had helped her to dismount and handed down the basket of clothes. As Rowena made her way up the steps to the keep, she was forced to contend with the open admiration for her ample figure, now fully revealed. She was able to block out the more demeaning comments because they were spoken in Norman French. She murmured another prayer in thanksgiving for her mixed blessings: She understood and spoke their language only slightly.

Further dissociating herself from the remarks, Rowena made the erroneous assumption that Runnolf found her lacking. She had little knowledge of men other than her father, who had been open and forceful. She had no understanding of Runnolf's iron control or his distrust of women. Nor could she read much from his few facial expressions. To her, Runnolf's behavior demonstrated that he did not find her attractive, that she was his varlet and that was all she would ever be to him. The knowledge hurt but made it easier to function normally. She tried to convince herself that the only people about whom she cared, the only people whose opinions mattered, were her father's people.

Once in the solar, Rowena hastily hung the damp clothes up to dry and then prepared to assist the servants in the preparation of the coming meal. She took only enough time to brush the dust from her clothes. She did not bother with her hair because it would take too long to brush out the tangles and braid it again.

Chapter Eight
✦✦✦✦

RUNNOLF TURNED HIS back on Rowena as she went up the steps of the keep. Yet he was unable to put her out of his mind as he rode Leben the short distance to the stables. Where her body had jolted next to his during the ride, there was now an emptiness.

However, there were more important matters at hand than a beautiful, deceitful woman. Methodically Runnolf groomed Leben, assuring himself that the destrier had plenty of grain and water before closing him in the stall for the night. He then went in search of Norbert. He must find fitz Giles's steward and question him more thoroughly. If the daughter, as well as her beauty, could be hidden so well under his very sight, then what else was hidden from him?

"He is still sleeping," Owain said when Runnolf entered the cottage unexpectedly. "Elaiva, my wife, has given him something to help him sleep through the pain."

"Sleep is good but too much is dangerous," Runnolf replied as he crouched down beside the sleeping man. Carefully he removed the light piece of cloth that was spread over Norbert's back to keep the flies off.

"Elaiva knows what she is about. She was taught by Lady Margaret," Owain answered defensively. "On the morrow, when the pain is less, she will allow him to waken."

"Who are you?" Runnolf asked, now directing his attention to the older man.

"I am Owain."

"What position do you hold here?"

"Whatever you order, Sir Knight."

"The occupants of this keep play word games. Answer me straight! What position do you hold here, now and before our coming?"

"I was huntsman and forester to Sir Hugh," Owain replied promptly. "Now I have no position except to care for the boy."

"How long were you with fitz Giles?"

"We came here together."

"How long?" Runnolf repeated quietly, all the while having difficulty keeping control of his temper.

"Ten, twelve years. A lifetime. In truth, I know not. They were good years and one does not count happiness."

"Only when it is rare and long apart," Runnolf added, more to himself. "Conduct me throughout the bailey. Show me its strong points and its weak ones. Tell me the history of the place. And I warn you, tell me no lies and play no more word games. Speak truth and fear nothing from me. Speak false and you will regret it."

"There is no history to this keep." Owain rose slowly and waited for Runnolf to precede him out of the cottage. "Many of us came here of free choice with Sir Hugh and Lady Margaret. I, for one, have never regretted it.

"As for strengths and weaknesses," Owain continued, "you are the king's knight. You know better than I."

"Your words are flattering," Runnolf snapped. "And there is no need for flattery."

"I intend no flattery, my lord," Owain bristled. "You are the king's seneschal. That speaks for you."

Standing outside the cottage, Runnolf could see the man clearly now. There was no slyness about his face. His light blue eyes were clear and steady in his weathered face. The squint lines about them attested to his years of service out-of-doors, and the lines around his mouth, which were now firm, also showed an upward turn, an indication of a happy disposition.

"Why were you not with your lord in battle?" he demanded.

"He ordered me to stay. If necessary, I was to counsel Norbert in the defense of the keep and ultimately add protection for the Lady Rowena. Norbert is very capable, but I know better the ways of the forest and the trails. I would be able to find her shelter if he could not."

"You too were part of the lie?" Runnolf probed, as he continued his second inspection of the stores in the bailey.

"There was no lie," Owain answered, looking at Runnolf directly. "We are duty bound to defend the Lady Rowena from any . . . and all."

There was no need to challenge Owain's words, but Runnolf did not miss the implication that the folk of the keep were still pledged to their dead lord.

"How?"

Runnolf saw the stubborn set of the man's jaw and the levelness of his gaze and knew no answer would be forthcoming. And truly, none was needed. A forester lives in the forest, makes his living from the forest. Therefore they would take Rowena to the forest to live.

"Since I act in the king's name," Runnolf continued, "why did the Lady Rowena hide from me?"

"She is very beautiful," Owain answered simply. "A man could be tempted beyond his strength."

Runnolf did not respond to this simple but truthful statement. The Lady Rowena was in fact very beautiful, and Runnolf himself had already been tempted but not yet beyond his power to refuse. "What are the weaknesses of this keep?" he asked, abruptly changing the subject.

"The greatest weakness is fire. Drought and starvation second."

Runnolf nodded. "And its strong points?"

"The well has not gone dry in all the years we have been here. Even in this heat, the well still holds water." There was a long pause before Owain continued. "And there is not a man here, untrained though he might be, who would not die for Lady Rowena."

"I noticed the sharpened plows and scythes. Were they trained to use them?"

"A little, but not enough to be of use against knight and destrier. Unless, of course, they could get close enough to kill the destrier or to unhorse a knight . . ." He shrugged, leaving the rest unsaid. "In truth, only afoot against your pikemen would they stand much of a chance," was his too-honest reply.

"Yet they would have tried if she had ordered it?" Runnolf persisted, even though the grim picture Owain painted brought chills to his spine.

"Yea, if she had ordered it. But she did not. She chose to protect them from such a catastrophe."

Runnolf was impressed. He recognized the truth in Owain's answers and respected him for it. The two continued to inspect the bailey, and when Runnolf was satisfied, he led the way to the storeroom beneath the keep.

"Is there a hidden escape?" he asked as he

walked off the dimensions and searched with a raised torch for any sign of the unusual.

"Nay, my lord. If there were, we would have insisted Lady Rowena use it upon your arrival."

"What alliances did fitz Giles have with his neighbors?"

"He taught the Welsh to respect him, both in battle and in fair trade," Owain responded proudly. "Until your coming, he had alliance with none."

"What did my coming have to do with it?"

"Sir Hugh did not trust de Witt but was forced to form alliance with him to defend his land."

Runnolf remained silent as he continued to examine the barrels of flour and vegetables for anything suspicious. "Is there anything that I have not yet seen?" he asked finally.

"Nay, lord."

"Is there anything that I have seen, that is not what it appears to be?"

Owain studied the king's knight before answering. "All here is as it is supposed to be," he answered honestly.

"Verily," Runnolf said at last.

Momentarily satisfied that he had searched as diligently as possible, Runnolf ascended to the hall, where he found that Rowena had made good her word. The meal of unbroken meats awaited him, and she stood beside the bench and table he preferred. Many called greetings to him as he entered and crossed to his seat. He returned their greetings with goodwill and seated himself.

While Runnolf expected another evening of

clumsiness and challenges, Rowena instead brought the basin, pitcher, and napkin and knelt demurely beside him as he had instructed her the night before. As he washed his hands, he was acutely conscious of what a beautiful woman she was.

Her eyes were downcast, their long brown lashes fanning her cheeks. The soft peach color of her bliaud as well as the ride in the sun had given her cheeks a blush of color, while the untamed strands of gold from her loosely braided hair framed her face. Unbidden images of her in the pool swept over him, and he felt desire for her stir deep in his loins. Her femininity was obvious. He could not understand why he had not seen it before. But then, he reminded himself, he had not been looking before.

The talk around the hall centered on the training that was planned for the morning, but Rowena paid it no attention. She was more concerned with the grumbling of her stomach. She had eaten little this day, and her stomach protested loudly at her neglect.

Runnolf's confusion at Rowena's submissive behavior and his attempt to control his memory and mounting desire caused him to be even more gruff than usual when he spoke to her, reinforcing her conclusion that she held no interest for him as a woman.

"A varlet eats when his lord is finished," Runnolf rasped as he slid back his bench and stood up. "There is no need to go hungry in the midst of all this plenty. Nor does a varlet need his lord's express permission to eat if his knights are still at table."

Rowena stared at him in disbelief. Was there nothing he missed? Her pride screamed at her. Did he truly know everything as his eyes said he did? She flushed crimson yet accepted his lesson with stoic fatalism. No one could keep secrets from the king's seneschal.

Runnolf's gruffness caused comment among his knights, and even he knew he was being unreasonable in his behavior toward her. He was not normally a gregarious man, but he was fair in his dealings with his subordinates. When the meal was over, Runnolf lingered amongst his knights as was his custom, speaking with one, then another. He watched a chess match but his mind was not on the game. From under lowered brows, he watched Rowena to be sure she ate. He also studied her as she moved about the hall, directing her servants as they cleaned the tables and stacked them against the wall for the night.

He saw her dismiss her servants when all was to her satisfaction and then look about the hall as if in some doubt. Then he saw her square her shoulders and resolutely begin walking in his direction. Seeing this, he left the hall and ascended the stairs to the solar. From the determined way she moved, he was convinced that she was up to some mischief. The meal had gone too uneventfully, and he did not want her to have an audience to her next challenge.

Rowena saw him leave and knew he had seen her coming toward him. She was perplexed by his strange behavior, yet she knew she must follow if she were to find out what next was expected of her. She picked up one of the candles near the stairwell and lit it from a flambeau on the wall before following him. He had told her that, as his varlet, she must be within calling distance. But where was that? Surely not in the hall with his knights! She shuddered. She would not be able to endure it if one of them came to her bed in the middle of the night.

As she slowly ascended the stairs, she heard a few remarks, which she tried to block from her mind. But as hard as she tried, she could not do so with much success. She knew that they expected her to share Runnolf's bed. Did he expect the same?

Her hands were trembling by the time she reached the solar and her mind was a jumble of incoherent thoughts. She stepped into the room. Without difficulty, she located Runnolf's shadowed form near the wall, darker than the rest of the shadows because of his dark clothing. The nearness of him, the reminder of her own undefined desire so recently put into crude words by the knights, nearly unnerved her as she stood reeling at the top of the steps.

"Sir Runnolf?" she began hesitantly, not knowing how to ask her question.

"It is past time you arrived," he snapped, in an effort to forestall her mischief. He stood with his back to her, pretending to stare out the window, because of her effect on him. "The candle has not been lit for the night. The bed has not been turned down, nor are—"

"I have been serving at your table below," she protested, surprised at his attack. "How can I be in two places at the same time?"

"A varlet's duty is to his lord, even if he must be in ten places at one time," he intoned in his teaching voice.

"How many times must I tell you—" Rowena began. She was finding it difficult to carry on an argument with his back. Her jaw tightened in frustration, her eyes squinted against his uncompromising authority. "I do not know the duties of a body servant! I cannot know what you expect if you do not tell me."

"That is why I came up here," he explained coldly. "So you would not have to be reprimanded before others. Now, one of your duties is to see that the night candle is lit. Another is to see that I have clean clothes for the morrow, and another is to see that the bed is turned down properly. In winter you will see that a bed robe is close at hand."

"In winter! You are to be gone by then! You said you would be here only a short while."

"I do not remember putting a limit on my stay," Runnolf answered thoughtfully. "But it is of no consequence. I have not yet heard from the king."

Rowena stamped across the room, jammed the candle into the empty holder on the coffer, and jerked back the covers, ignoring the bolster when it fell to the floor.

"And remove these clothes you have allowed to lie scattered about. This is not a laundry yard."

Rowena, angry and defiant, grabbed the garments and threw them into his travel basket before slamming the lid down hard. "The solar is no longer a laundry yard," she hissed through gritted teeth. "Your bed has been turned down like a small child's. Your candle has been lit so you can find your way in the dark. Would you also like me to undress you?" Rowena held her breath in shocked surprise at her own boldness. Before his coming, she would never have dared to speak so.

"A varlet's duty is to help his lord dress and undress," Runnolf intoned, aware of two meanings to her question. He was also aware of her angry beauty. Her breast heaved with suppressed emotion and her usually soft brown eyes glittered. He felt his desire for her mounting again but fought to control his dishonorable thoughts. "But you seem to have difficulty in learning the simple things," he continued. "We will forgo that phase of your training until you have progressed further.

"By-the-by, who helped arm your father?" He would need this information so that he could replace her. Owain's words echoed in his mind. If she was constantly too near, he was not sure he would be able to honor his pledge.

"When I was very young it was Swayn and Lady Margaret," she answered promptly. "Later, he taught me."

"Those are all the instructions for tonight," he said dismissing her. "Unless there is something you do not understand."

Rowena blushed as she remembered the question she now must ask. "Last night . . . I mean, this morn . . . you said . . . I was to always sleep . . . within your call." Her voice choked in her throat. They stood across from each other, separated by space yet each feeling the presence of the other.

Runnolf heard her unasked question with growing alarm. Yesterday, when he did not know of her physical beauty, he had not cared where she slept as long as she was within call to act as his varlet. Today was another matter altogether.

And then he thought of the many court intrigues he had witnessed and the wily maneuvers of the women, and he became suspicious of her innocent question. Had she not offered to undress him for bed? This was in complete opposition to her modest behavior at the pool. "Where did you sleep before?" he demanded.

"At the foot of the bed." Instantly she became frightened by the implication of her answer. "In my truckler bed," she hurriedly explained as she went to pull it out for him to see.

Runnolf studied her as she stood near her bed. As with all things at the keep, the literal truth was in front of his face. But whether or not he should believe it was up to him. He would have to test the situation to find out.

"That will do," he answered in a hoarse croak. "A varlet rises before his lord and retires after all his chores are completed. Tonight, there will be an exception. I will examine the keep before retiring as is my duty. Be abed before I return."

Runnolf was pleased with the strategy he had devised. If Rowena hoped to gain anything, she would have to make the first move. If he came back and she was not in his bed, he would know that the modest woman at the pool was Rowena and he would hold her untouchable.

Runnolf made the rounds of the keep, stepping over sleeping bodies and inspecting sentries. He even went to the stables and looked in on the horses, delaying his return to the solar as long as possible. When there was no longer an excuse, he turned his step in the direction of the keep.

Quietly he climbed the last set of steps and stood motionless just inside the solar. The bedside candle was lit as well as the larger night candle. He could see that the covers had been turned aside but that his bed was empty.

Slowly, cautiously, he walked over to Rowena's truckler bed and bent down beside it. He could dimly see the outline of her body in the shadows, but he knew she was not asleep. Her breathing was erratic and she was trembling; despite the heat, she was buried beneath the covers.

Her fear disquieted him. He sighed again, more heavily than before, then stood up, walked around to the side of the bed, and sat down. Fatigue washed over him as he undressed. He stretched out full length upon the bed and laced his fingers behind his head.

He took several deep breaths, attempting to calm himself enough to sleep. But sleep was a long time coming. He could not dispel the glorious vision of Rowena at the pool, her wet kirtle clinging to her body, her wet hair dripping silver streams across the secret places of her womanly body.

It was almost dawn when he finally began to dream.

Chapter Nine

✦ ✦ ✦ ✦

THE DURATION OF the sweltering heat was extremely unusual. The inhabitants of the keep watched the sky for rain, but it remained bright, hot, and cloudless. Temperatures rose within the buildings and tempers were short.

A truce of sorts existed between Rowena and Runnolf, but it wore on their nerves and strained their control. Within themselves they were secretly torn between the desires of the body and the noble ideals they held so dear. And for Rowena, there was another obstacle placed there years before by Father Dominic and his incessant preaching: the fear of sin and damnation.

The two adjusted their lives to the necessities of the keep, staying away from intimate situations. Rowena slept in her kirtle on the truckler beside his bed, and despite the heat, she had a covering over her when Runnolf returned from his patrol of the keep before retiring. And she was up and dressed before he awoke in the mornings.

For his part, Runnolf made a habit of returning to the solar late. He tried unsuccessfully to assuage his needs with a willing woman from the village, but it was only a physical release and therefore temporary. Rowena was ever present in his mind, and when he saw her huddled in her bed with the covers tightly drawn under her chin, the need and the desire rekindled anew.

The coupling with the other woman helped to forestall any attempt on Rowena's virtue, but it also intensified the strain between them. He was never truly content, while Rowena dreamed incomplete dreams of what might have been had Runnolf come in peace and been accepted by her father in friendship and blood bonding.

Rowena was usually a very fair-minded person, but the events of the past weeks were overwhelming and beyond her control. She had to blame someone, so she blamed the king and his seneschal for her father's death. And she still blamed Father Dominic for his part in her discovery as well as for his part in betraying Norbert. And because of this lack of forgiveness, she could not in good conscience participate in the masses offered by Father Dominic or Runnolf's chaplain, Father Bruno.

Late one afternoon, as Rowena was preparing to descend to the hall to oversee its readying for the night meal, she heard a low rumble as of thunder. Thinking the long-prayed-for rain had finally arrived, she rushed to the window, but the sky was still as clear as it had been for days and the air, although moving slightly, was hot and dry.

Straining, Rowena looked as far into the distance as possible from the window as the thunder persisted, then raced to another and another. From the east window, far off down the valley she saw a large dust cloud but she could not see what caused it. Her feet barely touched the treads as she rushed down the spiral staircase to the hall and out onto the top steps that led to the bailey. She paused, momentarily confused by the lack of alarm and the casual way the knights gathered on the palisades around the bailey. She heard a familiar whistle and her heart sang. Ecstatic, she searched the dust for her father's dapple gray destrier.

"Cheval!" she shouted when she spotted him. He was a little ahead and to the far side of the herd, allowing himself to be led by the groom assigned to his care. Yet it was difficult to judge who was being led. Cheval knew the valley and was nearly pulling the groom to the pasture where grass, shade, and fresh water awaited them. She watched him move with the grace and carriage so familiar to her.

Cheval, like Leben, had been especially bred for agility, stamina, intelligence, and fighting instinct. As was the way with their breed, the gray deliberately picked up his large feet in a quick, snapping motion that showed off the soles of his enormous hooves. His head was held high as he whistled welcome.

"Where has he been?" Rowena asked those around her, her face flushed and alive, her eyes dancing for the first time in days.

"They have been at de Witt's," Runnolf's deep

voice answered from behind her. "I left orders for them to remain there until they recovered from their injuries."

"He was injured?" Rowena's voice was high in alarm.

"Some deep cuts that will heal. His worst complaint is his age."

"He is very old," Rowena replied sagely as she studied the gray from a less personal level. "He is older than I."

Runnolf stifled a laugh at her remark. True, Rowena was old not to have been married or betrothed before now, but she was not too old to be considered extremely desirable. Runnolf forced his attention back to the horses.

Rowena decided that despite the gray's age, he moved with no sign of infirmity, no sign of strain from the journey. Reassured, she was again filled with the happiness of his homecoming.

Her father had set great store by the gray, choosing him over a younger, less experienced destrier. His intelligence and battle skills had been the deciding factor. But Rowena loved him because of his grace and gentleness. Now she watched in fascinated silence as he galloped down the road past the bailey, muscles rippling through his great body.

The only thing to mar the occasion was the absence of her father. Rowena, wiping a tear from her eyes, refused to give in to grief at this happy hour. Suddenly she had an overwhelming desire to share her joy with the destrier, to somehow feel her father's presence through his favorite war-horse.

"Cheval, wait! I am coming!" she called as if she expected the gray to hear above the noise of galloping hooves. Wrapping her skirts about her legs, Rowena jostled her way through the knights who lined the steps and made her way across the bailey.

Again she heard Cheval's familiar whistle, but this time there was an answering, angry response from the stables that froze her to the spot, sending cold chills of foreboding through her.

"Leben!" The name held frightening implications. Stallion! Leader! Challenger! *Life!* Rowena's mind whirled.

Cheval had been accepted as leader by the herd that just arrived. It was obvious by the way he positioned himself in front of the others. Even his groom rode in his dust. And this was his home.

When Rowena heard Leben's frenzied scream of challenge, she was propelled into action. The sound of splintering boards galvanized the men. They began running toward the stables, and Rowena could distinguish Runnolf's powerful voice above the din and chaos.

"Close the gates! Close the gates before—"

Rowena repeated his orders at the top of her voice. Over and over again, she cried them out as she herself hurtled through the slowly closing portals and raced over the bridge and onto the road.

In a fog, Rowena watched Cheval lunge away from his groom, his ears flat against his head. The groom was nearly jerked off his palfrey but he clung tenaciously to the lead rope. However, his valiant effort was wasted when Cheval turned in aggression, viciously lunging at the lesser horse and almost knocking it to its knees.

Having gained his freedom, the gray destrier moved into the open and screamed defiance at the unknown intruder.

The heavy oaken gates had closed too slowly. Leben had escaped! He brushed Rowena aside in his rush to meet the challenge of the old destrier.

Too concerned for Cheval's safety to think of her own, Rowena scrambled to her feet and chased after Leben into the still swirling dust.

"No! Oh, no!" she cried in despair, her lungs near bursting. When Rowena felt herself caught up from behind, she fought with all her might.

"You can go no farther," Runnolf panted in her ear. "It is too late for us to interfere. Needs must they settle this themselves." His voice was filled with emotions that were unrecognizable to Rowena.

For Runnolf, the past few minutes had been filled with too little action, taken too late. He cursed himself for not foreseeing this inevitable conflict and its catastrophic outcome. Yet he exalted in the willingness of both destriers to fight for supremacy. He gloried in Leben's willingness to challenge as much as in Cheval's willingness to defend, though to him, the outcome of the battle was a foregone conclusion. Youth, strength, and rest would overcome intelligence, experience, and old age.

Runnolf's exuberance was touched with sadness for Rowena as she pitted her meager strength against him, fighting for freedom to assist Cheval. Wildly she looked about for assistance, but of the knights and villains present, none offered any. Everyone's attention was on the two monarchs.

Realizing her struggles were futile, Rowena too turned toward the combatants. Through the thinning dust she saw the two destriers facing one another, still as statues, each measuring the other, each trying to outstare the other, each testing the other's will.

Gone was her father's gentle giant. In his place stood a brutally aggressive war machine incited by the natural instinct to do battle with a rival and claim victory.

Rowena stifled a scream of alarm as the two mighty warriors unexpectedly surged forward. Their screams reverberated off the hills that protected the valley. They reared, surprisingly agile for their weight and height, their forelegs pawing, striking indiscriminately. Teeth bared, they lunged at each other's throats, each maneuvering to get a death grip on his opponent.

With raking teeth, Cheval bit Leben on the shoulder. It was a deep, ripping tear, but the gray could not maintain his grip long enough to do mortal damage. Instead he left a deep, ragged wound that sent the black destrier screaming in rage.

Kicking out with hind legs, they strove for

positions that would enable them to deliver a fatal blow. Again they reared, black mane and gray whipping in the air as they struck again and again before dropping to the ground on their forelegs to stare at each other, waiting for the other to submit.

Cheval feinted an attack to Leben's legs and with a scream of triumph jerked his head up, catching the black under the jaw. The force of Cheval's upward momentum lifted Leben off his front feet. With the black off-balance, Cheval swiftly repeated his last maneuver, lifting the mighty black higher into the air, trying to expose his underbelly.

Agilely Leben whirled away, shrieking in anger that Cheval's years of experience had twice caught him unawares. Yet the older destrier was tiring. His movements were not as quick and as sure as before. Cheval struggled for breath. Still he refused to give ground.

Without warning, they lunged again. The sound of hooves striking bodies made Rowena and Runnolf groan in unison. Cheval turned and kicked, putting every ounce of power into the blow. Had it landed, it would have seriously injured the black; however, Leben saw it coming and instinctively shifted his massive body. Again his agility saved him. He was grazed, off-balance and stumbling, but he did not go down. The gray stood, his sides heaving, pulling great gulps of air into his lungs, allowing Leben to regain firm footing.

They reared and kicked, bit and battered each other until, at last better positioned than Cheval, the black landed a crushing blow with his mighty hind hooves to the gray's ribs, knocking him off his feet.

Rowena screamed in agony as Leben savagely reared and dropped his full weight onto Cheval. Her stomach heaved, and she could feel the bile rise in the back of her throat as the sound of breaking bones filled the air. Again she fought to be free, but Runnolf still held her captive.

"No!" she screamed in protest as Leben again reared over the mortally injured opponent. Her heart broke as she watched the gray struggle, refusing to acknowledge defeat. But he could not rise.

Victorious, Leben stood over him, his eyes blazing in the afterglow of blood lust and triumph. He trumpeted in victory, listening as it resounded off the surrounding hills. When no further battle challenge was issued, he wheeled and galloped toward the pasture where the other horses waited, exchanging nervous and tentative neighs. Even in their fear of him, they did not move away from his approach. They must accept him or issue challenge. None challenged.

Rowena felt Runnolf's arms tighten about her once again, calling her attention away from Cheval to the triumphant Leben. She watched spellbound as the black picked up speed with every stride. There was a perceptible change as he prepared to vault the hedgerow, a swelling of his chest as his lungs inflated.

She felt Runnolf's muscles bunch in anticipation as the black gathered himself, thrusting away from the ground to soar over the barrier.

His motion was so smooth and landing so cushioned that it seemed one fluid movement instead of the feat of poetic, muscular achievement that it was. Magnificent in his triumph, Leben had cleared the barrier, his legs tucked well beneath him, with room to spare. He cantered amongst the waiting horses, shaking his head with excitement and triumph.

When Runnolf released his hold on her, Rowena raced toward the gray, who was still struggling to rise. There was a bloody froth on his muzzle, and his breath rasped in his throat, ending in an agonized cough.

"Oh, Cheval, you were magnificent!" she cried as she threw herself at his head to keep him down. She knew his injuries were fatal, yet she shrank from doing what was necessary.

Owain and the villains were beside her as she ran her hands along the heaving side of the giant. She looked once to their sad faces, knowing that they confirmed her opinion. There was no choice. The tears flowed down her cheeks unchecked as she withdrew her poniard from her belt.

"Owain, take Rowena back to the keep," Runnolf commanded as he neared them.

But Rowena was too intent on her obligation to her father's destrier to notice him. She felt carefully for the large jugular vein that ran along the powerful neck. Swiftly she cut deeply across it with her small poniard, allowing Cheval's life to pour out upon the ground.

"Your Leben, is he seriously injured?" Owain

asked, exhibiting genuine concern for the safety of the other's destrier.

"Nay, he is bloody and there are many open wounds that will need to be stitched. He came to my call only long enough for me to be sure there were no broken bones. He would tolerate my presence no longer than that.

"Rowena," Runnolf said softly as he tried to lift her to her feet.

"You intrude on our grief," she screamed, pulling away from him. "You are not wanted here."

"A fine destrier such as your father's does not deserve to die in agony," Runnolf responded reasonably. "He has earned a swift, painless death."

"He has already received it," she retorted. "More swift than the one you have condemned this demesne to."

"Your grief confuses you," Runnolf said soothingly.

"My father died because of you. Swiftly and with honor, you have told me. You were supposed to destroy his keep the same way, but for some perverse reason you are destroying it a piece at a time."

"Rowena, you do not know of what you speak," Runnolf said gently.

"Do I not?" she shrieked. "I know better than anyone! This is my home you delight in destroying. Instead of cutting wood from the forest to open new meadow or farmland, your woodsmen are cutting down the orchard because it is closer and not as much work.

"The crops are ready to harvest, but they stand drying in the heat because you would rather have the villains count wagons. Soon they will be of use to no one, not even the wild animals. Your huntsmen have brought back more game since you have been here than Father took in a summer . . ." Rowena did not finish. Her shoulders sagged and her voice dropped to almost a whisper as she slumped to the ground and tried to lift Cheval's head to her lap. "What is the use? It will all be dead soon," she whispered as she lay her head against the lifeless neck. Tears slid down her face, mingling with the dust and blood of combat.

Runnolf was shaken and did not know how to respond.

"She has not properly mourned for her dead," Elaiva told him kindly. "It is finally time for her to do so."

Runnolf waved all those who were witness to Rowena's grief to move away and allow her privacy. He was the last to leave, her soul-wrenching sobs filling his ears while her words filled his mind.

Chapter Ten

✦✦✦✦✦

LATE THAT EVENING as the sun set, Runnolf slowly walked back to the two figures lying in the dust of the road. His mind was occupied with the fear that Rowena had again used her knife to bring a swift, painless end, this time to herself. The thought was an insult to her youth and her up-bringing, yet it seemed a possibility. Fleetingly, Runnolf experienced what it would be like without her, and he felt a perplexing sense of lone-liness.

From the time he could truly call memory his, he had been alone and had not particularly thought of it. Even though there was no bond between himself and the girl, she had been a constant part of his waking days and many sleepless nights as well.

Cautiously he knelt beside the recumbent fig-ures. The destrier was stiff and still in death, but Rowena's shoulders moved in steady rhythm. He exhaled slowly, not aware until he did so, that he had been holding it. Gently he lifted her. She did not wake but moaned. Cradled in his arms, she snuggled into his strength like a child untouched by the realities of the adult world. The walk back was short, but the memories of the past weeks flooded his mind.

He remembered most her eyes: fierce, glitter-ing brown, alive with inner fire when she was angered and defiant, as they were the first day when she sat on the floor of the hall, challenging him.

That memory was replaced by the vision of her eyes when they mirrored her inner conflict before challenging him. There was a squint, as if coercing herself to do so took great effort.

Again another pair of eyes, still hers and yet so different, flooded his memory. Soft, doelike brown, when she spoke of her father. The adoration for him was visible to all. Runnolf mourned for his own life, which held no future of wife and child.

He cursed fitz Giles for dying and leaving his daughter unprotected. He cursed Henry for sending him here in the first place to destroy this adulterine keep. He cursed his own fate.

He looked down at Rowena as she lay in his arms, her eyes now closed in sleep. He could see the trails of her tears as silver threads across her cheeks. She looked so young and vulnerable, and he felt the need to protect her swell within his breast. He berated himself for his impersonal conduct toward her. He wanted to be her friend so that he could console her in her grief.

Runnolf carried Rowena effortlessly down the road to the bailey, up the countless steps to the keep, and from there to the solar. The room was lit by the large bedside candle and another larger candle, which stood in a stand of twisted wrought-iron bars beside a tub of warm water. All was as he had asked, but he had intended it for her use while awake, not asleep.

Should he wake her? He dismissed the thought of her sleeping in her bloodstained clothes and sought another plan. None of the servants seemed to be about. If he went in search of Elaiva, the water would become cool.

His breath caught as he realized the choice left to him. He must bathe her himself or wake her. She is only a child, he reminded himself. If you can remember that, it will be easy. He made his decision. He would bathe her himself and not wake her. But the stirrings of his body mocked the noble intentions of his mind. He walked over to the stool beside the tub, sat down, and balanced Rowena upon his lap.

With trembling hands, he untied the laces that held her bliaud together at the sides and shoulders. He ignored her weak, sleepy protests as he tried to slip the kirtle over her head. Finally he removed her shoes and stockings, dropping them with her other clothes in a heap upon the floor. She lay in unguarded innocence on his lap, no part of her denied to his gaze. The dark smudges under her eyes and the trail of tears across her cheeks reminded him of her grief, and again he was overwhelmed with a desire to protect her from all harm.

The night was very warm, but not warm enough to account for the sweat standing on Runnolf's forehead. His loins began to ache from his need for her. He took deep, painful gulps of air, trying to control his desire as he cursed himself for his poor decision. Her innocence, her trusting behavior was all that protected her from his mounting hunger.

Cradling her in his arms, he knelt beside the tub and cautiously lowered her into the warm water. He was awkward in his movements and wished for three hands as he tried to settle her carefully in the tub without getting her braids wet, but he was only partially successful. He rested his arm across the back of the tub, supporting her head so that the rough wooden rim would not bruise her neck or shoulders.

Satisfied with his maneuvering thus far, he wet his free hand and brushed away the trail of her tears with his calloused fingers. He continued, gently stroking her cheek, feeling the softness of her skin with the back of his hand. Reluctantly, he drew his hand away. Cupping it, he scooped water over her, thoroughly wetting her body. Holding the tiny morsel of soap in the palm of his large hand, he rubbed her gently, starting at her neck and shoulders, then down her arms, murmuring soft words of reassurance lest she waken.

The water was warm, his large hand gentle and his deep voice soothing. Rowena languidly opened her eyes and looked about her. Runnolf! She was again in her secret dream. Only this time the dream was better: She could feel his presence. Only a dream! Knowing it was a dream, she would do nothing to awaken herself from its wondrous sensations. Happily she relaxed, allowing Runnolf to continue his ministrations.

Runnolf was hardly aware of Rowena's semi-wakefulness. He was too busy trying to control his soaring desire and keep his eyes from inflaming him more with forbidden sights. He breathed a prayer of thanksgiving for the willing partners he had found these past nights, otherwise he doubted if anything would have protected Rowena from him.

As he ran his hand over her breasts, he felt her nipples firm and inviting. Glancing down at her, he saw the pink buds of pleasure teasing him through the soapy lather. His body ached, and he hastily removed his hand from temptation only to let it slide down her belly to the valley between her thighs.

He heard her sharp intake of breath and hastily looked at her. "Rowena!" His voice was a croaking whisper of its former self.

"Runnolf," she sighed as she dreamily lifted her arm from the water and caressed his cheek.

"Rowena!"

"Shush," she breathed, placing a wet finger on his lips. "Do not spoil the dream with words."

In growing fascination, Runnolf watched her close her eyes in a serenely sensual action. Her lips parted as she confidently laid her head on his shoulder. He could feel her soft, warm breath on his neck, and it sent chills of raging desire through him.

He swallowed hard, trying to concentrate on the strangeness of her behavior. His distrust of women was learned long ago and not easily forgotten. What kind of game was she playing— was she asleep or only pretending? He watched the rise and fall of her breasts as they bobbed gently in the soapy water and decided that it was faster than normal, yet even and regular.

"If she wanted to share my bed, she had

plenty of opportunity before now," he mumbled aloud.

He finished washing her, only now, more swiftly than before. He rinsed her, again using his large hand to cup the water. If she was not pretending, he did not wish to waken her further, nor did he wish to linger in so dangerous a situation, especially if she was truly as devoid of guile as he so desperately wanted to believe.

"Rowena, listen to me," he whispered. "You must stand so I can wrap you in the towel." But her only response was to cuddle closer against his neck. Cursing softly, he put the towel in front of him like an apron, holding it in place with his chin. Then he stood up, lifting her to a standing posture.

Water splashed onto the reed-covered floor and his chausses, but he did not notice. She stood only as long as he supported her and then she would lean against him, her wet body drying itself against his sherte. In the brief seconds before she would collapse against him, he tried to wrap the towel around her. But he was too awkward to make the maneuver work.

Her face lifted to his, her lips softly parting and inviting. It was too much! Runnolf pulled her closer and kissed her deeply. Hesitantly at first, Rowena returned his kiss. Lost in her dreams, she instinctively raised her arms around his neck, pulling herself more tightly against him. And when he became more demanding, she timidly followed his lead, savoring the taste and feel of his lips against hers. His tongue swept the inside of her mouth and hers met his, making more gentle demands of her own.

With ragged breath, Runnolf broke their embrace. If he did not flee now, he would take her and the damage would be irreparable. But Rowena had unrealized desires of her own, and she did not relinquish her hold about his neck.

"Please, my lord, do not leave me," she whispered. "Please, do not let the dream end."

The battle was lost and temptation had triumphed! Runnolf only half heard her words. His needs were raging out of control as he tore off his own clothes and then pulled Rowena close to him again. She felt his body beneath her hands and sighed contentedly. Stretching, reaching instinctively to feel every part of him, she rubbed her body against his, feeling the shaft of his manhood rubbing against her belly. She wanted to giggle at the feel of his beard against her neck and shoulders as he trailed kisses to her breasts, but she only moaned softly, deep in her throat, like the purr of a cat.

She sighed, contented, as he lifted her and laid her upon the bed before covering her with his weight. Without conscious thought, she opened her legs to accommodate him as he sought entrance. Suddenly, she was torn by pain. Opening her eyes, Rowena stared at Runnolf in betrayed confusion. He loomed over her, his face contorted with his own needs as he moved in great surging waves within her.

In desperation she tried to free herself from the pain. Pushing against his chest, she twisted and struggled, but it only seemed to make him move faster. She could feel his huge hands holding her buttocks off the bed, forcing her body closer to his, deepening the pain. And then his massive body shuddered and convulsed before lying still.

Rowena was too frightened to move. What had happened?

"You were a virgin," he snarled as he flung himself from her. Rolling onto his back, he stared into the shadows of the bed curtains, cursing himself. He had felt her maidenhead, but by then it was too late to stop. "The way you encouraged me, I would not have known it."

Rowena struggled to sit up. Her large brown eyes mirrored her pain and confusion, and Runnolf could not look into them. "Why did you hurt me? My father . . . never hurt my mother like that. They always laughed and . . ." Large tears fell from her eyes and sobs choked in her throat.

"The first time is always accompanied by pain," he answered tonelessly. He was not speaking from firsthand knowledge, only repeating what he had heard many times. "What did you hope to gain by this?"

"Gain?" she repeated. "I do not understand."

"Do not play games," he answered wearily. "You behaved as one accustomed to the company of men."

"No one has come here before you," she whispered.

"There is Norbert," he snarled at what he thought might be an act of feigned innocence.

"But Norbert is . . . was father's steward," she protested. "Father would not have allowed—"

"What is the price of your virginity?" he interrupted her.

"Price?" She could hardly believe her ears.

"If you expect marriage, you can wipe such thoughts from your mind. I have no intention of marrying unless so ordered by the king. I do not need the encumbrance of a deceitful female."

Rowena sat in stunned disbelief, wiping the endless stream of tears from her eyes.

"Where are you going?" he demanded as she swiftly and unexpectedly moved across the bed.

In truth, she did not know. She could no longer tolerate being in the same bed with him— maybe even the same room—she had not thought that far. All she knew was that she needed someplace familiar, someplace safe and close, where her state of undress would not be seen. "To my own bed!" she cried when he demanded an answer.

"There is no use to it now," he said in exasperation. "The damage is already done."

But Rowena would not hear him. She pulled out her truckler bed and crawled beneath the sheet, pulling it up over her head. She needed the comfort of its familiar hollows, the safety of its small size to help ease her pain.

Runnolf lay awake, listening to Rowena's muffled sobs, fully aware of the hurt he had done to her and the irreparable damage. The bed felt strangely empty, its wide expanse of space crying out for her occupancy. "How was I to have known?" he demanded under his breath. She had not been aggressive, but she had responded so willingly.

Cursing, he climbed out of bed and scooped her into his arms. She fought him, scratching his chest severely before he dropped her onto his bed, pinning her down. He took her two hands in his, holding them on either side of her face, glaring at her.

"The damage is done," he repeated, his face only inches from hers. "There is no reason to have separate beds. And false repentance ill becomes you."

"I will not willingly give in to you again," she screamed back, unsuccessfully trying to mask her fear.

"We shall see," he said as he turned her on her side, her back to him. He also lay on his side and pulled her close. "We shall see what the morrows bring. And I promise you, each time it will hurt less until you too will enjoy it fully." He controlled his breathing, taking deep, even breaths to soothe her into relaxation.

For a time Rowena lay stiff and unyielding in his arms. She did not want her body to touch his but escape was impossible. He was holding her too close, his body wrapped about hers as if he were protecting her from some unknown harm. Slowly fatigue overcame her resistance, and her body melted to fit his. Finally, she slept.

Once Runnolf was sure she was asleep, he allowed himself to sleep also.

Chapter Eleven

✦ ✦ ✦ ✦ ✦

ROWENA WOKE ONCE during the night to the crash of thunder and the flash of lightning. It was as if the elements had been waiting for the inevitable to happen. Now that her fate had been fulfilled, things could return to normal and continue as they were meant to be. Carefully she tried to move from the circle of Runnolf's arms, but he pulled her closer, molding his giant body to hers.

Rowena heaved a deep sigh, almost a sob of self-pity as she watched the flashes of lightning illuminate the sanctuary of her childhood. But sanctuary it was no longer to be. As long as Runnolf remained it would be her prison. Even while he slept, his presence was everywhere. His travel baskets stacked in the corner no longer held any mysteries. She had washed and mended all of his clothes and moped over the unfinished shertes she wished she could embroider. His clothes, and now hers also, were strewn about the room in an intimacy that frightened her.

Again she sighed, sleepy now as the rain washed the dust from the landscape and refreshed the parched ground. Closing her eyes, she listened to the beat of the rain and the rolling thunder as it echoed against the mountains.

She slept late, awaking slowly, hesitantly, as if afraid to face the daylight. Thankfully she was alone. Her body ached from shoulder to toe on her left side, but that pain was inconsequential compared to the ache between her thighs and the pain in her heart as she remembered again that last night's dream had turned into a nightmare that daylight would not banish.

Rowena groaned as she tried to sit up. Her movements were slow and painful as she slipped her feet over the side and struggled with the sheet that encumbered her. She heard Runnolf's tread upon the top steps and her heart thudded in fear. Forgetting her pain, she flopped onto her stomach and buried herself under the sheet and bolster, burrowing deep into the mattress.

Runnolf saw her childish effort to hide and scowled. She was more child than woman this morning, and he was not sure how to deal with her. He had expected her to be weeping and bemoaning her lost virtue, not hiding from him. No matter what reaction he anticipated, what behavior he expected from her, she exhibited another. She was definitely not the type of female with whom he was accustomed.

"Rowena, the morn is half-spent," he called as he strode across the room. There was no regret in his voice, no remorse for what had happened to her. Neither was there any gloating, only a simple acceptance of what was. "Come, it is time to greet the day, and I have need of your help," he continued as he sat on the side of the bed and gently pulled the cover away from her.

He expected her to remain obstinate and thought he would have to coax her into getting up. All such thoughts were banished from his mind when he saw the bruises on her shoulder. He began to swear loudly and long.

"I am no uglier in the daylight than in the

dark," Rowena retorted, surprised. Turning, she grabbed the sheet from his hand and pulled it over her head, burying her face in the mattress to hide her new-sprung tears of hurt.

"Your shoulder!" he exclaimed, and pulled the sheet completely from her. "Your hip and leg! They are bruised!" With his guilty conscience, Runnolf immediately assumed that he had inflicted the injury.

Had she been more worldly and less honest, Rowena might have been able to manipulate the situation to her benefit. "It must have happened when Leben . . . when I fell on the road," she explained, wincing in pain as she tried to roll over and pull the sheet about her again.

Runnolf's mind spun as he remembered that Leben had nearly run her down in his savage rush to reach Cheval. He chastised himself for not seeing the injury last night. If he had . . . maybe it would have been enough to discourage him. Maybe, but he doubted it. Especially not when she had returned his kiss with such ardor.

"Have you anything to soothe your injuries?" he demanded.

"In the small chest inside my coffer," Rowena answered, baffled by his concern.

Runnolf rose from the bed and brought the chest containing the medicines. Opening the lid, he found three pots, held securely in their own compartments. "Which one is it?" he asked, resettling himself on the side of the bed.

"The large pot," she answered, her eyes wide and apprehensive.

Runnolf set the chest on the coffer beside the

bed and removed the pot she indicated. Inside was a smooth white salve with a pungent odor. Carefully he dipped three fingers into the mouth of the pot, extracting a goodly amount of the salve.

"Roll over," he commanded her quietly.

Suspiciously Rowena obeyed, all the while trying to watch him over her shoulder.

"Lie flat," he soothed as he began to smear the salve across her shoulder.

Rowena was instantly aware of the size and warmth of his hand as he gently massaged the salve onto her shoulder. His gentleness amazed her. This was a different side of the man she feared. She could not reconcile his actions with those of the night before.

The silence between them was heavy. As Runnolf worked, he could feel the tenseness in her muscles begin to relax. If his interpretation was correct, her fear of him was diminishing also, at least for a little while. Determined to take advantage of the opportunity, he decided to find out as much about her as she was willing to tell.

"What do the pots contain?" he asked casually, trying to put her at ease.

"The large pot contains agrimony to ease the pain of bruises and sprains," she answered. "The smallest pot is for the skin in winter when it chaps and is especially good for deep cuts."

"It has a pleasant aroma," he commented as he lifted the lid.

"It is made from the calendula flower," she answered, surprised at his interest.

"And the other?"

"It is a small amount of chamomile flowers to use in the bath to rid the body of pests," she answered. "There are more medicines in the still room behind the kitchen, but these are the ones I use the most, so I keep them here."

"Your mother taught you these things?"

He felt her stiffen, her muscles instantly tense at his personal question. He smiled in satisfaction.

Rowena's heart began to race. Why was he asking about her mother? What treachery did he expect to blame on Lady Margaret? Yet what harm was there in answering with the truth?

For a long while he did not think she would answer, but at last he felt her relax somewhat and her breathing became more steady.

"Yea," she answered simply.

"She has been dead a long time?" he asked, more a statement than a question.

She stiffened perceptibly but answered, "She has been . . . she died almost five years ago. A lifetime ago."

"Have you been lady here alone ever since?" he asked as he continued massaging her neck and shoulders.

"I was trained to be," she answered defiantly, rising up and glaring over her shoulder at him. "And I have been!"

"Sheathe your claws, little one," he chuckled as he gently pushed her back into the mattress. "You seem to have done very well," he continued without flattery, thinking of the smooth running of the keep and its servants. "Have you had no help?"

"Elaiva is all that is left of Lady Margaret's women," she answered sadly. "The rest were older. Some died before her and some died after her."

"Tell me of Elaiva," he coaxed.

"She came with Lady Margaret and Father," she began. "So did Owain. Father permitted them to marry and gave them a cottage in the bailey. They are very happy together," she said, casting him a meaningful glance over her shoulder. "Their only sorrow is that they have no children."

They have you, he amended for her silently. This entire keep was one family, molded together by their love and respect for Sir Hugh and Lady Margaret, and their love and devotion to Rowena.

"And have you always slept at the foot of this bed?" he asked unexpectedly.

"Yea, ever since I can remember, my bed has been there," she answered. "Why all of these questions?" she demanded in turn.

"I am trying to understand the way of things," he answered truthfully. Her answers explained her innocence. With her mother dead all these years, she would have the memories of childhood but they would have no relationship to the real world.

"Did your mother or father ever tell you what to expect between a man and a woman?"

"I know about breeding and birthing, if that is your question," she answered, blushing even though she was not facing him.

"But do you know of men and women the first time?" he persisted.

"I know how it was between my parents!" she answered adamantly.

"And as you found out last night, there is more to it than that," he added softly.

"My father never hurt my mother as you hurt me!" she protested angrily, trying to get away from him. But he held her firmly to the mattress with his hand at the small of her back, and her struggles were useless.

"Did your father ever sleep below," Runnolf asked, "with his men?" He had continued to massage her shoulder, including her upper arm and uninjured shoulder. Never once did he cease his ministrations lest she become afraid of his touch.

"You mean did he ever take another to ease his needs? Is it not part of the life of a man?" she asked scornfully, somehow anticipating where his question was leading. "Verily he took others. But never any who were unwilling," she added pointedly.

There was a long silence and then Rowena continued on her own. "But he rarely did so here. He went to the great market. There are women there who sell their bodies because of the needs of men."

Runnolf was momentarily surprised that she knew of the needs of men and yet was so naive concerning the act itself.

"What plans did your father have for your marriage?" he asked at last.

Again there was silence as she considered how much to tell him. There was nothing in her dream of the future to violate any secret, so she decided to tell it to him. "He said a knight would come, one who would love the land as we do. One who would be willing to fight to keep the land," she added defiantly. "Even against the king!"

"This great knight, where was he expected to come from?" There was a hint of scorn in his voice, but Rowena did not notice. She was lost in the magical tale of her future. The future that was no longer possible.

"Oh, he would not be a great knight," she answered. "A great knight would have lands of his own and would not be interested in ours. It would be the second or third son of a good family, one who had nothing of his own but would be willing to stay here with us."

"What would you do if you found out your husband went to the great market and availed himself of these women who service the needs of men?" Runnolf was becoming curious. Her combination of worldliness and naivete intrigued him.

"I would not wish to know," she answered softly. "I would wish that he keep it his secret."

"Why would you allow it?"

"My husband would marry me for the land," she answered realistically. "He might not be pleased with the entire bargain."

For a moment Runnolf was angered by Rowena's lack of self-worth. But then he reminded himself that prearranged marriages, and marriages in general, were not made for the pleasure of the two involved. Marriage was contracted to benefit the families. "And if you were not pleased with the bargain, would you also seek another?" he demanded sharply.

Unexpectedly Rowena turned on him, her fingers clenched in clawlike daggers, striking for his face. "You have insulted me for the last time!" she screamed, catching him totally unprepared. Her fingernails did not find their target, but it took Runnolf several seconds to gain control over her flailing arms.

"Rowena," he whispered, his breath coming in short bursts. "For one so small, you are very strong. Now be still." She struggled a few moments longer and then went limp from exhaustion. "I have not intentionally insulted you," he continued softly. "I was only curious as to what else about life you were taught."

"I was taught to honor my vows," she spat at him, her eyes sparkling in defiance although her body was subdued. "To obey my husband and lord . . . and never to bring dishonor to his name."

"Life is not always what we wish it to be," he offered as consolation. "Now roll over, and I will finish putting salve on your hip. Unless you offer me solace after your unprovoked attack," he added huskily as he gazed longingly at her breasts.

Rowena glared at him a few minutes. She was still too angry to fully understand his meaning. Once she did she was overcome with embarrassment. Hurriedly she turned onto her stomach, trying to hide from him again.

Impulsively Runnolf nuzzled the back of her neck and she felt the tiny tremors of beginning pleasure sweep gently through her. He used the silence to think on her answers. His large hands spanned her back, neck, and shoulders, massaging the renewed tenseness away. As the tension eased, he moved his hands down her ribs, over her waist to her hips and then her thighs. Then lingeringly he massaged upward until he could almost encircle her waist with his two hands. She appeared so fragile, and yet he knew this to be another deception. When she was fighting, it took all of his strength to subdue her without injury.

He fought the growing tension in his loins. It is too soon, he reminded himself. Go slowly, very slowly. You must try to understand. He forced his mind back to her words. Her perceptions of life were intriguing, but how could she have learned so much and yet not understand what she knew?

Rowena was becoming alarmed. He had been using both of his large, powerful hands to massage her whole body. His ministering had soothed and comforted her, and she almost wanted to go to sleep. But she dared not. She still did not quite trust his strange behavior, and she could no longer bear the waiting or the silence. She needed to distract him and herself as well. The warmth of his hands was both soothing and dangerous, and her breasts felt tender against the sheets.

"You have need of my help?" Rowena at last broke the silence.

"It will wait," he answered, absorbed in his task. He delighted in the unprotesting feel of her. His mind absently toyed with a dream of what the days ahead could be like with her sharing his passion.

"Leben? Is he . . . well?"

"He has allowed me to move him to the stables. I had them built stronger."

"There is little need now," she said dully. "What will become of the horses, once they return to health?" she asked, hoping to get his thoughts fixed on the horses.

"A knight needs three horses for his immediate use," he explained. "He needs his packhorse for his personal belongings, and it travels with his servants, either immediately in his company or with the baggage wains." Runnolf had unconsciously fallen into the toneless voice of teacher, but she did not mind this time, because it was information she found fascinating. More importantly, she hoped talking would make him forget whatever he was planning to do to her.

"A knight needs his destrier by his side at all times, especially now, with the countryside so unsettled. And he also needs a good riding horse, one for everyday travel, for the hunt, for pleasure."

"Those destriers killed or severely injured are replaced by those confiscated through the dissolution of the keeps. The best are sent to the king, and the rest are sold."

"And the land?" she whispered, almost afraid to hear his answer.

"The land that belonged to King Henry I, grandfather of our king, is returned to the king. It was his property, rightly so, and therefore returned to him." He emphasized the last, hoping she would better understand her father's unlawful position. "The keeps without license are destroyed . . ." He paused, trying to find words to make the telling less difficult, and decided there were none. "The property found in those adulterine keeps . . . is divided amongst the knights for their maintenance."

There was a long silence. The words of truth Runnolf spoke confirmed what Rowena already knew, but the telling did not ease the pain or make it any easier to bear.

So far, Runnolf had offered her no threat. She lay still, allowing the warmth and power of his hands to lull her into acceptance.

Suddenly she was aware that the tips of his fingers were teasing the sides of her breasts. Her heart began to beat in alarm as his warm breath on her neck sent shivers across her flesh. His beard tickled her shoulder. Her body stiffened as panic seized her. She was too frightened to think rationally as his large, calloused hands slipped beneath her, cupping her breasts while he continued to trail kisses along her spine. In an effort to escape from him, to protect her back from his gentle assault, she rolled over, placing herself in worse jeopardy. He kissed her belly and tickled her navel with his tongue before looking up at her.

Her breathing had become ragged with fear and her breasts heaved in rhythm to her near-hysteria. "Rowena, listen to me," he panted, trying to hold her without hurting her. "Stop fighting me and listen!" he commanded.

The authority in his voice penetrated her panic and she lay still.

"Please," she pleaded. Large tears filled her eyes. "Please, do not hurt me again." She hated herself for begging, but she could not still her tongue before it betrayed her fear.

Runnolf's ardor was momentarily dashed, but his desire prevailed. He understood that if he was to keep Rowena willing in his bed, he must teach her to overcome her fear. But what did he know of virgins? His instincts would have to guide him. He must proceed slowly. He must teach her what to expect, so that the pain would not overpower her.

"Only a little pain this time," he whispered, determined to keep his promise. "Next time, even less." Her nipples felt his determination first as he lowered his head to began teasing one and then the other with his tongue.

"Nay! I pray thee, do not!" she cried, her hands wrapped in his hair, fighting to pull his face from her breasts. There was a warming in the nether region of her body, accompanied by a dull pain. He was causing such strange feelings to possess her. She must make him stop. She began to whimper in protest.

His beard tickled as he smothered his face in the deep valley between her breasts. Yet she had no desire to laugh. He blew gently on the moisture of his kisses, and her nipples became even more firm, more sensitive. Softly and then more urgently, he suckled on their firmness until Rowena moaned in spite of herself.

He knelt above her, his legs between hers, and

raised his tunic. He would have preferred to remove his clothes, to feel her body next to his, but he was afraid to break contact with her. Rowena shut her eyes so as not to see the weapon that had caused her pain. He lifted her buttocks to meet his need and positioned himself at the threshold of her innocence. Slowly, carefully, he entered her, feeling her body tense. A protest escaped her lips.

But before the pain he withdrew, massaging her buttocks with his powerful yet ever-gentle hands. This was the first time he had ever taken extra time with a woman, and the strain was evident. His body was covered in sweat and his tunic stuck to him, and he trembled as much in anticipation as in frustration at the need to proceed slowly. He forced himself to study the woman-child who was at his mercy, and her obvious fear helped his control.

Again he entered her, going deeper until he felt her stiffen, but she did not cry out. Once more he withdrew and then entered. Each time his patience was rewarded as he saw the changes in her. He watched in fascination as her chest and neck reddened and her lips opened slightly as her chest rose and fell in a faster rhythm, almost matching his own.

Once more he withdrew and waited, but then he could wait no longer. He plunged deep within her. He heard her cry out but he could not help her now. He felt himself exploding and then he lay still, his head cradled on her heaving breast.

He could hear her heart beating swiftly, but he could not tell if it was still from fear or if she too had felt some exhilaration, if only for a few moments. Softly he held her, stroking her shoulder, soothing her. He became aware of the lesson he had just learned. Gentleness and care had almost won her. It was his own speed and lack of control that had caused her discomfort.

"Next time," he promised, his breath ragged and hoarse. "Next time it will hurt even less."

He looked into her face and saw tears seeping from her tightly closed eyelids. He was overcome with a desire to kiss them away. "Go back to sleep," he whispered kindly as he succumbed. "Go back to sleep and I will see you later."

Rowena felt the loss of weight from the bed as Runnolf got up but refused to look at him. As soon as she heard him descend the stairs, she struggled to a sitting position and then moved her arm and shoulder carefully. The salve had eased the pain, and she was able to leave the bed. Stiffly she walked to the basin and poured herself fresh water. And then diligently she washed all sign of his presence from her body.

Rowena had difficulty dressing and found the stairs almost impossible, thankful to find the hall nearly empty as she crossed, with only a few knights sleeping on their pallets in a corner. In her shame, she had forgotten that the fall in the road would be all the explanation necessary. She was convinced that everyone would know immediately that she had failed to withstand Runnolf's seduction.

Unbeknownst to her, her fear was groundless and entirely unnecessary. Runnolf's knights assumed that she had been sharing his bed since her first night spent in the solar. And the servants also believed it was inevitable. She was, after all, very beautiful. They did not consider it one way or another—it was simply a fact of life, such as had happened to them before their coming to fitz Giles's service.

Rowena paused on the top step of the keep and looked to where Cheval had lain, but all that was there was a mound of freshly dug earth beside the road.

"Father's people," she whispered to herself, wiping a fresh tear from her eye. "They could not bury him properly, so they buried Cheval."

She looked past the cottages clustered near the fields and was surprised to see the villains harvesting the crops. She could not believe her eyes and rubbed them as if she had just awakened. She listened for the sound of axes from the orchard, but the woodcutters were silent.

Bewildered by these changes, Rowena forced her bruised body to descend the endless steps to the bailey. From habit, she stopped by the kitchen to see if there was anything that needed doing. She found Elaiva in the rear of the shed making pies, but when she offered to do them Elaiva insisted that she do nothing until she was properly healed.

Rowena stiffened in alarm and then blushed in shame. She had hoped that she had behaved as if nothing unusual had happened. More tears sprang to her eyes and she turned away, hoping Elaiva had not seen. But that was expecting too much from someone who loved her as if she were her own.

"What is it?" Elaiva asked worriedly, rushing to her mistress.

"Elaiva . . ." Rowena tried to control her sobbing. "It is . . . I cannot . . . the shame of everyone knowing."

For a moment Elaiva did not understand Rowena's distress. Sir Runnolf had left orders that Rowena was not to be disturbed because of the injuries she had received from her fall, but he had mentioned nothing else.

"Sir Runnolf told me you were sleeping and that you were sorely bruised from your fall yesterday," Elaiva began. But when Rowena would not look her in the face she guessed what had happened.

"My lady," Elaiva crooned as she enfolded her arms about her mistress and held her to her ample bosom.

The young, bewildered child in Rowena responded. "How can you be so kind and understanding?" she cried against the older woman's shoulder.

"Hush, child," Elaiva soothed as she rocked Rowena. "Life is sometimes harsh. But one learns to live through it."

"Can you ever forgive me?" she sobbed. "If father knew . . ." She could not finish, as her throat choked closed with her rising tears.

"There is nothing to forgive, child. It was inevitable when he saw how lovely you are. It is only surprising that it took so long."

"I do not want to be lovely," she cried defiantly. "I wish I were ugly and—"

"Hush!" Elaiva ordered her. "You are lovely.

God has made you so. And you are as lovely and as good as the Lady Margaret. Sir Runnolf will see that and do what is right by you."

"He said he would not marry unless the king ordered it," she wept. "He said he would not be saddled with a . . ." She paused, trying to remember his exact words. "He did not need the encumbrance of a deceitful female," she finished.

"He is undoubtedly used to the women at court," Elaiva explained. "Ask questions about them and you will find out what he does not like. Then you will not be that way."

Rowena already had some idea from the things Runnolf had said. "Is that not also deceitful?" she asked, not sure she wanted even to consider marriage with him. The past night had been so brutally strange.

"If you knew your lord did not like venison, would you serve it at his table?" Elaiva asked reasonably.

"Verily, I would not! But . . ."

"Then . . ."

The older woman knew that Rowena would not be able to carry out a deliberate deceit for any length of time. She hoped instead to distract her mistress from dwelling on Runnolf's past sins and to have her concentrate on a possible future. But if Sir Runnolf would not marry Lady Rowena, then she, Owain, and Norbert would simply carry out their original plans to protect and care for Rowena after his departure.

Yet Rowena was disturbed by the suggestion. A lie was what had precipitated this predicament in the first place. If she had met Runnolf at the gates of the keep as Rowena, daughter of Hugh fitz Giles, she would not now be varlet and . . .

"He was looking for scissors and thread to stitch the wounds of his destrier," Elaiva interrupted her thoughts. Though Rowena might harbor ill will toward the black destrier for the death of Cheval, Elaiva knew the girl's kind heart would allow no animal to suffer needlessly. "Mayhap you should go to the stables and see if all goes well. By all tales, that black beast has suffered for his triumph over Cheval.

"Splash some cold water on your face," she suggested. "It will wash away the stain of your tears."

Rowena went to the well and drew fresh water. Washing her face with her hands, she then soaked her wrists to cool herself and give herself time to calm her inner turmoil. She looked absently at the sky and saw a few small clouds scudding across the vast expanse of blue. They were the first clouds she had seen in many days, and she whispered a prayer of thanksgiving for the rain during the night.

The two women embraced one more time before Rowena reluctantly walked to the stables to look for Runnolf. Elaiva watched her for a few minutes and then hurried to the solar to set the room to rights. It would not do for Rowena to return and find the bloodied sheets. It would only remind her more of her loss.

"Almighty Father, why must the child suffer so?" she prayed as she wiped her own tears on the sheet she held so tightly in her hands. At any other time Elaiva would have rejoiced to be the one to show the sheets after Rowena's wedding as proof of her virginity. Not now and never in the future would anyone have that honor. "Let another one of us suffer," she begged. "She is too young, too innocent."

Chapter Twelve

＋＋＋＋

ROWENA HEARD A shrill whistle of alarm from inside the stable. She hurried to the large, low door and stopped just inside, trying to adjust her eyes to the dim interior. Her heart raced in dread of what she might find if the anger voiced by the destrier was accompanied by violence. Faced with the possibility that Runnolf might be injured, she forgot her fear of him.

What she heard was the thud of shod feet against solid wood, combined with Runnolf's curses. She was relieved when she realized that such violent oaths could not come from a seriously injured man.

In the dim light of a lantern hung from a peg, Rowena could distinguish Runnolf's head above Leben's darker shadowed rump. The destrier had pinned his master to the wall and was holding him there with his great bulk.

"Are you hurt?" In spite of the shadows, she could see his face darken. She could not be sure if it was anger or embarrassment that prevented him from answering. "Are you in any danger?" she persisted.

Rowena reassured herself that Runnolf was not hurt, nor was he going to answer her.

In the past week Rowena had discovered that she had a mischievous sense of humor. She had always been a happy person who enjoyed the pranks of others but had never participated in any herself. Now she was in a position to enjoy the discomfort of the man who had turned her innocent dreams into a living nightmare.

"Could you use some help?" She winced as she stooped to climb through the slats of the stall. "You seem to have lost something," she continued as she knelt in the ankle-deep straw to retrieve the pot of salve.

"God's feet, woman! Be careful, or you will be trampled!"

"He cannot hold you to the wall and step on me at the same time," she reasoned logically, intent on enjoying his immobility as long as possible.

"What were you about, to get yourself into such a predicament?" she asked as she returned the pot to the small chest. She recognized the set as the one from the solar but made no comment.

The value of a good destrier had been impressed upon her since childhood. In fact she knew, from many stories told by her father, that sometimes destriers were treated better than wives and children. This was because a wife could always be found to replace one lost and children could be bred at any time. But a knight's life ultimately rested on his destrier, and good ones were hard to find and very expensive. A good destrier could sometimes cost as much as a small keep.

"I was cleaning his wounds," Runnolf answered sharply and then swore as he tried to shove Leben aside. But the giant would not budge.

"How far did you get?" she asked, running her hands gently along Leben's off side.

"He has been brushed." Runnolf panted because he could not get a good lungful of air. "Most of his wounds have been cleaned except for the one on his shoulder. He will not let me near it."

"You washed them in salt water?" she asked as she withdrew a tiny pair of scissors from the coffer.

"Verily!" he answered, surprised that she knew anything about the care of destriers.

"Father had a groom once who would never clean a wound properly before medicating it. The wounds healed but it took longer, and there was usually scarring." All the while she was talking, she was deftly clipping the hair around each of Leben's wounds to ensure quick, clean healing and then repacking them with salve.

She spoke calmly but her heart was racing. Runnolf was practically at her mercy. If she could get Leben to cooperate, she could have her revenge. All she had to do was jab him with the scissors and the giant would crush Runnolf against the wall. Her stomach revolted and she could taste the bile in her mouth as she pictured Runnolf severely injured by his friend.

Murder! It would be murder of the simplest kind. No honorable death for him and no honor in the deed for her. The thought was fleeting but it left her knees weak. She could not bring herself to do it. And Leben, she rightfully guessed, would never do more than harass his master on occasion. Not even serious injury would turn him against Runnolf.

Besides, if Runnolf were to die, what treatment would she receive at the hands of his men? They treated Runnolf with good-natured teasing, but in all things there was a deep underlying respect, coupled with fear, that kept them faithful to his command.

"Now, let me see the other side," she said to Leben as she slipped under the black's massive head. There was barely enough room for her, so she knew how tight the space must be for Runnolf. She almost giggled out loud at his discomfort.

"Cheval had very sharp teeth," she said soothingly as she packed the wound on his neck with salve. There was only a slight sob in her voice when she spoke of her father's destrier. When she tried to probe the wound on his shoulder to see how deep it was, Leben snorted irritably and pressed Runnolf tighter against the wall.

"Stop prodding him!" Runnolf commanded. "The wound troubles him greatly. I will have to gather the knights and the farrier."

"What will happen then?" Rowena asked,

alarmed by the vague implication of so many men to handle one destrier.

"We will hold him down and you will do your treatment of his wounds," he answered irritably.

"But that will not work!" she protested. "The wounds on the other side of his body will get dirty, and they may become worse."

"Then we will hold him to the wall," he answered in exasperation.

"I cannot see in this light," Rowena complained softly. "I must bring another lantern."

Before leaving to fetch another lantern, Rowena pressed a handful of salve into the open shoulder wound. Leben kicked out irritably and snorted a warning, letting her know of his displeasure, still not allowing Runnolf enough room to push free.

Returning with the second lantern, Rowena hung it on the wall. "You are truly brave," she said, standing at the black's shoulder, studying the wound. Carefully she toyed with the salve, smearing it on the places she missed. She was encouraged, for each time she returned to the wound, she was able to do more and more. The salve was drawing out the pain.

"If I leave the wound open," she was explaining to the destrier, "it will take longer to heal and you will be of no use to your master for several weeks. It needs to be stitched to heal properly," she continued. "If the salve softens the skin enough, maybe . . . just maybe it will not hurt so much."

Runnolf watched the two, seemingly forgotten. Rowena's gentleness with the giant and her lack of fear were extraordinary. No women of his acquaintance would ever be found in a stable, even if they rode and hunted regularly.

The entire time she was talking, explaining the wound, Runnolf had the impression that Leben understood her. But what was unusual about that? he chided himself. Did he not also speak to the horse and expect him to understand?

"Father always said that destriers are more intelligent than man and more noble," she said, as if she read his mind. "If you explain to them what is to be, and they trust you, they will usually offer you no harm, allowing you to tend them properly."

As she talked, the destrier stood quietly, permitting her to continue work on his other wounds. Once, when she ceased her soliloquy, Leben became irritable and restless, paying more attention to Rowena than to Runnolf, and he was able to slip away from his imprisonment against the wall.

"If you are truly more noble than men," she continued, "then you will not be concerned for your appearance. But if you are as vain as men, then you will want to be stitched so that you will have few scars to detract from your beautiful coat. And this wound will leave a very ugly scar."

There was a movement at the entrance to the stables and a small boy walked slowly down the aisle between the stalls carrying a bowl carefully in his hands.

"Wiellas, is that you?" Rowena called quietly over her shoulder.

"Yea, my lady," came the soft reply.

"Did Elaiva fix the herb as I told you?"

"Yea, my lady."

"Bring the bowl as close as you dare and then put it on the railing. Then quietly back out as you came," Rowena instructed him.

Surprisingly the boy brought the bowl to the entrance of the stall before Leben made his objection known.

"We can but try," she murmured, more to herself than to either Leben or Runnolf. "Fetch me the needle and thread Elaiva gave you," she ordered Runnolf without thinking. Taking them she deftly threaded the needle and began stitching. Her fingers were swift, sure, and steady. The giant destrier stood perfectly still, prepared to stop her if she should inadvertently hurt him.

"Fetch the bowl," she ordered Runnolf again.

Runnolf went to the railing and looked at the glutinous concoction with distaste, then held it out to Rowena.

She dipped her fingers and placed the gummy substance directly on the stitched injury. "The wound is as clean as I can get it," she said as she put her things away. "He should not be ridden until it is fully healed. Put him out to pasture if you like. There is plenty of grass yet and the water is fresh and cold."

She stepped back to survey her handiwork and was thoroughly pleased. She had cared for Leben, while Runnolf had not been allowed to do so. The heady feeling of her pride was a little overwhelming.

Runnolf studied her carefully, now thoroughly bemused. She had spoken to him with authority and knowledge; there was nothing of the hurt and tearful child of the morning, nor the mischievous, gloating child she had been when she first entered the stables. She stood proud, pleased with the task just completed. Yet suspicion dies hard. Again he felt somehow deceived.

"What brought you to the stables?" he demanded as he opened the gate to lead Leben out.

"You said you had need of my help, and I came to see what it was," she answered, bewildered by his brisk attitude. In her pride of accomplishment, she had expected him to thank her. Obviously he would not. Dejectedly her shoulders slumped and she turned to leave.

Runnolf saw the hurt in her eyes before she turned and was instantly sorry for his hasty words. "I will need to choose another destrier to ride while Leben is recovering," he said as if nothing had happened. "Needs must I return Leben to the pasture. While there, I will choose another destrier. Do you feel up to the walk?" he asked.

Rowena's heart raced in excitement at his invitation. "The walk would be very pleasant," she answered, looking at him with surprise and happiness. Truly it would not be a pleasant walk, except that she would be with Runnolf. The sun was high and there was no sign of rain. But she would not say nay and break the thin thread of peace that he offered her.

Elaiva watched Runnolf and Rowena leave the bailey, leading the black destrier. They were deep in conversation. Elaiva looked at the sun, saw that it was nearly midday, and frowned. Apparently they were unaware that it was almost time to eat, and that was not like Rowena.

Then she smiled indulgently at her mistress and gave orders for the fires to be banked and the sides of meat to be set aside until later. She sent a child to climb to the top of the keep as a sentinel to watch for their return. She hummed softly to herself, a smile playing about the corners of her mouth as she continued the preparation of the meat and vegetable pies to appease the hunger of the rest of the knights.

Elaiva did not have time to worry about the future. The present occupied her time; she would leave the future in the hands of God.

As they walked Rowena and Runnolf spoke of horses, and Rowena continued to astound Runnolf with her knowledge and common sense.

"It might be wise for you to isolate the mares Leben has selected," she suggested. "When it is time to take them to market, they will bring a higher price if they foal one of his get."

As if Leben understood their talk, he hurried down the road, tugging and pulling Runnolf along, nearly jerking his arm out of its socket. He wanted to be free to roll in the green grass, to wade in the cool water of the stream and rest in the refreshing shade. He had fought for these things and won. He would not give them up willingly. And for once he did not prefer Runnolf's company to all others.

And for the first time, Runnolf also preferred another's company. He was with Rowena, and for the moment, he was satisfied. Runnolf tried to hold Leben to a slow walk, but the destrier would have no part of it. He wanted his freedom and Runnolf wished to remain with Rowena.

The decision was easy. Sensitive to the needs that inspired his destrier, Runnolf released the lead rein and let the black go. Without a backward glance he galloped toward the pasture, his inky mane flying out behind him like the ribbons of a pennant whipping in the wind.

Rowena held her breath when she thought the destrier intended to crash through the gate, then squealed in delight as he unerringly sailed over the obstruction like an arrow shot from a taut bowstring.

"He is as vain as all men," Rowena laughed as if reading Runnolf's mind. "Why do something as simple as waiting for the gate to be opened when you can jump it and impress everyone?"

She climbed the gate and hung over its side, watching as the black approached each of the destriers. She held her breath lest there be another battle, but they stood quietly, their tails tucked close to their bodies, heads drooped. When none showed aggression or challenge to his leadership, Leben re-marked his territory before herding his chosen mares away from the others.

Runnolf stood beside Rowena. She was alive with enthusiasm, her cheeks flushed with excitement as she watched Leben. Runnolf wondered where her thoughts were. Did she dream of riding one of the mares as they raced about the

pasture? She had said that she did ride to hunt.
He would have to remember to ask. And he
would like to make a gift of one of the mares to
replace her loss. It would be a pleasure to ride
with her as she went about her duties.

Runnolf forced his attention from Rowena and
concentrated on the issue at hand. He must find
a temporary replacement for his beloved black
destrier. His greatest problem was to find one
that would accommodate his own great size and
weight as well as the additional weight of his
hauberk, sword, lance, and shield. All of the
destriers in the pasture were large, muscular
horses, but he was able to eliminate many of
them immediately because they were not yet
fully recovered from the battle.

Rowena centered her attention on Runnolf as
he climbed over the fence and strode into the
pasture. His movements were graceful and sure
as he moved about the meadow, looking over
the horses. He selected three, one a dapple gray,
darker than Cheval, and two bays.

"The gray, I think," Rowena remarked carefully as she followed close behind. She was having as much trouble selecting only one as
Runnolf. "He is older, should have more experience, may have had more than one rider, so he
might adapt more easily to your ways."

Runnolf looked at her strangely, surprised that
his thought paralleled hers. "I will try him, and
if he does not suit, there are these other two.

"You told me that you rode to hunt," Runnolf
said. "What became of your palfrey? I saw no
horses in the stables when we arrived."

"When father rode out . . . to meet you, he mounted everyone who could sit a horse," she answered calmly.

"Would you care to choose one for your use now?" he asked.

"Yea, may I?" she responded gleefully, already having one in mind. At the nod of Runnolf's head, she turned her attention back to the pasture, searching for the mare that had captured her attention earlier. "That one!" She pointed excitedly to an elegant chestnut with extremely delicate lines.

Runnolf looked to where she pointed and saw the chestnut mare. And she was indeed beautiful! But as Runnolf went into the pasture to bring her out, she shied away from him, trotting out of reach. Runnolf tried for her several times more, but she successfully evaded him each time. She was as fleet-footed as she was elegant.

Runnolf was pleased with Rowena's selection—the two would look well together—but the mare was too fractious at present. It would take much patience to calm her and school her properly to be a lady's palfrey. Regretfully he did not have time for that now. His first obligation was to do the king's bidding, and he could not without a destrier.

His patience at its end, he made his own selection. He searched out and found a more sedate mare that would give Rowena no trouble during a ride. He looked her over carefully, then satisfied, led her out.

"That is not the one I selected," Rowena protested as Runnolf led out a white palfrey, older than the chestnut but still in her prime. The mare rubbed her nose on Rowena's hand while she waited for Runnolf's explanation.

"The chestnut is not well schooled," he explained. "She would be too dangerous for you and I have not the time now to school her."

"But I could—"

"I do not have the time," he interrupted. "Mayhap later," he half promised as he hooked a lead rein to the mare's bridle. Runnolf was too busy with the mare to notice Rowena clamp her jaw shut on her angry retort. Nor did he see the squint of determination in her eyes. If he thought the mare was too unschooled, then she would train her and show him how mistaken he was in both of them.

Reluctantly Rowena turned her attention to the palfrey. She could not take her hurt out on the innocent mare and unconsciously crooned to her as she took the lead. The mare followed docilely along as Rowena walked about slowly, hoping to find some reason to refuse her. But, as in most things, Runnolf had chosen well. Reluctantly Rowena admitted that the mare was of good, sound breeding even though nonspirited.

It was nearly dark when they rode through the gate to the bailey. They were met by Owain.

Rowena told him of Leben's selection of mares, instructing him to meet her in the morning, and she would accompany him to the pasture to assist in marking them for market. What she did not tell him, or anyone for that matter, were her plans for the chestnut mare. She also had in mind to make friends with the mare, the first step in the training of a horse.

"Norbert is recovering well," Owain added, interrupting her thoughts. "On the morrow, he should be well enough to begin some of his duties." But then he paused, embarrassed, and shifted his attention to Runnolf. "That is, of course, if Sir Runnolf has no other duties for him."

"We shall see what the morrow brings," Runnolf commented, watching the two carefully. He still did not trust them overmuch, although he allowed Rowena to remain as chatelaine. He watched for any signs that would cause him alarm.

Rowena blushed, grateful that Runnolf had not reprimanded her in front of her faithful retainer.

"Owain, please," she called him back when he would have departed. "Tell my father's people how grateful I am that they buried Cheval. Father would have wished it," she continued. "It is also a great comfort to me to have it so."

"But, Lady, we did not bury him on our own," he responded guiltily. "It was Lord Runnolf's command. He also sent the villains to the fields to harvest and even sent the teamsters to help carry it back for storage."

In a state of confusion, Rowena bid Owain good night, then turned to Runnolf. "I do not know how to adequately tell you . . . ," she began formally, trying to express her feelings. She could not fathom his behavior. Surely her outburst the day before could not have caused this change in him. "The harvest . . . the woodcutters . . . they were absent today," she stammered. "Cheval . . ."

She was standing several steps up from the bailey, putting her at eye level with him. They stood so close that she could see him as clearly as if it were full sunlight instead of dusk. "Thank you, my lord," she said earnestly as she unconsciously placed her hand on his arm and looked into his dark eyes.

There was no change in Runnolf's expression, but his eyes began to glitter from the desire that lay just beneath the surface. This look of tenderness, of open emotion, was what he wished to see in her eyes for him at all times. Afraid his voice would betray his mounting emotions, he motioned her to precede him up the long flight of stairs to the hall.

Chapter Thirteen

✦✦✦✦✦

ROWENA REALIZED HOW tired and sore she was when her legs cramped halfway up the stairs. The muscles in her thighs felt like gelatin. Her feet felt as if they were covered with clods of mud that grew heavier with every step. Stubbornly she was determined that Runnolf would not know of her weakness. There were so many things she hoped to prove to him.

But Runnolf was more aware of her than she knew. He noticed the hesitancy of her step and the slowness with which she climbed. When she stopped at the table beside the hall door to wash, he saw her hands tremble as she poured the water into the basin. He saw the discomfort she tried to hide, and it gave him the opportunity to countermand her position as varlet without causing undo resistance on her part.

"If you will be seated, Sir Runnolf, I will serve your table as usual," Rowena protested as Runnolf took the basin from her and poured his own wash water.

"That will no longer be necessary," he responded. "I will begin looking for a new varlet and you will sit by my side."

"But why? I am as capable as before."

"I will hear no naysay," he said adamantly.

"But they will know—"

"They have known for a long time," he interrupted her.

"But how?" she protested in amazement as he led her toward the high table. "Only last night . . . it happened," she stammered in bewilderment and embarrassment.

"People believe what they want to believe," he said enigmatically. He pulled out the bench for her.

"Sir Runnolf, please. I—"

"Give orders to your servants to begin serving the meal," he commanded her sternly.

Chagrined, Rowena realized that she did not

have the strength or the courage to call more attention to herself by causing a scene, and motioned to Elaiva to begin serving. As if nothing unusual had happened at the keep, Elaiva ordered the servants about. Rowena could not look at her directly for the shame she felt at sitting with Runnolf. The compassionate looks of the servants as they waited on her were harder to bear than the leers and smiles of the knights.

Runnolf was pleased that Rowena had acquiesced. She sat in silence, her eyes downcast, her face wan and her hands trembling. Runnolf knew that only a small part of her distress was her embarrassment. The rest was her fatigue and bruises. He swore silently to himself that he would not couple with her this night. She was in no physical condition to respond. He must wait. Somewhere in the back of his mind was the all-consuming desire that she respond to him willingly. He made a conscious decision to place her well-being first, a decision that would have far-reaching effects on his life.

Runnolf did not like what his knights were saying about the obvious change in Rowena's status, although he knew enough about human nature not to make an issue of it. They could think what they pleased; he could not control that. But he could respond to each comment by changing the subject.

If Rowena had not been so lost in her own shame, she would have been pleased by his efforts, and she would have realized that the servants were trying to give her encouragement, not condemnation. They were, after all, people of the earth, used to hardship and reality, with little time for high ideals and guilt over the inevitable.

But Rowena was her own worst enemy, constantly striving to live up to the perfection she believed her father expected of her: the perfection of her mother's image, long glorified by an early death.

And now she had failed to live up to that image. Never would Lady Margaret have been thwarted in anything she had set out to do, as Rowena had been with the chestnut mare. Never would Lady Margaret have allowed herself to be brought so low as to share the bed of any man without the sanctity of marriage. Never would anyone have been able to disparage Lady Margaret in her own hall without being challenged for it.

Disheartened, she forced herself to nibble at the choice morsels Runnolf placed on her trencher, but she could not swallow. Her food stuck in her throat, and she was forced to wash it down with cider.

"Give orders to your servants to have bath water carried to the solar," Runnolf commanded her halfway through the meal. "And be sure you have those flowers for the bath that relieve the pain of bruises."

She stared at him with her mouth slightly agape. How did he know? How could he have guessed her thoughts? Again she was awed by his apparent ability to know all things. Guiltily, lest he read the other secrets she concealed, she forced herself to stare at her trencher.

When the meal was over, Runnolf stood beside Rowena's bench waiting for her to stand.

"Are you not to join your knights this eve?" she asked, her voice barely above a whisper. "I must see to the cleaning of the hall," she added when he did not move.

"Elaiva will see to the hall," he answered patiently.

The blood raced past Rowena's ears, making hearing almost impossible. Slowly she stood up and allowed him to lead her to the steps. Before climbing to the solar, she tried once again to disengage herself and proceed alone, but he would not allow it. The candles were lit and the room orderly. Rowena's bed robe was lying on the foot of the great bed. On the coffer beside the bed was a pot of salve along with a pitcher of cider, a hunk of cheese, and fruit.

"I am not the only one to see that you did not eat," he commented. "Your servants are exceptionally well trained," he complimented her.

"It must have been Elaiva," Rowena answered, blushing to the roots of her hair.

The bath was inviting, but she could not sink into its healing warmth as long as Runnolf was present. Rowena trembled from head to foot. She was so tired, her aches so deep, that she was nearly in tears.

"Hurry and undress," he commanded gently. He was standing beside her, watching her intently, unmoving. "Your bath is ready and getting cold."

"Please . . . I cannot bathe with you . . ."

He moved closer, so close she could hardly see

his face, because of his height, without leaning backward. The warnings of temptation were flowing sharply through her being, reminding her that the powerful attraction she felt for him was a sin.

"Let me help you with your laces," Runnolf offered.

"Nay . . . please . . . ," she whimpered in distress.

"I will not intrude," he promised as he stepped away from her. "And when you are finished, I will have my bath."

True to his word, Runnolf moved away, looking for some distraction. He settled on the menial task of preparing her bath water to his satisfaction.

Rowena's hands trembled so that she knotted the laces of her bliaud. Unconsciously she whimpered in frustration and fatigue.

Within a heartbeat he was beside her, moving her fingers from the hopeless tangle. She stood stiffly in front of him as his powerful hands gently unlaced her bliaud. His eyes glittered in the candlelight, yet he controlled his growing obsession for her. Rowena undressed slowly, partially from the stiffness of her muscles and partially because she could not match Runnolf's detached attitude.

"Hurry or the water will be cold again," he called over his shoulder. He was fighting to keep his voice level and his demeanor nonthreatening.

Rowena stood only in her kirtle, her hands clasped tightly together at her breast, unconsciously causing the fabric of her kirtle to tighten, outlining the pink tips of her nipples. Her hair, now unbraided, hung to her waist, shimmering in the flickering light of the candles.

"How many of these flowers do you put in the bath water?" he croaked, his voice strained from the battle raging within him. He dipped his hand into the large jar beside the tub and waited for her to answer.

"A handful," she answered quietly.

Rowena tried to stifle a nervous giggle as he withdrew a massive fistful of the dried flowers and dropped them in the water, then swirled them around. His handful was almost the entire jar!

"Well?" he demanded when she had not moved.

"I should . . . wash my hair first," she stammered, desperate to postpone the moment when she must completely disrobe in front of him.

"I will wait." Runnolf stretched out on the bed, his arms propped behind his head. He pulled his knee up, trying to hide his bulging manhood from her view. He did not know how he was going to get through the evening without touching her.

Rowena quickly knelt at the side of the tub, her back to him, hoping that to block him from view was to block out his presence. She bent over the rim of the tub so that her hair fell into the water, her bottom thrust into the air and wiggling provocatively as she vigorously soaped and scrubbed her hair. She was having trouble rinsing it when the large pitcher was lifted from her hand.

"You should not be so stubborn," Runnolf's voice rumbled in her ear as he poured for her. "I do not mind assisting when necessary."

Rowena trembled anew, worried over his behavior. This man was one contradiction after another. Hastily she wrapped her hair in a towel and looked up at Runnolf. When she was kneeling at his feet, her feeling of extreme vulnerability was intensified by his giant proportions.

"Here, let me help you with your kirtle," he volunteered, satisfied with their tentative domesticity. "Modesty is a virtue taught to children," he said when she hesitated to accept his offer. " But in the tub, there is little space for it. And between us, even less." Actually he found her modesty pleasing. It was a refreshing change from the brazenness of whores and the false modesty of others.

"Sir Runnolf, please." She tried once again to get him to leave so that she might bathe in privacy.

"Little one, let me help you," he whispered huskily as he impulsively knelt beside her.

His deep, throaty voice was like a caress, swaddling her in a warm cocoon of safety. She allowed him to remove her kirtle. Runnolf sensed the delicacy of the moment, the slim line of balance between her wanting to trust him and her desire to flee. He held his breath as he took her arm to support her while she stepped into the tub. He expelled his pent-up breath only when she sank into the water.

With great difficulty, he tore his gaze from her soft, enticing breasts as they bobbed lightly in the water. He almost staggered over to the bed, flinging himself upon it with as much nonchalance as he could manage. Once he heard the tiny splashes, he could no longer keep his good intentions. He opened his eyes to slits and enjoyed the picture of her in her bath. He was able to maintain this pose until she stood up, the water cascading off her body, shimmering in the wavering candlelight.

Rowena, oblivious to his subterfuge, completed her bath in relative peace. It was not until she stood up to dry off that Runnolf's deep moan of desire startled her. Instinctively she grabbed the towel to her breast and stood as motionless as a fawn in the forest. Her large brown eyes stared at him as if waiting for him to pounce so that she would know which way to run.

Her obvious fear gave Runnolf the control he needed. However it was the one thing he disliked about their relationship. It was bewildering to him that she could have spent the entire day unafraid and happy, but the minute they returned to the keep, she had become deferential to the point of being submissive.

As nonchalantly as possible, Runnolf began to undress in preparation for his own bath.

"I will call a servant for fresh water," Rowena stammered as she wrapped the towel around her.

"Nay," he answered firmly. He did not want anyone to disturb the mood of tranquillity he was trying so desperately to establish between them. "You were not that dirty, nor is the water that cold." Swiftly he finished his own disrobing and climbed into the tub.

The tub was just barely adequate for Runnolf's frame. His knees were drawn up close to his body, and he displaced much water onto the rush-covered floor. But he was determined that Rowena have ample time for her ablutions without his intimidating presence.

While Runnolf sat quietly in the tepid water, Rowena unwrapped the towel from her hair. She had forgotten to rinse it with cider vinegar, and the snarls were overabundant. Unrelenting, she set about combing them out. The act held such familiarity that it brought some measure of calm to her. She worked diligently on the snarls until her hair fell in long, glistening strands of new gold in the soft light.

"Come and wash my hair," Runnolf commanded when she had finished.

Rowena came to the side of the tub and knelt down beside him. This was not what she wanted to do, but it fell within the realm of a varlet and she had resigned herself to it. The bath had eased some of her aches and somewhat refreshed her, so that her hands were steady and sure as she soaped his hair and scrubbed it vigorously. She let the long, thick strands slip through her fingers only to recapture them to do it again. Having him sit docilely under her care sent waves of warmth surging through her. Her stomach felt like a covey of swallows seeking a nesting place.

Taking the large pitcher, she dipped it into the

bucket of clean water and carefully poured it over his head, rinsing the soap from his hair. The suds and water ran down his face, over his tightly closed eyes, and into his beard, then cascaded down his chest and back, creating small rivulets in the fur on his upper body. Once satisfied that his hair was rinsed properly, she began to dry his face with a clean towel.

"God's strength, woman!" he swore at her as he abruptly snatched the towel from her hands. "How much temptation do you believe I can stand?"

Rowena choked back a startled cry. What had she done now to provoke him so? Runnolf suddenly stood up. From her position, kneeling beside the tub, she was on eye level with his masculinity, and there was no doubt at all what was on his mind. But instead, he dried off and wrapped the towel about his waist.

"If you will lie upon the bed, I will put the salve on your bruises," he whispered in a hoarse voice.

"Do not trouble yourself," she murmured, barely able to keep her gaze from his camouflaged yet protruding member. "I will have Elaiva do it in the morning," she continued as she darted to the foot of the bed and fumbled with her truckler.

"I have already told you," he whispered as he moved beside her, "one bed is all that is needed."

"Surely you do not . . . I . . . every night . . . !"

"Yea, I do mean . . . you and I . . . every night!" he softly mimicked as he gently slipped his hand behind her neck and leaned down to kiss her softly on the forehead. He unwrapped the towel from around her and gazed longingly at her body. "Now, go you willingly?" he asked more harshly than he intended.

"Please, Sir Runnolf," she pleaded as she tried to back away. "There must be others who are willing to satisfy your needs."

"Yea, there are," he answered truthfully as he held her gently, his hand still behind her neck. "But they do not suit as well as you."

Rowena was stung by his words. She suspected that in the past he must have relieved himself with someone, but never before had it been mentioned aloud. The spoken knowledge hurt her more than she thought possible, filling her with shame at the comparison between herself and the other women who catered to him.

But his words were not meant as comparison. He simply did not lie. In his own way, he had paid her another compliment: He preferred her innocence to another's experience. But Rowena was too unworldly to understand.

Runnolf scowled as Rowena let out a groan of fright mingled with dread and darted for the bed. Scrambling under the sheet, she pulled it up to her chin and lay watching him apprehensively. He became more determined than ever to win her trust and affection.

"If you will turn over," he said softly as he sat on the side of the bed and took the pot of medication from the coffer, "I will salve your bruises."

Rowena lay stiff under Runnolf's gentle massage, dreading what was to come. His hands were gentle as he smeared the salve first on her shoulder, then her hip, and finally her thigh. At some point, her body began to rebel against her fear and she felt herself relax.

Runnolf felt the tension leave her body and was pleased that she seemed to be drifting off to sleep.

In sleep, Rowena's innate innocence and trust resurfaced. She wanted to love and be loved, to be accepted and cherished, to give obedience and honor to her husband and lord. Of her own volition she responded to him, rolling over, moving into the warmth and strength of his persistent hands.

Runnolf's heart beat erratically at this change in her. The half smile of contentment on her sleeping features was too much for him to resist. He began to massage her breasts. Her awakening nipples were an invitation to his mouth. He bent his head to caress them with his tongue and nibble them softly.

"Rowena, waken to me," he whispered, and he was greatly pleased when she looked at him without fear.

The pain of anticipation was absent. She was infused with a warmth in the nether regions of her body that added to the peace his calloused hands had brought her. Trustingly she lifted her hands to his damp hair, entwining her fingers in its thickness, holding his head to the places that aroused her. She arched her back, thrusting her breasts closer to his seeking mouth, and her legs parted for him.

She rubbed her hips against his, trying to maneuver her body to his so that he would satisfy the deep need, the physical ache that was growing within her. But instead he pulled her legs closed and held them so with his own. Frustrated by this strange turn of events, she whimpered as her mind cried for release from the sweet torture. She could hear the blood racing in her ears. Her cheeks burned with a heat that spread down her neck and throat.

And then it was over! She had hardly felt him enter her when he shuddered, exploding in his own release, and she was left behind. She moved against him, trying to reach her own release. When she could not, she sobbed in frustration. She was too innocent to do it alone, and he could not help her now. In trying to control himself to the last possible moment, Runnolf had lost sight of his own goal and the growing needs he had awakened in her. Now he realized that once awakened, she would not be fulfilled as easily as himself.

"We are both learning," he whispered as he held her closely against his shoulder. "We will learn together," he promised and let her cry herself to sleep.

But sleep did not come as readily for him. She had brought him to more awareness than any other woman. And he was learning as much from her innocence as he hoped she was from his limited experience. Once he taught her to come willingly to his bed, he would find perfect contentment.

Before now, all those who came to his bed without pay were there because of his position in the king's household. Or they were trying to better their station by snaring him into marriage. And marriage, he reminded himself, was the thing he wanted least. He was the king's knight, pledged to serve without land of his own.

Land would be a gift of mixed blessing for a knight such as Runnolf. It had been many years since he had allowed himself to dream of owning a demesne or even being castellan to one of the kings. But this, as were all long-range thoughts for himself, was fleeting. He had never been properly trained to manage a demesne. His sword and his life were the only things of value he had to offer his king. He was pledged to do battle. That was one of the reasons he had let this keep go so long without noticing things that were in need of being done. Stewardship had never before been his responsibility. He followed the king's orders to defend the king's property, not to manage it.

But Rowena had been so trained. She had proved it on several occasions. A new plan emerged in his sleepy mind. He would return stewardship of the keep to Rowena while he trained his men and awaited further orders from the king. That he knew how to do, and do well.

Chapter Fourteen

✦✦✦✦✦

THE NEXT MORNING, Rowena was awake first. She moved quietly through the solar, completing her morning toilet before dressing, all the while glancing over her shoulder to where Runnolf slept. But he was, in fact, already awake and watching her.

He gloried in her young body, its slender, muscular firmness. He remembered it beneath him last night and wished to have her so again. But for now, he would settle for the sight of her preparing for the day. She had twisted her long hair into a loose coil, which she draped over her shoulder while she washed her face. When she was finished, she moved closer to the bed to retrieve her kirtle.

"There is no need for you to stare so hard in hopes of wakening me," he whispered, trying to tease her a little. "If you desire to lie longer with me, I will not forbid it."

She had been so intent on not waking him that when he spoke, she was so startled that she jumped back from the bed. Hastily she grabbed her kirtle and tried to put it on.

"Rowena, listen to me," he commanded as he sprang from the bed and stood beside her. He pried the garment from her trembling hands and tossed it aside. "Listen to me," he said as he held her firmly by the shoulders so she could not turn away from him. "What has happened between us, has happened. I will not pretend that I am sorry. I am not. You meet my needs and give me pleasure. I intend to keep you by my side . . . for now," he added hastily, not wanting to promise more. "Let me also give you pleasure as your father gave your mother."

Father Dominic's voice, warning of damnation, was clear in her mind, yet Runnolf promised her happiness, happiness such as her parents had. She stood staring at him, fighting the fear that overshadowed her. But would it be the same as her parents? They were married!— would that make a difference? In her innocence, she wanted to accept him, to test the truth of his words. Such a promise was more than she could refuse.

He stood looking down at her, watching the vein pulsing in her neck. He had almost given up his patience when he saw it rewarded.

Tentatively she reached out her hand to touch the furry mat of hair on his chest. Her fingers played delicately across his muscles.

Runnolf held his breath as Rowena looked up from his chest to his face. He watched her dark eyes shimmering with intense concentration as she battled her conscience. Slowly he saw the fear recede and her eyes become misty with desire. Her lips parted slightly and he bent his head to kiss her, gently, as if asking permission to continue. Timidly she returned his kiss, opening her mouth to his, allowing his tongue to explore its depths. She met his advances with her own tongue, flicking it across his and then following it into his mouth when it retreated.

He ran his hand down her shoulders and over her hips. Cupping her buttocks with his hands, he pulled her close against him, lifting her off her feet. With her body held thus, she could feel his shaft against her thighs, and she trembled in anxious anticipation.

"Rowena!" he breathed in her ear as he carried her back to the bed.

"Yea, my lord," she answered softly, shivering as his voice vibrated through her.

"Rowena," he whispered again as he sat upon the bed with her in his lap. He delighted in the tremors that coursed through her when he called her name.

He loosened the coil of her golden hair. Beginning at her temples, he pulled his fingers through the silken strands as far as he could without tugging. He moved the blond screen over her shoulder, displaying her breasts to his hungry gaze. By the soft morning light he could see the slight bluish tint of her veins under her skin. Responding to the soothing sensations of his fingers on her scalp, Rowena laid her head back, exposing her neck and the hollow at the base of her throat, tempting his lips to caress her there. She was so vulnerable, so inviting. She was everything he desired.

Arching her back, she thrust her breast out to him, unconsciously enticing him to kiss her there, also. Succumbing to her allure, he took the nearest nipple into his mouth while rolling the other between his fingers. A moan of pleasure escaped her lips as she thrust hard against him. As he suckled, she felt a deep warming in her lower belly, in harmony with the sensations he aroused in her breasts. This new feeling was similar to what she had felt before, but now it was a deeper ache that begged for more.

"You are a morning star," he murmured against the fullness of her breasts, and then laid her down upon the bed. Her legs parted willingly so he could kneel between them.

"My lord, please do not leave me behind."

Runnolf felt no anger at Rowena's request. He had understood from her tears last night that she had not been content.

Gently he lifted her buttocks to meet his manhood and entered her carefully. She was ready for him, and he matched his movements to hers, then increased the pace until her chest was a blotch of arousal. Her breathing was almost as ragged as his own, but still he held the rhythm steady, pacing himself to her slower climb to the heights of surrender. Through each phase of ecstasy he moved with her, increasing his own passion and hers along the way until she cried out to him for release.

But instead of releasing her, he slowed, then carried her higher still until she screamed his name and dug her nails into his arms, trying to escape from the frightening heights. Again and again she shuddered as spasms of abandonment racked her body. And then they exploded together, falling to the bed sweating and exhausted.

Runnolf rolled to his side but would not let go of her. He caressed her, calling her name over and over until at last she was calm. He held her to him, listening to the rapid beating of his own heart.

Rowena was shattered by the experience and thoroughly frightened. She knew she had allowed him to take control of her body, but she had not expected her body to overwhelm her mind. That truly terrified her. He had transported her out of herself to experience sensations she had never dreamed existed. If he could do that once, he could do it whenever he pleased. Worse, she now desired to know those feelings, those sensations, that lack of control, again and again.

And then the reality of their situation stole in to ruin her happiness. She was not married to the man who brought her to such ecstasy. And he refused to marry anyone unless the king so ordered. Before, she had been his reluctant paramour. Now she would be his whore, and by her own desires. For the first time, she thought of what would become of her once he was gone from her life. Would she become one of the women of the market, serving the needs of other men, or would Runnolf be the only man to command her? And what if she carried his seed— what then?

And what if you do not? her conscience demanded. You can stop this now. You have found out what you wanted to know. You need not do it again!

"To sin in the mind is to sin with the body."

The words belonged to Father Dominic. Now that she knew what his words meant, she knew that she would never be free of her sin. Runnolf would always be in her mind and in her heart. He would always be a fire in her body.

She must speak with Father Dominic, but she realized she could not. To seek forgiveness through confession, to be granted forgiveness through penance, one must promise to sin no more in thought or in deed. How could she promise, knowing the way she felt? All Runnolf would have to do was ask her and she would willingly grant him anything.

"You are so sad, little one," Runnolf whispered, his breath tickling her neck. "Was it so terrible that you continue to grieve for your lost innocence?"

"Nay, my . . . nay, Sir Runnolf," she answered truthfully. "It was not so terrible."

He was aware that she had yet again almost called him lord but had changed it to Sir Runnolf. His own feelings of pleasure and contentment slowly slipped away as he perceived the deep sadness within her.

"If you do not mourn, then why the melancholy?" he persisted.

"There is no melancholy," she answered again truthfully, since she would not have described her feelings in such terms.

He waited for her to say more but she did not.

"Your father, fitz Giles, trained you in the

management of this keep, is that not so?" he asked as he reluctantly climbed out of bed.

"Yea," she answered softly, unsure where his question would lead her.

"Then you will continue to manage it, giving orders about harvesting and whatever. If you need any help from me, simply ask." As he dressed he watched her from across the room as she lay on the bed, the sheet covering her.

"What will you do with your day?" he asked, in an effort to find out what might be on her mind.

"First I must see to the preparation of the day's meals. Then I will take Owain out to the mares and mark them—"

"If you do not get out of bed soon, the day will be over," he chided her teasingly.

Runnolf scowled as Rowena hastily scurried from the bed and began dressing. He had made the comment in jest trying to lighten the mood between them, but she had misunderstood, taking his comment for an order. He knew he was not an adept courtier, but neither was he so tyrannical as her behavior indicated.

"How do you intend to mark them?" he asked, trying to ease her nervousness.

"We will brush their manes out and braid them," she answered hastily. She knew that he was displeased by something she had done, but she did not know what it was. Had she not obeyed him instantly? She hurried along with her explanation, hoping to placate him. "They will be the only ones braided, and any of the grooms will be able to spot them without difficulty. Even if they come partway unbraided, that part closest to the crest should hold.

"The monastery holds market every feast day," she rushed on breathlessly. "And there should be a ready market for the destriers your men do not choose. We . . . your men could choose those they want and keep them separate—if there were another pasture."

Runnolf noticed her correcting herself from using the word "we" and it disquieted him. "We" sounded supremely appropriate coming from her lips.

"Smithfield, outside of London, has the best horse market," he told her.

"Whatever you think best," she responded immediately. Her voice had lost a spark of animation when she answered, and it confused him further.

"The destriers will go to Smithfield," he decided. "The palfreys to the monastery. And a select group of mares will be left for Leben. Once they carry his foals, they can be taken to Smithfield also.

"After the harvest, turn the horses out to graze," he continued. "That should keep them separate."

"But that should not be done!" she protested, pausing in the process of pulling a yellow bliaud over her kirtle. "Unless, of course, it is your will," she amended submissively. Again she saw him scowl and did not understand its cause.

"Explain!" he demanded, her submissiveness beginning to wear on his nerves.

"The cattle must be turned out for fattening before butchering," she answered. She was positive in her knowledge, but she did not understand why he was asking unless he was testing her.

"When the harvest is complete, set the villains to clearing the land of your choice," he said, reasonably well satisfied with her answer.

"The woodcutters could clear the land while the villains harvest their own crops," she suggested, not sure why he did not suggest it himself.

"Then tell them your wishes!"

"What is the point of all this?" she cried as she picked up her hairbrush and unexpectedly threw it across the room. She was frustrated by the questions, confused by his apparent need to test her, and angry that he did not give the orders himself. "You question me. You scowl when I answer. You scowl when I obey. And even if I do all of these things for the demesne, it will all be for naught and be destroyed as soon as you leave."

Runnolf took a long moment before responding. He wanted to reassure her that her efforts would not be wasted, but he was afraid to build her hopes too high. The king had not yet responded to his messages. And how could he tell her why he scowled, when he truly did not understand it himself. It was not that she obeyed him—obedience was expected—it was the way she obeyed, her quick, scurrying movements that smelled of fear.

"It is my wish that you do so," he explained simply, coming to stand in front of her and resting his powerful hands on her shoulders. Bending down, he kissed her deeply, yet tenderly, breaking the embrace only when she began to respond. He had too much to do to be tempted.

"Come, it is time to break our fast. Are you ready?"

"I must finish my hair," she managed to answer breathlessly.

"Fetch your brush and I will wait."

Shamefaced, Rowena retrieved her brush from where she had flung it and finished brushing her hair. She did not have time for the elaborate braids she usually wore, so she braided it in one loose plait that hung down the middle of her back.

As Runnolf studied her, he again noted how swift and jerky her movements were, so different from the graceful gestures he had admired when she thought him asleep.

When she was through, they descended to the hall. There was not much left on the table. But there was still enough for them to help themselves to generous portions of cheese, fruit, and cider.

"While you see to the mares, I will work with the gray." Runnolf munched on a wedge of cheese. "It will take a full day to work with each before I will be able to make a choice."

"Where are your other horses?" She remembered Runnolf telling her that each knight needed three. "Have they been injured so you do not have them with you?"

"Until now, I had need of none other than Leben," he responded. "But I do have a pack-horse to carry my belongings. Usually my squire cares for it along with his own horse. However, since Odo's death, I have left his care to Ferrand."

Rowena wondered what he chose for his share of each disseized castle but knew it was none of her affair.

"When do you wish the horses ready for market?" she asked, changing the path of her thoughts.

"However long it takes to sort them out to everyone's satisfaction."

"The mares should not be taken from Leben until he is sound and you have need for him again," she ventured. "It will assure that he has . . ." she did not finish but blushed unreasonably. To speak of such matters had held no embarrassment for her before.

"Take Sir James with you if he is available." Runnolf missed her moment of embarrassment as he started for the door. "He has a good eye for horses. If he is not available, then Sir Lyle."

Rowena followed Runnolf to the top of the stairs leading to the bailey and then paused. It had rained again during the night, the soft gentle rain that nourishes the soil and gives new hope. She inhaled deeply, tasting the fragrant air. From her vantage point, she could see that the dust had been washed from the grass and leaves, leaving them almost new looking.

Runnolf, however, did not have her feel for
the land and all its moods. All he knew was that
it was a good day to begin a strenuous chore. He
immediately proceeded to the stables to fetch the
gray and begin training.

Reluctantly Rowena left her aerie and went in
search of Sir James and Sir Lyle. But first she
stopped at the cooper's cottage and ordered a
new tub made for Runnolf. It would take some
time, but she shyly asked that it be done as soon
as possible. She was embarrassed on so personal
an errand, but she was determined that he be as
comfortable as his great size would allow. Her
reticence, coupled with the love the cooper held
for her, placed the new tub high on his list of
priorities.

She spent the rest of the morning searching
for Sir James and Sir Lyle but never finding
them. She was constantly distracted by first one
minor catastrophe and then another as the keep
began to make space for storing the harvest.

Rowena shyly joined Runnolf at table for the
main meal of the day. She so wanted to enjoy his
company as much as possible in the short time
before the king demanded the destruction of the
keep. And she would ignore the sly glances of
the knights and their comments. She would live
with the knowledge of their thoughts, but she
would not let it interfere with her new-found
joy.

"Did you find Sir James and Sir Lyle?" he
asked when they were seated.

"Nay, Sir Runnolf," she apologized. "I was
searching for them but—"

"It is of little import. They are here now." He spent the rest of the meal explaining his plans for the horses to his knights.

During the meal, Runnolf showed no outward affection for Rowena. He was attentive to her needs, seeing that her trencher was full of the most delicate slices of meat and vegetables, and when appropriate he included her in conversation regarding the demesne.

After the meal, Runnolf returned to the stables to work with the gray, while Rowena and Owain accompanied Runnolf's knights to the pasture. Selections were made for the knights as well as for those of Sir Hugh's garrison who were to join Runnolf's troop.

Rowena took the opportunity to bring an apple for the chestnut mare. Occasionally throughout the afternoon she tried to entice the mare to accept her gift, but the high-spirited horse would have none of it. She tossed her head disdainfully, refusing. Just before returning to the keep, Rowena placed the apple on the ground and walked away.

"Just in case you change your mind," she called cheerily.

The mare appeared to ignore it until one of the other horses came to investigate. Still behaving as if it were an object of scorn, she blocked the other's approach.

Rowena was pleased at the mare's possessive behavior. "Do not let anyone spoil your treat," she laughed as she mounted the white palfrey and rode away.

Rowena returned to the keep tired but happy.

Things were falling into a hectic rhythm that was challenging as well as satisfying. For now the villains were safe, the harvest was being gathered, the horses being sorted out, and she was looking forward to her private time with Runnolf.

They shared a light meal with the rest of the keep and then Runnolf escorted her to the solar. Again Elaiva had seen to their every need.

Timidly Rowena turned to Runnolf. "May I assist you, my lord?" she whispered, blushing at her boldness.

"Anon," he breathed as he pulled her into his arms and kissed her. "I have been wanting to . . . do . . . this . . . all day, " he murmured as he kissed her lips, her eyes, and her temple. He could feel the throbbing of her blood against his lips, and he thrilled to see that it was not for fear that her blood raced so.

"Oh, little one, you make me so happy," he whispered as he began to unlace her bliaud. "I never thought to have such contentment."

She melted against him, molding her body to his, her breath coming rapidly. She felt his shaft press against her belly and snuggled even closer. "Must we wait?" she pleaded, her own needs as demanding as his own. She had been in the pasture most of the afternoon and had witnessed Leben with the mares. As hard as she had tried, she could not help but think of herself and Runnolf, their lives paralleled in so many ways.

Runnolf groaned with his desire for her and needed no second invitation. Lifting her into his arms, he carried her to the bed, laid her down, and covered her with his own body. He would have been patient but she met his kisses with her own, demanding and insistent. He could not wait or he would loose his seed. Lifting her skirts and his tunic, he entered her. To his surprise and delight, she was ready for him. He tried to prolong her pleasure, but they were both in too much of a hurry.

When they were sated he cradled her closely, feeling the heat of her body, tasting the sweat of her brow. He was in no mood to leave her nor was there any need. Momentarily content, he leisurely finished unlacing her bliaud and helped her to undress. She lay on the bed beside him, her skin glistening in the candlelight.

She was so beautiful. She made him so very happy. And in his happiness, he wanted her to be happy also. He remembered her words when describing her parents: *He made her laugh.*

Playfully he nibbled the budded nipples of her breasts and licked her salty sweat. She giggled gleefully as he gently ran his thumbs down her sides and over her pelvis.

"It is truly like my father and Lady Margaret," she breathed, perfectly content to remain by his side and never leave the bed again.

Her laughter was like music, and he was determined that it would always be so with them. Every time they coupled, he would not forget to make her laugh. It would be done until it was so without conscious effort.

This was a side of the king's giant that Rowena would never have believed existed if she had not been a witness to it. He was everything her father had been to her mother. Strong when necessary. Gentle when possible. Virile . . . She blushed, unable to form words, although the image of his aroused desire was in her memory and in the memory of her flesh. They were so indelibly impressed upon her, along with the memories of her home, that she knew she would never forget no matter where she went. Many times that night new memories were added to the ones already stored.

Chapter Fifteen

✦ ✦ ✦ ✦

ROWENA WAS HALFWAY across the bailey, heading toward the stables, when Norbert hailed her. She had not known that he was healed, and her negligence made her blush in embarrassment.

He was dressed in the simple tunic of the villains, with woolen chausses and cross garters. His body and hair were clean, his beard gone. Rowena knew that Elaiva had been taking good care of him during his recuperation.

"Lady Rowena, wait," he called breathlessly, his eyes alight with devotion. He took her hands in his and held them tightly. "You tried to save me," he stammered, overcome by emotion. "I remember . . . you came . . . afterwards . . ."

"How is your back?" she asked, concerned by the stiffness which which he still moved, and his limp. She wondered how she might remove her hands from his grip without seeming cold or heartless, but she could not think of a way.

"I am fine now," he answered, beaming. "Soon I will be as good as new." And then his expression changed to deep sorrow. "Rowena, I am very sorry for the death of your father. It is more than you—"

"Please, I do not wish to dwell—"

"I understand," he interrupted. "And I have good news for you," he exclaimed, his eyes again shining. "I have just spoken to Sir Runnolf. I have asked to serve as his varlet in your stead."

"But your back! You will not be able to bend or stoop, fetch or carry without reopening your wounds," she protested, trying to dissuade him. He had not been in the hall since his injuries, so he did not know of her change in status. Nor did she know how to tell him of her shame.

"I promise to be gentle in my demands," Runnolf said, coming up behind her. His face was immobile, but there was a slight edge in his voice that betrayed his anger at the intimacy they exhibited.

Startled, Rowena pulled her hands from Norbert's grasp and looked down as Runnolf placed his hand on her shoulder, then slowly, deliberately, ran his finger up and down the column of her neck, watching the effect his presence had on them both.

Rowena felt waves of shame emanating from her body as the implications of Runnolf's actions registered on Norbert. Despondently she watched his shoulders sag and the happiness drain from his face. His chin sank to his chest, and his arms hung limply at his sides as if he had no strength to hold them to his body. Beseechingly she raised her hand to him, begging for understanding, but he did not see the gesture. She looked to Runnolf for comfort, but all she saw was cold indifference to her plight. Totally distraught, she fled from them both.

Tears filled Norbert's eyes as he looked from Rowena's fleeing form back to Runnolf's cold visage. He understood that in reality Rowena was physically safer in Runnolf's care than in his own, but it did not assuage his guilt. He had failed Sir Hugh, and now Rowena was forced to pay for his failure with her shame. "She was left to my care and I failed her," he wept. "How can she ever forgive me?"

"Seek not her forgiveness but God's," Runnolf answered curtly.

For the first time in his life Runnolf witnessed total disgrace, not the disgrace reflected through others' opinions but the disgrace felt from the soul. Norbert knew that he had failed in his ultimate responsibility and would never be able to make amends to his dead lord.

Runnolf did not hold Norbert in any way responsible for what had happened between himself and Rowena. Yet he understood words would not change the man's feelings of guilt or ease the burden he must now carry through life, nor would any penance the priest would give him.

Runnolf recognized the deep devotion Norbert held for Rowena and was disquieted by it. The steward's close association with Rowena would always leave him uneasy. He shrugged it off. In reality, he must accept Norbert's devotion as a weapon to ensure Rowena's future safety.

Runnolf studied the heartsick man, hoping to find a way to channel his despair into something useful. "You may begin your penance"—he began slowly, deliberately, so that his words would penetrate Norbert's guilt—"by serving me faithfully." He continued gruffly, unaccustomed to being so deeply involved in another's personal life. "By protecting my back in battle. By seeing that no harm comes to me, you guarantee that no further harm will come to her."

"I do not understand," Norbert stammered. "How does a varlet—"

"Not as a varlet, but as my squire!" Runnolf emphasized. Norbert was deaf to Runnolf's words and only stared, sad-eyed and openmouthed. "Take you to my chaplain. I saw him last with the baggage wains. Tell him your sin and my words."

"I will never leave her," Norbert whispered huskily. He was thankful that there was a way he could still be of service to Rowena, but he must also make Runnolf aware that his first obligation would always be to his lady. "I will remain by her side no matter what befalls. And when you send her away, I will still be there."

The two men looked deep and long at each other, studying the core of determination each possessed. Runnolf was the first to give ground, acknowledging Norbert's commitment to Rowena. "So be it." Not until then did Norbert go in search of the chaplain.

Runnolf watched Norbert shamble away and then dismissed him from his mind. He had done what he could. He had offered him a way of redemption and now it was up to Norbert. He slowly walked toward the keep, dreading his next encounter with Rowena. Mentally he reviewed the ways of dealing with a crying female and realized he knew of none. But nothing could have prepared him for Rowena's greeting.

"You cannot have him for varlet!" she shouted as he entered the solar. Her eyes were red from weeping, a trail of tears evident on her cheeks. However there were no tears now.

He would have told her of Norbert's elevation from varlet to squire but his bewilderment turned to anger, preventing him from doing so. Rowena may administer the keep by his permission, but she did not pick and choose his servants!

"I have need for a varlet and he has asked to serve," he answered tonelessly, trying to mask his bewilderment. He had expected to find her crying; he had not expected her to turn shrewish.

"Father found better use for him as steward. He must have had good reason."

"I have already accepted him. Unless he proves unworthy, he remains."

"What will his duties be?" she demanded.

"A varlet serves his master whenever and wherever. Norbert is a man grown, so I may use him in any capacity I see fit." The jealous image of Rowena and Norbert in the bailey surfaced in his mind and his voice grew cold and deadly with growing suspicion. "Are you more concerned for his welfare or mine?"

"And he will sleep within call of your voice?" she asked, ignoring his question. Runnolf stared at her, unable to understand the odd question. When he did not answer, she continued. "Let him serve you in the hall," she pleaded, her voice melting to supplication. "Or wherever else that suits you, but not in the solar."

"Part of his responsibilities will bring him to the solar," he explained. Her erratic behavior bewildered him anew, and he strove to maintain temperance while he sorted things out. "He must arm and disarm me, see to my clothes—"

"Let me do those things for you," she pleaded.

"You have your own responsibilities—"

"I will not tolerate him in the solar," she screamed unexpectedly.

"You will do as you are told!" he thundered as he advanced on her, now completely out of patience. "You will tolerate what I tell you to tolerate!"

"I will not have him sleep at the foot of the bed!" she shrieked. "I will not have him hear how I cry out to you in my need. Is it not enough that he knows me as your whore? Must he also be witness to it?"

Runnolf halted in midstride. He did not know whether to slap her for her defiance or wrap her in his arms for the joy her unexpected words brought him. But it was not a hard decision. He scooped her up and swung her about in delight.

Rowena was as mystified by Runnolf's change in attitude as he had been by hers moments ago. A heartbeat past, as he had advanced on her, she had expected to receive a severe beating for her rebelliousness. In fact it had taken all of her willpower not to cower from him. And now she found herself crushed to his chest in an embrace so strong she almost could not breathe.

"Where did he sleep before?" Runnolf asked as he buried his face in her neck, smelling the warmth of her skin.

"In the hall, where your knights now sleep," she answered breathlessly.

"I will forbid him the solar," he whispered. "As long as he sleeps in the hall."

"Verily, my lord?" she asked, desperate for confirmation.

"Verily," he answered and kissed her deeply.

Rowena returned his kiss with vigor and intense relief. She had prevented Norbert access to the solar! Her shame might be known, but the depth of her sin was still her secret.

"We should have words more often," Runnolf chuckled as he released her. "Your fire is high and I would gladly indulge you, but we do not have the time."

Rowena blushed, but it did not hide the slight burn about her lips from his beard.

"Is there time before the meal for Norbert to shave me?" he asked, rubbing his face thoughtfully and glancing out of the window to judge the hour.

Rowena's heart jumped at the thought of him without a beard. She had never seen him otherwise, and somehow she felt that he would not be completely dressed without it. "Your beard is very pleasing to me," she ventured, again flushed at her daring. "It only lacks trimming."

"It leaves marks upon your fair skin." He traced his finger lightly about her lips, mesmerizing her with his gentle touch.

"As you wish, my—Sir Runnolf," she whispered, slowly raising her hand and gently placing her fingertips on his lips. As if in farewell, she touched his beard softly. "I will summon . . ."

Again she had nearly called him lord, and Runnolf was tempted to ask her why she had not. Somehow he knew that such a question would spoil the mood. He was also intrigued by her fondness for his beard. "You like my beard?" he whispered, turning his face into her hand and kissing her fingertips.

"It is very soft," she whispered in response, as if divulging a secret. "It looks as though it would not be, being as dark and thick . . ." She ran her fingertip softly along his cheek. ". . . It tickles."

"I have never cared for a beard . . . before now," he answered hesitantly. In truth he did not particularly like a beard and mustache, especially when he was in the field on the king's business. It was too hot under the helm and needed too much care and attention for his tastes. He had not shaved since coming to this keep because he did not have a squire and because other things, especially Rowena, had occupied his mind. But if it pleased her, for now, he would allow it. "Does Norbert—"

"I will care for it," she volunteered, her eyes large and luminous as she gazed into his, continuing to caress his beard with light, swirling strokes.

"Have you ever . . ." Her mood was heavy upon him. All he wanted to do was sweep her up into his arms and carry her to the large bed.

"Nay . . . I have not," she responded sadly. Her shoulders slumped in dejection. "Father and all his men shaved. The only ones who do not are the Welsh. But I will shave you if you like," she volunteered. She was falsely cheerful, as if trying to convince him that it did not matter.

"If you do not mind the beard," he began hesitantly, "at least for a little while. And if you think you can trim it yourself . . ." He let the sentence trail into nothingness as his mind examined the sweet possibility of having Rowena's undivided attention. "But I want my hair trimmed short."

"Settle yourself on the stool," she commanded happily as she hurried to fetch her scissors. They spent the rest of the morning in domestic bliss.

* * *

Rowena's days and nights were a mixture of sadness and euphoria. Sadness came only in the daylight and only when she allowed herself to dwell on her future. She had long since stopped hearing the warning voice of Father Dominic in her conscience along with his preachings of chastity. Now she heard his voice promising eternal punishment and damnation for her unrepented sins. However, the grimness of those thoughts was overshadowed by the new heights to which Runnolf transported her as he taught her the joys of the flesh night after night.

For Runnolf also, the nights and days were vivid contrasts. For the most part he was able to concentrate entirely on the present, relegating all else to the future and the king's whim. But sometimes at night, after Rowena had fallen asleep, the future would crowd in on him. Especially troubling was Norbert's promise to remain with Rowena. Runnolf would lie awake for hours remembering Norbert's shame as well as his prophecy. "When you send her away I will still be there."

Before Norbert's avowal, Runnolf had not allowed himself to dwell on the time when he must send her away. But now it had been brought home to him that he might have to. What was he to do with her if the king should command him to disseise more castles for the crown? He held no land on which to keep her in safety. Would she consent to follow him? If so, she could travel in the baggage wain. Or could he afford to hire some mercenaries to be her guard and have her follow separately?

Runnolf knew that winter was not far off, so the chance of being sent out again was slim yet not impossible. They might have the winter months to themselves here, if Henry did not order the destruction of the keep. If he did, where would they pass the winter? Would he be commanded to travel with the king? Would the king allow him leave for the winter? He had asked very little from Henry all these years; would having Rowena be too much?

Occasionally he was able to wipe out his questions concerning the future by remembering the morning that Rowena had declared her passion for him. The only thing to mar that memory was her calling herself a whore. That had shocked him. But he was even more shocked when he realized that might well be what she thought of herself. She was so innocent, so vulnerable. Surely she must know that he did not feel that way about her. She held meaning and tenderness; she filled a place left lonely so long that he no longer recognized it as being empty. She was many things to him but certainly not whore!

When the day finally arrived for Runnolf's final inspection of the horses, he decided to send Sir Lyle and Sir James to the market without delay.

The next morning dawned clear and bright. The bailey was in chaos as the grooms sorted out their charges and prepared to lead them out. Rowena watched from the top step of the keep. She heard Sir James call his knights to mount. Then to her surprise he turned to salute her. Bemused, she turned to see whom he might be waving at and realized she was alone. Hesitantly she waved back. After receiving her answering fare-thee-well, Sir James kicked his mount into a trot and the troop rode sedately down the green valley.

Rowena blushed becomingly. The man had acknowledged her as if she were truly Lady of the keep. She would have been content to stand and watch them out of sight, but it was not to be.

"Gather your medicines," Runnolf called to her, interrupting her contentment. "And accompany me to the pasture. It is time to see if your stitches have held."

Rowena hurried to do his bidding. On her way past the kitchen, she also picked up several apples and stuffed them into her apron pocket.

In the pasture Rowena watched as Runnolf was reunited with his destrier. His other duties had kept him from visiting, so his excitement was great. But her mind was on the chestnut mare. On her last visit not only had she been able to feed her an apple from her hand, but she had begun to groom her.

In the following week, each day when Rowena and Owain went to the pasture, the mare tolerated her more and more, and the progress could be seen in the chestnut's coat. The mare's head and shoulders, chest and barrel shone brightly in the sun, but her flanks and tail were still dull and roughly combed.

Days passed. By the time Rowena had the mare's coat thoroughly combed, brushed, and shining, she had gained enough confidence to attempt to put the halter on her.

"I am sorry I tricked you," she apologized as the mare backed away from her, tossing her head and trying to dislodge the annoying straps around her face. "Please forgive me," she continued sweetly. "But you would not have let me if I had not. And if you do not let me train you, Sir Runnolf will sell you at the market and we will not be able to be friends anymore."

Rowena spent every afternoon in the pasture with the mare, while Runnolf trained his men and rode patrol. Eventually the mare allowed her to take the halter off and put it back on again without fear. Each time, she rewarded the mare with a handful of the oats she carried. She worked ceaselessly, repeating the lessons, rewarding her for good behavior, constantly reinforcing the mare's confidence in her goodwill and love.

"Today is the day," Rowena told the mare late one afternoon after she had been groomed and lessoned. "Today you will show me how smart you are," she continued as she led the mare outside the pasture with the saddle blanket now in place. Rowena's heart raced as Owain approached from her left side carrying the saddle. He had never before left the gate to come near the horse, and she sidestepped away from him.

Never once did Rowena stop talking as Owain raised the saddle over the mare's back and gently set it in place. The chestnut turned nervously in a circle as he struggled to get the girth straps through the buckles.

"Oh, Firelight, you are just being contrary!" Rowena whispered in exasperation. "You are just like Leben!"

It was the first time she had called the mare by name. During the long hours of training, Rowena had agonized over a proper name for such a beautiful animal. "Firelight!" she repeated, testing the new name. "Firelight, the name fits you. Why did you not tell me that was your name?"

Firelight's ears perked forward as Rowena continued to call her by her new name, distracting her.

"Be sure the girth is tight," Rowena reminded Owain. "She may have held her breath on you."

Again Owain approached the prancing chestnut. He was able to tighten the girth another notch but no more. "She was too nervous to hold it long," he said in satisfaction. "It should be tight enough now."

Chapter Sixteen

✦ ✦ ✦ ✦ ✦

ON THE DAY that Rowena chose to saddle the mare, Runnolf was working his troop on the hillsides. He was not paying attention to the scene below but was concentrating on Norbert, guiding him among the trees where there was no true trail.

Training in such terrain was not the normal practice for knights. But Runnolf was a hard taskmaster and never allowed an opportunity or an exceptional situation to go unexplored. He knew by reputation the unusual battle tactics of the Welsh, as well as their fighting ability and tenacity. He wanted his troop to know as much as possible of the land and to be adept at fighting in it.

It was not until they came to a small clearing where they were able to rest that Runnolf had time to survey the demesne. Slowly the presence of Rowena with the chestnut mare penetrated his reverie. At first his mind would not register what his eyes beheld. Then in horrified disbelief he watched as Rowena prepared to mount.

"Sir Hugh said she was the best horsewoman he had ever seen," Norbert said in expansive pride.

Before Runnolf could find his voice to answer, Owain gave Rowena a leg up. She had not enough time to seat herself properly before the mare pitched her off. Runnolf let out his breath in an explosive oath as she went sailing through the air to land forcefully on the ground and lie still.

"She is not hurt," Norbert whispered in a prayerful voice. "She will be up anon."

Runnolf felt a breathless aching in his own body as he watched Rowena slowly climb to her feet, sway slightly, and lean heavily upon Owain. He turned back to his troop, unable to look any longer.

"See! I told you! She is not hurt and she will try again!" Norbert cried out in excitement.

Runnolf spun around, now utterly aghast. He watched as Owain boosted Rowena back into the saddle. This time, however, she was prepared. The mare reared, and again he vicariously experienced the teeth-jarring impact of the horse's action as the mare came down hard, her front hooves hammering the ground. Runnolf's heart pounded in fear for Rowena's safety as the chestnut bolted across the open field.

"Now you will see!" Norbert shouted, ecstatic beyond control as he watched his beloved Rowena. His excitement was contagious, infecting the others to admiration and animated wagering. Those who had no firsthand knowledge of Rowena's ability with Leben wagered against her. Those who had seen them together wagered in her favor.

Runnolf felt the reckless urge to rush to Rowena's rescue, to save her from the danger of riding a horse so apparently out of control. Yet, practically, he reminded himself that he was too far away and could not possibly make his way down the trackless hillside with any speed.

Momentarily forced into inactivity, he stared as Rowena and the mare fought for control. It appeared that Rowena would win the contest, but instead she relaxed, blending her body to the mare's and allowing the animal's long, powerful strides to carry them toward the keep. Rowena's legs were a white blur as she used her knees to mold herself to the mare. Her blond braids mingled with the long chestnut mane as the two fused into one spirit.

Once the two disappeared behind the bailey wall, Runnolf could be still no longer. He steadily worked his way down the hillside, his original fear for Rowena's safety turned to cold anger. Her stupidity, her total lack of regard for her own safety, was appalling to him. By the time she and the mare came back into view, Runnolf was waiting by the side of the road near the pasture.

If he had not been so concerned for her safety, Runnolf would have seen that the mare had ceased her breakneck speed and had settled into a well-paced run, her step light and sure. But he had received a good fright and had not yet recovered enough to make such observations.

Rowena's heart raced in rhythm with the pounding hooves of the mare, and there were tears in her eyes as she rode back to the pasture. She did not know if they were from exhilaration or the sting of the wind. Her cheeks were flushed, and her eyes danced with sparks of life and happiness.

Norbert rushed to assist her dismount. He had nothing but words of praise for her ability, but they fell on deaf ears. The only person Rowena saw was Runnolf. The only praise she wished to hear was from him.

"Oh, my lord! Isn't she beautiful? Truly as magnificent as your Leben!"

"Give orders to Owain to walk the mare until she cools and then come with me," Runnolf commanded without commenting upon the horse or her ability to ride.

Rowena's happiness evaporated at the soberness of Runnolf's demeanor. She could rarely read his daytime expressions, since he kept such tight control over himself, but this time there was no doubt that something was drastically wrong. The corded muscles in his neck stood out alarmingly, and his brow was drawn together in a dark and forbidding appearance.

"Sir Runnolf, what news?" she asked as she waved Owain to obey Runnolf's commands for the care of the mare. She was fully concerned that something serious was amiss, and she gave her entire attention to him.

Runnolf was angry, but not so angry that he failed to notice the instant change in her. In the excitement of her ride, she had called him "lord". But now that she was once again exerting control over her emotions, she had reverted to calling him "Sir Runnolf". This change in her angered him more.

"Norbert! Assist your lady to mount her palfrey!"

Reacting as if shoved, Norbert hastened to do Runnolf's bidding. Once Rowena was astride, he hurried to mount his own horse and followed discreetly behind as Runnolf led the way to the keep without another word passing his lips.

In her mind, Rowena went over what had happened. Was he truly so furious over her riding the mare? She had tamed her! Was it not a true accomplishment? Or perhaps he had found the money and jewelry in the hems of her bliauds? She immediately discounted that thought because she never wore them anymore, and by the look of him he had just returned from training, not from the keep. Had he discovered that she had sent some of the cattle away so they would not be butchered? She also dismissed that idea because he paid so little attention to the actual running of the demesne. And to her knowledge, the hiding place of the animals was farther from the keep than his troop usually traveled. Had he heard from the king? Her heart suddenly felt as heavy as lead within her breast. She searched no further for an answer to his dark mood. Runnolf must now destroy the demesne and leave. She rode the rest of the way trying to muster the courage to say good-bye to everything she loved.

At the bailey Runnolf tossed the reins of the gray to a groom. He completely ignored Rowena, allowing Norbert to lift her down while he stormed the two flights of stairs to the solar. Rowena raced after him, dreading to hear the words from his lips yet knowing the future must be faced.

Once in the solar, Runnolf turned on her in anger. "What were you doing on that horse?" he demanded as he threw his helm across the room.

"Did you not know that you could have been killed?"

"What has Firelight to do with the king?" she demanded, confused by his outburst.

"What king?" he demanded. "I am talking about you riding the mare."

"You have not heard from the king?" she persisted.

"Rowena! What were you doing on that dangerous animal?" he demanded, towering over her in frustration and rage.

"Firelight is no more dangerous than your Leben," she answered, relieved.

"Did I not tell you that horse was not well schooled?"

"You said you were too busy to work with her, and that was what I have been doing."

"By what right . . ." he began as he flung himself onto a nearby stool. "Unarm me," he commanded, forgetting to finish his question.

Rowena did not usually disarm Runnolf, but she did not hesitate to obey. She pulled the hauberk over his head, finding that its exceptional size was almost more than she could handle. She struggled under its weight, carrying it over to the corner, where she laid it on the floor. Even her lack of strength was not enough excuse to allow her to mishandle the valuable property belonging to another. Next she helped him with his gambeson and laid it on top of the hauberk.

"Rowena, you are the most—" he began in exasperation.

"You think that I am like the women at court," she interrupted, trying to be reasonable. Yet her

relief that the king had not sent for him was hard
to keep hidden. A little smile kept surfacing
about her lips that was hard to suppress. "But I
am not like them. I am capable of running a
keep. I have proven that to you. I am capable of
riding a horse astride. I have proven that also,
although I have not been able to prove my ability
on a hunt. I am capable of training my own
horse: I was trying to prove that to you."

"I told you not to ride the mare!" he thundered, ignoring her arguments.

The signs of her own growing anger were becoming visible as he persisted.

"By what right do you tell me what to do?"
she cried in unrestrained frustration. The entire
conversation was becoming an escalating confusion of emotions.

"I am lord here," he warned her menacingly.

"You are lord here," she answered. "But you
are not my lord. I am only your whore."

Incensed by her reckless disregard for propriety, Runnolf backhanded her, sending her flying
across the room to slam backward into the wall.
Slowly her legs collapsed and she slid to the
floor, straining for the breath that was knocked
from her. Her face was ashen except for the
deepening scarlet imprint of his hand, and her
eyes watered, but not with tears of contrition.

Alarmed that he had struck her so hard, Runnolf strode to her side and unceremoniously
lifted her to her feet. Yet he would not apologize. Nor was he, in his mind, unjustified in
disciplining her. She had deliberately disobeyed
him, had placed herself in jeopardy, had refused

to recognize her error, and had argued with him about it. Finally, she had resorted to the most unladylike language. He would not tolerate such behavior from her.

Once steady on her feet, Rowena pulled away from his support and faced him. Her breasts heaved with the effort to gain air into her lungs. Her renewed fear of him was obvious as her whole body trembled. But it was the pain in her eyes that made him cringe inwardly, for they revealed her deep despair that he would ever take pride in her.

"You are not my husband and lord," she rasped, emphasizing the words *husband* and *lord* to mean one and the same. She had clenched her jaws together to keep her teeth from chattering, trying not to show him how frightened she was.

"I am not your husband," he snarled, angered that he had lost so much of her trust and seeing the effort it took her not to cower from him. "Yet you are lady here by my word. All here obey you by my will."

"I am unquestionably obeyed by my father's people because I am his daughter, but I am not considered 'lady' by your men. If you were not present, they would not obey me. I am nothing more than your—" She stopped abruptly as Runnolf deliberately raised his hand to strike her again.

"Never say that word to me again or I will beat you until you pray for death!" he promised her coldly. He wanted to argue the point with her, but he knew in some measure that her words held more truth than exaggeration.

"You once asked the price of my virginity," she whispered fiercely. "I have found my price. I want the mare!"

"Nay!" he thundered, afraid that if she kept the mare she would be killed. "The mare will be a gift to the king, and if I find you near her, I will have her destroyed."

The threat to destroy the mare was as strong a blow to Rowena as if she had been struck.

"But why? Your king has everything! What need has he for one more horse?"

"I have spoken!" His fear for her safety made him blind to her needs.

"Where are you going?" he demanded as she walked toward the solar steps. "I have not given you permission—"

"To the kitchen. I will earn my place there."

"I forbid you the kitchen. You will stay here, at my side as before!"

Deliberately Rowena moved back into the room, walking toward her coffer. Carefully she laid out her old blue and brown bliauds along with Elaiva's large brown one.

"Now what are you doing?"

"I am leaving," she answered as she removed the dark green riding outfit she had been wearing and began pulling on her blue bliaud.

"And where will you go?"

Rowena shrugged. She truly did not know. All she knew was that she must leave. In her swirling, conflicting thoughts, she believed his refusal to give her the mare meant that as his whore, she was so inadequate, so low in his esteem, that he need not pay for her virginity, or for her services.

"I forbid it!"

"You cannot," she answered naively. "I am neither serf nor slave, nor wife. I am the daughter of a knight, and therefore free."

Runnolf knew this was a gross exaggeration. No woman was free. First she was subject to her father, then her husband. And upon his death someone else would be her warden, be it king or kin. But he was too surprised by her behavior to argue the point with her.

"You cannot leave this keep without my permission! Any man who allows it will be severely punished. Any who assists you by subterfuge will be executed!"

Rowena stared in horror at the man she loved. He was the same and yet not so. The man standing before her was the one all feared. He was cold and unyielding, even to her. In the tranquillity of her love for him, she had forgotten how terrifying it was to oppose him. She summoned every particle of her courage.

He watched in disbelief as she pulled the second bliaud over the first. Her hands shook so badly that she could not lace it properly and was forced to let it go.

"I forbid you to leave," he repeated menacingly.

"You cannot," she answered stubbornly.

"And why not?" he demanded, incredulous that she was now pulling the largest of the bliauds over the others.

She turned to face him while tying the leather girdle about her. Again her body was encased in the bulky clothes of their first encounter. As he looked at her, he wondered if he had been truly blind when first he came to the demesne. Even in her disguise, if he had truly looked, he would have seen her narrow waist topping sturdy hips, her slender hands and forearms, her pale complexion so different from outdoor villains, and the large soft eyes that were so expressive of her emotions.

"Even a woman of the fair is paid for her services," she said, nervously interrupting his intense scrutiny of her. "You think so little of me that no payment is necessary. But, I . . . I must see to myself." Large tears formed in her eyes as she spoke and were now falling unchecked across her cheeks.

Runnolf stood rooted to the spot. Her voice was so low that he could not breathe for fear of missing her words. He almost offered her Firelight, but he immediately dismissed the notion. He would not fall into her trap. Angered beyond all restraint and logic, Runnolf moved toward her, reaching her in two powerful strides.

"You wish to be a woman of the fair?" he thundered. "You wish to be treated as they?" He swung her to him, crushing her against his long body, kissing her savagely, bruising her lips. But there was no response, only tears of anguish and pain as he savaged her tender mouth.

Rampaging in frustration and anger, he threw her upon the bed. Viciously he began ripping her clothes, tossing them aside in an effort to reach her body, desperately hoping that with her clothes gone, so would be her defenses. But she remained motionless.

He took her as he would assault an enemy. But even this outrage solicited no response. Despite his frustration and passion, he knew he was irreparably severing whatever was left of the bonds between them.

In agony he rolled away from her and stood at the side of the bed looking down. "I will have you willingly or not at all!" he snarled as he replaced his unspent member within his clothes. "You may not leave this keep without my permission. Nor will you return to the kitchen. You are expected to sit by my side at table. You are expected to remain in my bed." He paused to see if his words were having any effect on her, but there was no sign of acknowledgment.

"Do you hear my words?" he demanded as she lay unmoving on the large bed.

"I hear," she whispered.

"Do you obey, or must I hold your people hostage to your word?"

"I obey," she answered in absolute dejection.

He bent to retrieve her torn clothes and felt the heaviness of the hems. He was not all that familiar with women's clothing, but the weight of the hems was definitely unusual. Bewildered, he hefted them, feeling the hems, then looked to her for an explanation.

"Well?" he demanded.

"You hold the treasure of the keep," she explained slowly, sitting up to the side of the bed. "My mother's jewels, my father's, what coin we had, are sewn there against the day of my freedom so that I would not have to beg or become a . . ."

"What else?" he demanded as he stood in stony silence, waiting for her to continue.

"I sent the best of the breeding stock into the mountains," she continued in the same dead voice. "To our Welsh neighbors . . . to hold for us until your departure."

"Why?"

"So there would be enough food during the winter for Father's people. Hopefully, some of the stock would survive to give birth in the spring for the coming year. You will want these things also for your king. I will send for them."

Runnolf's feet and legs felt as if made from lead.

"Now you have all there is," she continued. "The keep, the treasure, Firelight, the winter food, and my . . . virginity. There is nothing more for you to find, to destroy, or give to your king."

Runnolf stormed from the solar, his mind exploding in turmoil. He was all the way across the hall when he realized that he still held one of her bliauds. He stood undecided. Should he return it to her? And the treasure it held? If he did, he would have to ascend the stairs and face her again. He did not have the energy.

He remembered the strangeness of her behavior after his assault. There was no resignation, no acceptance, only a barrenness, a deadness of spirit. Impulsively he bolted up the stairs. He burst into the solar to find Rowena standing by the washstand, slowly bathing her swollen face. Her beauty was undeniable as she stood naked before him. It took all of his willpower not to rush to her and take her in his arms. He remembered the other times he had seen her so. On those few occasions that he had seen her without covering, she had blushed enticingly from her hairline to the pink buds of her nipples, causing him to wish to protect her from the hardships of life. Even that innocence was now gone.

She stood before him, her complete lack of concern for her own nakedness leaving him feeling a despoiler of life. Hastily he looked around the room until he found her poniard, still lying on the coffer where she had lain it. Reading his thoughts, she walked over to the coffer and picked it up.

"My soul is being punished for the lust I shared with you," she said, her glance lingering on the small knife. "But I will not condemn myself to the eternal fires of hell by committing the unforgivable."

In the face of her defeat Runnolf was helpless. Her words only slightly reassured him. Her lack of spirit was depleting his own; being with her was too much for him. He tossed her torn bliaud onto the bed and left.

True to his word, Runnolf commanded Rowena's presence at table that night, but nothing that was said seemed to ease the strain between them. In fact, it worsened. She sat stiffly beside him, her cheek discolored and swollen, barely picking at her food. Several of Runnolf's knights congratulated her on her ability to ride the mare, but their praise brought scowls of anger from Runnolf and listless replies from Rowena.

It was Sir Lyle who finally made matters worse

by comparing Rowena's ability with the chestnut mare to Runnolf's ability with Leben, even calling the mare hers.

"Firelight is not mine," Rowena interrupted him with fresh tears in her eyes. "Sir Runnolf . . . is to give her to his king."

Without waiting for permission to leave the table, Rowena dashed from her seat and ran to the solar, leaving the hall in stunned silence.

Until that moment everyone had assumed that the bruise on Rowena's face was from her fall. Now they suspected otherwise, and the room became charged with tension. There was a swift movement. Runnolf turned to see Norbert being forcefully restrained by two knights.

Norbert's eyes glittered in anger, his face suffused in crimson. "Why?" he cried in rage and disbelief. "She gentled her! She rode her! Even Sir Hugh acknowledged her a better horsewoman than his wife!"

"What is between us concerns you not!" Runnolf thundered.

"The boy speaks words from his heart," Sir Lyle said emotionlessly as he took Norbert by the arm.

Before Runnolf was aware of it, the hall had emptied of all except the servants, who were yet frantically clearing the tables. None lifted their glance to him. In their silence and the emptiness of the hall, Runnolf felt censure and disapproval.

Slowly, laboriously, he drew himself to his feet to follow after Rowena. He felt like an old man, crippled by life and weighted down with too many responsibilities. He moved deliberately, one foot in front of the other, one tread atop the next, until he reached the solar.

His eyes searched the gloom for Rowena until he found her lying on the bed, lost in the covers piled over her. The bed was large, accommodating his body adequately, and it had given them much space for sleeping in comfort and romping in freedom as young children might. But now it dwarfed her with its vastness.

The candle beside the bed had been extinguished, but the candle on the large table where he kept his papers was still lit. Listlessly he walked over and dropped heavily into his chair. He noticed a small pile of coins and jewels laid atop his papers. He studied the meager treasure, one piece at a time, without truly seeing it. With a great effort, he pulled himself from his own desperation and forced himself to concentrate. Maybe there would be a clue to her relatives, whom she refused to acknowledge.

There were several coins, a few ornate brooches, a leather girdle studded with gems, and a signet ring with the head of a wolf on it. It was very old and worn, and undoubtedly belonged to Sir Hugh's family. The sentimental value far outweighed the actual value. Rowena's expectation to live on so paltry a sum again bespoke her innocence, and with renewed vigor Runnolf cursed Hugh fitz Giles.

Drained emotionally and physically, Runnolf stripped off his clothes and climbed into bed beside Rowena. She did not acknowledge his presence, although he suspected that she was still awake. She simply lay still, indifferent.

Chapter Seventeen

✦ ✦ ✦ ✦

THE NEXT MORNING Runnolf asked Rowena to go to the pasture to remove the stitches from Leben's shoulder, but she reminded him of his stricture not to go near the mare or the animal would be destroyed. Caught in the trap of his own angry words, Runnolf was forced to bring the stallion to the bailey himself.

The giant destrier shook his head in welcome to Rowena, but she responded lethargically. He butted her playfully as if trying to cajole her into better spirits, but she remained indifferent to his efforts. He sensed a change in her and whistled in alarm, prancing away. Runnolf had to resort to force to hold him still as Rowena methodically cleansed the wound before removing the stitches.

Once Leben had been pronounced sound, everyone expected the black destrier would again become Runnolf's chosen mount, but it was not so. He was returned to the pasture and Runnolf continued to ride the gray.

During the ride from pasture to bailey, he had been reminded of the important place the horse held in his life, and he was conscious of the great pleasure of which he was depriving Rowena. He suffered with her, but pride, jealousy, and fear are vicious enemies of a man when out of control. And Runnolf's emotions were as out of control as they had ever been in his entire life. By his angry words, Rowena was not to have the chestnut mare. And even though he might wish to do so, Runnolf did not know how to back down.

So the days progressed. He continued to ride the gray, and Rowena continued to withdraw deeper into herself. As mysteriously as they had disappeared, the animals were returned to the pastures. Runnolf could relax his vigilance against the Welsh since the raider of missing livestock had been Rowena. The villains went about their affairs suspiciously watchful lest there be punishment for their complicity in hiding the cattle. And they waited anxiously for the return of Rowena's good spirits.

Rowena was not willing to have Father Dominic hear her confession because she was not repentant for any of her actions. She was filled with a deep emptiness, an all-consuming coldness of despair that sprang from within. Soon she felt nothing, saw nothing, and did not look at anything unless forced to do so. Her life became a blur of shadows and faraway sounds that held no meaning for her.

Seeing her so was torture for Runnolf. He had damaged Rowena's spirit, of this he was sure, but he could only guess how deeply. And in all honesty, he did not entirely understand why it had happened. He could understand her not trying to escape, because it would subject her people to his wrath and punishment. But how would that affect her spirit? He worried it around in his mind and decided that it did not. After all, she had protested and defended their honor, their loyalty, and devotion on numerous occasions. She had witnessed Norbert's whipping, because of his defense of her, and it had not affected her so. He was convinced that her lethargy had nothing to do with her people.

He could understand her anger for being deprived of Firelight. But why would that leave her thus? If she wanted the mare badly enough, she could wheedle it from him or find another way to gain her will. Yet he knew that was not her way.

He had struck her, true. But that should have reawakened her fear of him, not destroyed her spirit. Beside, one slap was not overmuch. It had not been delivered as punishment for lack of obedience or mismanagement of the demesne, things in which she took great pride at doing well.

Then what was it? he kept asking himself. She had taken pride in the many things that she did well, but especially in her stewardship of the demesne. Now she ignored everything. If it were not for the groundwork set by fitz Giles and the love of the villains for her, the keep would have fallen into disrepair overnight. Runnolf felt he had half the clues to Rowena's behavior, but he could not fit any of them together to form an answer.

The worst was that he knew it was he who had caused this change in Rowena. She ate little or nothing. Deep hollows formed in her cheeks, and her bones became prominent. Her hair became as dull as her eyes from lack of care. She reminded him of the wanderers, the peasants along the roads who had no place to go, not enough to eat, and no hope for the future.

She never left the solar unless she was summoned. Her pale skin became wan from lack of sunlight. Several times Runnolf commanded her to accompany him to the bailey, hoping she might feel the love and concern of her people. But she only shrank deeper into herself.

There were dark circles under her eyes, and Runnolf knew that she did not sleep. Night after night he held her unresisting body in the circle of his arms, offering her warmth. But she lay cold and huddled. Even extra covers on the bed, which caused him to sweat as if fevered, helped her not at all.

While Rowena lay unresponsive beside him, Runnolf scoured his mind for a remedy to the damage he had done. Did she demand marriage? He did not believe so. He had told her from the beginning that he would not marry unless ordered to do so by the king. And instinct told him that was not the solution. But on occasion, in desperation, he considered broaching the subject to her.

Other times he would leave their cold bed and pad over to the table to search through her treasures seeking the answer. He began to wear the signet ring in hopes its constant presence would help him. He knew an answer lay somewhere close, but it continued to elude him.

All the while, words kept running through his mind. Rowena seemed to possess nothing. She always referred to the people of the demesne as her father's people. She had never said "my people." Several times, in the beginning, she had said "we" but quickly changed it. She had called him lord only when she forgot herself in the jubilation of riding the mare and also in the excitement of their coupling. And worse yet, she no longer considered herself a lady but believed herself his—He could not bring himself to say the word.

Others never doubted that she was Lady of the keep. Even in her present state, the villains, and his own knights as well, continued to look to her daily to resume her responsibilities. Runnolf felt a deep obligation to find the way to set things to right.

But life on the demesne continued worsening all the while. Patrols were mounted, harvesting continued, the new field was being cleared, and Runnolf's new tub was finished and delivered, but all was done as if in quarter motion, while all mourned the death of their lady's spirit.

Her decline was turning the entire keep into an armed camp. Tempers were short and harsh words were spoken, although no one could ever remember the cause. Runnolf was the worst. Everyone stayed out of his way. The training sessions had to be canceled because there were too many injuries, minor ones, to be sure, but the atmosphere was dangerous to all.

The guards on the palisade walls alternately swore and prayed that the spell over the demesne would lift so they might go about their lives in the service of their king without thought or worry about anything but survival. The villains and servants prayed with resignation for their beloved Rowena. Runnolf too prayed that something, anything would happen to break this terrible state of affairs.

One day, as if in answer to their prayers, the king's messenger arrived. Runnolf watched from the high steps of the keep as the man rode down the valley. He had almost wished the king would forget them completely, or at least for as long as it took to solve his problem with Rowena.

Descending to the foot of the steps, he accepted the missive before dismissing the man to seek his rest. Even though it was unnecessary, Runnolf personally gave orders to the groom who took charge of the messenger's horse and watched as the animal was led to the stables. When there was no further excuse for postponement, he slowly climbed the stairs to the solar, carrying the unopened commands of his king with him.

At any other time, Rowena would have been avid with curiosity at seeing the large piece of parchment with the double-sided seal of Henry, King of the English, but she watched with little interest as Runnolf walked across the room and slumped into his chair near the windows to read.

"Rowena?" He studied her, watching for some sign of understanding. "Rowena, I have been summoned to the king. He is on his way to Winchester and commands me to meet him."

At last the waiting is over! Rowena's mind shouted, waking from its self-imposed stupor. He will be leaving and the fires will be set.

Large, silent tears formed in her eyes and slipped past her thick brown lashes. She did not know what hurt her most—his leaving or the destruction of her home, *their* home for such a brief time. It was the final straw. The dignity and reserve that she believed she had maintained these past days was shattered. In panic her glance darted from object to object, gathering one last look at her home and possessions.

She stumbled about the room, moving from one precious item to the next, running her hands over each as if saying farewell to old friends. Her behavior was clouded with despondency, yet Runnolf hesitated to interfere since this was the first initiative she had exhibited in the uncounted days since she had ridden Firelight.

Unexpectedly she rushed at him, throwing herself at his feet and grasping his legs as if she were afraid to let go.

"My lord," she whispered, her lips trembling as she tried to formulate her words. "My lord, may I . . . leave first?" Gasping, she tried to continue. "I could not bear to watch."

Runnolf felt a sudden fear at her odd request. What possessed her?

"Father's clothes," she continued in anguish. "Might I give them to Sir Lyle?"

Even as his concern mounted, irrational jealousy crept into his heart. "What is Sir Lyle to you?" he demanded, gripping her upper arms fiercely.

"He and father are of a size," she began, oblivious to the pain. "I—"

Runnolf did not wait for her to finish. The sight of her groveling at his feet disgusted him. He flung himself out of the chair and strode to the top of the stairs, bellowing for Sir Lyle.

"You sent for me?" the knight panted as he stopped at the entrance to the solar, his face flushed from the hasty climb.

Before Runnolf could answer, Rowena scrambled to her feet and rushed toward him. She clutched the front of his tunic. "Sir Lyle," she began, the tears spilling unchecked down her cheeks, "my lord Runnolf has allowed me to give you my father's . . ." She choked on a sob and could not finish. Instead she fled to the huge coffer that held her father's possessions and tried to drag it across the room.

The two knights looked at each other. In spite of their alarm, they moved as one to assist her.

"The chest too?" she begged Runnolf, gripping his arm. "Lady Margaret had it made especially for him. I could not . . . his belongings . . . hers . . . divided and burned."

Runnolf nodded mutely, and then her words "divided and burned" brought home to him the meaning behind her strange behavior. He was as stunned as if she had struck him with a mace. Rowena believed that he was going to set the keep afire and destroy it before leaving!

"I will help you carry this below," he told Lyle, his mind furiously trying to think of a way to explain his plans without giving her false hopes.

"Pack your own clothes," Runnolf commanded, more harshly than he intended, as he struggled with the heavy chest.

"Yea, my lord," she answered obediently, backing toward the stairs. "The travel baskets . . . Father's are in the storeroom . . . May I . . . ?"

"Yea," he mumbled.

Rowena bobbed him a brief curtsy and rushed down the stairs in a fit of frantic activity. Now that her future was upon her, her capacity for unquestioning obedience took over, crowding from her mind the private hell she had created for herself.

"Why are we moving this chest?" Runnolf demanded. "I am not going to fire the keep! The king's letter gave no orders to do so."

Sir Lyle stood staring at his leader, bewildered.

"Here, move the chest out of the way," Runnolf commanded as he picked up one end. "Move it anywhere out of sight." They carried it to the far corner and dropped it heavily.

"The chest and its contents are yours," he told his confused companion. "I do not have time to explain. I am summoned to the king. You will stay here to garrison the keep and defend the villains until I send for you. After we depart, you may remove the chest or leave it here, whichever suits you," he said in dismissal.

Rowena returned to the solar and began packing. She started with Runnolf's belongings while Runnolf paced deep in thought.

"You will ride with me," he began, still searching for an appropriate explanation.

"I am to accompany Owain and Elaiva," she protested, more like her old self. "It has been arranged so."

"And Norbert?" Runnolf demanded, remembering the man's vow to remain always with Rowena.

"He is your servant now," she replied, for once looking into his eyes as she answered. "Owain will—"

"Rowena!" Her name choked in his throat as he

saw the depths of despair hidden there. For the first time in days she willingly melted into his embrace, molding her body to his, pressing herself as close to him as possible. "Rowena, we are going to join Henry. You are coming with me."

"Nay, please," she protested, slightly pulling away from him, her fingers plucking nervously at the sleeve of his sherte. "I know that I have been . . . these past . . . please forgive me. You have been so—"

"I have been nought," he interrupted, nearly overwhelmed by suppressed desire. She was so soft and pliable in his arms. "I have been waiting for you to come to me freely and without force."

"I could not," she answered sadly.

"Rowena!" It had been so long, and now it seemed she was retreating again. "You will accompany me!" he said stubbornly, as he began to kiss her lips. "Will you, nill you!"

"I will not bring more shame to my father or to you," she whispered in anguish as she tried to evade the tender caress of his lips.

"Stop gibbering and explain your meaning," Runnolf snapped, becoming angry. "My brain is sore unto death from trying to understand what you say and do not say."

"I am not your wife. I am no relation to you. How will you account for me to your king?"

"Why should he ask?"

"What will I answer people when they ask my price?" She continued as if he had not answered her question. She kept her eyes firmly downcast and would not raise her glance to meet his as she continued. "Should I say that you think so little of my . . . services that you refuse to pay me? That would shame us both."

Runnolf was appalled. He dropped his hold on her and stared in disbelief. She had no concept of what she was saying. He was sure of it. She had confused things to such a point that he did not know how to straighten them out. And as was the case lately, the demon of jealousy lurked in his mind, ready to pounce and destroy the fragile bond between them.

Why was she so concerned with price? Would she seek another to replace him? Someone of higher standing than he in the king's household? Someone who could afford to be more generous?

"You see," she persisted. "You cannot answer me. How can you answer your king?" She turned her back on him to resume her packing, fresh tears glistening in her eyes.

"God's Blood, woman! I thought you gave your love to me freely and without price," he swore in a strangled voice. "But you are like all women! There is always a price! I do not want love that is bought," he continued bitterly, for the first time exposing his innermost pain aloud. "I can buy any woman at court simply because I am of the king's household. I can buy any woman in the kingdom with the ceremony of marriage and sufficient monetary inducement to her family. And I refuse!

"Now tell me once and for all, why are you concerned for your worth?!"

"I pray thee," she pleaded, as she backed away from his tirade, "do not torture me with questions I do not have answers for."

"Answer me!"

"You asked me once the price of my virginity . . ." she stammered, her brown eyes now wide with fear. "I wanted Firelight for my own as you have Leben . . . I wanted Firelight, and I thought that was the way to have her."

"That does not explain why you are concerned for your price if any should ask. No one can give you Firelight but me."

"You do not feel my virginity is worth the value of the mare . . . and I wanted . . . needed to know what value you place on me." Her voice was weak but she continued the last in one gulp of breath.

"I cannot place a value on your virginity," he answered solemnly, now vaguely understanding her need. "To me, it is beyond price," he said. His honest words were rewarded by a smile that brought life back to her face. Her eyes cleared of their deep pain. But his jealousy also needed appeasement. "While at the king's court, will you offer your affections to another?"

Runnolf waited in silence, dreading her answer. Rowena did not know what to say.

"I am not . . . what I gave to you I can give to no other," she whispered. "I am your wh—but I love you above all else . . . no matter what price you . . . I do not wish to be parted from you. But I know someday . . . the king . . ."

Runnolf had heard enough. He scooped her up in his arms and crushed her to him. His heart filled with joy, knowing that one more obstacle between them had been overcome.

"I have written the king, telling him of this

land," he whispered, holding her fiercely. "I thought to have him keep the demesne as it is. If he does, he will need a castellan. I will ask for that position. Or he might allow me to purchase it for us. Either way, you will be with me."

"I will not purchase this land at the price of my father's honor," Rowena answered sadly, pushing away from him. Seeing the bewilderment in his eyes, she hastily tried to explain her reasons. "If I go with you, and the king grants your request, all will know that my father's tenure to the land was not valid. His tenure is just! Ask your king only to recognize his tenure. After that, I care not what befalls the land."

"What of your people?" he asked, searching for some basis to refute her statements. He only half believed her. He knew her well enough by now to know that she cared about the land deeply. Everything she did proved it. It had been ingrained in her since her birth. He was sure of it.

"My father's people have served you with honor," she replied. "If the king accepts this land, he will need them and you can ask him to let them stay."

"Nay!" Runnolf thundered. "I will not allow you to abandon your obligation to your people."

"But they are not—"

"They are your people," he interrupted, shaking her until her head bobbed dangerously upon her neck. "They are your people and you are responsible for them now! You dishonor your father by abandoning them."

"I have not—"

"You have! Your father is dead! You are alive! Yet you have slunk around this solar like a wraith. You have your people frightened for your life. You are the only one left to do for them. You are the only one left to pass his honor to your sons and daughters."

Rowena unconsciously let her hand drift to her abdomen and blushed crimson. Was she now carrying his child? They had certainly been together long enough. The possibility struck her forcefully. Her eyes began to sparkle with interest and excitement at the possibility. Maybe he would not marry her, but he would certainly want to know his son.

The thought also brought pause to Runnolf's tirade. If she were carrying his child, it would complicate matters greatly. But if that was what she needed to hold onto herself, then so be it. He would do everything in his power to see that she was, and soon. And the thought did not bring him displeasure. If she were to carry his child, he would petition the king for any position that would allow him to marry Rowena.

"I will not buy your love," he finished quietly, more aware of the probability of marriage than ever before. "I want your love freely given, with price in yourself, not self-pity."

Slowly Runnolf released her. They had been so long apart, it felt like a tearing now. But his thoughts were on the future.

"Needs must I see to the preparation for our departure. We leave at first light."

Chapter Eighteen

❖ ❖ ❖ ❖ ❖

HOURS LATER, RUNNOLF returned to the solar unable to contain his anxiety. He did not know if his words had returned Rowena to her despair or if they had succeeded in bringing her fully back to him. He admitted to himself that he desperately needed her to welcome him as she had before.

His heart beat heavily as he slowly mounted the stairs. She was wrapped in her bed robe, her golden hair hanging loose and flowing about her. The only sign that things were not entirely well was a frown that creased her brow as she stared into the rising steam of the bath water.

Runnolf was not the only one worrying about their reunion. Elaiva had come to the solar shortly after Runnolf's departure. She was greatly relieved to see Rowena again aware of her surroundings. They embraced fondly as if they had been separated by a great distance for some time, which was, to some extent, the truth.

Rowena listened in stunned silence as Elaiva, in good-natured fussing, recounted her behavior of the past days. In no way did Elaiva intend her chatter to be considered chastisement or blame. Her only intent was that Rowena know how much she was loved, and how worried everyone had been for her well-being. She was eloquent as she related the distress of the keep and the happiness Rowena's recovery would bring to everyone.

Rowena asked hesitant questions, to which Elaiva readily responded concerning the demesne. Her answers, meant to reassure, only added to Rowena's guilt. She let Elaiva ramble on from one topic to another, now only half attuned to her words. She felt unworthy of such devotion. Later, when Elaiva had gone, she continued her examination of conscience as she packed and prepared for the night.

"All is well?" Runnolf spoke softly, not wishing to startle her.

"Welcome, Sir Runnolf," she greeted him guiltily, unable to look at him directly. She rose gracefully, waiting for him to say or do something to indicate his present mood. She was trembling from suppressed desire and guilt, not knowing what to expect.

He could not speak to her, so overcome was he with his own conflicting emotions. Over the past days he had come to realize how much he needed her, yet now he sensed reserve in her manner. He had hoped so desperately, wanted so badly, and was now monumentally chagrined at her lack of spontaneity.

To Rowena, his silence was unnerving. And she blamed herself.

"Your bath is ready," she said, striving to bridge the gap she believed was between them. "May I help you disrobe?" she offered.

Her voice was soft, and she was so beautiful in the candlelight, it made Runnolf's desire burn nearly out of control. He did not want a bath! He wanted her in his arms! He wanted to devour her!

"Elaiva has sent some broken meats and ale," she offered as she stepped aside so that he might sit on the low stool she had just vacated.

Runnolf moved across the room and sat down, still not knowing what to say to her. He studied her but could find no clue to what was amiss. She seemed well and behaved almost normally, except for the undefined restraint hidden in her submissive demeanor.

She knelt before him, unwinding his cross garters and removing his chausses and shoes. "All is in readiness for the morrow?" she asked as she slipped her arms around his waist to grab the hem of his tunic. As he lifted his hips, she lithely stood up between his thighs, pulling the tunic over his head.

"Yea," he answered gruffly as his head cleared the folds of material.

She tossed his garments aside and then trailed her hand in the water, splashing it around. "The water is warm and inviting," she whispered. She was so very aware of his masculinity and her desire for him that she felt as if bands of steel were encompassing her chest so that she could not breathe.

Without haste, Runnolf stood and stepped into the tub. It was the new one that had recently been delivered, and he luxuriated in the added space it afforded him. He lay back as far as possible, soaking in the heat of the water, his eyes half closed, watching her.

His mind was awhirl. They had resolved several matters before he left the solar. Did he need to reaffirm them, or was there something else?

And he had another matter on his mind that must be settled for all time. Yet as important as these things were, he did not know how to broach them or break into the restraint with which she had shielded herself.

Runnolf watched in consternation as Rowena knelt beside the tub. Her eyes were large, brown and soft as they watched him avidly. Runnolf had the feeling she was memorizing him lest she forget some one of his features. Boldly she took the cloth, wet it, and trailed water over his chest, watching fascinated as it trailed through the hair and wet his skin.

Lovingly she bathed him, washing his hair, his back, his chest. She felt his rigid manhood and looked at Runnolf with love-glazed eyes.

"Rowena?" His voice was a rough croak as he leaned toward her, his lips parted to kiss her gently.

"Sir Runnolf, please," she sighed, placing her wet fingers upon his lips. "When you are refreshed and have eaten . . ." Vague ideas had been swirling about in her mind since Runnolf's return to the solar. She must somehow confess her many transgressions and beg his forgiveness.

Reluctantly he slumped back against the rim of the tub. Apparently she also had important things on her mind and was searching for a way to broach them. Not knowing how to approach the delicate matters himself, he allowed her to proceed at her own pace.

After his bath, Runnolf, wrapped in his bed robe, settled into his favorite chair. He accepted a cup of ale and waited for Rowena. He watched her over the rim of his cup as she moved deliberately about the solar, putting things away. He did not prohibit her from calling the servants to remove the tub and water, nor did he rush her in any way. It was so nice just to have her moving about with intent instead of sitting staring at nothing.

Rowena folded the last of Runnolf's clothes into his travel basket and laid out his clothes for the morrow. Beside his shoes lay his belt. Hesitantly she picked it up and studied the thickness of the leather. She shivered thinking about it. Yet this might be the way to forgiveness. Reluctantly she folded the belt and then squared her shoulders.

Rowena came to stand in front of him and then knelt. "Sir Runnolf," she began hesitantly. There were misty tears in her eyes, tears of remorse and contrition. "Elaiva has reminded me . . . of my negligence. I have also been very disobedient. I beg forgiveness," she whispered as she handed him his large belt.

Runnolf sat looking from her to his belt and back again. His stomach knotted as he realized her intent. Except for the tears, her eyes were clear and bright; there was nothing left of her previous state of withdrawal or disorientation. She knew well what she asked of him. She believed herself guilty of disobedience and neglect and expected to be punished. He silently cursed himself for threatening her so many times with a beating. He did not want to punish her! All he wanted to do was love her, care for her, protect her, not harm her.

Yet he was afraid that if he did not comply, she would construe it as a lack of forgiveness and again slip into that limbo of nonliving from which she had just escaped. And if he did, he was afraid he would hurt her, she was so small, so delicate, so vulnerable.

"I cannot discipline you," he ground out between clenched teeth. "I am not your husband . . . and you deny me the place of lord in your life." This was the matter he had wanted to discuss with her. She never called him lord except when, in excitement or passion, she forgot. Now he was glad she had not. It might be the way to avoid this unpleasant situation.

"Do you not want to forgive me?" she asked, bewildered and more hurt than if he had used the belt upon her. She knelt as stone, staring at him in disbelief. How could he possibly not know that she called him lord in her heart?

"That is not the point," he tried to explain. "You have denied me that right."

"Nay, not so," she protested. "You know—"

"I know that you only call me lord when you forget it is I you are speaking to. Never do you—"

"But you must know how . . . I could not otherwise," she stammered, at a loss how to explain her feelings for him. "Please, my lord. You are my lord! You are my only lord! Please forgive me." Tears coursed down her cheeks as she knelt, waiting for Runnolf to take the proffered belt so that she might be forgiven.

Runnolf was not her confessor. He shrank from the role in which she cast him. Yet he knew

Rowena well enough by now to know that she did nothing by half measures. She gave herself wholeheartedly into everything; her emotions either spiraled to the heights or plummeted to the depths. It was obviously the same with her guilt. She felt it full measure, and her soul demanded forgiveness.

The church and its priests taught him atonement and punishment went hand in hand for the remission of sins. There could be no forgiveness without repentance, no forgiveness without penance. And penance was useless without atonement. If Runnolf sent her to the priest, the worst penance he would probably give her was forty days of fasting on bread and water, and those days would be scattered throughout the year—certainly not enough to expunge the sins of which Rowena believed herself guilty. Once her spiritual nature was forgiven, she might even be sent back to him for her corporal punishment, since he was lord of the manor. Then he would be faced with this dilemma all over again.

Rowena kissed Runnolf's hand as he reluctantly accepted the belt. Almost gaily, her step already lighter, she moved to the foot of the bed. She turned her back to him and removed her bed robe, letting it fall about her feet. Under any other circumstances, her actions would be considered supremely stimulating, even erotic. But not now, not to Runnolf.

With a sinking heart he watched her coil her hair and then pull it over her shoulder. If she would only turn and ask him, even hesitate a fraction of a moment . . . if she would only indicate she wanted him to forgo her punishment, he would willingly do so. She did not. She gripped the bedpost for support, and he knew by her stance she was not expecting a light chastisement.

Sweat stood out on Runnolf's forehead as he stared at her beautiful, unmarred back. He cursed himself again for his loose tongue as he searched frantically for any reason, no matter how weak, to refuse. Finally he was forced to accept the fact that he could not refuse. Reluctantly he gripped the belt by its buckle and let the leather fall loose. Never in his whole life had anything felt so heavy.

Runnolf drew back his arm. It took every ounce of willpower to bring the belt across Rowena's back and shoulders. He heard her gasp for breath as the leather connected with her bare skin, and his own back prickled with empathy. His arm trembled as he brought the belt across her back for the second time. He watched her rise up on her toes, instinctively trying to move away, trying to diffuse the pain. His heart beat rapidly, his gorge rose in his throat as he struggled to do his duty by her. He heard her muffled cries, and tears clouded his vision.

Enough! He threw the belt aside and rushed to her side. "Rowena! Little One!" he nearly wept with her. He cradled her in his arms, burying his face in her neck, lest she see his weakness.

"Am I forgiven . . . all?" she whispered between her tears. "Please, my lord?" She turned onto her side, burrowing herself into his comforting arms.

"You are forgiven . . . all." His voice broke with his own emotions, now nearly out of control.

And she smiled, so beautiful and happy now that she was assured of his forgiveness. "My lord," she whispered.

"Yea?" he answered as he looked into her tear-stained face.

"I love you," she said, with all the love and devotion she could manage.

Runnolf crushed her to his breast, rocking her and glorying in her declaration. He kissed her, tasting the blood from where she had bitten her mouth. She returned his kisses a thousand times over for each one.

Runnolf was bone weary but thoroughly satisfied the next morning when he descended to the hall with Rowena by his side. She was slightly stiff from her beating, but that did not mar the morning because the rest of the night had been all things made from dreams.

They broke their fast in companionable silence, and the keep sighed collectively in relief when they saw that whatever had separated their lord and his lady had somehow been resolved.

Norbert armed Runnolf as Rowena watched. Her eyes glittered with pride as she watched his muscular body easily carry the heavy hauberk and remembered the night before, when that same body had covered hers in fierce tenderness.

Their eyes met. Rowena blushed and shyly dropped her glance lest someone see the desire that dwelt there. But others did see it and rejoiced for them. Even Norbert, who still loved her deeply, rejoiced. It was obvious that Runnolf was as enamored of Rowena as she of him.

Norbert was resigned never to possess his lady. He should never have aspired to such an exalted position in the first place. His dreams safely relegated to the past, Norbert now dwelt in the present and the future. He was ever determined to care for her as long as his body held breath. It was a vow to Sir Hugh, Sir Runnolf, and to himself that he would never break.

When he was fully armed, Runnolf extended his hand to Rowena and led her down the steps to the bailey. Together, as one, they entered a world of ordered chaos as the knights and their servants prepared for the long journey to meet the king. Each knight was in full armor, carrying his shield and wearing his helm. Each of the servants who would be leading the packhorses was also fully armed, as were all the other miscellaneous persons who accompanied the cavalcade. Packhorses milled and balked as they were loaded with last-minute items. The great destriers were in a state of excitement, eager to be on their way.

The order of travel had been decided the night before, when Runnolf had selected his troop. Each man was chosen for his fighting ability and his loyalty. No man was chosen who had a loose tongue that would cause Rowena embarrassment.

Runnolf assigned Owain care of the mare. He was the one most familiar with Firelight and knew well the care Rowena would demand for her.

He also set Elaiva in charge of Rowena's absence, so all would be done with the same attention as if she were present.

Runnolf was in a particular hurry to meet the king. He was anxious to settle the matter of fitz Giles's land and to know how he was to spend the winter. He fervently hoped that all would be settled to his and Rowena's satisfaction.

Rowena shoved the past out of her mind and settled on the coming journey. She was excited and more than a little worried. This journey to the king would be the most important journey of her life, even more important than a journey to meet a husband and a new home. The lives of everyone within the keep and those living upon the demesne depended upon the decision of the king. She could not think about the ramifications without feeling overwhelmed.

When the time came, Norbert hastily lifted her to her palfrey and she nervously adjusted her dark green riding outfit. Once properly seated, she withdrew an old pair of leather gloves she had tucked into her belt and pulled them on her hands for protection.

News travels swiftly in a small community, and the villains were waiting outside the bailey gates to wish Rowena God's speed. Runnolf slowed the pace enough so that she could speak to them, to reassure them all was well.

Runnolf was riding Leben again, but not without guilt. He watched Rowena upon the solid, plodding palfrey, gallantly making the best of the situation. There were no recriminations, no comparisons, no protests from her. Instead of easing Runnolf's discomfort, Rowena's behavior made it worse. Whenever he was able, he tried to think of a way to take back his angry words over Firelight, but so far he had not been able to think of any.

Runnolf rode beside Rowena the first day, in spite of his momentary qualms about Firelight, enjoying her companionship. The slow pace of the palfrey ensured an abundance of time with no hindrance to conversation. Leben was forced to adjust his gait to match the palfrey, and the troop did likewise, moving steadily but with maddening slowness for those used to speed.

Runnolf watched Rowena carefully to be sure that she did not relapse into another depression, especially on the third day, when they neared the burned-out shell of de Witt's keep. However, she only voiced her resentment toward de Witt's cowardice for abandoning her father when he was unhorsed.

Much to his delight, Rowena was more interested in the way the land renewed itself even without the aid of man. Runnolf would not have been as pleased if he had known that she was storing this information against the day that she might find herself turned out and her own keep destroyed.

But what occupied her attention even more was the way the servants prepared camp every night, setting up the cook fires and the tents for the knights. They seemed tireless in their endeavors, and Rowena was greatly impressed with their stamina and abilities. She asked so many questions that on occasion Runnolf threw up his hands in mock horror and ordered her to change the subject.

If there was anything to cloud her happiness, it was the fact that, within the tent they shared, there were separate cots. One was large, old, and battered, and had undoubtedly been built to accommodate Runnolf's huge bulk; the other was newer and obviously designed for her.

Not once did Runnolf invite her to share his cot, or repeat his oath that one bed would be sufficient for them both. She worried that she might have done something to anger him, but she could think of nothing. Or it could be that with the nearness of their meeting with the king, their paths would soon be taking new directions, and maybe this was Runnolf's way of preparing her for their parting.

Or it could be that he had not truly forgiven her. Was her beating not enough? Would there be another? She shuddered as she remembered the burning pain of the leather as it crisscrossed her back. Yet she would have welcomed a beating if she could have his undivided attention for just a little while. She would even welcome his anger, but what she feared most was his disregard, his indifference. He had already removed her physically from his bed; she feared he was now prepared to remove his good opinion of her as well.

Once Runnolf had led them past the lands that

he had charted, he ordered Rowena to the center of the cavalcade for safety and he began to take a more active role in the leadership of the troop. He did this without explanation, forgetting that Rowena had never traveled far before and would find this change unsettling. Had he but taken a few minutes to explain, he would have saved her untold hours of suffering.

However, shortly after assigning Rowena to safety within the troop, Runnolf noticed an unusual quietness. And during the nights she tossed and turned upon her cot, gaining no rest. Runnolf, now more closely attuned to her moods, did not find rest either.

"What ails you?" he demanded, finally unable to tolerate her behavior any longer. It had been a quiet day with fine weather, but the past nights with little or no sleep made him gruff and abrasive.

"It is nought," she lied as she tried to still her restless body. His outburst had startled her badly, since she was not aware that he had been listening to her restlessness almost every night. In her bewilderment at their separation, Rowena believed his outburst one of anger rather than one of concern.

"Rowena, I know better," he said as he climbed out of his cot and moved toward her. "Are you still sore?" he continued as he sat down on her cot.

She could not answer him; her throat was locked in a vise of dread and longing.

"Roll over," he said quietly. Rowena had started wearing an old kirtle to sleep in since beginning the journey. It was a mark of modesty of which Runnolf approved. But her tossing and turning had entangled it about her hips and legs.

When she obeyed, he untangled the cumbersome garment, moving it over her thighs and laying it high across her shoulders. He noticed that the welts had lost much of their swelling and were now only slightly red. He again heaved a sigh of relief that he had not broken the skin.

Once reassured that all was well with her back, he lightly massaged her legs. He feared that she might be falling into another depression, and he did not believe his sanity or hers would survive it.

Rowena lay quietly under his insistent ministering. She felt his immense hands move to the top of her legs, then to her thighs, sending swirls of desire swelling within her. Silently she prayed that he would not stop with her thighs but would continue to that private place within her that caused her to lose all control.

They had discovered that secret place seemingly by accident one night. She remembered it as vividly as if it were now, and she pressed herself against the bed, trying to still her growing need for him. She fought not to remember, but she could not forget. He was with her now, touching her, getting closer and yet not deliberately teasing her as he had done on that previous occasion.

"Rowena! I will not tolerate half truths from anyone, especially you. There is trouble in your mind, and I will know of it."

The sternness of his voice hurled Rowena back

into the present, while the pulse in her neck beat in rhythm to the spasms of her lower body. The musky aroma of her desire perfumed the night air. In desperation, her throat locked in fear lest words escape her tongue to betray her as had her body.

"Rowena! Answer me!"

His words had been meant to be kind and reassuring, but his concern for her made them more demanding than he intended. Rowena, raised to instant, unquestioning obedience, blurted out her fears and desires in a jumble of half-formed sentences.

"You wish to share my bed?" he demanded, only half believing his ears. He had ordered the separate cots, remembering how she had refused Norbert the solar. He had thought to spare her, but now it seemed she did not wish to be spared. "You wish all to hear as you call my name?" he demanded again, reminding her with her own words the secret she had tried so hard to hide from the people of the keep.

"Let me hear your voice," he coaxed her gently, almost gleefully. He had sorely missed her these past nights and wanted to be sure that her wishes were the same as his.

"Yea, my lord," she answered slowly. "My shame knows no bounds where you are concerned. Soon, too soon . . ."

Her words stabbed into his mind and he started, remembering the unpredictability of their future.

"My lord, what have I said amiss?" she cried in despair.

"Nay, you have said nought amiss," he soothed her, banishing the future and concentrating on the present. "You have said everything aright." He lifted her in his arms and carried her to his cot. He laid her down and lay beside her, savoring the feel of her body so close to his for the first time in days.

"Does ought else disquiet you?" he asked as he kissed her temple. "Answer me truth," he insisted. "I will have no more secrets."

"I have so many questions," she answered hesitantly, "and I have no one to ask when you are not with me." Said aloud, the complaint sounded like a whine from a spoiled child, yet during the past days, the complaint had grown out of proportion, causing her great distress. "I am sorry, my lord. I do not wish to burden you with . . . but I have never been . . . and there is so much I do not understand . . . it causes me . . . to fear." She tried to finish her thoughts aloud, but Runnolf interrupted.

"Do you fear me?" he asked, misunderstanding her.

"Nay, my lord, I fear not being with you."

"You are well guarded. That is why you are in the center of the cavalcade," he answered, bewildered by her fear.

"Nay, my lord, I fear a life without you."

Runnolf claimed her mouth with his. Her passion already spent, Rowena languidly returned his kiss. Content, she snuggled toward the warmth of Runnolf's body and slowly began to drift into sleep. But sleep was not what Runnolf had in mind.

"Nay, Temptation," he whispered into her hair. "You are not so easily ignored."

Gently he began to slide the kirtle over her head. She lay beside him as he ran his hand hungrily over her hips, across her abdomen to her breasts, awakening them to the forthcoming demands of his mouth. Deliberately, tantalizingly, Runnolf began to rouse her. His mouth suckled insistently on her nipple, then unexpectedly released it so that he might swirl his tongue around the entire mound of her breast.

Rowena arched her back so that her breast would not lose the tender torture of the incessant sucking. But he nuzzled her neck instead.

"My lord, do not stop," she panted. Unconsciously she supported her breasts from underneath with her hands, holding them as an offering to him. The magic words "my lord" held him captivated to her smallest wish. At this moment she could have asked for Firelight, and the mare would have been hers.

Carefully, tenderly, Runnolf brought Rowena to peak after peak of pleasure while still trying to protect her as much as possible. He smothered her outcries with his own mouth, absorbing them, tasting them, feeling them as if they were his own. Finally he allowed himself to join her in one last powerful union before they slept.

At dawn Sir Roger would have wakened them, but others, those older and more worldly-wise, would have them sleep longer, until they were finally awakened by the morning noises of the camp, somewhat exaggerated to penetrate their sanctuary. Runnolf was the first to stir and then shake Rowena awake. They dressed hurriedly, breaking their fast with cheese and cold meats while they rode.

The happiness of the keep had again been returned to them, and the knights were exuberant. Their leader had always been stern but fair. He commanded their deepest respect. Yet none had ever seen him happy before Rowena came into his life. True, none of them had ever seen him unhappy either. He simply had been pledged to the king, moving as a chess piece upon the king's board. His new happiness was recognized as a blessing, even though all understood such blessings carried a great price.

Runnolf's duties now demanded his entire attention, so to keep Rowena occupied he sent Ferrand, the oldest of his road servants, to ride beside her and answer all the questions he knew were brewing in her mind.

Rowena's thoughts and questions might have been alarming to Runnolf, although they would have greatly reassured him of her devotion. As long as Runnolf desired her, Rowena was determined to find a way to remain with him, even if she had to be a servant traveling with the baggage wains that followed him from place to place. And she was determined that this trip would be her training ground.

Hour after hour, day after day, she listened as Ferrand expounded upon the necessities of this item and that. Eventually he was convinced that she intended no criticism of him, and he became more expansive about the years he had spent in Runnolf's service.

Finally she had the confidence to give him a direct order. And that order was evident to Runnolf the moment he entered their tent that night: her cot was missing!

"It is extra work for the servants to set up my cot every night and then take it down every morn," she stated stubbornly, "especially when it is not slept in."

They were standing close together in the tent as he looked from her to the vacant place once filled by the cot, then back again to her. The telltale signs of her resolve were apparent as he studied the aggressive jut of her chin and the squint about her dark brown eyes. Her color was high and visible even in the shadows of the tent.

"Did I say thee nay?" he asked, pleased with her demonstration of love.

"Nay, but—"

"Waste not your resolve on things that I do not oppose," he instructed her contentedly. "Instead, welcome me to your bower."

Joyfully Rowena melted into his arms.

Over the next days the rains became their companions in a conspiracy to prolong their journey into love. They were an excuse to start late, stop early, and on a few days, not to go at all.

Their path took them past many homeless men, women, and children as they worked their way south along the old Roman roads. Runnolf never gave them his attention other than to consider them a potential source of danger. Once he had assessed them harmless, he did not look at them again. He did not see them as individuals, but Rowena did, and her heart cried for them.

The hamlets and villages they passed through held nothing much better than hovels. However, no matter how poor the dwellings, they were surrounded by orchards and gardens that somewhat softened their deprivation.

Rowena's instinctive revulsion at these living conditions was real, for in truth she saw the people as human beings, possessing souls from Almighty God, beings placed on this earth by the same God to serve a purpose in the larger scheme of His plan. And that plan, as she had been taught by the priests, was to serve the nobility. In turn, her place in God's plan was to provide for those placed in her care.

She drew a comparison between these people here and those on her father's land. And these people fell far short. Her father demanded a certain standard of hygiene, not nearly as stringent as for himself and his keep, but definitely better than what these pathetic people experienced. Coupled with that, he ensured that all shared in the bounty of the keep and its farm. Full stomachs were a necessity. What she saw along the roads was a waste!

Many of the women were too undernourished to feed the children at their breasts or give birth to healthy, strong babies. Their teeth were rotten and missing. Folklore said you could tell how many children a woman had borne by the number of teeth she was missing. Rowena had never believed it before now, but she could see the truth of it in some of the young women.

And the children themselves would never grow up strong enough to work a full day. Another waste! It would take two of these malnourished people to do the work of one.

If they all lived by her father's standards, all would be reasonably clean, well fed, and healthy. Disease would be less prevalent so a man could work more days in the fields. The strong would work harder and longer, while the women would deliver healthier children who stood a better chance to outlive the rigors of childhood.

As they passed through these settlements, some of the braver children would trot beside Rowena's palfrey, occasionally trying to touch her to prove their courage and to see if she were truly real. Few had seen anyone as brilliantly clean or as beautiful.

In the sunlight, Rowena's hair was like plaited gold that hung below her waist. Her complexion was flawless, touched lightly by the sun, reflecting back its warm rays. Her eyes were soft and merry, and her smile was a quick reward for the boldest who succeeded in his endeavor.

It was such times as those that Rowena thanked Runnolf's stubbornness in selecting the palfrey. The antics of the children would have set Firelight to prancing and kicking. Sometimes, when they stopped at a well to drink, the women would approach her in much the same manner as the children. They would shyly exchange pleasantries, and she would compliment them on the bravery of their sons or the beauty of a child carried in a mother's arms. The fact that she spoke their language set her even higher in their regard while banishing some of their reticence.

Runnolf also found Rowena's behavior exemplary. She was not arrogant nor repulsed by their poverty. Nor was she frightened by them. She genuinely cared for their plight and wished she could bring all of them to the valley to show them how to live properly.

Chapter Nineteen

✦✦✦✦✦

AS THEY REACHED the more populous areas of England, Rowena occasionally saw a stone castle far in the distance, but Runnolf merely passed by them. When she asked why, he explained that the king's banner did not fly from the battlements, so there was no need to stop.

"But if you do not stop to ask after the king, how will you know where he is?" she persisted.

"I have sent messengers ahead, and they will tell us where he lodges," he answered confidently.

Rowena took assurance from Runnolf but with some reservations. This was a very large country for so small a party to find the king.

They worked their way ever southward, using the old roads, which dated from the time of the

Roman invasions almost a thousand years before. They were the only roads that connected the country from one end to the other, all else being mud lanes and worse.

Their progress was interrupted by a day-long interlude at a local fair, where Runnolf happily bought many items for Rowena. He bought her several pieces of velvet and sendal, as well as fine chainsil for his shertes and her kirtles. And as a special gift he purchased a fine mantle with vair lining. They were entertained by minstrels and jugglers and acrobats. And they feasted on honeyed pastries and cider.

They were a strange group, one lone woman guarded by a troop of the king's most formidable knights. But they dallied for only the day and were off again the next morning, still in search of the king.

Midafternoon many days later, Runnolf spied the castle of Oxford sitting on the river outside the walled city bearing the same name. He squinted against the glare of the sun and saw the king's pennant still flying from the battlements.

He was again flooded with mixed emotions. The pleasant journey was now at an end. They would no longer be able to postpone their future. If they pushed on now, they would arrive by dark. If they made camp, they would only delay the inevitable. Reluctantly Runnolf ignored his own desires, as he gently urged Leben forward.

Runnolf led them through the gates of the town and past a large church. They traversed a long, narrow gravel street that barely gave them enough space for two horses abreast. A few feet into the canyon of houses, Rowena was forced to draw her palfrey to the rear of Leben.

The twilight of evening was lost once they entered the street. Eventually they came into an open area where the houses were far apart, forming a square. Runnolf led the way across it and plunged into another street at the opposite end.

They made no turns, and Rowena realized that even though the street was narrow, it must lead directly to the castle. Again they broke out of the darkness into an open area. Ahead of them loomed a high, level wooden drawbridge and behind that, the forbidding shadows of the castle itself.

Runnolf drew rein at the foot of the bridge. His voice reverberated through the empty street as he hailed the sentry in the watchtower. They exchanged a few words before Runnolf led them across and under the portcullis.

Rowena shuddered as she passed beneath the heavy oak and iron gate with its spikes on the downward end. Nervously she held her breath.

Once in the immense bailey, Rowena was again assailed with doubt. The imposing stockade walls surrounded and dwarfed her, making her feel a captive with no chance of parole. Until now she had not realized how small her father's keep was and equally how small her chances of success might be, if the comparison of sizes was any measure. Rowena was seized with an irrational desire to flee. What chance did she have, one person against the King of England!

"Rowena?" Runnolf's voice penetrated her moment of fear.

They were at the stables, and Rowena could smell the numerous odors that identified it. The aroma was welcoming to horse and man alike, and Rowena felt slightly more calm for it.

Night had already fallen. The bailey was nearly deserted except for those necessary to the castle watch and those stable lads who now stood about, waiting for the knights to relinquish their destriers to their care.

"Give orders to the king's groom on how Firelight is to be cared for," Runnolf commanded as he lifted her to the ground. The strength of his arms and the steadfastness of his character gave Rowena the courage to obey.

"How are you known?" Rowena asked the youth who stood before her.

"Iwdeal."

"From the yew tree valley," she translated his name for him, but he did not seem to understand her English.

"Iwdeal, Firelight is a gift to the king," she began slowly, testing her Norman to its limits. "She has not yet been properly schooled. You will need care when you approach her, especially now that she is tired. She can be unruly. She has barely become accustomed to the saddle and has not had a bit in her mouth since I . . . since her training began."

The lad listened eagerly, sensing Rowena's care for the mare, and expressing his desire to do well for his king.

"Someone has caused her injury," Rowena continued. "She needs love and patience."

Rowena watched anxiously as Iwdeal preceded Owain to the stall that would be Firelight's new home. A tremor of apprehension shook the mare as she paused to paw the straw at the entrance. In spite of her fatigue she made an effort to back away, but Owain held her firmly.

Rowena's worry faded as Iwdeal moved to Firelight's side, stroking her, soothing her as he calmly boasted of the excellence of her new surroundings.

Firelight cautiously entered her stall, examining every aspect as if to test her groom's word.

Rowena was momentarily alarmed when the groom slipped out of the stall, leaving Owain to begin the grooming. But she instantly regretted her doubts when Iwdeal returned with a bag of oats and offered a handful to his new charge.

Rowena watched as Firelight tossed her head, rejecting so paltry an offering. She smiled as she remembered that was the same behavior the mare had used on her when they were making friends. Of course the groom must prove himself worthy, but right now he was too coaxing and the tidbit too tempting. Firelight tossed her head again, then daintily she accepted the offering.

By the time Runnolf was finished grooming and feeding Leben, Owain was out of the mare's stall and the young groom seemed to have been fully accepted. He led them across the deserted bailey toward the great hall. The massive doors swung open, and they were assailed by the noise and laughter of many people. Rowena hesitated to enter, but Runnolf had a firm grasp on her elbow and ushered her inside.

They were greeted by a harsh voice, rising out of the tumultuous air and startling her. "God's eyes, Runnolf! Is that you behind that beard?" A powerfully built man in his early twenties strode across the hall to greet them. He had close-cut red hair, and his clean-shaven face was ruddy and freckled.

Runnolf steered Rowena toward the man with the unusual voice, and his knights followed closely behind. As they neared the friendly young man, Runnolf and his entire troop unexpectedly knelt in greeting. Hastily Rowena did likewise, although she was not sure why. Curiosity rather than arrogance kept her head erect, and she was able to witness the warm greeting exchanged between the two.

"My liege," Runnolf exclaimed, taking the extended hand and bringing it to his lips.

The king accepted this act of homage and then immediately greeted Runnolf by raising him to his feet and thumping him heartily on the back. "You are well come!" the king boomed, and Rowena doubted that this man ever spoke in a soft voice. Irreverently she wondered if the entire keep knew when he whispered words of sweetness to his wife.

"And who is this lovely young woman?" the king rasped, bringing full attention to Rowena in her travel-weary condition.

"Sire, this is Rowena, daughter of Hugh fitz Giles," Runnolf said, introducing her.

Rowena took the king's hand and kissed the back of it as she had seen Runnolf do moments before. Even though he clasped her hand gently as he lifted her to her feet, it was not a malleable hand. It was strong and manly, calloused and weather toughened, bespeaking a man not immune to hard work.

"You are all well come!" the king boomed again in his forceful voice. This time he included all of Runnolf's troop in his greeting. The king acknowledged each man's homage and greeted him by name, enquiring about his health and latest adventure.

"Who are these two strangers?" the king asked, indicating Owain and Norbert, who still knelt in the rear of the group. The quick gray eyes missed nothing, especially when it came to the people who served him best. And Runnolf had served him long and well, as had the others.

"This is Norbert, my squire. He was once steward to fitz Giles. And this is Owain, liege man to Lady Rowena."

Henry waved the men to their feet after accepting their homage and turned back to Runnolf. "Have you eaten? I do not suppose so, if you just arrived," he said in answer to his own question. "Find a place and be at ease," he said, dismissing them all.

He then moved on, in what Rowena would

learn was restlessness caused by boundless energy. Standing so near the king had left Rowena breathless. But she did not think it was simply because she was impressed with his being the king. It was the energy and enthusiasm that emanated from his very being that had left her so. She looked around at the knights who had just greeted their king and thought she saw the same awe on their faces that must appear on her own.

After the king had moved on, Runnolf dismissed his knights to seek their own ease and to renew friendships. He guided Rowena to a quiet corner of the great Norman hall. Norbert and Owain stayed close by their side. Their unfamiliarity with the language caused them to view their new surroundings with skepticism and slight alarm.

Runnolf viewed their behavior, his emotions at cross purposes. Their devotion to Rowena was evident in their protective stance, and in these strange surroundings she would be well served. He only hoped that their unfamiliarity with the language would not cause undue trouble. He had spent as much time as possible trying to teach them Norman French, but their conversations had been limited by the necessities of the trip. He shrugged realistically. He had done what he could to help them.

Runnolf stopped a scurrying servant to demand food for them and then prepared to wait.

Standing with her back to the rough-hewn planks of the wall, Rowena tried to sort out the emotions and sights that threatened to overwhelm her. But her first concern was for Runnolf's comfort. He still wore his armor, and she wondered why no one had been sent to offer them baths. Nor had he commanded Norbert to disarm him.

While they waited for their refreshments, Rowena had time to survey her surroundings. Even in her nervousness, her trained glance noted familiar things that gave her comfort. Servants moved about the room freely, albeit in great haste. The floors were covered with rushes. The room was warmed more by the press of people than by the fire that burned invitingly in a large, free-standing firepit set on a stone hearth in the middle of the floor.

Rowena had not allowed herself to envision anything about her meeting with the king. And in fact she did not know what she had anticipated, but she was pleasantly relieved. She had met the king and he was friendly. Now all she had to do was find an appropriate time to ask him about her father's land. Yet she was too excited to relax at the thought.

Her glance roamed the hall, from one brightly clad figure to another. She studied the clothes of the men, judging Runnolf's wardrobe against those in the room and finding it sorely wanting. What things he had were well made and expensive but not nearly as elaborate as the others. And yet she did not think that he would wear such flamboyant colors. Everything he had was dark and subdued, somewhat matching the heavy control he placed upon himself. She would content herself with the dark colors he seemed to prefer, but she would be sure that they also contained some color such as a blue velvet. She would need to spend many hours sewing if she were to create a wardrobe to match these others. And the material already purchased would not be enough. She would have to find a way for him to buy more.

Once that determination was made, Rowena let her attention drift to the ladies of the court and their clothing. What first caught her eye was that the majority of women wore coifs that covered all or part of their hair. Rowena was later to learn that this new head covering was called a barbette, a fashion highly favored by Queen Eleanor.

And then there were the women's bliauds. The material used was apparently extremely soft, placing emphasis on the body of the woman wearing it. They were full skirted, with fine pleating that clung to the breasts and hips and then fell in elegant narrow folds to the ground. The folds were held in place by double girdles. Rowena would have liked to inspect them, because they seemed to be made of the finest embroidery. A few wore simple girdles of bright-colored silk cords that she found equally attractive.

Studying the bliauds, Rowena almost giggled. Except for the texture of the material, they would be as loose and as large as Elaiva's. She had been in style all the while she was in disguise and only now found it out.

As she continued to watch the women, Rowena became distinctly uncomfortable. She felt like a villain fresh from the fields. But she refused to dwell on her lack of wardrobe. She was here to see the king, and as soon as the matter was settled, she would return to her father's keep.

But you want to stay with Runnolf! her mind scolded her. How can you stay with him if you return to your father's keep, and if the king keeps him by his side?

Rowena's conflict did not have time to fully occupy her mind before the servant returned. He seemed disgruntled as he thumped down the stool he was carrying and dropped the tray of food upon it. He spilled some of the wine from the pitcher and nearly knocked over Rowena's flagon of cider. Rowena was forced to bite her tongue to keep from delivering a severe reprimand to the man, but she reminded herself that this was not her keep and she would not give offense by disciplining someone else's servants.

Runnolf had been watching her out of the corner of his eye, trying to gauge the impact the king and his court were having on her. He had noted with some apprehension her rapt attention when she met the king and her careful surveillance of the hall with its occupants. He was slightly reassured that the opulence had not overwhelmed her when he saw the flash of anger that sparked her normally quiet eyes. Runnolf had never seen Rowena discipline one of her servants, since the need had never arisen. But he was sure that Rowena would never have allowed such disrespectful behavior.

Somewhat mollified, he picked over the poorly cooked meat and handed one of the better pieces to Rowena before helping himself to a large bone. He then nodded to Norbert and Owain to help themselves.

As Rowena slowly chewed on a piece of dried-out meat, a man several years older than Runnolf approached them. He was heavy of body, elegant of dress, and his eyes were candid and friendly.

"Earl Richard," Runnolf greeted the man quietly.

There was nothing special about the greetings exchanged, but Rowena sensed that a gentleness had softened Runnolf's eyes, and his posture was relaxed though not inert. His mouth was full of unchewed meat, and in deference to the man's presence, he tried to swallow his food whole. Unfortunately he began to choke on it.

"I know you are pleased to greet me, but you need not choke yourself to prove it," the older man chided as he thumped Runnolf upon the back. "Here, drink this and see if it helps," Earl Richard de Lucy commanded, handing Runnolf his flagon of wine. He waited for Runnolf to wash the rest of the meat down before speaking again.

"Have you found sleeping space yet?" the earl asked.

"We will never find space among all these people," Runnolf answered, shaking his head. "I should have stopped in the town and made inquiries."

"It is too late tonight, and on the morrow the king hunts in the royal forest. You will not want to miss the sport. Besides, it would have done you no good, everything is full to overflowing."

Rowena watched the two men as they discussed sleeping arrangements. If she were not so in love with Runnolf, she might have felt slighted that he did not introduce her to his friend. As it was, she was doubly impressed with the affability of the important looking man.

Their apparent forgetfulness of her presence gave Rowena an opportunity to study him. Runnolf of course was the larger of the two, probably the largest man in the entire hall. But de Lucy was also a powerfully built man with no sign of inactivity about him. He was magnificently dressed in a richly embroidered dark green tunic that reached to his ankles. He wore dark hose and shoes of soft leather. A chain of gold links hung about his neck, and a large ring adorned his left hand. His hair was beginning to gray at the temples, and he was clean shaven like the king.

Rowena was abruptly brought back to the conversation when she heard her father's name.

"So this is fitz Giles's daughter," Sir Richard remarked, then continued when Runnolf nodded assent. "The queen has gone ahead to Winchester, so there must be room for her in Lady de Vere's bower. If you do not mind sharing my chamber for a night or two, that will solve your immediate problems."

"And you will have a chance to pick my brain of all the information you think I have stored there," Runnolf added soberly but without rancor.

"My friend, you have a mind like a coffer. Once something is inside, it never again sees the light of day unless it is needed. I would see what is stored there.'' Sir Richard smiled. All secrets were safe with Runnolf, and he acknowledged this noteworthy trait. Yet that did not keep Runnolf from divulging information that was vital to the king, in this case the condition of the countryside that he had traveled through while on the king's business.

Rowena's eyes widened in surprise, and then her face lost its color as fear swept over her. Runnolf had accepted Sir Richard's offer without consulting her. She could accept all the strangeness so long as Runnolf was by her side to guide her. But what if she should make a mistake or unwittingly cause some embarrassment?

Runnolf saw her momentarily overcome with fear and whispered to her in English. ''For a short time only. Be without fear. I will not be far.''

The harshness of the English was softened by Runnolf's concern for Rowena, and this did not go unnoticed by Sir Richard. Nonetheless he was momentarily surprised. This was a new side to Runnolf. Nor did Rowena's immediate obedience and demure acknowledgment go unnoticed. There was more at stake here than the tenure of the land.

Sir Richard quickly concealed his surprise by summoning his page and sending the lad to search out Lady de Vere.

While they waited, Rowena listened to the two men exchange information. She learned that as the winter neared, more and more of the knights were returning to the king to report their assignments completed. Over five hundred adulterine castles had been destroyed and all of the king's castles had been restored to him.

One phrase stuck in Rowena's mind as she listened to the discussion about the return of the king's castles. ". . . Had held in the year and on the day upon which King Henry, his grandfather, was alive and dead."

Somehow that phrase was important to the king in deciding what property was his and must be returned and what was not. Rowena was too tired to figure out if it would apply to her father's tenure of the land, and she wanted to ask Runnolf, but this was not the place.

Within a short time a matronly woman arrived at Sir Richard's side. She was dressed in the finest of materials, with the new style barbette about her head. Her movements were quick and sure as she curtsied before de Lucy.

"Lady de Vere," Sir Richard said, bowing as she straightened up. "You remember Sir Runnolf?"

"Yea, Sir Runnolf . . ." she smiled, and her face was alive with friendliness and welcome.

"And this is Rowena, his ward." There was only the slightest hesitation as Sir Richard settled Rowena into her designated position at court.

Rowena blushed uncomfortably as she curtsied to Lady de Vere. She had heard Sir Richard's slight pause and was discomfited by what she considered a judgment upon herself.

But she was mistaken. Sir Richard had read

between the lines of Runnolf's reports and had made several surmises on his own. At first he had attributed Runnolf's concern for the land as a desire to possess it for the king. But as the reports became more eloquent, he suspected that Runnolf wanted it for himself. Now, after seeing him with Rowena, he was not sure. More than likely the matter was much more complicated.

In any case, he knew both Runnolf and Rowena were innocents at court intrigue. Therefore it was necessary for him to use his experience in court matters and find a way of protecting them from any slander that might weaken their standing in the king's eyes. Sir Richard shook his head mentally. It appeared that this would be a full-time endeavor, especially since Rowena had accompanied Runnolf halfway across the kingdom without her ladies in attendance.

Lady de Vere's blue eyes never lost their friendliness as she acknowledged Rowena's introduction. If she found Rowena's travel-begrimed clothes distasteful, or if she noticed de Lucy's pause, she did not betray it.

"Sir Runnolf will share my chambers," Sir Richard explained. "Until he can make other arrangements. But tonight it is not feasible, and on the morrow we are to join the king's hunting party. Have you room amongst your ladies for Rowena?"

"There is always room for another," Lady de Vere responded without hesitation.

Rowena watched unhappily as Lady de Vere accepted the arrangements. She realized that the best was being done for them and that she should be highly honored, but it did not fill the emptiness that threatened to overwhelm her.

"It grows late," Lady de Vere smiled, noting Rowena's dejection and attributing it to fatigue. "I must be up before the king to assure that all is in readiness when he returns from mass."

In a friendly fashion, Lady de Vere took Rowena's hand, pausing only long enough for her to curtsy to Runnolf before leading her to the back of the hall. Behind the dais was the entrance to the private chambers of the king and his household. Anticipating Rowena's curiosity, Lady de Vere explained the different rooms as they passed. She slowed their steps so Rowena could glance inside where the doors were open.

"This is the king's chamber," she explained as they walked past. "It is the only room with a fireplace. Earl Richard and Sir Runnolf will share the room immediately across . . . Robert de Beaumont and Robert de Ilchester, this one . . . Thomas à Becket, this one."

Rowena followed Lady de Vere as she retraced their progress to the steps immediately inside the private entrance. "These steps lead to the solar, where you will stay with my ladies."

They climbed the steps into a room overflowing with sleeping cots, where whatever floor space remained was covered with pallets. The majority of the cots were vacant, awaiting their owners who were still below. The older, more experienced servants were sleeping, curled up in corners or anyplace out of the way.

"Beyond the door is my chamber, which I share with Lord Aubrey."

Rowena was awed by the expanse of the building. She should have been prepared for the extent of the private quarters, since the main hall was so large, but she had never before seen anything so mammoth.

"If the queen is not present . . . and the castle is still so full . . . where does everyone sleep when she is here?" Rowena blurted out, then blushed from her boldness.

Lady de Vere did not respond as if Rowena were too bold. "That is a very good question." She laughed as she patted Rowena's shoulder. "I have often wondered that myself, and I have been here and should know the answer." She paused, as if thinking, and then answered slowly. "There are some small rooms above for servants, but they must use a ladder to reach them. Most of the knights sleep in the hall on pallets, while some prefer to sleep in their tents. When the queen is here, she occupies the chamber that I now share with Lord Aubrey, and I sleep on a cot in the queen's chamber. He shares a room with one of the other barons . . ."

Lady de Vere shrugged her shoulders in bewilderment. "Somehow or another, everyone finds a place."

Rowena shook her head. She did not think that she would like to travel too much in the king's company. There would be too little time with Runnolf.

"It is not really so bad," Lady de Vere contin-

ued, reading the expression on Rowena's face.
"To be with the king and queen is a very great
honor. And when we move on to another castle,
one larger than this, my lord and I will sometimes have a room to ourselves. If the castle is
smaller, he will lease a house in the town near
where we are staying. And if they are traveling
too far, I will stay behind and make preparations
for when they return."

"Lady Anne?" a sleepy voice greeted them
from the doorway of Lady de Vere's private
chamber.

"Fanchon, this is Rowena, ward of Runnolf le
Geant," Lady de Vere said. "She will be staying
with us until Sir Runnolf can make arrangements
for quarters in the town."

Instinctively Rowena curtsied to a plump
young waiting woman, a little older than herself,
with a round face. She was dressed in her bed
robe, her lustrous black hair falling in long silken
strands to her hips. Her pale green eyes, which
moments ago were beclouded by sleep, were
now alert, sparkling with friendship and interest.

"Will you be so kind as to take Rowena into
your care while she is here?"

"Verily, my lady. But first I will help you prepare for bed."

"Nay, I will manage for myself," Lady de Vere
answered, waving her aside. "Rowena is more
tired than I. I am sure she would appreciate a
bath before retiring."

"Madam," Rowena called hesitantly. She
wanted to thank Lady de Vere for accepting her,

a stranger, without protest, but a simple thank-you seemed so inadequate.

Lady de Vere saved Rowena any embarrassment in the awkward situation. "Rowena, all of my ladies call me Lady Anne," she responded kindly. "You are now a member of my bower until your guardian removes you from my care."

"Thank you," she whispered, her eyes misty with fatigue and gratitude.

Once the door was closed behind Lady Anne, Fanchon woke a maid and sent her for fresh bath water. Almost immediately a tub was brought and the water poured while Rowena undressed. Before long, Fanchon had Rowena bathed, her hair washed and towel dried, and had helped her into a linen chemise and snuggled her into her cot.

"On the morrow, when you are rested, I will take you about, so you will not feel so lost and confused," she promised as she climbed into a nearby bed.

Rowena felt twinges of guilt as she closed her eyes. What will happen to their friendliness when they find out that I am not Runnolf's ward? she worried. But her guilt was as tired as the rest of her and succumbed instantly to sleep.

Chapter Twenty

✦✦✦✦✦

ROWENA SLEPT SOUNDLY until she was shaken awake the next morning by Fanchon. She had anticipated a fretful night without Runnolf beside her, but her body was just too tired.

"You must hurry if you are to attend mass," Fanchon said as she settled the pleats of her bliaud about her plump waist. Her hair was already brushed and braided. "After that, we will break our fast and see to getting you properly settled."

Her own dressing finished, Fanchon helped Rowena with her hair. Once dressed, the two young women hurried down the stairs and out through the large hall, picking their way around the sleeping knights.

"By the time mass is over," Fanchon explained as they entered the bailey, "all the knights will be awake and food will be set out for all."

At first Rowena did not see any building that resembled a church and was further confused when Fanchon led her toward a large keep with watchtower. But once inside, she recognized the ancient aroma of burning candles and incense. Looking around, she was sure this building had never been anything else but a church. Fanchon led her to a quiet spot and they knelt on the wooden floor. The comforting aroma of sanctity, the quiet press of bodies brought a familiar feeling of peace as Rowena closed her eyes to pray.

She had so many things to ask the Almighty

that she did not know where to begin. Her first thoughts were, of course, for her parents, as she prayed for her father so recently deceased and asked for eternal peace for his soul. She could not find the words to beg forgiveness for her present sins. She tried to feel remorse but she only felt guilt—guilt that she was not ready to give up Runnolf and could not, therefore, ask forgiveness.

As Rowena remembered her sins, there was a disturbance within the church. From her attitude of prayer, Rowena watched the king and his party arrive. She tried to search for Runnolf but could not see him with her head bowed. Sighing heavily and resigned to her damnation, she raised her head and looked directly into his eyes from across the room. He had been looking for her also.

When the mass began, Rowena reluctantly focused her eyes upon the altar and tried to concentrate on the liturgy, but she could not, first, because her mind was centered upon Runnolf, and second because of the king. Henry's character was such that he never remained idle, even in prayer. During the entire mass he was constantly whispering to one or the other of his liege men, remembering this and then that, reminding them of things yet to be done.

No matter how quietly he whispered, his voice carried about the church. Rowena was afraid that if the priest was anything like Father Dominic, he would retaliate by pronouncing the prayers more slowly, so that everyone would be forced to remain on their knees in penance for the disturbance. But then, she reminded herself, Henry was king. Who but God would dare chastise his behavior?

When mass was finally over, everyone made their way back to the hall to break their fast. But the king instead called for his horse, anxious to be on the hunt. Those who had not eaten were faced with the choice of going without or missing the hunt. Most chose to go without, to be with the king.

Rowena had no time to speak with Runnolf before he went to the stable to saddle Leben. Then he was off, leaving her feeling lost and desolate. She would like to have been a member of the hunting party. Many of the women of Henry's court were included, but she knew that her palfrey would never have been able to keep up.

"If you will be traveling with the king," Fanchon said, coming to stand beside her as she watched them ride away, "you will have to become accustomed to his energy. He is up before everyone and goes to bed after everyone else. He is constantly doing, and hunting is his passion."

Rowena was only momentarily disheartened. She would use this time to break her fast, find her travel baskets, and begin her sewing. Humming softly to herself, she followed her new friend into the hall.

She met Norbert and Owain just inside the door as if waiting for her, and she was surprised that they had not accompanied Runnolf—Norbert, at least, as Runnolf's squire, should have.

"Sir Runnolf ordered us to stay behind," Owain answered her question. "He thought you might have need of us."

Rowena did not at first know what she would need them for until she realized she did not know where Ferrand was. "Do you know where Ferrand can be found?" When they nodded, she continued, "Go to him and bring my travel baskets."

"We did that while you were at mass," Norbert answered. "They were given to the maids to carry to the solar. Sir Runnolf had us fetch his, also."

"Have you seen the horses—how is Firelight?"

"The lad Iwdeal slept in her stall all night," Owain answered, pleased that they had successfully anticipated her. "All is well there."

"Break your fast and then spend your time getting acquainted," she said, dismissing them. Things were progressing well, and she happily joined Fanchon, who waited for her beside one of the tables.

Rowena, anxious to be about her sewing, wolfed down her food, not truly tasting it but eating enough to assuage her hunger. Together, she and Fanchon climbed the steps to the solar and went immediately to Rowena's travel basket to freshen her wardrobe.

The sight of her new vair mantle brought oohs and ahs from those present. It was truly a magnificent garment, and Rowena was very proud of it. Fanchon pronounced the material for the blue mantle to be also superb.

"I will make a mantle for Sir Runnolf with it," Rowena said shyly.

"And the pink and the brown?" Fanchon asked.

"They are mine," she replied.

"They are also very fine. Whoever selected these knew her material. And the colors will flatter your complexion," Fanchon added as she continued to sort through the second travel basket.

"I do not wish to speak ill of your guardian's generosity," she said, taking Rowena's hands in her own and looking frankly into her eyes, "but is this all the wardrobe that he provided for you?"

"It is all that I have," Rowena answered. And in truth it was all that she possessed. She did not count the coffer at the keep that contained her mother's belongings. She had never considered them hers, nor had she ever thought of wearing them. Besides that, she had given them to Sir Lyle.

"Was Sir Runnolf planning to purchase everything anew for you in the newest fashion once you arrived?"

Rowena was speechless at Fanchon's persistent inquiries. She could detect no viciousness in her new friend's behavior, but her questions bespoke very poor manners.

Seeing Rowena's confusion, Fanchon hastened to explain. "If you are going to be at court for any length of time, you will need more . . . appropriate . . . an entirely new wardrobe," she stammered.

"I will not be at court long enough to need a new wardrobe," Rowena answered. "I am here to petition the king to recognize my father's tenure to his land. After that—"

"If you are to wait for the king to make up his mind about land, then you had better be prepared to be at court a long time. On some matters, our king can be instantly decisive. But when the issue is land, he is very deliberate."

"I do not have to wait at court," Rowena protested. "I can—"

"If you do not wait at court, then how will he be reminded?" Fanchon asked. "Soon the court moves to Winchester and you will want to meet the queen," she continued, cajoling Rowena into recognizing her need for a greater wardrobe.

"I do not believe that the queen will notice—"

"The queen notices everything," Fanchon interrupted. "And while she may be too polite to comment on your lack of wardrobe, there will be others who will not be so kind. Jealousy is a fatal weapon in the hands of some women."

"Jealous of what?" Rowena demanded, bewildered.

"You are very lovely," Fanchon answered truthfully. "Many would be envious of your unmarked complexion. You do not need to add false hair to make yours appear thick and luxurious. They would viciously use your lack of wardrobe to make you appear less worthy than others."

"I have materials that I can sew," Rowena replied pointing to her pink and brown material.

"But you do not wish to spend all of every day

sewing. Then you would not be able to wear the clothes you make nor will you be able to tell your children and their children about the king," she continued.

"Yea, children," Fanchon teased, her voice imitating the squeaking quality of an elderly woman. "I was at Oxford Castle with the king. But I was so busy making clothes to wear that I did not see him at all.

"You would not want Sir Runnolf to be japed because you are not suitably attired," Fanchon added. She had seen the looks Rowena had directed at Runnolf and had heard her deep sigh during mass.

Rowena could feel her ears burn with shame. Fanchon had already guessed the relationship between herself and Runnolf. Now she would no longer be her friend. She hung her head in shame, waiting to be dismissed. But Fanchon had only guessed at the love Rowena held for Runnolf and no more. Runnolf kept too tight a control on himself for a casual observer to read his emotions. Rowena felt Fanchon's arms around her shoulders giving her a warm hug of affection.

Fanchon was the youngest daughter of a family of daughters. Her father had been a liege man to Sir Aubrey during the entire reign of Stephen's anarchy, and Sir Aubrey treasured the man's loyalty highly. To honor him, Lady de Vere had taken Fanchon as one of her women.

Fanchon had been in Lady de Vere's service since the king's coronation. During that time, she had made a point of studying the king's court so that she might become invaluable to Lady de Vere. She had resigned herself to living her life through the court's intrigues.

Fanchon was pleasant looking but no beauty. She had no real prospect for a well-placed marriage since she had no dowry. She had adjusted to these facts and was now suitably placed with her ladyship. She was a maid yet, but she dreamed of passion. That is why she wished to help Rowena in any way possible. Also, Fanchon realized that Rowena was very naive when it came to court necessities. In this also she was determined to help her new friend.

"To love is a marvelous experience," she whispered dreamily. "But to be loved in return is even better. We will set out to capture his heart."

Rowena looked up, bewildered by Fanchon's words.

"You love that stone-faced giant, do you not?" Fanchon asked bluntly. When Rowena nodded, she continued. "Together, we shall snare his heart. He will have eyes for no other, even though others are attracted to him."

A stab of jealousy hit Rowena, as physical as a blow from a mailed fist. "I have some money," she began, remembering the coins and jewels that were her inheritance.

"What need have you for money?" Fanchon asked with mischief dancing in her pale green eyes. "He is your guardian. We are out to capture his heart. We will charge the bill to him. Is that not appropriate?"

"Nay, I will not!" Rowena was so adamant that she startled Fanchon, making her jump.

Here was court treachery, which Runnolf hated so much. She would not be a part of it. "I have some money. I will buy my own cloth."

Fanchon was a little surprised that Rowena thought she had control of her money. Rowena might be an heiress, but as she was Runnolf's ward, he had control of everything of hers, including herself, her land, and her money. However, she held her tongue. She had succeeded in getting Rowena to admit to the need for new clothes, and she was not going to push her further.

One of the chambermaids, who had been in the room during their entire conversation, came forward. Plucking all of her courage together, she curtsied before them. "My ladies," she whispered. "My name is Eada and my uncle is a mercer," she blurted out before she lost her nerve. "His merchandise is very fine but he is not well known. . . . All the important mercers will be too exp. . ."—she too had seen Rowena's small wardrobe and did not believe that Rowena could afford some of the more popular mercers— "too busy to do anything right away," she amended. "There might even be a long delay before they could answer your summons. And my cousin sews a fine stitch. . . . She could help—"

"When will be the soonest your uncle may come here?" Fanchon interrupted, seeing an answer to their dilemma.

"Sometime on the morrow," the girl answered, thinking of all the work she had to do before she would have any time to herself to run the errand. "But if you would come with me . . ." She hesitated. If she was with them she would not get into any trouble for not doing her chores. "I could take you there . . . now." She brightened. "You can make your selections and then you will have them sooner."

"Rowena, do you have the time now?" Fanchon asked, caught up in the plan to ensnare Runnolf's heart.

"Verily!" Rowena answered enthusiastically, knowing that Runnolf was hunting with the king. Once she had made up her mind, she wanted no delay. If what Fanchon said was true, she would need many more clothes. No wonder Runnolf had wanted her to have more material for clothes. If only he had told her more about the king's court and its customs. Well, if everyone believed Runnolf her guardian, she was determined to put him in a good light. She was more than anxious to set out.

"We cannot go without an escort," Fanchon wailed. "I was so excited, I nearly forgot. We will have to ask Lady Anne if she can spare us someone."

"I have two liege men," Rowena said as she took her money from her travel basket. "They are below." She grabbed her cloak and waited at the stairwell for the others.

They hurried down the stairs. As they entered the hall, Rowena spied Owain and Norbert in conversation with some young pages. She motioned for them to meet her outside. As the women crossed the noisy bailey, Norbert and Owain fell into step behind them.

"Should you not be riding?" Norbert demanded when he realized that she was going outside the castle walls.

Rowena discussed his question with Fanchon and Eada. Eada apologized, but she did not know how to ride. She assured them that the walk was not that far. Furthermore, there would be no place to leave the horses while they were at her uncle's.

Rowena relayed the maid's answer to Norbert, who accepted her decision with ill grace but said no more.

They crossed the drawbridge and walked into the open space in front of the castle gates. Then they walked down the main gravel street toward the large market square that she had ridden through the night before. Dogs, pigs, and rats were everywhere, feeding on the garbage that littered the streets. Rowena noticed that the stench of decaying matter was more noticeable in the warmth of the day than in the chill of the night.

Rowena and Fanchon were forced to lift their skirts as they carefully picked their way over the debris. But the debris on the ground was not as bad as the unannounced offal that came hurtling down from the upper-story windows. Soon it became a gamble as to whether to watch where one placed one's foot or to watch above so that one might have time to duck. They had already had several small mishaps that had left their bliauds stained and spattered with foul-smelling residue. On one occasion, Owain had to catch Fanchon when she slipped and nearly fell in the filth.

"On Sundays, after mass, my uncle opens a booth here in the market place," Eada volunteered, aware of the distress of her two companions and trying to ease their misery. "It isn't much farther," she encouraged them as she led them into the other half of the main street. She hurried along, afraid if they delayed overlong they would change their minds. Then they would never do business with her uncle.

Rowena was once more lost in the dilemma of where to look when she heard the muted thunder of horses' hooves. Instinctively she moved closer to the wall and looked up to see that she had miscalculated, because the street was clear of all pedestrian traffic. Eada had hurried ahead to the nearest alley and was motioning them to follow.

Rowena looked down the street and was alarmed at the inconsiderate speed of the oncoming horsemen and their utter disregard for the townspeople. Her attention was drawn to a movement at the entrance to the alley across from her. At the mouth of the alley was a small child. Rowena's heart stopped beating as she watched the child toddle directly into the path of the oncoming horses.

Without thought for her own safety, Rowena dashed into the street. The startled horses screamed in anger as she raced in front of them. There was not enough room for the heavy destriers to maneuver, and the one closest to Rowena reared up in rebellion against the tight rein of its rider. Its foreleg struck Rowena on the shoulder, sending her falling into the muck of the gutter.

The angry screams of the horses, the curses of the knights slurred into swirling black unconsciousness as Rowena lay in the gutter, clasping the child to her. Once the giant animals were under control, the knights continued toward the castle without looking to see what damage they had caused to the child or to the woman.

Pandemonium broke loose in the street. On the wings of the wind, word spread of the accident and of the woman who had tried to save the child. Crowds gathered to gawk and to gossip, to see the blood and mutilation.

Owain gently turned Rowena over and she nearly fainted again from the excruciating pain. She felt strong hands searching her body for injury and slowly opened her eyes to Owain's tear-stained face.

"The child?" she whispered, afraid to speak the words aloud for fear of cursing her luck.

"Fainted," he answered. "Maybe her leg is broken."

In falling, Rowena had cradled the child to her, and even now, as Owain inspected Rowena for broken bones, she held the child and would not release her. Through her pain, she felt Fanchon's presence on her other side. She turned her head toward her new friend, who was kneeling in the gutter, oblivious to the garbage. Her eyes were moist with unshed tears as she waited for Owain to make a determination of Rowena's injuries.

"No bones broken," he mumbled in relief. No bones were broken, but he did not know how to look for internal injuries. How he wished that Elaiva were there to help him!

"My lady," an elderly man addressed her. "Are they dead?"

"Who are you?" Fanchon demanded, thinking it was someone looking to spread fresh gossip.

"Mannfrith, my lady. Rebecca . . . the child is my granddaughter. I was supposed to watch her while her mother delivered some sewing . . . a customer came . . . I turned . . . She is the only child of my dead son . . ."

Fanchon's hostility instantly vanished as she spied the tears running down his cheeks and heard his explanation. "They are not dead," she consoled him kindly, "only injured. Where may we take them?"

"Our house is at the corner." He pointed to the alley from whence the child had come.

"Send for a leech to see to their injuries," Fanchon ordered. "We will await him there."

"Eada!" the mercer cried in relief. "Eada, do you hear? They are not dead, only injured. Go! Fetch Joseph. Tell him what has befallen and bring him back anon!"

The young maid peeped from behind Norbert, listening to the good news. She brushed her tears away so that she might see for herself that Rowena and Rebecca were not dead. Rowena smiled encouragingly at her, and then Eada hurried on her errand.

Rowena reluctantly released her precious burden to Norbert, who was still badly shaken. Owain lifted her in his arms and followed after

Fanchon and the old man. The two were carried into the mercer's shop, then up a steep flight of stairs to the second story that was the family's private living quarters.

In spite of her resolve to mask her pain, Rowena moaned whenever her shoulder was bumped. She could feel Owain tremble each time, and she smiled at him weakly to reassure him that all was well. Times change but people do not, Rowena realized. How many times, when her father was not available during her years as a child, had she been held, comforted, and cared for by Owain. And now again Owain cradled and comforted her in his strong arms. For a man of advanced years, Owain was a miracle of stamina and resourcefulness, and she thanked God for his loyalty.

Rowena asserted herself when Owain would have placed her on the bed. "I am too filthy," she protested. "The child, place her on the bed so that the leech will have room to tend her."

Reluctantly Owain stepped aside so that Norbert could put the child in the center of the bed.

"Owain, please, put me down," Rowena begged, trying to make light of her own pain. "I cannot help the child from your arms."

Owain reluctantly set her upon her feet and held her steady while the room spun about her and she was caught in a spasm of nausea.

"Go below," she instructed them when the room had stopped spinning and her stomach had returned to its rightful position. "Ask the neighbor women to help you prepare a bath for the child and me. But, first, bring a kettle of hot water. I will begin the child's bath immediately."

Fanchon helped Rowena strip off her soiled clothes down to her kirtle. They tossed them aside into a pile on the floor. Through her own pain Rowena, with Fanchon's help, undressed the child, who now lay on the bed. Her heart lurched when she saw the awkward angle of the child's leg and the bruises that were surfacing from the fall. She hoped the leech would be capable, because she did not think that she would be able to set the leg properly. She knew her own shoulder was not broken, but it was severely bruised. If she did not possess the proper amount of strength, she would cause the child a deformity for life.

While they bathed the little girl, she revived from her faint and began to cry. Mannfrith knelt beside the bed, next to Fanchon, crooning softly to his granddaughter. She quieted somewhat so that they were able to bathe her, except for her injured leg. Eventually they left the child to Mannfrith's care and spent time cleaning themselves.

A young woman hurriedly climbed the stairs and rushed to the side of the bed. Without hesitation, Mannfrith relinquished his place to her. "I am her mother," she whispered. She tried desperately not to cry, but her lower lip trembled uncontrollably and her voice cracked. "Thank you for saving her life."

Rowena was embarrassed by the woman's sincerity. "She would not let us wash her leg,"

Rowena said as she brought the wash bowl and cloth to the bedside. "Maybe you will have better luck."

"Joseph!" Mannfrith greeted an elderly man, who was now climbing the stairs. He walked unsteadily toward the newcomer with outstretched arms.

"I met Blythe on the way and took a few minutes to calm her," the old man called Joseph said by way of greeting. "I trust all is as Eada said."

In response to Mannfrith's eloquent silence, Joseph moved to the foot of the bed and studied the child who lay before him. His sharp dark eyes missed nothing of the broken leg, nor the kind treatment of the blond woman who sat on the bed holding the wash basin for Blythe.

"Blythe, I will need a cup of sweet wine. Fetch it for me."

Rowena noticed that his voice was kind but held authority, which the woman did not hesitate to obey.

"What is your name?" he asked Rowena.

"Rowena, daughter of Hugh fitz Giles. Are you the leech? Would you like to sit here so that you can examine the child?"

"You are not from here," Joseph continued, ignoring her offer. "You are from the north, close to the Welsh borders?"

Rowena was surprised that he knew this of her, but she was in no mood to be distracted by chatter. "If you are the leech," she said imperiously, "then I suggest that you assume your responsibilities."

"I am a physician," Joseph chided her gently.

"There is no need for you to give up your seat. You are doing everything that I would do, and the child is not overly distressed by your presence."

Rowena was only somewhat mollified by his compliment. As if in answer to her unasked questions, the old man began to explain.

"You have washed the child of filth except for her leg. Has she cried out in pain in any other place?"

"Nay," Rowena answered positively.

"She breathes regularly, with no winching or rattling in her chest?"

"Her breathing is strong and steady," Rowena affirmed.

Blythe returned with the cup of sweet wine and gave it to Joseph. He poured a small packet of powder into it and stirred it well before handing it back to the mother, with instructions to give as much of it as possible to the child and then bathe the injured leg thoroughly.

"Now, young woman, let me have a look at your shoulder."

"I am fine," Rowena answered stubbornly. "Take care of the child first."

"The potion Blythe is giving Rebecca will let her sleep deeply while I set her leg. While we wait, I will see to your shoulder."

Reluctantly Rowena stood. She moved toward Joseph and was able to see him more clearly. His skin was swarthy, and his bushy white eyebrows hung over dark eyes that were compelling yet tempered by deep lines of humor that smiled when he did. He was a tall, thin man, with a prominent nose, and his back was straight despite his advanced years. His long beard was white upon his chest and was accentuated by the fine quality of his somber tunic.

"My name is Joseph," he said introducing himself. "I am a Jew and a physician."

Rowena's eyes widened at being in the presence of a heretic. But once the shock of his statement passed, she tried to remember everything she had ever heard about Jews, which was not much. Until today, all her knowledge had come from either her father or Father Dominic. Her father had become greatly disturbed whenever Father Dominic would condemn the Jews for the death of Christ. It wasn't that he condoned what they had done to his Savior, but that he had met many in his travels and liked some of those as individuals.

"I have never met a Jew before, nor a real physician," she answered honestly. But in truth she was more interested in his being a Jew.

"Do you have objection to my tending your injuries?" he asked bluntly.

"Nay," she answered without hesitation. "My father has met your people in the Holy Land. He speaks well of some of them. He says to judge people as individuals by your own knowledge and not by the word of others."

Joseph smiled, encouraged by her lack of guile.

"I am not from here but the lands south and west of Chester," she replied to his earlier question. "How did you know?"

"It is a game I play between myself and my

patients," Joseph said as he examined her shoulder. "It keeps their mind off their injuries so I can examine them thoroughly. Over the years, I have gotten fairly good at it." As he talked, he was pressing his fingers firmly but gently across the shoulder bone itself and then her back, searching for broken bones. His examination was interrupted by Norbert's entrance.

"Lady, your bath is finally ready. I was able to borrow this tub. Where do you want it?"

Rowena had no desire to give orders in another's house. Hesitantly she looked around the room for Blythe, who was busy with her child and completely ignoring everything else.

"Put it in the corner, over there," Fanchon directed him both by motion and by slowly spoken word. She had little knowledge of English and she had not yet heard Norbert speak very much Norman French. "A blanket can be held about for modesty," she added, more for herself than for anyone listening.

Norbert set the tub in the indicated place but refused to leave the room as Joseph continued his examination of Rowena's shoulder. It was left to Owain to carry the buckets up the stairs and deliver them to Fanchon, who poured them into the tub. All the while, Norbert stood against the wall, out of the way, but watching as the examination continued.

He eyed them suspiciously as Joseph had Rowena put her arm up as far above her head as she could, while he examined her back again. He kept his hand on his sword as Joseph's hands strayed to Rowena's neck or shoulder, glaring at the physician as if he expected the man to do her harm.

"A warm bath is more what you need than anything," Joseph pronounced as he studied the growing bruise through Rowena's torn kirtle. "You are very fortunate that it is not broken. Yahweh has found favor with your charity toward others."

Rowena blushed at the compliment, but her guilty conscience would not allow her to acknowledge it. Yet she did not want the conversation with Joseph to end.

"May I help you?" she asked timidly.

"After your bath," he answered, smiling like a kind father bribing his child.

Rowena saw the smile and did not take offense. In nothing the physician said or did, would Rowena find offense. She smiled in return and then frowned.

"We will both need clean clothes," Rowena whispered. "Will Blythe be able to spare . . ."

"Blythe is a mercer's daughter. She must always be at her best for the customers. Therefore she has extra," Joseph answered kindly. His respect for Rowena was mounting. Rowena understood Blythe's station in life, and her desire not to impoverish her was commendable. Not many would have cared. However, a mercer's family was rather fortunate. Some women only had two dresses, one for church and holidays and the other for everyday wear. But Blythe had a few extra to show off her talent for needlecraft.

"Take your bath before the water cools," Joseph prompted her.

Rowena stepped behind the blanket Fanchon had hung and into the tub. The warmth of the water reminded her of how badly she needed the bath, and she was grateful to Owain and Norbert for providing her with it. She slid as far into the tub as she could without spilling the water and let its soothing warmth ease some of the pain and stiffness from her shoulder so that she would be able to help Joseph.

"What was in the wine you gave the child?" she asked over the blanket barrier. She was fascinated at how peacefully the child was sleeping in spite of all the strangers in the room.

"A sleeping powder made from the poppy. She will not feel the pain when I set her leg," Joseph answered.

"I will need two pieces of wood and some long strips of cloth," Joseph told Blythe when she brought clean clothes to Rowena and Fanchon.

"Owain cut some pieces of wood that might be suitable. You will have to look them over carefully and make your selection," Rowena called over the blanket barrier. "And Lady Fanchon tore some cloth from the shop into long strips to hold the leg in place."

"You have done this before?" Joseph asked, only a little surprised. He had noticed that Rowena was very knowledgeable and self assured unless she felt she was encroaching on someone else's area of responsibility.

"Not very often and never a leg," Rowena answered. "That form of injury is rare among my people." She said "my people" without even being aware of it.

After her bath, Rowena dressed in the clothes that Blythe had laid out for her. It was well that fashion called for fuller cut bliauds or Rowena and Fanchon would not have been able to wear Blythe's clothes, since she was shorter and thinner. They were clean but coarse against the skin. But neither was in any mood to find fault with so minor a detail.

Chapter Twenty-one
✦ ✦ ✦ ✦

RUNNOLF RETURNED FROM the hunt in high spirits. The hunting had been poor but the chase had been magnificent. With the king in residence for nearly three weeks the forest was already nearly empty of easy game. All the animals left were wily in the ways of hunting parties and therefore a true pleasure to pursue. For their trouble the king had a large hind as reward.

A large group gathered to welcome the hunting party, amongst whom were the stable hands who were to take charge of the horses, those well-wishers of the king's court who had not been able to attend, as well as many idlers from the town hoping to get a glimpse of their king.

Leben had been ridden hard and long but was in fine spirits as he harassed the frightened stable hands who hesitantly offered to help Run-

nolf unsaddle and groom him. Runnolf eyed
those about, thinking he might permanently employ a stable lad to relieve him of some of his
duties. Then he would be able to spend more
time with Rowena.

His woolgathering was interrupted as Lady de
Vere hurried through the jovial throng with the
red-faced maid, Eada, in tow. In her agitation,
Lady de Vere failed to do deference to the king
and went instead directly to Runnolf, blurting
out the maid's story.

The cold hand of fear encircled Runnolf's heart
as he fought to control the images of Rowena
lying in the filthy gutter of the town with a rearing destrier looming over her.

"Where is she?" Runnolf demanded. Although Runnolf's face had remained immobile,
his voice was cold with the effort to control his
apprehension. And he had inadvertently taken a
menacing step toward the already frightened
maid.

Eada squealed in fright, darting behind Lady
de Vere for protection and forcing her mistress
to answer for her. It took all of Lady de Vere's
courage to answer without wavering before le
Geant's anger. She mentally crossed herself and
sincerely prayed that he would not turn its full
force upon his ward.

"How do I find this—?"

"I will lead you!" a town youth volunteered
from the crowd. To say that the lad was brave to
draw Runnolf's attention was not exactly true.
He was wily in the ways of life and saw an
opportunity to advance himself in Runnolf's fa-

vor and from there possibly to the king's attention.

Runnolf nodded curtly, and the lad ran off toward the town. Without even a parting word to his king, Runnolf remounted Leben and cantered after the youth. He had all he could do to restrain himself from running over his guide in his impatience. Their approach sent pedestrians scurrying for protection as they entered the gravel streets and crossed the town square. The short time it took to reach the alley of the mercer was an eternity of swirling impressions and fanciful images in Runnolf's mind as he fought to keep his fears for Rowena's safety at bay.

Dismounting at the head of the alley, Runnolf was met by Norbert and Owain. Their pale countenances did nothing to relieve his anxiety as he glared at them in silent accusation.

"She is above," Norbert answered as Runnolf tossed the reins to him. "She is—"

Runnolf did not wait for any further explanation. He entered the shop door that Owain indicated. The narrowness of the stairs forced him to climb sideways, his hand on his sword to keep it from banging noisily against the wall.

He forced himself not to dwell on Rowena's possible injuries but to wait to see for himself. His mind obeyed, though his body did not. His hands were cold, his palms sweating on the hilt of his sword.

Pausing at the top, he surveyed the crowded room. He was somewhat reassured when the only occupant of the bed proved to be a small child whose leg was swathed in bandages, but he continued to search anxiously for Rowena.

Rowena, who had been in conversation with Joseph and Fanchon, had heard his deep voice below and his heavy tread upon the stairs. When his head appeared above the floor she darted across the room, throwing herself against him, nearly knocking him back down the steps.

Her heart beating with relief and excitement, Rowena gave herself over to the physical pain of greeting as Runnolf's powerful arms encircled her, crushing her breath from her and reminding her of her injuries.

The relief that Runnolf experienced the instant Rowena was safe in his arms was overwhelming. His throat was dry and closed against any utterance. His elbows felt too weak to support his arms, which had grown heavier with each moment. And his knees were wobbly under his great bulk, causing him to nearly lose his balance upon the top step.

Rowena's cries of greeting mingled with her tears of relief as she tried to explain all in one breath. But she was caustically interrupted by the voice of the king, directly behind Runnolf on the stairs.

"God's knees, Runnolf, will you get off these stairs before I run you through!" Henry bellowed. "It is so close here that I cannot turn around, and you block the way up!"

Hastily, Runnolf moved into the crowded room, never letting Rowena leave the protection of his arms. Since hearing of Rowena's injuries,

Runnolf had forgotten everything else. He stood in bewilderment as Henry climbed the rest of the stairs into the room.

The room had been barely adequate for the family. With the addition of Joseph, Fanchon, and Rowena the room was crowded, but with Runnolf's huge frame and the king's now invading it, the room became overburdened. And when Henry was recognized, the room became a bowing, curtsying mass of bodies, mumbling greetings to their king. Henry impatiently waved those formalities aside and demanded an explanation.

"It was all my fault," Rowena began, facing the king and wiping the tears of greeting from her cheeks. "I hurt the child when we fell—"

"That is not so, Majesty," Fanchon interrupted. "Rowena tried to save the child from being trampled. They saw her! I know they did! But they would not stop!"

"But when I fell . . . her leg was broken . . ." Rowena said, waving her hand despondently in the direction of the bed. "Afterward, they did not even stop to see to the injuries."

"Silence!" Henry commanded the cacophony of female voices.

"Sire, may I explain?"

"Who are you?"

"I am Joseph, a physician."

Henry nodded permission and Joseph related the tale succinctly. "The child, Rebecca, wandered away from her grandfather and out into the street. She was nearly trampled by some of . . . some knights. Lady Rowena saw the child's danger and saved her life. In so doing, they fell. The child has a broken leg and the lady suffers severe bruising to her shoulder."

Upon hearing Joseph's account, Runnolf found himself torn between his admiration for Rowena's courage and his anger at her complete lack of caution for herself. Looking down at her, his eyes softened as he gently touched her shoulder. He noticed absently that his hand shook, but not as much as his stomach when he saw her flinch before forcing a smile of reassurance to her lips.

"And how did you come to be in the street at that moment?" the king demanded, drawing their attention back to himself. He recognized Fanchon as being one of Lady de Vere's women, and she would have no reason to be outside of the castle. And Rowena was new to the town, so she would have even less of a reason to be absent.

Rowena hung her head and refused to answer. She remembered Fanchon's words about her inadequate wardrobe and believed she would bring Runnolf embarrassment if she spoke of it.

"It was my doing," Fanchon answered. "I bedeviled her about her wardrobe, and Eada suggested that her uncle might be able to fashion one for her."

Henry grunted in disgust at the female reason for the near catastrophe, and Runnolf glared menacingly at the two young women.

"Gather your belongings. We will return to the castle," Henry ordered abruptly.

"Where did you leave your horses?" Runnolf demanded, remembering that he had not seen them below in the alley.

"We did not ride," Fanchon answered timidly. "We walked."

"Walked!" both Runnolf and the king bellowed in unison.

"It is not very far," Rowena interrupted, wishing to distract Runnolf's angry outburst. "It is not farther than the orchard—"

"Enough!" The king silenced her, losing patience with the entire matter.

"Good merchant," Henry said, addressing Mannfrith, "I am truly grieved that the inconsiderate behavior of my knights has caused you and yours grief. I sincerely wish your granddaughter a swift recovery."

Henry held out his hand in parting, and Mannfrith fell to his knees in homage. The king stomped down the narrow stairs and left Runnolf to hustle the two women after him. Runnolf gave them no chance to say farewell, but no one seemed to notice. They were too preoccupied by the king's unexpected visit to their home.

As she carefully descended the steps, Rowena could hear the people as they greeted their king. Word had spread rapidly of the king's presence, and the town crowded the street and alley to cheer one who cared enough to offer his encouragement to the parents of the injured child.

Henry was already well liked by his subjects, and one of the reasons for his popularity was that he was not afraid to mingle with them. His popularity increased a hundredfold that day.

Outside Rowena noticed that the king was not the only one to have followed Runnolf from the castle. In the sea of faces she recognized Sir Corbert and Sir Roger, who had been part of her escort to Oxford, as well as others whose faces she had seen last night.

Norbert was holding Leben's reins, but the crowd of people made the task nearly impossible. The plunging, snorting destrier kept the people at bay, allowing room for the king to mount unencumbered. But that was the only benefit of his behavior.

Rowena waited apprehensively, afraid that Runnolf would make her ride pillion behind Sir Roger or Sir Corbert because of Leben's fractious behavior, but Runnolf's weight and hand of authority instantly calmed the mighty war-horse.

Norbert assisted Fanchon to the pillion position behind Corbert and prepared to help Rowena mount behind Runnolf. But instead of behind him, she found herself settled in front of him. What signals passed between the two she did not know, but she was grateful, for there was not another place she would rather be. Once safely within the circle of his powerful arms, she forgot all the things she had wanted to say earlier and settled herself, her head resting on his shoulder, her uninjured arm slipping back around his waist.

Rowena felt a stiffening of Runnolf's posture at her presumption, and she momentarily experienced panic. She was bewildered as always that his concern for her so easily turned to anger. But when she herself stiffened to sit upright, he pulled her roughly against his chest, and she was bewildered anew. His roughness was no longer frightening to her, although she would have liked him to be as gentle with her in public as he was when they were alone.

Runnolf was still torn between his pride in her courage and his anger at her recklessness. Intensifying his anger was the knowledge that the entire incident had been precipitated by a wardrobe he had wanted to buy her but which she had refused.

The ride was too brief. Rowena's sense of security and contentment vanished as they entered the bailey and rode toward the stables. She was startled from her sanctuary by Firelight's frightened whinny and the angry cursing of men. The cry of distress was as familiar to her as Runnolf's own voice, and she immediately sat up to find what danger threatened the mare.

Rowena spied Firelight plunging away from two grooms, who were attempting to saddle her. Frantically looking about the outbuildings, Rowena searched for Iwdeal, and they saw each other simultaneously. Breaking from the protection of the stable, Iwdeal rushed toward her. As he neared, she saw the smeared blood beside his mouth.

"They would not listen," the lad shouted above the chaos.

Without having to be told more, Rowena wiggled from Runnolf's grasp and slipped to the ground. She cried out in pain as she jarred her shoulder, but she ignored it as she made her way toward the mare.

Runnolf watched in alarm as she confronted the grooms. He knew she was in pain from the way she cradled her arm to support her shoulder. But the pain in no way diminished her anger or distracted her from rescuing Firelight.

"You there!" she commanded as she neared the two. "You there! You are not the grooms assigned to this mare. Away with you!"

The groom with the saddle backed away from her instantly, but the other had his back to her and did not see her righteous expression. He only heard her heavily accented speech and judged her to be someone whose words he need not heed. Nor did he see the king and his party standing behind her.

"The mare was assigned to Iwdeal," she stated firmly. She had never interfered with the discipline of another's servant, but she would where this man was concerned, no matter whose servant he was.

"I am head groom here and I did not assign him," the man snarled.

"I assigned Iwdeal!" Rowena said, glaring at the arrogant man's back.

"Out of my way and tend your pots," he snapped, ignoring her and yelling to the second groom to bring the saddle.

And there he made several very serious errors. The king was a just individual in most matters, be it justice for his people or treatment of a prized possession. And Runnolf, who was dangerously possessive of Rowena, held a long memory. Where a slight to himself might go unnoticed, one to Rowena would not.

At that very moment Runnolf would have interfered, but the king waved him still. "I will see the mettle of my people," he commanded.

The king's command was unusual, considering the way most men felt about the capabilities of women. But Henry's mother, the Empress Matilda, was a very aggressive woman. And now he was married to a woman as intelligent as himself and every bit as tempestuous.

Runnolf reluctantly resettled himself and watched. He had to keep reminding himself that Rowena was accustomed to giving orders, and he should not interfere unless she needed him. While he watched, he also came to realize that she would not bend to the norm. She would always follow the dictates of her heart where justice and love were concerned. Had she not proven that almost every day they had been together?

The blood pounded in Rowena's temple as she strained to control her temper so as not to further frighten Firelight. But it was a losing battle as the groom continued to jerk on the bridle.

"If you do not know how to handle a frightened horse any better than this display I am witnessing, then you do not belong in the stables, even to muck them out."

Since the groom with the saddle had been removed from her sight, Firelight had stopped her sidestepping. But she was still nervous and continued to strain against the reins. She whickered shrilly, trying to pull away, but the groom was past patience at the mare's behavior and the interference of the unknown woman. Viciously he jerked on the bridle, causing the mare to scream in pain as the bit hurt her already sore mouth.

Rowena could stand no more. Unexpectedly she jumped for the reins, catching the groom by surprise and shoving him aside. He would have retaliated against her but Iwdeal careened into him, sending him sprawling. In the confusion of bodies and the frantic steps of the now thoroughly frightened mare, one of her hoofs came down solidly on the groom's hand.

The groom screamed as his hand was crushed. The unexpected scream from under her hoofs caused Firelight to rear. Rowena, her reflexes attuned to the mare, did not allow her to rear more than a few feet into the air before she was putting her weight on the reins to bring her back down. Rowena tried to maneuver the mare away from the stricken man, and barely succeeded. But she succeeded enough to allow others to pull him to safety.

Once the man was out of the way of the plunging hooves, Rowena concentrated solely on the mare. Crooning softly, yet holding the reins firmly, she began winding them about her hand until she was close to the bridle that the mare found so threatening.

"Beautiful Firelight," she crooned. "Do you see Iwdeal standing over there? He will fetch your own bridle for you. Be patient."

Rowena prayed that the lad would understand her direction and was happily rewarded when he brought the bridle. Her approval of the stable lad increased as he slowly approached the trembling horse, offering his scent to her so that she would not be frightened further.

"I told you he was a smart lad," she crooned. She noticed that Iwdeal was matching her own soothing melody but with no words of his own, just a soft hum of comfort. Slowly yet confidently the lad approached, even as the mare laid her ears back and prepared to defend herself against the newcomer.

"If you will be still but a moment more," Rowena soothed as she wrapped her good arm around the neck of the still frightened mare, "Iwdeal will take the painful bridle from your mouth."

Following Rowena's instruction, Iwdeal released the bridle and bit, then slipped the mare's own bridle on her. Standing quietly at her head, they waited for her to relax. Satisfying herself that there was no further danger, Firelight leaned against Rowena as a frightened child might do with its mother.

Rowena stroked the mare with her good arm, still crooning soft words of comfort and sighing in relief mingled with pain.

Runnolf had watched the entire incident with trepidation. Instinct told him that Rowena knew what she was doing and that he should not fear for her. But his heart raced as fast as if he were exerting himself along with her. His arms hurt from the strain of remaining motionless and his inability to assist her.

As the mare quieted, so too was Runnolf able to relax. He slumped in the saddle, utterly exhausted from the emotional upheavals of the afternoon. Yet he was beginning to see Rowena with new eyes. All his small impressions and unrelated opinions of her were now coalescing and forming a complete picture that he had only guessed at before. To Runnolf, she was no longer a young woman to be cosseted and protected, to be pampered and humored. She was becoming a capable and talented woman. He loved her and would no longer try to fit her into the mold of his old beliefs.

Runnolf ached to take her in his arms, to congratulate her on her newest triumph with the mare, but he was afraid to compromise her. She was disheveled, her hair pulled from her braids. Her clothes were torn under the arms and down some of the seams from her struggle to rescue the mare. To others she might have appeared as a peasant, but to Runnolf she was as regal as the queen. And then he stiffened in guilt as he saw Rowena lead the mare toward the king.

"Come, my precious beauty, there is someone that you must meet," Rowena crooned as she led the mare toward the king.

Runnolf's heart froze in his chest as he realized that Rowena was going to give the mare to the king. He wanted to call back his hasty words. He had waited too long looking for a logical way out and now it was too late.

"Your majesty," Rowena began hesitantly, not knowing where to begin and not wanting to do so at all. As if sensing Rowena's reluctance, the mare laid back her ears and refused to go farther.

Henry was intrigued by the drama unfolding

before him and now was not displeased to see that he would also play a part in it. He dismounted and walked slowly toward Rowena, being careful not to frighten the mare by any quick, unexpected actions.

"Your majesty, Firelight is a gift . . . from Sir Runnolf. I . . . she has not been well schooled, yet. She needs a gentle hand."

Rowena looked about for Iwdeal. "That young groom," she said, pointing to the lad, "was patient and gentle with her last night, and he knows how to obey orders rightly given."

The king was impressed with Rowena's abilities and did not doubt her judgment of the young groom. He motioned the youth to join them and watched appreciatively as the lad approached facing the mare, again offering his scent to her before facing the king.

"You cared for Firelight last night?" the king inquired, making a definite effort to keep his voice quiet. When Iwdeal nodded affirmatively, he asked how he had happened to lose charge of her this morning.

"Unwin would not listen to the instructions the lady left," Iwdeal answered slowly, fearful that his words would cause more trouble for himself once the king returned to the castle. "And he is the head groom."

"Take the mare back to her stall. Follow Lady Rowena's direction. You and the mare will come to no hurt," the king assured him.

Slowly, carefully Iwdeal took the reins from Rowena and led the mare back to the stables. It was as if the entire bailey had held its breath

during the incident. Once Firelight was safely
within the stable, pandemonium broke loose.
That a young woman, a very small young
woman, would be able to calm the frightened
mare amazed them all—all, that is, except the
knights of Rowena's keep. They had seen her
with both Leben and Firelight and were not surprised. In fact, they were very pleased with her.
She had won them large sums of money. And
now, as they collected, they told and retold the
stories of her and the horses.

With the crises over, Rowena became aware of
the sharp, throbbing pain in her shoulder, and
she cradled her arm against her body to ease it.
But it did not help. She hardly knew if her physical discomfort was more than her emotional
pain at losing Firelight. Engulfed by a spasm of
self-pity, Rowena was no longer able to suppress
her feelings. Tears began to seep past her eye-
lashes and trickle down her cheeks.

She looked toward Runnolf for comfort, but all
she saw through her tears was his stony expression. It hurt her even more to feel the chill of his
imagined displeasure. Her self-pity was too great
at the moment to read concern for her in his
eyes.

Henry saw the tears and gently brushed them
aside. His sympathy and gentleness threatened
to overset her control all the more. She fought
hard to suppress her tears and to focus her mind
on something else, but Firelight was predomi-
nant in her thoughts.

"Your majesty?" Rowena began, and then
hesitated as the tremor in her lower lip slipped

into her voice. "Your majesty, I would not interfere with your servants . . . but the groom Unwin . . . I must speak my thoughts on the
matter."

She waited for permission to speak, and when
the king nodded, she continued, her voice thick
with tears. "He needs to be replaced. No one of
his . . . heavy-handedness should have such responsibility."

Rowena knew it was no easy matter to replace
a servant. They held their positions from father
to son and mother to daughter. It would be easier to have the man killed than removed. Yet she
had to make an effort to have the man removed.

"Do you not think that his injury and your
reprimand are sufficient?"

"He will only take his temper out on those
who cannot defend themselves . . . a young stable boy . . . or another animal."

"What would you suggest?"

Even though the king had granted her permission to speak on the matter of his stable hand,
Rowena was surprised that he would then ask
her opinion of his disposition. Nevertheless, she
answered as she would if her father or Runnolf
had asked. "He is simply not suited for the care
of fine horses . . . or any other animal, for that
matter. I would recommend a change of duties
. . . to a place where he can do no harm."

"Nought else?" the king asked, studying her
closely.

"That is sufficient to the deed," Rowena answered firmly. "He did not injure the mare past
healing."

"I will speak to the marshal." Henry smiled as he gently took her arm, placed it chivalrously upon his own, and led her toward the castle.

Runnolf was seized with an overwhelming sense of guilt and foreboding as he watched Henry lead Rowena from the stable yard toward the castle. He had not missed the king's concern for Rowena's weeping and had seen his gentle gesture. Recriminations rushed upon him. He had let his pride deprive Rowena of the mare, and it was now too late to take her back. He wondered if she would hold the deed against him or could she forgive him his folly? Would she turn against him altogether and seek solace from the king?

Runnolf knew so very well how Rowena could appear worldly when she was, in fact, blind to reality. And he knew of Henry's penchant to roam from his marriage bed whenever the queen was not present. Valiantly he tried to suppress his growing alarm as he led Leben into the stables and began to groom him without his usual patience and good humor.

As the king led Rowena back to the castle, she tried in vain to catch a glimpse of Runnolf from over her shoulder. But all she saw was his back. Henry tried to make conversation with her, but the usual plays at gallantry fell upon deaf ears. Noticing her distraction, he glanced over his shoulder to see where she watched.

At first he frowned when he realized that another had her attention; he had thought it might be the mare. And then he smiled. So, le Geant is in danger of being snared by this small young maid, he mused to himself. It would prove great sport to watch one so small scale the defenses of one so large and in utter control as le Geant. It would break the monotony of the long winter. But then Henry's fairness interfered with his sense of mischief and he became concerned for his faithful liege man. He owed more than one successful campaign to the diligence and ferocity of Runnolf le Geant, and to allow him to be duped would be poor recompense for loyalty.

"Why are you here?" Henry demanded unexpectedly, bringing Rowena's attention back to himself.

"Surely my lord Runnolf has told you," Rowena answered, startled by the question.

"I know what he has told me," Henry answered. "But I wish to hear from you all you wish to gain."

Rowena blanched at the bluntness of the question and then blushed when she thought of all she wished to gain. Nonetheless she plunged ahead, explaining her primary reason for being at court was recognition of tenure for her father's land.

But Henry was not satisfied with her answer. "And Sir Runnolf?"

Rowena paused on the top step of the castle entrance and stared at the king. To voice such private desire was almost beyond her ability, but she tried. "I wish to remain by his side for as long as he will allow it," she answered slowly, remembering Runnolf's earlier advice to always answer the king truthfully. "He refuses to marry without an order from you, but I do not care. I will share his bed whenever he wishes it. If for this reason you wish me to leave your court, I will do so," she added naively yet belligerently.

Contrary to her expectations, Henry smiled with honest pleasure. "Your truthfulness is refreshing, and I will not order you from court for doing what everyone else does."

"They are married!" Rowena added sorrowfully.

"But not to each other." Henry chuckled as he led her inside.

"Would you like me to order him to marry you?" he asked mischievously.

"Nay, your majesty! He would detest such a deed. I am satisfied."

Henry heard a tinge of bitterness as she spoke. He knew no woman was content without marriage, but if she wanted Runnolf enough to pretend that marriage was unnecessary, then so be it. At least for a time, at least until he found out how Runnolf felt. He led her to the stairs of the solar. "You are more than welcome at my court," he murmured, kissing the fingertips of her hand. "And thank you for the mare," he said in parting.

Henry could not guess at Runnolf's feelings toward Rowena, but he would soon know. Her courage and youthful honesty were very refreshing. "If she does not stir his loins as she does mine"—the king chuckled half out loud—"then he deserves a lifetime of loneliness."

Chapter Twenty-two

✦ ✦ ✦ ✦ ✦

LADY DE VERE met Rowena at the head of the stairs and bade her welcome in a very formal and angry tone of voice. Fanchon stood in the middle of the room, still in her borrowed clothes, her lower lip trembling.

"And what punishment did you receive from your guardian?" Lady de Vere demanded. She was not a vindictive person, but she knew Runnolf had no experience with young women and wanted to help him set his authority so no more unfortunate episodes would occur.

"He has said nothing," Rowena stammered, surprised at Lady de Vere's interference. It had been so long since any woman had interfered with her life that Rowena was not sure what to expect. Her first inclination was to rebel, but her better judgment prevailed. She had been assigned to Lady de Vere's care, and apparently Lady Anne took her responsibilities very seriously.

"I will speak to him. He cannot allow this episode to go unnoticed. Where is he?"

"He is in the stables, grooming Leben," Rowena answered.

Lady Anne left the solar with an air of righteous crusade. Rowena moved closer to her friend, Fanchon, and then noticed that Eada was not among them.

"Where is Eada?"

"She is about someplace," Fanchon answered. "She is not in any trouble," she continued, seeing Rowena's concern. "Lady Anne is holding us responsible for her deportment."

"What will she do?" Rowena whispered as they continued to wait for Lady Anne's return.

"Do not worry about her discipline. A switch is the most I have ever seen her use on anyone. But what of Sir Runnolf?"

Rowena shook her head in bewilderment. She truly did not know what he would do.

After a period of time that was a lifetime to those who waited, but in actuality was only minutes long, the door at the top of the solar steps opened to admit Lady de Vere.

Rowena sighed in relief. Lady Anne had returned with Runnolf's verdict! Then Rowena gasped in shock as Runnolf followed Lady de Vere into the solar.

Instantly everyone curtsied and murmured greeting to Sir Runnolf. After the amenities were observed, Lady de Vere dismissed her women, shutting the door firmly behind them.

Runnolf's face was somber but his eyes were wary. He did not like being in the women's solar. It was not the proper place for a knight of his low standing. In fact, he would not have agreed to Lady de Vere's suggestion at all if Sir Aubrey himself had not given his permission.

Runnolf stood motionless but Rowena noticed that he periodically clenched his fist as if his arm or hand was stiff from an injury. Her heart beat erratically and her eyes misted at the thought that he might have sustained an injury during the hunt and had gone all this time without proper attention.

"Has my lord injured his hand?" she inquired softly, her own hands cold with fear for him.

"Do not try to becloud the matter," Lady de Vere commanded before Runnolf could answer for himself. "That tactic will not work."

Rowena's face turned crimson at the injustice of the accusation, and her jaw clamped shut in a stubborn jut that foretold rebellion.

Runnolf did not miss her momentary flash of outraged innocence. He shared her feeling that Lady de Vere should not interfere between them, but this was not the Marches. They were no longer alone. This was the court of Henry of England, at which certain proprieties must be observed.

Lady de Vere motioned Runnolf to her own chair near the brazier and stood waiting in silence beside him.

"I would hear the entire tale," he commanded as he gingerly sat in the seat that was too small for him.

"It is as we said at the mercer's," Rowena began. There was only a slight tightening of her jaw as she strove to remain calm in the face of his intense scrutiny. "There is nothing more to tell."

"I do not understand your reason for going to the mercer's shop, nor do I understand the reason for walking when you have your own palfrey," he stated stonily as he sat forward, leaning his arms against his thighs.

"That was my doing," Fanchon blurted out in

her hurry to answer. She was intimidated by his presence. In the privacy of Lady de Vere's solar, she felt the full strength of it directed entirely at herself, and she was frightened. "I was helping Rowena . . . freshen her wardrobe after her journey . . . I felt that it was ill suited for the court . . . I told her so."

"How Sir Runnolf dresses his ward is no concern of yours," Lady de Vere berated Fanchon.

"She did not want me to embarrass you," Rowena interrupted in her friend's behalf.

"Your friend's motives are exemplary," Runnolf responded coldly. "But you told me your wardrobe was sufficient for your needs. You befooled me."

"Nay, my lord," Rowena pleaded, taking a step forward and raising her hand in supplication. "I believed it was."

When Runnolf offered her no consolation, Rowena hung her head in embarrassment, remembering how he had offered to buy her so many things and how she had refused. Now her refusal had caused all this new grief and brought her new miseries.

"Now you do not?" he demanded unexpectedly.

But Rowena would not look at him or answer his question. Runnolf studied her silent form and judged that there was need for privacy to settle this matter, and several others, to both their satisfaction.

"Lady de Vere, I would have words with Rowena in private," Runnolf commanded coldly.

"Sir Runnolf, please," Fanchon began, fearful

that the privacy Runnolf asked for meant that
Rowena would receive a beating for her behavior. But her courage nearly failed her when his
cold, unyielding glance again centered on her.
"Her wardrobe may . . . have been sufficient
before . . . but here . . . appearing before the
king and his court—"

"Why is it necessary for her to—?"

"Sir Runnolf," Lady de Vere interrupted. She
had walked to Rowena's travel baskets to examine the contents, since they seemed to hold the
entire explanation for the episode in question.

Runnolf glared at her impatiently and the
words nearly froze on her tongue. Where once
Lady de Vere felt punishment was necessary,
she now felt protective toward both young
women. Now she also feared what form his punishment might take. Not that both of them did
not deserve a sound thrashing, but Runnolf was
so large and so powerful.

"I have been looking through Rowena's ward-
robe," she said despite her fear. "And I am afraid
Fanchon is correct in her assessment. Wearing it,
Rowena would be an embarrassment to you.

"But it can be put to rights," she hurried on
when she saw Runnolf's face turn red in anger
and his fingers turn white where they gripped
the chair arm. "I can set my women to sewing
this material and I can find some things that will
fit her amongst my own things."

"Nay! She will have new, from outside in!
Now leave us! I will have privacy!" Runnolf's
tone brooked no argument, and Lady de Vere

hurried Fanchon out of the room, shutting the door tightly behind them.

For a long time Runnolf sat in silence, staring at Rowena, who refused to look at him. Dressed in the ill-fitting clothes that were now torn under the arms and side seams, she appeared forlorn and lost.

He had all he could do to remain still and not pull her into his arms to soothe her pain. But he reminded himself of his duty to chastise her for her disregard of her own safety.

Rowena fought valiantly to control the trembling of her lip and the tears that threatened to break the dam of her control. But it was no use. Her spirit crumbled in the face of all her imagined trespasses. His silence was worse than his anger. She could stand it no longer and threw herself into his arms, crying miserably and clutching convulsively at his tunic.

"My lord, please, forgive me. I have brought you shame. But everything is so different," she wailed in misery.

He did not hear the rest of her babbling words as he crushed her close to his heart, muffling her voice. As the first wracking sobs subsided, he pulled her onto his lap, holding her until she cried herself to silence. Gently releasing her, he bent to place a kiss on her still-trembling lips, but she pulled aside enough so that he kissed only the side of her mouth.

"Are my kisses no longer pleasing to you?" he demanded, as horrifying images of Rowena with the king flashed through his mind.

"I desire nothing more in this life," she whispered. "But I have shamed you and must be punished."

"And what punishment do you desire?" he demanded. His heart stood still in his throat waiting for her reply. He prayed feverishly that she did not feel she merited another beating. He did not think he would be able to do it again.

"I desire none," she whispered, her body trembling in fear. "In truth, I fear your anger. I did not intend to bring you shame. I had hoped to please you and make you desire me above all others."

"What others?" he demanded, bewildered.

"The ladies of the court," she answered, her cheeks crimson.

"Have you seen me desire another?" he demanded, outraged by her accusation. "Have I had time to even look at another since arriving?"

"Nay, my lord. Nor did I want to give them a chance to catch your eye."

Runnolf's anger was replaced by genuine pleasure, but it did not wipe out the image of her walking with Henry.

"And the king? Do you intend to catch his eye also?"

"Fanchon said I must stay in his sight or he will not remember my father's land," she answered truthfully.

"You will not find the king's bed a very warm place," he snarled. "He is rarely in it."

"My lord, you are hurting me!" Rowena cried out. "My lord, please, I do not understand."

"The king! I saw you with him!"

"He asked about my being at court. He wanted to know my intentions toward you," she cried, protesting her innocence.

"And?"

"I told him!"

Runnolf eased the pressure on her arms, but he did not release her.

"What have I done? You told me to speak only truth to the king!"

"You have done nought amiss," he assured her. "I am overset by the incident at the mercer's."

"And Firelight?"

"What about the mare?" he demanded, again feeling the pangs of guilt.

"Are you angry?"

"Why should I be angry about the mare?" he asked as he wearily sat back into the chair, pulling Rowena onto his lap again. Deep discussions with Rowena were confusing and tiring to the extreme. Why, oh why, could they not converse easily?

"You forbade me to go near her ever again. But I could not allow the groom to mistreat her."

"Nay, I am not angry about the mare," he assured her. "And you have not shamed me about the wardrobe," he continued softly. "But I allowed you to dissuade me from purchasing other material for you. This I will not allow to happen again. Do you understand?"

"Yea, my lord," she purred as she lay softly against his chest, listening to the powerful beat of his heart.

And with each beat of his heart, Rowena's

guilt lessened and her passion began to rise. Her blood raced through her body, warming her, setting her on fire as she waited, hoping he would kiss her again.

"You will incur my anger if you do not return my kiss while we still have privacy," he commanded gruffly, his voice hoarse with desire.

Happily Rowena lifted her face to his and clasped him firmly about the neck with her uninjured arm. Hungrily, deliberately she returned his kiss, feeling the searing pains of passion swell within her.

"Please, my lord," she whispered in his ear, the vibrations of her voice sending ripples of tension along his skin. "Please, hurry and find a place for us to be together."

Runnolf moaned in reply, his face buried at the base of her throat. He ran his hand down the length of her and then back up her side, stopping at her breasts. He brushed his hand gently around them, feeling her desire-hardened nipples straining against the tight-fitting bliaud. Encouraged, he slipped his fingers into the torn seam of her bliaud, feeling the fullness trying to escape the tight confines of her borrowed clothes. He was spurred to more fervent caresses as she thrust herself against his calloused fingertips.

It had been less than two days since their last shared intimacy, but to the two of them it felt like two years of celibacy. But Rowena's good name and reputation were not far from Runnolf's mind. He was the first to be brought back to the harshness of reality by a persistent scratching at the door. He swore mighty oaths of blasphemy and hastily set Rowena off his lap.

Rowena staggered from his abrupt movements. Her head pounded, her knees were weak, and her breath was ragged from thwarted passion. Shakily she moved to the nearest chair and leaned against it, struggling to orient herself. With trembling hands she put her own clothes to rights as she waited for Runnolf to regain his own control. His surcoat hid his aroused state while his eyes, no longer glittering with passion, flashed anew with anger at their interruption.

After a curt nod from Runnolf, Rowena moved to the door and opened it. Lady de Vere surveyed the room from the safety of the entrance but would not enter. Even through the thickness of the wooden door she had heard Runnolf's muffled voice. Having no way of knowing the relationship between Rowena and Runnolf, she assumed Runnolf's stiff posture and glittering eyes, and Rowena's red ones, were from his anger and the discipline he had meted out. Shuddering in fear and concern for Rowena, she nonetheless addressed Runnolf.

"Sir Runnolf, I beg pardon for intruding, but the supper will be served in a short while and my ladies and I must see that Fanchon and Rowena are made presentable."

Runnolf bowed stiffly to her, recognizing that if he had stayed any longer, Rowena would have been sorely compromised.

He walked stiffly to the door, and Lady de Vere hastily stepped aside for him. Before leaving, he remarked to Rowena, "Whatever punishment is settled on Fanchon will also be yours." And then to Lady de Vere, "You would be doing me a great boon if you would see to her wardrobe. Spare no expense and see that the bills are sent to me."

Lady de Vere curtsied in acknowledgment of Runnolf's wishes and then sighed in relief as he purposefully descended the steps. After his departure, she ushered Fanchon and the rest of her ladies back into the solar, where she became a bustling burst of energy.

"Clare, you and Alyce measure Rowena. On the morrow you will begin her new wardrobe."

"Nay!" Rowena cried as Lady de Vere withdrew the piece of blue velvet from her travel basket. "That is to be a mantle for Sir Runnolf!"

Lady de Vere was taken aback by Rowena's behavior. Moments before she had been the epitome of a chastised child, but now she fiercely protected the property of her guardian. Lady Anne smiled tolerantly. It well bespoke Rowena's upbringing and promised good fortune for her future husband, whomever le Geant should choose.

"These?" she asked, as she held up the brown velvet and the sendal.

"Yea, my lady. They were purchased for me." Rowena blushed and dropped her glance.

"The color suits you," Lady Anne murmured and set the material aside. "And the chainsil?"

"Half for my lord's shertes and the rest for my kirtles."

Lady Anne nodded. "When my ladies have

finished their measurements, wash your face and come with me," she commanded as she entered her own sleeping chamber. "Fanchon, when you are changed into more appropriate clothes, I will need your assistance."

By the time Rowena and Fanchon joined her, Lady Anne had her bed strewn with clothes. "Help Rowena out of those clothes and give them to Eada to wash, mend, and return to . . ."

"Blythe," both young women answered in unison.

While Lady Anne sorted through her own wardrobe, Fanchon helped Rowena off with her borrowed clothes. As her kirtle was removed, Fanchon's sharp intake of breath brought Lady de Vere's attention back to them.

Lady Anne studied the nasty bruise on Rowena's shoulder and the fresh bruises on her upper arms. She rightly believed that the bruises on Rowena's arms came from Runnolf's temper, but she said nothing. Apparently le Geant had already punished Rowena to some extent, and she did not feel that further punishment was necessary.

After much deliberation, Lady Anne selected pale green hose, a dark green bliaud of finely woven wool, and an orange kirtle of linen for Rowena to wear. From another chest, she withdrew a white linen barbette.

"Alyce, on the morrow, send word to the leathercrafters for shoes. Also send to the mercer for materials."

"Please, my lady," Rowena interrupted. "Please, send for Mannfrith. The merchant that you would normally use would be too busy to make my clothes, and your ladies have other responsibilities beside sewing for me."

Lady Anne glared at Rowena and then Fanchon, although the latter had said nothing. In silence she walked to the door and motioned to Eada to bring Blythe's clothes for closer examination. She tested the seams for the smallness of the stitching and their strength.

"I will seek Sir Runnolf's permission at supper," Rowena volunteered.

Still Lady Anne stood in silence, examining the clothes. She did not need further permission from le Geant. He had entrusted her to see to Rowena's wardrobe, and that included choice of mercer as well. But was it not wise to consider cost? How much could Runnolf afford for his ward? How valuable an estate was she to inherit? She and Eada exchanged a few words and then Lady Anne reentered her chamber without further comment.

"Needs must you wear your own shoes," Lady Anne remarked ruefully. "Mayhap no one will notice they do not match the bliaud."

Rowena glanced down at her feet to see what was wrong with her shoes. She shrugged, noticing that her shoes were sturdier, more suitable to the keep than to castle life. And they were the natural brown of leather, not dyed to match her clothes.

When Fanchon and Rowena were finally dressed to Lady Anne's satisfaction, she led them out to join the others. Grandly she swept into the great hall to see to the last-minute preparations for the meal, while her ladies were released to seek out their own friends, husbands, or eating companions.

Chapter Twenty-three

✦✦✦✦✦

SIR CORBERT, WHO was standing with Runnolf, recounting the wagers he had won, was the first to see Rowena and Fanchon enter the hall. Since his stay at the keep, he, like so many of the others, had become a great admirer of Rowena's.

Runnolf scowled as Sir Corbert abruptly broke off their conversation and moved to intercept the two young women. In spite of his earlier resolve, he was continuously being assaulted with spikes of jealousy.

Nonetheless, Runnolf followed after him. Yet they were unable to get near her, because all the knights of Henry's household had surrounded her, especially those who had lost money wagering against her. The stories of her ride at the keep, coupled with those of witnesses to her feat at the bailey, were spreading and embellishing on her reputation with horses.

Rowena stood rooted to the spot, overwhelmed by the attention and not knowing how to respond. But Fanchon replied to their advances with playfulness and wit, helping her new friend as much as possible.

Fanchon was a favorite of Lady de Vere's women because she had no illusions for her future. She accepted the inevitable and did not bemoan her unmarried fate. This ability made her a sought-after dance partner and frequent listener to love poems and verses, especially those inspired by the love of others.

In some ways, Fanchon felt she had the best of it, especially when she saw some of the husbandly behavior of the barons. She, at least, would be spared the humiliation of a black eye or flaunted affair. And she assiduously guarded her heart lest some young swain catch her eye, intent upon an immoral liaison that would result in her banishment from Lady de Vere's household.

As Rowena and Fanchon moved farther into the hall, surrounded by their escorts, they passed close to another group who were avidly listening to an exuberant knight eloquently bemoaning the disreputable behavior of the Oxford populace. Rowena's group also stopped to listen.

Rowena was shocked by the tale's viciousness as the knight blamed an unknown woman who had nearly overset riders in the streets. Mayhap she had misunderstood, she cautioned herself, since she had only heard part of the telling. Mayhap it was a different incident.

Making her way through the crowd of listeners, Rowena asked the speaker to repeat his story in its entirety. "Sir Knight," she said, addressing the slender man, "I could not help but overhear some of your tale. Would you be so kind as to repeat it?"

"Hubert de Lund," the young man said as he bowed gallantly, introducing himself. "A pleasure to do your bidding." Happy to be the center of the group's attention again, including the attractive newcomer to court, he retold his tale, embellishing it with exaggerated mannerisms.

Rowena found his affectations repulsive. She clamped her teeth shut on her tongue until de Lund had finished his boastful speech. Her cheeks flushed a deep crimson as he magnified the stupidity of the townspeople while adding generously to the injuries to his friend and his destrier.

"It is not the stupidity of the townspeople that caused the injury," she told him coldly at the conclusion of his story. "But the ignorance of those who should know better."

Sir Hubert's mouth hung agape at her sudden change and her charge of stupidity.

"If your friend had not been riding without thought and care, he would have been able to rein his destrier in time so the incident would not have occurred. It was his carelessness that caused the accident, not the child's."

"What child?" the perplexed knight demanded.

"The child your glorious friend nearly trampled to death in the street," Rowena answered, her voice dripping with scorn.

"There was no child in the street," de Lund

protested. "Only some crazed woman who darted in front of the destriers."

Runnolf had been watching Rowena and the very confused young knight. He would have laughed outright, except that would have insulted de Lund more. He wondered absently if he looked as confused when he and Rowena spoke at cross purposes.

"Never tell a tale if you are missing the whole of it," Runnolf said to him, as he firmly took Rowena by the arm and led her from the group of startled onlookers.

The glitter of anger in Rowena's eyes instantly softened to pools of adoration as she looked into Runnolf's steel gray ones, and her pride in him swelled. To her mind, he had firmly chastised that arrogant knight for besmirching the dignity of the townspeople. By so doing, he had lived up to the code of chivalry by defending the innocent.

Hoping to help Rowena attract Runnolf's attention, Fanchon tried to draw the three of them into conversation. She was only partially successful. Sir Corbert answered her carefully yet easily, while Runnolf remained silent and Rowena answered only in monosyllables.

Rowena was too conscious of Runnolf's presence beside her and the pageantry around her to reply sensibly. The blazing colors of the clothing, the opulence of the jewels, the overloud and explosive sounds of the crowd so overwhelmed her senses that conversation, at that moment, was nearly impossible.

The glitter of gold shone from the king's table

and was reflected in lessening degrees by the tables close to his, while down at Runnolf's table and those around it, the glitter had disappeared. Even though Runnolf was a favorite of Henry's, he sat with the large body of untitled knights in the king's service. Their tables were simply set with trenchers, wooden spoons, and earthen flagons.

Rowena stood in wide-eyed attention as the court waited for the king to signal the beginning of the meal. While they waited, servants with pitchers and catch basins moved among the guests so that hands could be washed and dried.

Rowena looked back to the king and his guests who were taking their seats on the dais. She noted that behind each stood a page with pitcher and basin, waiting for them to be seated. Once they were seated, the pages knelt beside their lords' chairs and poured water over their hands. Rowena's cheeks burned with shame as she remembered how she balked at this practice. She had once again misjudged Runnolf's intentions, when he had only tried to teach her the ways of courtly life.

When the hall was silent, the king's chaplain intoned the grace. Quick on the last syllable of Amen, a piercing blast from the trumpeters announced the first course to be served.

The unexpected fanfare ending the solemnity of the prayer startled Rowena, and she gripped Runnolf's arm convulsively. He looked down at her, reassuring her that all was well by covering her dainty hand with his massive one and giving it a firm squeeze before releasing it. Blushing happily, Rowena basked in the pleasure of the intimate gesture.

The noise accompanying the continuous lines of servants entering the hall drew Rowena's attention, and her eyes widened in amazement. Vast assortments of food were being carried in. Even the stories of royal banquets that her parents had told in her childhood prepared her not for the immensity of it all.

Rowena noted that the king's table was served first with the best and most elaborate dishes. After the king's table, each succeeding rank of barons was served. By the time the servants reached their table, the most exotic dishes were gone, but Runnolf was careful to select the best of what was left and place them on the side of his trencher, closest to Rowena, so that she might taste them all. There were herons and sea gull, oxen and bulls, sturgeon and turbot, eels in a paste and oysters. There were delicacies of jelly, and custards, both hot and cold. The variety of beverages was also as great, if not as tasty. There was ale, beer so thick that the guests had to filter it through their teeth, acidic wines flavored with honey and spices, and fruit juices.

Inquisitively, Rowena tasted of every dish until, reluctantly, she was forced to refuse more. The desserts, fresh fruits, and nuts she left untouched.

Runnolf noticed her studying the king and his dignitaries seated on the dais. No matter how hard he tried not to, he continued to suffer momentary stings of apprehension that Rowena might have an ulterior motive in mind. After all, they could offer her so much more than he could. He forced himself to dismiss so unworthy an idea by reminding himself that she had never before seen so august an assembly and would, therefore, be naturally curious to know who they were.

"Beside the king, on his right, is Thomas à Becket, the chancellor," Runnolf explained, fighting to keep the tightness from his voice. "Beside him is Robert de Beaumont, Earl of Leicester and probably the most powerful baron in the realm. Next is Robert de Ilchester, another of the king's councillors. On his left, you know Lady de Vere, then Sir Aubrey, and Sir Richard."

Rowena nodded in acceptance of the information and continued to look around her. She was impressed by the splendor. There was a chaotic confusion associated with everything and yet, in that confusion, there was also order as everyone went about his own chores.

"You are very quiet," Runnolf remarked. For himself, he found her silence among so much noise very pleasing, but he must know her thoughts. Before now, he had never cared for court life, preferring the field of honest combat to the field of conniving that he perceived in the king's presence.

Runnolf especially loved the excitement of a battle well fought or hard won. He fought well and took great pride in that excellence. He had no lineage, no patrimony. He had only that which he won with his sword—a reputation for honesty and loyalty, great respect as a man and fighting machine, and some money. However, he was realistic enough to know that since he wanted Rowena, he must assume the responsibility for her safety. And her safety would not be found on the battlefield.

Did she desire to remain at court with all its intrigues? He did not believe so. However, he would try to adjust himself to it if she so desired. In truth, he missed her father's keep and its solitude. There was work there to keep everyone busy, new land to be conquered for his heirs, and that land to be cultivated by the villains.

His heirs! He breathed deeply, trying to control the tremor of desire and pride that surged through his body at the thought. This was not the first time he had considered children, but it was the first time he had considered them in respect to land and succession. This was also the first time such a thought had taken precedence over his desire to spend his life in the service of the king.

"Is this not a magnificent gathering?" he prodded when Rowena did not answer.

Rowena studied everything around her before answering. The great hall was filled with guests. The minstrels sat in the oriel above the entrance to the hall playing their instruments, which were barely heard above the noise. Servants by the hundreds moved about the tables serving the throngs of diners. The king's hawk sat with other favorite hunting birds, high on the wall near the dais. The hunting hounds wandered freely, stealing scraps from the tables and from each other, giving the king and his knights something else to bet upon.

Suddenly Rowena was filled with a great longing to be home, away from all the pandemonium and strangeness that surrounded her. She missed the quietness of her home, its orderliness, its purpose. She closed her eyes, trying to fight the momentary surge of homesickness. When she had her emotions again in control, she opened her eyes and tried to answer Runnolf's question.

"I have asked Lady Anne and she could not answer me," Rowena began hesitantly, forcing herself to concentrate on her surroundings. "If the queen were here, how many more people would there be and where would they stay?"

This question had been nagging at the back of Rowena's mind since her arrival. The answer would indicate her ability to remain at Runnolf's side and, more importantly, in his bed.

Runnolf, intently watching her, noted the tenseness of her body, the stiffness of her back, and knew the question was not asked in idle curiosity. "The queen has as many followers as the king," Runnolf answered thoughtfully. "And if she were present, we would not be seated so close to the king's table. Her courtiers would push us farther down the hall."

His answer was as vague as Lady Anne's had been. Somehow she was not asking the question that would gain her the answer she needed to know.

"Why do you ask?" Runnolf demanded when his answer did not seem to satisfy her.

Rowena gazed intently into his eyes as if she could convey the reason for her question with-

out words. The intensity of his gaze was as deep
as her own and she blushed, thinking he had
read her mind. They were saved the embarrassment of having to voice their thoughts by the
approach of the king.

Henry, as was his habit, ate sparingly and
then moved from table to table, visiting and con-
versing with all the members of his court.

He paused a time at Runnolf's table, exchanging pleasantries and asking after Rowena's injury. However, the majority of his inquiries
centered on Firelight, since he was greatly impressed with Rowena's ability.

"I am told, by those who know, that Hugh fitz
Giles considered her one of the best horse-
women of his acquaintance," Runnolf volunteered, startling Rowena into speechlessness.
She had never heard her father say such a thing
although she knew he was not dissatisfied with
her abilities. She also knew that Runnolf did not
lie, so the compliment held great significance for
her.

"Who began the training of the mare?" the
king asked.

"Rowena," Runnolf answered when she remained silent. "She gentled her and had progressed as far as riding her one time before . . .
I decided to gift the mare to you."

"She was magnificent!" Corbert enthused as
he remembered that fateful day. "The two were
as one, riding down the valley and back." And
he retold the entire incident for the king's benefit. It was not the first time the king had heard
the story that afternoon, but Corbert's honest

admiration left Henry spellbound and visually aware of every move of horse and woman.

"It is very unusual to have such a rapport between a woman and her horse," Henry admitted judiciously. "Especially on a first ride."

Henry watched Rowena intently during Corbert's recital of her ride and was surprised when she did not participate in the narrative. By her subdued manner and the aura of sadness that hung about her when the story was complete, Henry suspected that there was more for him to know.

His gaze shifted to Runnolf, who also was not participating in the lively telling. There was a stillness about him, similar to the iron calm he enforced upon himself before battle.

As if reading the king's unasked question, Runnolf hesitantly offered an explanation. "The reason I gifted you with Firelight was because I trusted not Rowena's ability and feared she would do herself an injury."

"And you do not care if the mare harms your king," Henry teased.

Runnolf's face did not betray his teasing response when he answered, except that his eyes had lost their coldness. "If the king can tame a kingdom, then he will have no problem with a country mare. Or he could gift her to one of his enemies in hopes he will break his neck on the first ride."

The king laughed uproariously and then everyone followed suit. Runnolf's wit was not well known except to a very few, and those around him knew not whether he was serious or not.

"And do you still doubt her ability?" Henry demanded unexpectedly as he probed deeper into the wound he perceived between Runnolf and Rowena.

"I still fear for her safety," Runnolf answered slowly. "But with time, she would have schooled the mare."

The fact that he had spoken so truthfully of his error in judgment reinforced the king's faith in his vassal. If nothing else, Runnolf was honest to a fault. Where Rowena's presence might complicate matters, it did not diminish his veracity.

"Then why did you not give her back the mare?" Henry demanded explosively.

"I had already given my word," Runnolf answered adamantly.

"And your word, once given, is your life," Henry acknowledged, satisfied that Runnolf's honor was in no way changed by Rowena's presence.

Rowena had remained quiet, almost unbelieving, as Runnolf admitted to her ability. It was something she had long since despaired of hearing, and his words were a joy to her ears. Waves of pleasure, almost physical in their intensity, coursed through her body. To hear these words spoken by Runnolf was worth the loss of any mare.

"Are you satisfied with his word?" Henry demanded of Rowena.

The king watched the momentary surprise flutter across Rowena's face. Until now she had not been included in the conversation, and his question had caught her off guard. She lifted her emotion-filled eyes to look at Runnolf, and the king knew instantly her total commitment to le Geant.

"My lord's word is my life also," she answered clearly as she placed her hand on Runnolf's clenched fist.

"If all were as faithful as the two of you, we would have eternal peace," Henry said as he covered their hands with his own before abruptly moving on.

Eventually the guests finished their meals, and the king's almoner collected the leftover food for distribution to the poor who waited at the castle gates. The tables were cleaned and stacked against the walls while everyone milled about in conversation.

Rowena again found herself the center of attention from the young swains of the court. Slowly, following Fanchon's lead, she bantered carefully with those who surrounded her while staying close by Runnolf's side, never letting him out of her sight while he was occupied with comrades of his own. It was not that she was a coward or in the least bit backward. Left to her own devices, she would have survived the ordeal of making new acquaintances, but she gained strength and assurance from his towering presence.

Rowena listened with half an ear to the talk of the men that involved the Welsh. She tried to hear enough to determine if it pertained to her own lands but could not.

The evening grew long, and Lady de Vere motioned for Fanchon and Rowena to join her as she retired for the night. The two young women reluctantly curtsied to Runnolf and then followed Lady Anne to the solar.

That night Runnolf lay sleepless. The night candle had been lit by the foot of the large bed where Richard de Lucy slept, and was casting shadows upon the walls. The convolution of shadows mimicked the thoughts that plagued Runnolf's peace of mind.

Lying upon his cot, Runnolf was filled with a fierce anger against the knights whose carelessness had endangered Rowena. Yet he could not comprehend why she would risk her life for an unknown child. If she would do so much for the child of a stranger, what would she do for a child she loved? How possessive and caring would she be for a child of her own body? What foolish risks would she take to protect a child of her own?

"Last night you assisted me by sharing your knowledge of the Marches and its people," Sir Richard said from the depth of his curtained bed. "May I now assist you?"

"I did not mean to disturb you," Runnolf apologized. He felt great warmth toward Sir Richard for offering his counsel, but he had experienced such a fright earlier today, and was now reliving it, that his voice sounded cold and unfriendly.

"Do not think to frighten my concern away," de Lucy warned him sternly. "In the past year, I have come to know you well. You may speak your mind openly and without fear that my tongue is loose on both its ends."

Runnolf lay still, wanting to unburden him-self, but what could he say without compro-mising Rowena's reputation? "Many things trouble me," Runnolf replied, sighing deeply. "The first of course, is Rowena . . . the Lady Rowena and her land," he corrected himself. "But even before that is her father, Hugh fitz Giles."

"What troubles you about fitz Giles?"

"Why would he ride out to do combat and leave his only daughter unprotected? Why did he not withdraw behind his walls, demand safe conduct to the king, and present his plea for tenure to the land?"

"He had warning of your coming?" Sir Rich-ard asked quietly.

"A full summer."

"Then he had his spies out, searching for your weaknesses and strengths. He knew your repu-tation for fairness and honor."

"All the more reason to have withdrawn to his keep."

"It is hard to fathom the mind of a desperate man."

"He was not desperate!" Runnolf protested. "Desperate is having nought else to rely upon. Fitz Giles had options open to him."

"Name them."

"Return to his family and take his people with him . . . or withdraw to his keep, as I said before. In either case, he could plead his cause before the king and his daughter would be safe."

"With him dead, his daughter became your

responsibility," de Lucy said as he tried to reason as fitz Giles might. "You are favored with the king's respect, and therefore you would have more chance to ensure the daughter's protection by making her a ward of the crown. As ward, the tenure secure, a satisfactory marriage could then be arranged with the property remaining intact."

"He had no way of knowing I would do that," Runnolf protested. "Every keep I destroyed, I sent the women back to their families. I did not make any of them wards of the crown."

"Why did you not send her back to her family?"

"She either does not know or will not tell me of her parents' family," Runnolf answered, miserable. In truth he had never asked her until after he found her out at the pool in the orchard, but Sir Richard need not know that. "There is some mystery involved that I did not think to straighten out. Even the servants who know will not say."

"Was there anything at Fitzgiles Keep to indicate Sir Hugh's parentage?" De Lucy had innocently given the keep its formal name.

"Amongst his possessions was a signet ring with the head of a wolf, the same for his shield as I explained when I wrote about the land."

There was a long pause before Sir Richard went on thoughtfully. "The land, you say, is beautiful and productive . . . Rowena is also beautiful . . . both are beautiful enough to warrant your placing them under your own personal protection. And now you are asking the king for his recognition."

Runnolf did not answer. A wave of guilt passed over him as he was reminded that Rowena was protected from everyone but himself.

"I have sent messengers to some of the older barons in hopes that they will recognize the device you described and name the family. Once that is discovered, her other problems may also be solved."

"What other problems?" Runnolf demanded.

"Her future, of course," Sir Richard answered innocently. "She is nearly past marriageable age and should be soon settled so that you may go on with your own life."

Runnolf was beyond words. To his knowledge, no one of the court beside the king knew of his relationship with Rowena. Therefore de Lucy must be sincere in his desire to assist Rowena to make a suitable marriage. But it upset him greatly to think that she might be shuttled into a marriage without her consent and without his own. It must never happen!

Runnolf knew that rarely were marriages arranged with the consent of the parties involved. They were made by guardians and parents who were interested in political realities, blood bonds, and the acquisition of land. Runnolf knew this, but it was no longer abstract knowledge. It was personal—it concerned Rowena!

The thought of marriage for her conjured mental images that brought Runnolf physical pain:

Rowena in the arms of another . . . Rowena in the bed of another . . . Rowena with children fathered by another. He groaned aloud and drew himself into a fetal position, trying to block out the pain of his thoughts.

But you are her guardian! a small voice of reason shouted from the depths of his despair. He had already proclaimed himself so. If a marriage was to be arranged, he would do so and it would be him she married.

But what if her grandfather was found? Or another member of her family? The questions made him nauseous with dread. Would they accept her once they knew she was no longer a maid? And if they did, who would marry her under those circumstances? And what if she were carrying his child? Would he be allowed to marry her?

Runnolf was experienced enough at court to know that if her family was highly enough placed, they could buy her a husband who would overlook her condition. And if she were carrying his child, and if her family refused to acknowledge her, then she would carry the stigma of whore, and her child, bastard. The only option open to him was marriage. But how could he care for a wife and child upon the battlefield? If she were mistress of her own lands . . . if she were granted Fitzgiles Keep . . .

Fitzgiles Keep! The name caught his attention amidst the swirling irrational thoughts. It was the way de Lucy had called it earlier. How fine-sounding was the name! It was no longer the property of Sir Hugh fitz Giles, but it would bear his name so all would remember that he had built it and nourished it with his blood.

The thought calmed him enough that he was at last able to relax and straighten his massive body upon his cot. Soon his breathing had slowed, become regular, and he drifted into a light sleep.

Sir Richard lay quietly, listening to Runnolf's fast breathing. He smiled benevolently at the giant who struggled in silence. He regretted planting such doubts and obstacles in his mind, but if they worked to his satisfaction all would be well.

As one of King Henry's chief councillors, his prime consideration was the benefit of the kingdom, and the Marches were a volatile border whose stability was necessary for the peace of the realm. They needed a man of Runnolf's loyalties. Sir Richard fervently prayed that he had read Runnolf and Rowena correctly and they were already bonded together. If they were, and Runnolf would accept marriage with Rowena, the king would benefit, the realm would benefit, and so would the wedded couple.

Chapter Twenty-four

✦✦✦✦✦

The next morning dawned rainy and damp, but the life at court went on as if the day were bright and sunny. Rowena and Fanchon accompanied Lady de Vere to mass, where Rowena found herself distracted from the liturgy while she searched for Runnolf among the worshipers.

Returning to the castle, they broke their fast still under Lady Anne's watchful eye. Rowena was almost resigned to not seeing Runnolf that morning when she heard his deep voice from behind her. Gleefully she turned but was bewildered when she did not spot him immediately. Her cheerful smile of welcome faded to perplexity as her glance settled upon the largest man in the hall. Obviously this giant must be Runnolf, as no one else was near so large. In fact, Runnolf had shaved off his beard and mustache, revealing a strong face slightly raw from the scrape of the barber's blade.

When she realized what had changed, Rowena felt a stab of worry. *Perhaps by shaving he means to tell me that we are to settle into court life permanently. That we are to leave our other life behind us, unmentioned and forgotten.* If so, then she wondered what did yesterday mean? Certainly in the privacy of Lady Anne's solar Runnolf had still wanted her.

Oh, if only we could be alone, she wailed to herself, *so that he might tell me of his plans.*

"Good day, demoiselle," he greeted her solemnly as she continued to stare at his face. "Do you find me offensive without the beard?"

"Nay, my lord," she answered as she curtsied in formal greeting to match his own. "Only different."

Rowena sought consolation in her few small duties. She cut a wedge of cheese and poured a flagon of watered wine. All the while she fought not to let her eyes betray her inner turmoil. However, she could not keep her glance from straying to his face and in so doing, to be found staring.

"Did Sir Richard's barber scar me beyond your tolerance?" he demanded gruffly, irritated by her strange behavior.

"Nay, Sir Runnolf," she whispered as she turned to look at him more closely. She lifted her hand to touch his cheek, wanting to put soothing ointment upon the rawness left by the blade. But such action might betray their secret, so she let her hand fall to her side. The only sympathy she dared offer was words. "Your face is scraped raw. Has the barber no salve to soothe your cheek?"

"I had not noticed the pain," he answered as he rubbed his cheeks absently. And in truth he had not. For one long used to inconvenience, hardship, and pain from battle wounds, the small abrasions on his face were only flea bites by comparison.

They stood a few moments in silence studying each other, each wanting something from the other by way of private recognition but neither daring.

Fanchon, who had been visiting pleasantly with Corbert, noticed Lady Anne gathering her retinue. Reluctantly she acknowledged her summons.

"Lady Anne awaits us in the solar," she said, interrupting the silence between Rowena and Runnolf.

Rowena hesitated to comply until she had permission from Runnolf. She waited silently, hoping that he would read her thoughts as he so often did at her father's keep. Barring that, she hoped he might have some duties for her to perform.

As a guest at court, Rowena had no responsibilities, not even the care of Runnolf's clothing. There were no meals to oversee, no servants to whom duties must be assigned, nor was there weaving to be done. And for someone who was bred to responsibilities as part of life, the lack of them left a rift in her daily existence.

But Runnolf did not read her hidden need. "The king sits in justice today and needs not my presence," he said thoughtfully, thinking to reassure her with his own plans. "I will take Norbert to the practice field and continue his lessons in arms. Owain will remain within your call."

Rowena was mute with disappointment. Yet there were alternatives. Since Runnolf did not command her presence, she would use the time to begin sewing his mantle. When she finished with that she had a whole basket of material to sew for him.

Out of the corner of her eye, Rowena could see Lady Anne standing by the solar stairs waiting for her to take leave of Runnolf. It seemed that Lady Anne was as intent upon keeping a close watch upon her all day as she had so far this morning. She did not appreciate such close scrutiny. She was used to her freedom, to coming and going as she pleased, asking no one's permission, not even Runnolf's, as she went about her duties. But here at Oxford Castle, she had no duties and no freedom.

Rowena curtsied deeply to Runnolf in parting and followed Fanchon to the solar. Lady Anne, conscious of Rowena's injuries, assigned her tasks that would put no strain on her shoulder, and true to her word, she had the leathercrafter summoned so that Rowena could be measured for several new pairs of shoes. Rowena protested the extravagance of more than one pair, but Lady Anne ignored her and issued orders as to style and colors.

In exasperation, Rowena went to her travel basket and withdrew the blue velvet material to begin Runnolf's mantle. Again Lady Anne intruded.

"He must be properly measured before you do any cutting," she remonstrated. "This material is too costly to be poorly cut."

Even though her reason was sound, Rowena was angry. She had set her heart and mind on sewing the blue mantle.

Lady Anne had no trouble reading the signs of rebellion written on her face and she knew that she must do something to curb Rowena's budding mutiny. Having managed many keeps and castles for her husband, she knew well the use of compromise and diplomacy.

"You will begin sewing the chainsil." Lady Anne withdrew the fabric from the basket. "For what purpose was it purchased?'' she asked although she already knew the answer.

"Shertes for my lord and kirtles for myself,'' Rowena answered belligerently, her chin jutting out in suppressed anger.

"He has shertes that are of good fit?''

"All of them,'' Rowena responded.

"Eada,'' Lady Anne called before Rowena could begin to challenge her further. "Take yourself to Sir Richard's chamber. If his squire is about, ask him for one of Sir Runnolf's shertes. If not, find it yourself and fetch it hither.

"You have decided what embroidery you wish upon the hems?''

"I beg your pardon?'' Rowena stammered, baffled that she was finally being allowed an opinion.

"I asked if you had considered what pattern you desire to use upon the hems of his sherte,'' Lady Anne repeated calmly.

"Horses . . . black horses . . . rearing . . . running . . .''

"While my ladies are cutting and sewing the garments, you may have my seat before the window. Begin with a piece of scrap and embroider several horse motifs. Then select the one you like best for his sherte.''

Why would Lady Anne give up her seat before the windows where the light was the brightest? Rowena wondered. Then she quickly forgot the question as her enthusiasm to begin work on Runnolf's new clothes returned.

In truth, Lady Anne only wished to see that

Rowena was kept out of mischief. She knew Runnolf's reputation as a fighter. And she instinctively knew that he had no understanding of women nor the responsibilities of being a guardian. Therefore, she was determined to help him as much as she could.

By observing Rowena at her stitchery, Lady Anne also would be able to guide her and evaluate her wifely potential. She hoped to draw Rowena out as well, to discover how extensively she had been trained to be chatelaine. Through her tutelage, Lady Anne hoped to spare Rowena embarrassment and her guardian shame.

So the morning was spent cutting and sewing and learning. Lady Anne made suggestions for the embroidered hems and instructed Rowena on new stitches to enhance the brilliance of the simple design Rowena felt would please Runnolf. Once the samples were judged, Rowena happily began to embroider a black destrier rearing in majestic pride, his forelegs pawing the air while his mane and tail furled out behind him in the imagined wind.

As Rowena lost herself in her task of love, Lady Anne's women, with the speed and accomplishment of experienced seamstresses, not only sewed Runnolf's shertes but cut and began stitching Rowena's brown velvet bliaud and her kirtle of sendal. As the companionship of the women wrapped Rowena in a cocoon of friendship, she freely told them of her father's keep, leaving out no detail except those concerning Runnolf and herself. Late in the morning, a small page attached to the king's court knocked upon the solar door. Lady Anne listened attentively to the message and then nodded in dismissal.

"Rowena, you have been summoned to the king's presence," she announced as she walked back into the solar.

"Oh, madam! Do you think he has made up his mind about my father's land?" Rowena asked breathlessly. Her color was high and her eyes sparkled in anticipation as she hastily brushed the wrinkles from her bliaud and tried to straighten her barbette, which had become askew during the morning.

"No one knows the mind of the king," Lady Anne answered truthfully. She did not want Rowena to build her hopes too high.

"Am I to go now? Do I have time for a bath? Do I look presentable? Oh, I am not prepared!" Rowena complained all in one breath.

"You must go now. You do not have time for a bath and you look very presentable," Lady Anne answered. She straightened the bliaud across Rowena's shoulders and tucked a stray hair into place. As she performed these soothing gestures that gave Rowena an added measure of calm, she tried to suppress her smile at Rowena's excitement. No matter how angry Rowena had made her, no matter how belligerent the girl could be, Lady Anne found her innocent enthusiasm a pleasure. In fact, all of Lady Anne's women were equally beguiled by her lively charm.

"Will you both accompany me?" Rowena asked, afraid that she might make an error and destroy the king's goodwill.

"We will all accompany you," Lady Anne nodded.

Rowena hurried out the door. Her excitement was so high, her anticipation so great, that all consideration of deportment fled from her mind as she sped down the solar steps without waiting for them to join her after all.

At the foot of the steps she paused, momentarily confused by the throng of richly clad people. Only by looking between the groups did she glimpse the king, who now sat in his great chair upon the dais.

Rowena recognized Becket standing beside the king's chair. He was a man several years older than the king who arrayed himself in even greater splendor than his lord. His garments were of the finest cut and enhanced his well-knit body. His jewels outshone the ones worn by Henry, and he held himself aloof from his surroundings. His pallid complexion held a hint of excitement that was a reflection of the intense interest of the king.

Also present were Henry's other ministers, de Lucy and de Beaumont. They were both men of middle years, although Rowena had no idea of their exact ages. And neither man seemed so struck by his own importance.

Rowena looked about the great hall for Runnolf, but she could not find him. As she hesitantly approached the king, she was surprised to recognize Mannfrith and Joseph, the physician, among a group of finely dressed men waiting to one side of the great room.

Rowena felt suddenly let down. Somehow,

without knowing how she knew, she realized
that her summons had nothing to do with her
father's land. Had not Fanchon warned her that
Henry took long and long to decide such matters? But joy at seeing her new friends overcame
her disappointment, and her worry over Rebecca
became her immediate concern.

Rowena curtsied deeply before Henry and
waited for permission to rise. Surprisingly,
Henry stepped from the dais and lifted her to
her feet. Not relinquishing her hand, he turned
her to face the assembly.

There was an air of expectancy in the hall.
Word had spread that Rowena was again involved in something unusual, and the hall was
filling fast with excited and curious onlookers.

Unconsciously Rowena held her breath, waiting but for what she did not know. Her heart
beat nervously as she glanced at the king, trying
to match her behavior to any clue he might give
her. His demeanor was grave yet his eyes twinkled with mischief. When the attention of everyone in the hall was centered on him, Henry
motioned to the group of men along the wall.
They advanced, made their formal obeisance to
their sovereign, then turned to Rowena.

"Rowena, ward of Runnolf le Geant, we, the
members of the Guild of Mercers, bring you
greetings," the guildmaster addressed her and
bowed formally.

Bewildered, Rowena curtsied.

"You have saved the life of Rebecca, granddaughter of Mannfrith. For this deed we thank
you. I, Fullere, on behalf of the members of the

guild, present you with these gifts as a token of our esteem."

Rowena's face colored crimson with embarrassment. She did not wish to accept any gift for doing what she considered proper and necessary. Frantically she looked to Henry for direction.

"Sire, I cannot—"

"Do not embarrass them by refusing," Henry whispered in her ear.

Normally Rowena's saving the child might have gone unnoticed by the community at large, but the king had come in search of her. He had entered one of the poorer houses, thus showing the deep regard he held for her. And if the king showed regard for Rowena, then the Guild of Mercers was intent on showing her, and the king, their respect for her too in a tangible way.

The guildmaster stepped aside, and several apprentices came forward carrying two large wicker traveling baskets. They set them at Rowena's feet and stepped back expectantly.

"Well, open them!" Henry encouraged as Rowena stood hesitant.

Obediently Rowena knelt to remove the lid from the first basket.

"Your majesty, look!" she cried in excitement as she beheld the contents of the basket. "Lady Anne! Fanchon!"

On the very top of the first basket was a piece of the most beautiful crimson velvet Rowena had ever beheld. The hue was so deep, so rich that it appeared many shades of the same color at once. The shadow of each fold was crimson-black while the peak of each was crimson-pink. As if mesmerized by its beauty, Rowena slowly, reverently lifted it for all to see, and then gently rubbed it against her cheek to feel the softness of the pile.

"And look!" she exclaimed again, when she saw the second piece of cloth in the basket. "Look at the green!"

Lady Anne rescued the piece of red velvet from Rowena's trembling hands so that she could examine the green, which was every bit as lavish. Under the velvets were pieces of the heaviest and finest wools, amply able to provide warmth in the coldest of winters.

By the time Rowena opened the second basket, tears of excitement were tumbling merrily down her cheeks and she was beyond speech. She found the second basket contained linens and chainsil as well as pieces of sheer silk and finest-quality damask.

"As you can see," Henry chuckled when Rowena could not articulate her pleasure, "the lady is very much pleased."

Mannfrith knelt on one knee before Rowena so he would be on the same level as she, and handed her a package. "My lady, Blythe and her friends sat up all night so that they might have these ready for you."

With trembling hands Rowena unfolded the package to reveal bliauds and kirtles. The first bliaud was of green wool with a long-sleeved kirtle of lighter green. Another was of lighter woven wool dyed light brown, and another was of peach-colored fustian, while yet another was of blue. The kirtles were pale yellow, dark brown, and gold. All the colors had been carefully selected to be interchangeable with the bliauds so Rowena would appear to have a larger wardrobe.

"They did not have time to embroider them properly," Mannfrith apologized. "So they decorated with fabric."

"They are beautiful!" Tears choked Rowena's voice so that it was barely a whisper, yet all saw the emotion written across her flushed face and the gleam in her eyes.

"I have seen your daughter's needlework. It is very fine and delicate," Lady Anne said, because Rowena was not able to do anything but cry. "All of the women are to be complimented on their needlecraft," she added.

Mannfrith smiled happily at the compliment.

"How is Rebecca?" Rowena was slowly recovering her composure.

"She is well and happy this morning," Joseph answered as he stepped forward and presented her with a small coffer of intricately carved wood.

"Oh, please. I cannot accept more!" she protested, yet her curiosity overwhelmed her at the same time. She lifted the lid and saw small packets, tightly wrapped in oiled linen. "What are these?"

"Packets of powder from the poppyseed," Joseph answered. "They may be of use to you. But be careful of their use, each packet contains enough powder to put a small child into a deep sleep. Be sparing with it and it will last you a lifetime."

Rowena knew not how to express her thanks to the physician. She clutched the chest to her breast and the tears again began to flow.

Henry carefully lifted Rowena to her feet.

"Words are not enough to express my gratitude," she stammered as she embraced first Mannfrith and then Joseph.

"For once a woman speaks truth," Henry said jovially as the merchants bowed deeply to him and then to Rowena before taking their leave.

Rowena stood beside the king, laughing and smiling as she watched the delegation and her friends depart.

"Come," Lady Anne said. "We must carry your gifts to the solar, where we can properly decide how best to sew them."

"I must tell Sir Runnolf," Rowena added breathlessly. "And I must ask Ferrand to make room . . ."

"See your gifts safely away as Lady Anne requests and then search out Sir Runnolf and Ferrand," Henry interrupted indulgently. Used to the more jaded tastes of the court, he enjoyed seeing Rowena so enthusiastic over such simple gifts as uncut fabrics and unadorned clothes.

Once in the solar, Rowena could not concentrate on sorting out the materials. She was worried about having enough room amongst the baggage to get her new possessions home. But more important than that was her desire to share her happiness with Runnolf.

"If you do not make your decisions with proper forethought, then your wardrobe will—"

"But the king said I could find Sir Runnolf and Ferrand as soon as we had taken the baskets to the solar," Rowena protested.

"You should save your glad tidings for your

meal. Happy news makes a pleasant dinner companion, especially if your partner is as silent as Sir Runnolf," Lady Anne scolded, handing Rowena her sewing and motioning her to resume her seat in front of the windows.

"I have rarely heard Sir Runnolf say more than a few words at most," Lady Genevieve remarked. "Not only is he le Geant but he is also le Geant *Muet*."

Rowena blushed at the gentle teasing and kept her head bowed so no one would notice.

"It is strange that he has never married," Alyce added. "He is a great knight and highly favored by the king. He need merely ask his majesty for an heiress and the king would grant it."

"Maybe marriage is distasteful to one so used to men and wars," Lady Clare added bitterly. "Some men do not take well to peaceful pursuits."

Rowena was alarmed at the bitterness in Lady Clare's voice until Fanchon whispered an explanation. "Her husband is one of whom she speaks. He is glad to see her when first he returns, but the quiet of the castle unnerves him. At the slightest provocation, he will beat her to ease himself. She is only at ease when he is away on business for Sir Aubrey or the king."

Rowena shivered with distaste and silently whispered a prayer of thanksgiving that Runnolf did not fall into such a category. She tried to concentrate on her sewing, but all she managed to do was stick her finger with her needle a hundred times.

"If you do not begin to concentrate you will

stain the cloth," Lady Anne admonished, looking over her shoulder. "Your stitches are not tight enough. If the thread tangles, you will have to pull them all out and begin again."

Rowena dropped her sewing into her lap and sucked on her tortured finger.

"I am sorry, my lady, but I do not know if there will be room among the baggage for my new wardrobe."

"Then send your man to find the baggage master and ask him," Lady Anne answered in exasperation.

As an arrow shot from a bow, Rowena flew from her chair and sped out of the solar before Lady Anne could order her to return. She rushed down the stairs, and out upon the steps of the castle. Owain was right behind her as she paused upon the steps to catch her breath.

"What trouble?" he demanded as he waited beside her, his hand on the small dagger in his belt.

"No trouble," she answered merrily as she took great gulps of air into her lungs. "I have been so long within that I could not wait to be . . ." Rowena almost answered "free," but she let the sentence go unfinished and babbled on. "The air is a blessing and the clouds so refreshing."

Owain continued to stand beside her, watching their surroundings for any sign of danger. He was not happy to be among so many strangers. He missed the quiet of the woods and the safety of Fitzgiles Keep.

"Did you see my gifts?" she asked breathlessly.

"Yea, I saw them," he answered briskly.

"I must find Ferrand," she explained happily as she skipped down the steps to the bailey. "I must know how much room he can allot me among the baggage."

"He will allot you what you tell him," Owain answered testily. When he saw the look of surprise on Rowena's face, he was instantly sorry for his harshness. But he was not used to her having to ask permission for anything. She was Lady of the keep, and as such she should not have to ask permission.

"Wait here," he said, shrugging his shoulders. "I will fetch him."

"Nay, I will accompany you," she answered. "After we find Ferrand, we will find my lord and tell him of my gifts," she continued, dreaming happily as she skipped along beside Owain.

Owain observed her from the corner of his eye. She was almost like her younger self on an outing with Sir Hugh. The sheds where the extra servants stayed when not about their duties were no place for her. After all, this was not their keep. But he kept his misgivings to himself, since she exhibited no fear.

"My lady," he said finally as they approached the practice field teeming with men, "Lord Runnolf and Ferrand will be somewhere about. You must wait for me here. You may come no farther."

There was a finality to his voice that Rowena had learned long ago would brook no argument. Now was one of those times. But Rowena was too happy to worry about his reasons. She was out of the solar, free, and looking forward to finding Runnolf and sharing her good news.

"This is no place for you," an older knight said, approaching her patronizingly. "Ladies belong with their kind in the solar."

"I have come looking—" She did not finish before he left her standing alone. He had thought her lost and wanted to return her to the solar without incident. But if she were protesting his help, he would leave her to her own devices.

"How did you manage to sneak away this time?" The voice of another drew her attention. "What prank are you about now?"

Startled, Rowena spun around and was relieved to recognize several people whom she had been introduced to, even though she could not remember all of their names and titles.

"Le Geant is occupied elsewhere," they told her mischievously. "May we be of service to you until he returns?"

"Nay," she murmured quietly. "I have come to watch my lord practice." He had been on the field, she was sure of it. She was supposed to await Owain and Ferrand. And he would be disgruntled if she continued to move about without him. "I will wait for Sir Runnolf, if you think he will return soon," she ventured.

"He will return when he returns. I am Jocelyn de Wyrick," one of them said as he introduced himself. He took Rowena's hand in courtly fashion and continued, "I am nephew to Robert de Ilchester. I have heard that you are here to secure the tenure to your father's lands."

"Yea," Rowena responded as she instinctively curtsied to the handsome young knight. He was splendidly attired in a new hauberk and wearing a new sword and scabbard. She used her curtsy to cover a stifled chuckle. He had a way of speaking, while looking down his face, that was most amusing.

"Sir Runnolf has told the king and I await his decision," she continued as she tried to withdraw her hand from his grasp.

"Mayhap I can be of some assistance and speed the king upon his decision," de Wyrick whispered as he kissed her palm. "For certain . . . ah . . . considerations."

For a moment Rowena was not sure of his meaning, until his hand purposely brushed her breast as he slipped his arm around her back. So sure was he of his position and prestige that he did not wait for her answer. Smiling silkily to his companions, he began leading Rowena toward one of the tents erected near the field.

Again Rowena was overwhelmed by strong emotions. Only this time the heat that radiated from her face was from anger. And with her anger aroused, she was indeed a very strong young woman. With all of her strength, she stamped upon de Wyrick's instep, then shoved him away from her. Having been caught unaware, the knight fell backward, landing full sprawl upon the ground. Looking up, he found himself surrounded by all of his friends, who were laughing loudly.

"Mayhap, Sir Robert is not placed high enough," his friends chortled. "Mayhap, she has eyes for the king. After all, he has shown her great attention these past days.''

"Who do you think you are?" Rowena demanded, her eyes flashing dangerously. "What makes you think—"

"You will find out who I am," de Wyrick snarled as his squire hurriedly helped him to his feet. "I will see that you do not get tenure."

Rowena stared open-mouthed. No wonder Lady Anne rarely leaves the solar, Rowena thought to herself. There are too many dangers, too much disrespect for a woman to go about on her own without an escort.

"You are no lady," the man continued maliciously. "If you were, you would not be out here. Even le Geant knows what you are or he would not allow your behavior."

"Lady, I have found him," Owain called out, running up to her with Ferrand right behind him, puffing and blowing. As they neared, Owain felt the tension between his lady and the angry young knight. Standing purposefully between them, he grasped the hilt of the small dagger in his belt and coldly surveyed the young man.

"Nor do you speak as a lady," de Wyrick sneered, looking past Owain as if he were not present. "You speak as the serfs, and if truth were known, you are probably one of them." So saying, he spun upon his heel and alternately cursed and limped from the practice field, surrounded by his cronies.

At that moment Rowena was overwhelmed with the desire to return to her father's keep, where all was ordered and safe. And then de Wyrick's words penetrated her thoughts. Spiteful and untrue though they were, they left her feeling bereft of all confidence.

"Lord Runnolf! I must find him! He will set things to right!" She looked around, panicked.

"I have erected Sir Runnolf's tent at the far side of the practice field," Ferrand panted as he tried to distract her. "When he finishes training, he goes there to rest without interruption. Come, I will take you there."

Jabbering incessantly over his shoulder that he was sorry that he had not been at hand to welcome her, he did not see Runnolf exit the tent and ran backward into him. Both men stopped in surprise and began to laugh. Ferrand laughed in relief. Runnolf laughed because of the look on the servant's face and his joy at seeing Rowena.

Rowena was in the process of curtsying to Runnolf, her calm somewhat restored again by being in his company, when she saw a coarse-looking woman exit the tent and stand beside him. She staggered slightly as she forgot her curtsy and was forced to take a step backward to regain her balance.

The two women eyed each other critically. Bold, worldly eyes pierced Rowena's innocence and silently mocked her. As if to make Rowena understand more completely, the woman moved next to Runnolf, molding her body to his in a suggestive manner while brushing her breasts against his arm.

Runnolf gave the woman not a glance and

shrugged her away. In truth, she was no more to him than a pesky fly. But Rowena's inexperience and lack of confidence magnified her to great importance.

"You could not wait?" she whispered huskily, tears of pain filling her eyes. Her face was ashen and her lips trembled as she fought to hold back the tears that threatened to wash away what little self-respect she still had left. But it was of no use. Her pain was greater than her control and she fled.

Runnolf took one step as if to follow and then stood still. What could he say? What excuse would she accept? Again he had hurt her. He let her go but motioned Owain to follow after, to see her safely back to the castle.

Returning inside the tent, he collapsed upon the cot that had once been hers. What a fool he had been, he berated himself silently. The small release of his body was not worth the pain he had given her. By his own stupidity, he had destroyed the trust he had so carefully nourished.

Half of his mind chided him for allowing Rowena's feelings to dictate to him. Either married or unmarried, it was not a woman's place to question her lord's behavior. It was not her place to approve or disapprove whom he took to his bed. Yet Rowena had not deserved such pain. And the worst of it was that the woman had not been worth the price Rowena had paid. She had exhibited no spontaneity, no joy of sharing, no happiness, no enthusiasm. In short, she had not been Rowena!

Chapter Twenty-five
✦✦✦✦

Rowena returned to the solar, barely in control of her emotions. Her eyes were red from weeping and her nose was red from her sniffles. She spent what little time there was before dinner ignoring Fanchon's anxious glances and Lady Anne's not-so-delicate inquiries. Regardless of their persistence, she refused them an explanation, letting them make what they wanted of her silence.

For her part, Lady Anne believed that Runnolf had duly chastised his ward for going unbidden into the masculine realms of the court. No proper guardian would tolerate such unladylike behavior, especially for so trivial a matter as clothes and materials. Fanchon believed somewhat the same. But no matter what the reason, she hurt for her friend, who was having such a difficult time adjusting to life at court.

Rowena tried to concentrate on her embroidery. But no matter how hard she tried, her mind would not cease its whirling imaginings.

Why had he not called her to him? She was more than willing to satisfy his need as well as her own. Was he tired of her inexperience already? But that is not fair! she protested to herself. Had Runnolf not promised to teach her how to please him? He had not given her enough time to learn! Had she failed to please him and he was looking for another?

Then, in the back of her mind, Rowena heard Father Dominic's droning voice expounding on the wages of sin and punishment. Feminine virtue was supposed to fight the baser nature of man, controlling it and channeling it into the marriage bed for the purpose of procreation. She had failed and was being punished because she had refused the chance to force Runnolf into marriage. She lusted after Runnolf both in her heart and in the flesh, and now she was to be punished by seeing his lust for another. Her needs would become her punishment, the beginning of the pains of hell.

Confession! Her soul cried out for confession, but she would not seek its solace. As yet there was no repentance in her heart. She could not repent now simply because she was losing him. And without repentance there was no forgiveness. She was not experiencing true contrition, and she knew it. She was only experiencing sorrow for her loss.

Rowena's sorrow was interrupted when Fanchon called her to freshen herself for dinner. Fatalistically she accepted her pain and focused her mind on the coming encounter with Runnolf. What was she to do? How was she to behave? Her mind reeled trying to decide until she calmed herself enough to partially reason. Her reasoning centered on her father—what would he have expected of her? Once that question was asked, the answer became simple. She must be ever obedient. She must be biddable and meek, ever willing to do her lord's will.

She made up her mind to be pleasant and attentive, not to mention the tears of the morning or their cause. After all, a woman, be she wife, mistress or ward, was not expected to challenge or berate a man. She was expected to blindly accept his behavior without comment. Therefore she would greet Runnolf as if this morning had not existed, and in this way she hoped she might be able to repair the breach growing between them.

With this slight ray of hope before her, Rowena washed her face and hands in the basin held for her by Eada. Suddenly a devastating thought crossed her mind. What if Runnolf did not accept her? What if she could not win him back? What if he ignored her? What would happen then? Her hands trembled in the shallow basin of water. She tried to take control of her fear. Squaring her shoulders, she forced herself to face that possibility. If she could not win his love back . . . Her mind would not proceed further, it was impossibly frightening. She would have to seek him out and see.

At least momentarily satisfied with her decisions, Rowena was able to dry her hands and face with only the slightest tremors showing in her hands. Her step was slow but steady as she followed Fanchon down the solar steps. She entered the main hall with Lady Anne and her women, surreptitiously searching for Runnolf. When the trumpets sounded, she still did not see him amongst the throngs of feasters. Feeling very much alone, she proceeded to the table they had occupied during the other meals. Corbert held the bench for her and Fanchon, but it was as if they did not exist. She seated herself in silent dignity, but all her resolve, all of her hopes were for nought. Runnolf was not present.

Where was he? Was he still with . . . her? Rowena wanted to scream with renewed pain. Runnolf's absence was another log on the already smoldering bier of dislike for the king's court. Resentment began to build as she silently raged at her plight. She spent the entire mealtime feverishly searching for a way to escape this hell in which she found herself.

Even the presence of the king, as he stopped to visit, did not distract her for long. Nor did his encouraging questions tempt her to speak more than monosyllables.

After the meal, Rowena immediately returned to the solar, where she sat suffering her abandonment. To her beclouded mind, Runnolf's absence meant he preferred the other woman over her. Desperately she tried to devise new plans for her future. First and foremost, she must secure the tenure of her father's land. She was the only hope her people had, and she would not desert them no matter how she herself suffered.

The words of de Wyrick and his friends invaded her thoughts, bringing new bouts of fear and doubt. Would the king grant justice only to someone who was willing to grant certain favors?

Was the king truly interested in her as they said? Mayhap. She tried to picture herself with Henry, but she could only see Runnolf. Angrily she dismissed her evil thought. Life at court was corrupting her. She was sure that if the king was interested in her, it was in a general way, as one of his subjects or because she was in love with his liege man.

Once she had set the king back on his throne, Rowena was able to make other decisions. She resolved that at the next opportunity, this very night, when the king stopped at their table, she would request a private audience. During the audience, she would explain her predicament and ask him to make his decision on her father's land immediately so that she might leave court.

Gaining strength with her new resolve, Rowena further decided that she would remain in the solar, leaving only for mass and meals. In that way she would not ensnare herself in any further indiscretions. She was finally beginning to realize that she could not, must not forget she was at court and that her home and freedom were far behind her.

Now that she had ordered her life as far as possible for the moment, she felt almost happy. Almost lightheartedly, Rowena devoted herself to the one manifestation of love not yet denied her; she continued to embroider the hems of Runnolf's shertes.

Outside the castle walls, in a small room over an ale house, secured by stealth and a great deal of money, Rolf de Witt was also awaiting the king's pleasure. He also had petitioned King Henry for tenure to his land, land to which he claimed only the Welsh had prior ownership.

De Witt had arrived at the king's court shortly after the battle that had taken fitz Giles's life.

Being a man of reasonable courage only when the outcome was a certainty, he was disturbed because, being new upon the throne, Henry was an unknown.

"Why the frown?"

Startled, de Witt looked up from his slumped position before his meager fire. Slouched in the doorway was Coleton, his manservant for appearance's sake but in truth his coconspirator in his quest to regain his land.

"God's shadow, Coleton! Must you always sneak about?"

"I do not sneak about," the other answered sullenly as he pulled on a lock of his sparse brown hair. "You simply did not hear me enter. Besides, one of the reasons I am of value to you is my . . . uh . . . ability to gather information. And one cannot gather information if one clomps around like a plow ox."

This last remark was a barb aimed specifically at de Witt for his lack of finesse. De Witt was well aware of others' opinion of him. It rankled, but at times it was also correct. Rolf de Witt was not stupid, and he knew he was not used to the cities, to court intrigues and the play for power in large households. It was for this reason alone that he put up with Coleton's arrogance.

Coleton, on the other hand, was a study in stealth and intrigue. He was the youngest son of a poor merchant. Not having the aptitude for honest business, he preferred instead to make his way by his wits, within the shadier elements of the populace. His eyes were a soft, innocent brown that belied the coldness of his soul. His generally nondescript appearance more often than not allowed him to skulk about, listening to tales, making use of the information and embarrassing incidents that, if known, could topple great families.

If de Witt were ever to regain his lands, Coleton knew, he would need a trusty ally to assist him at court and he would be forever grateful for that assistance. Coleton wanted the stewardship of de Witt's land. And it was this pending reward that kept him in the employ of de Witt, whom he considered a dullard and a simpleton.

For his part, de Witt was well aware of Coleton's ambitions, and he was not averse to using Coleton in such a capacity as stewardship. By fair deed or foul, both men were prepared to advance themselves.

Coleton waited patiently for de Witt to continue. If he probed for more information, he knew de Witt would wonder at his purpose. If he waited, pretending indifference, he knew that de Witt would tell him just to prove he had information the other did not. And as usual, his patience was rewarded.

"The other day when we were returning after the hunt . . . one of the local women darted in front of my destrier—"

"Yea, I have heard the story oft enough," Coleton snapped in spite of his attempt to appear uninterested. De Witt was in the habit of blaming others for his own misfortune, so he blamed the people of Oxford for the accident that lamed his destrier. "What of it?"

De Witt shot his companion a quelling glance

before continuing. "De Lund was telling of the mishap at court and was called all but liar by some slip of a girl and the king's seneschal, le Geant."

"Why?" Coleton demanded. If the king and his advisors were to believe de Witt less than honorable, they might doubt his claim to the land. Even if they but suspected some duplicity, they could postpone any decision indefinitely. And postponement would spell financial disaster for them both.

"God's brains! How should I know," de Witt swore. "All I know is they did!"

"Then what?"

"Then nothing. De Lund left in embarrassment."

"There was some to-do this morn," Coleton mused, thinking over the day's news. It was his custom to spend many hours of every day playing at dice and other small games of chance with the servants of the castle, gathering news, innuendoes, and gossip that could be used later. "The ward of le Geant was honored for saving someone's grandchild from being run down by a troop of knights."

"This could not be the same incident," de Witt protested vehemently. "There was no child, and the woman was trampled. I hope she died from the injuries after what she did to my horse," he added maliciously.

Coleton refused to argue, since de Witt was so adamant, but he had doubts there were two separate incidents on the same day. It was too much of a coincidence, and Coleton knew coincidences very well, for he was in the habit of making them happen.

"Well, what are you going to do about it?"

"Do about what?" de Witt snapped belligerently.

"The challenge, you fool!"

"I cannot challenge le Geant!" de Witt thundered in protest.

"You must! He has called you liar before the entire court."

"He is the king's champion! He is acknowledged the best of his knights!"

"Of course you cannot hope to win in an equal contest," Coleton sneered. "But if we tip the scales in your favor . . ."

De Witt's face lit up in mirthless glee and then faded into frowns of despair. "To challenge le Geant is ludicrous," he avowed. "Only someone in their dotage would take me seriously."

"Mayhap open challenge will not be necessary," Coleton murmured, thinking aloud as he twisted and twirled his stringy brown hair around his fingers. "Le Geant is in a precarious position. As the king's seneschal he must be beyond reproach. And he cannot participate in private feuds without bringing the king's wrath upon his head."

"So!"

"So! All you have to do is throw back the lie in his face. Stand before him without openly calling him liar and reavow your tale. After all, you were there, he was not."

"And?"

"And if he backs down, then he looks bad, not you. You have shown your courage by facing him. You have shown yourself to be in the right, not he."

"And the king will see me as stronger and braver than the seneschal!" de Witt preened, already anticipating his victory.

"Mayhap it is time that the king has a new seneschal for the Marches," Coleton prodded.

"When shall I do it?"

"At the soonest . . . tonight's meal."

Later that evening, Rowena entered the great hall for the light end-of-day supper. She searched the hall hoping, but not expecting, to see Runnolf.

Her heart beat heavily in her chest as she spied him off by himself, standing as still as an effigy against a wall. She hesitated to approach, but courtesy demanded that she greet her guardian. With such reasoning to uphold her pride, she moved toward him as a flower moves toward the sun. Silently she thanked the Almighty that the crowded floor gave her time to quiet her quickened breathing.

She snatched at the conflicting ideas that swirled in her mind: "used to the women of court . . . do not be as they . . . deceitful . . . lying . . . lack of honor . . . honest . . . obedient . . . biddable . . . meek."

Foremost in the litany of traits that Runnolf admired were honor and honesty! These were the things that Runnolf expected and respected in turn. Instinctively she knew she must be truthful in her dealings with him, using no subterfuge. There must be no scene to shame or embarrass him.

Too soon she was before him. "Good eventide, my lord," she murmured softly, dropping into a deep curtsy of obedience.

Runnolf grunted, a response that Rowena interpreted as permission to rise. From under lowered brows, she studied the planes of his face, trying to see behind the mask that hid his emotions even from her. No matter how hard she studied him, she could not detect whether he felt guilt for his behavior of the morning or annoyance at her presence now.

For his part, Runnolf had expected Rowena to shun him or at the very least to make some snide remarks about the morning. She had done neither. She had greeted him civilly and even called him lord, a word that held much meaning between them. Apparently she had not yet withdrawn her regard for him.

He was surprised and confused by her, which made him more aloof than normal. To those who braved his stony expression and had come to bid him good eventide he had been unusually abrasive. So they were left to themselves, no one wishing to incur his displeasure.

When it was time to be seated for the meal, Runnolf, in stilted but nonetheless courtly fashion, offered his arm to Rowena. He held his breath waiting for her to choose this time to rebuff him but she did not. And when she laid her small, delicate hand upon his arm, he felt shock waves of desire surge through his body, making it most difficult to remain in control. He wanted to sweep her into his arms and carry her to some private place where he could show her how sorry he was for the morning.

Rowena could feel the tremors of tension that ran throughout his entire body. Intently studying him, still hoping against hope for some clear sign of welcome, she obediently followed beside him as they slowly walked toward their table. She wished she could think of something witty to say to ease the strain, but she was too immersed in their weighty problems to think lightly.

Runnolf held out the bench and they sat together, but still neither of them uttered a word. His silence was as deafening as the crowded hall was loud. Yet for all his restraint and apparent aloofness, he was attentive to her needs, constantly offering her choice morsels from his own trencher and sharing his wine with her.

Rowena ached to speak to him, to ask, nay, to demand answers to all the myriad questions that were causing her distress. But she dared not. She did not wish to open the way for a true rejection. Instead she sat in silence, accepting the attentions he was willing to bestow upon her.

Fleetingly Rowena noticed that the hall was more crowded than the night before. More men of apparent importance were present, and the king's table held more places of honor. Listening with half an ear to Fanchon as she politely chatted to fill the heavy gaps of silence from her table companions, Rowena learned that many of the newcomers were barons answering their summons to meet the king at Winchester. The reason for the calling held no import to her. What was of importance was the scarcity of housing and privacy that plagued the king's court no matter where it went.

Privacy within the king's court was nearly an impossibility, as it was within the confines of most castles and keeps. However, compared to Oxford, Fitzgiles Keep had an overabundance of private places. The most obvious of course was the solar, but then, whenever she wished to speak to Runnolf alone, all she had to do was approach him and the others courteously moved away. Here there was no such courtesy, because no one knew they needed it or desired it.

Since private lodging was paramount to her needs, Rowena questioned Fanchon as to why these barons would want to stop at Oxford rather than proceeding to Winchester to secure what lodging was available. Fanchon advised her that the barons probably wanted the opportunity to have private conversation with the king on confidential matters. They knew there would be little time at their destination.

Rowena wanted to remind Runnolf of their need for a place at Winchester, but again she chose not to mention their future. She did not know if he intended for her to accompany him further or if he would be going out on the king's business soon again. There were just too many unknowns in their life for her to broach them.

The thought of telling Rowena what plans had

been made for her never entered Runnolf's head.
This was mostly because their plans were con-
tingent upon the king, and Runnolf did not wish
to build her hopes too high, only to have them
blow away as smoke. But also, he simply did not
think of it. Decisions were made by men, and
women were expected to obey without question.
So it was and so it was meant to be.

Sitting beside him, Rowena found herself lost
in his presence, feeling safe from all physical
danger and threat of danger. Even though she
doubted the depths of his concern for her, when
she was with him she almost did not care.
Watching his powerful hands slice the tiny
pieces of meat for her and offer her sips of wine
from his own flagon was almost enough to forget all her worries. He was here with her, now.
Nothing else mattered!

But it does! the voice of hurt pride shouted,
trying to foster rebellion. Why did he not stop
you from leaving the field? Why has he not demanded your presence in his tent? You know
you could have satisfied him—there would be
no need for another!

As the meal progressed, Rowena was torn first
by love and by pride. Her throat locked in frustration as the war within her raged on unre-
solved. She began to choke every time she tried
to swallow her food. Finally she was saved from
having to pretend interest in the meal by the
purposeful approach of two men.

One she immediately recognized as Hubert de
Lund, but the other she did not recognize, although there was a hazy familiarity about him.

He was of average build and well muscled from years as a knight, but there was a leanness about him that gave him the look of hunger, hunger of the spirit that put its stamp upon the body. She had to force herself not to stare as she tried to place the stranger.

As the two men approached, the hairs on Runnolf's arms and the back of his neck began to rise in warning. Sensing a confrontation of some sort, Runnolf set his poniard beside his trencher and waited for the men to make their intentions known.

"Do you have reason to doubt my word or the word of my friend?" the newcomer demanded of Runnolf without formality. He stood in front of them, leaning slightly over the table, forcing his presence upon Runnolf, crowding him at his own table.

"Your friend should not repeat a tale until he knows the all of it," Runnolf repeated quietly, as he let his glance travel from the speaker to de Lund and then back again.

"My friend knows the whole of it," de Witt swore. "For I gave it to him."

"De Witt!" Rowena gasped the name between clenched teeth. She had not recognized him without his beard and mustache, nor had she expected to see him at the king's court. It was his voice that she recognized. It was unmistakable, because it was so much higher than would be expected for a man full grown.

"Demoiselle?" De Witt acknowledged her unexpected intrusion. He had the feeling he should know her, but he could not place her face.

Slowly, deliberately, Rowena stood up, her breasts heaving in her agitation, her eyes glittering dangerously with hate.

"Coward!" she hissed. "Coward! Murderer!"

De Witt stood in stunned silence at Rowena's accusation. His face lost its color, and he stared at her in bewilderment. He had hoped to find trouble with Runnolf and was, in fact, searching for it. But this woman was another matter altogether.

De Witt was not the only one to be taken aback by Rowena's words. Runnolf was stunned. Before he could order her to silence, she cried out her accusation again.

"You murdered my father!"

"You are mistaken, demoiselle," de Witt replied, his voice one pitch lower than before. "I have never killed any man except in fair combat."

"Liar! When he was unhorsed and fighting for your land and his, you turned your back on him and left him to die. You murdered my father as surely as if you stabbed him yourself."

"Who?" he demanded.

"Hugh fitz Giles!"

Suddenly de Witt's face beaded with perspiration as he realized who she was. It had been four summers since he had seen her last, and in that time she had matured into a woman. A woman who was now dressed in the fashion of court, not riding higgledy-piggledy beside her father in the fields.

"Demoiselle," he began slowly, silkily, his mind frantically working to extricate himself. "I mourn with you for the death of your father, but he fell to the sword of the king's seneschal," he said, stretching the truth to the farthest degree.

"He would not have died if you had not deserted him," she persisted.

" 'He would not have died'," de Witt parroted sorrowfully. "That is the dream of a loving daughter," he continued. "I am truly sorry for his death, but it happened during a battle, and no one can be blamed for the will of God."

"You—"

"Rowena, enough!" Runnolf commanded her coldly.

"Enough!" she shrieked. "How can there be enough when the murderer of my father faces me!"

"If anyone is the murderer, it is the one who struck him down," de Witt added maliciously. He did not know why she was with le Geant, but he knew he must shift the blame from himself. "Look to the king's seneschal for your murderer," he repeated.

Runnolf heaved himself to his feet, knocking over the bench and towering over de Witt. His face was cold with fury, his body perfectly still, tight as a bowstring ready to discharge its arrow. He had been stunned speechless by Rowena's outburst. Now he was sickened by the way de Witt was able to turn whole truth into lies, not to mention the fact that de Witt was responsible for Rowena's injuries.

The silence of their witnesses spread across the hall to engulf even the king's attention.

"De Witt, your presence is unwelcome at this table. Take yourself elsewhere."

De Witt studied the giant who now towered

over him. Rowena's accusation, backed by the cold fury smoldering in the depth of le Geant's gray eyes, sent shivers of indecision down his spine.

"I forgive you, demoiselle," de Witt said, bowing gallantly to Rowena while trying to ignore Runnolf's imposing presence. "For your harsh words. Grief speaks for you and I choose not to hear."

As he walked away, de Witt knew it to be a stroke of genius to shift the death of fitz Giles to the fate of battle and to paint the daughter's accusation as grief. But he did not know how long he could sustain the image of the gallant neighbor if she continued to accuse him of cowardice. Someone in Runnolf's troop would soon remember that battle and recount their version, and all would discover that he had, in fact, quit the field too soon.

Rowena turned to Runnolf as de Witt walked away. "You cannot allow—" But she was interrupted by Runnolf's cold anger.

"Your tongue has taken on the proportions of a magpie," he snarled, furious that she had not instantly obeyed him as she had before coming to Oxford. "Your father's death was on the field of honor! He does not need for you to cry foul!"

"But de Witt is a coward!" she shrieked, now beside herself with renewed grief and rage. "How can one such as he be welcome to the king's court?"

"Your father died with honor!" Runnolf hissed, trying to keep her from further disrupting the court. "The king and all his councillors know of it. There is no need—"

"No need . . ." she cried bitterly. At this moment, she hated Runnolf as much as she had ever loved him. Her breast heaved with the effort of her breathing, and her heart hurt as if it were being crushed by Runnolf's giant hands. She glared at him. All of her bitter feelings since coming to court burst her control as she vented her outrage. "No need to die! No need to mourn! No need to have honor! Pray excuse my desire to see my father's death avenged," she added sarcastically. "If there is no need, then there is no longer a need for you in my life, coward!"

Frustration, guilt, anger, and two half-slept nights worrying over their future snapped Runnolf's iron control. Unconscious of witnesses, he grabbed Rowena by her upper arms and shook her until her teeth rattled together. Her head bobbed upon her shoulders, nearly snapping her neck. The ferocity of movement caused many of the pins that held her barbette and hair in place to fall out, letting her hair tumble about her in disarray. Her eyes rolled back into her head with only the whites showing, and her entire body went limp.

"Runnolf! Release her! Runnolf!" The king's deep, authoritative bellow penetrated the red mist of savage anger that clouded Runnolf's mind. He had listened to that voice for many years and knew it demanded his instant obedience. It was the only thing that saved Rowena from real harm. Slowly, as out of a deep slumber, Runnolf climbed to conscious thought, focusing his attention on the king.

"Release her!" Henry commanded in a lower tone than before.

Sweat beaded upon Runnolf's brow from the effort it took him to regain control. After an eternity of waiting, he heaved a deep sigh, then almost gently, he released Rowena. She slid to the floor, fighting to regain the breath that had been so cruelly shaken from her.

Carefully Henry lifted her semiconscious form from the floor and handed her over to Corbert. "Carry her to the solar. Lady Anne, see to her."

Once Rowena was safely on her way to the solar, Henry turned his full attention again toward Runnolf.

"Cool your temper," he commanded as he placed his hand upon Runnolf's arm. He could feel the tremors of his liege man's anger, although it was now fully under control. "I will summon you anon. Remain sober."

"I will be in my tent on the practice field," Runnolf responded tonelessly as he bowed in obedience to the king's command and then strode out of the hall.

Owain and Norbert remained behind at the foot of the solar steps, bewildered by all that had transpired. They were late witnesses to the altercation and could not follow all of the conversations. But it was blatantly obvious that Rowena had again incurred Sir Runnolf's wrath.

Corbert bore Rowena from the great hall as he would a treasured child. He followed Lady de

Vere up to her solar with Fanchon close on his heels.

"Lay her on her cot," Lady Anne commanded him as she pulled back the coverlid, and Fanchon added extra bolsters so that they might prop Rowena into a sitting position.

Once he had delivered his burden, Corbert backed as far as the door and waited for Rowena to regain her wits. He did not fault Runnolf for the discipline. It was Runnolf's obligation as guardian, but he wanted to be sure Rowena was not seriously injured. Corbert was confident that in spite of Runnolf's anger, he would want to know.

He waited while Fanchon removed Rowena's disarranged barbette and fetched fresh water with which to bathe her face. The blood raced in his own veins in apprehension as Rowena's eyes momentarily fluttered open and then closed again. With mounting concern he watched Lady Anne uncap a small vial and pass it under Rowena's nose. He saw her inhale deeply before turning her face aside.

"Rowena, whatever possessed you to behave so?" Lady Anne crooned half reproachfully, half sadly as she wiped her hot face with a cool, wet cloth. Rowena kept her face averted and her eyes closed.

Lady Anne assured herself that Rowena was not injured or unconscious and then began to lose patience with the unmannerly woman who had been entrusted to her care.

"Rowena, I know you can hear me. I expect an answer," she demanded quietly.

"Why would he not challenge de Witt?" Rowena asked in defiance, her voice harsh with grief and unshed tears.

"I do not know the whole of it, but I do know that Sir Runnolf is no coward," Lady Anne snapped. She had been completely unprepared for the outburst. She had expected Rowena to be subdued and repentant after her chastisement. Lady Anne was grateful that Fanchon was close at hand. It would take both of their skills to explain to Rowena the ways of court.

"He could not have," Fanchon soothed. "You know he could not or he would have."

"I know naught!" Rowena answered stubbornly as she flung her arm over her head and stared at the ceiling. Her eyes were dry, but her breath was ragged in her chest.

"Sir Runnolf is the king's man," Fanchon added. "He is not free to issue challenge."

That was the last thing that Corbert heard before leaving the solar. He knew that Lady Anne would not have snapped at Rowena if she had been seriously injured. He shook his head in disbelief. How could one woman possess so many contrary characteristics? At the keep, she was so obedient to Runnolf's commands. She seemed so capable, so . . . He almost thought *worldly*, but that was not a good word to use, he mused to himself. Worldly only as it pertained to her father's keep and the Marches, he corrected himself. For all else, she was abysmally ignorant.

As he descended the step, Rowena's education on court life continued.

"Then I will declare a feud against him!" Rowena persisted.

"If you are foolish enough to declare a feud against de Witt, one of two things will happen." For the first time since Lady Anne began talking, Rowena paid her absolute attention. She gazed intently into the older woman's eyes, her attitude so intense that Lady Anne was almost lost in their soul-deep sorrow. "If you declare a feud against de Witt," she said, struggling to regain her train of thought, "you also declare it against his kith and kin, his servants, free and unfree, as well as the entire community which might want to assist him and protect him."

"Who would want to protect a coward?" Rowena snapped bitterly.

"In this case, he has sought allegiance with Walter fitz Miles, Sheriff of Hereford," Fanchon added as if Rowena had not spoken. "He is now of the sheriff's household. Did you not see the colors he wore?"

"And Sir Runnolf is of the king's household," Rowena interrupted belligerently. "Certainly the king has more power than the sheriff."

"You are an orphan," Lady Anne continued dispassionately. "You have no kith or kin to carry your cause. You have no knights in your service to protect you. If de Witt accepted the feud, he would be at liberty to destroy your keep along with all of your people. They cannot defend themselves against his strength or that of the sheriff.

"But what is worse for you personally," Lady

Anne resumed, "he may choose to laugh it off as the mad ravings of a distraught daughter. You will look more ridiculous than you already have. And Lord Runnolf, as your guardian, would be open to ridicule because of you."

"But he is a coward and a murderer! How can the king allow such as he at his court?"

"He is here for the same reason you are here," Lady Anne continued. "He is hoping to pay a small fine to redeem his lands from the king. He claims tenure for the same cause as you. The land belonged to no one before his coming."

Rowena lay upon her cot, closing her eyes, tears slowly seeping down her temples into her hair.

"And if Sir Runnolf were to stand as your champion," Fanchon added, "he would have to cease being the king's liege man and stand alone. To my knowledge he has no kith or kin of his own."

"Needs must he remove himself from the king's service else the king be embroiled in your feud," Lady Anne explained further. "The king cannot take sides in a feud between two of his barons. If he did, there would be civil war again as we experienced with Stephen."

"Sir Runnolf is not a baron," Rowena remarked, still not willing to give up completely.

"All the more reason for the king not to involve himself," Lady Anne answered.

When there was no further argument from Rowena, Lady Anne arose from the cot and went to the small table near the brazier and poured a small flagon of wine, returning with it to the bed.

"Drink this," she prompted. "You are in need of sleep. All will be more understandable in the morning."

"But de Witt is a coward!" Rowena stubbornly protested.

"So you say," she answered in exasperation. "You also called le Geant 'coward,' and all here know that to be an untruth."

"Then I have lost all!" Rowena cried. "I have nought!"

To her listeners, Rowena's cries were those of a spoiled, self-centered child, but they did not understand how deeply she mourned. She was sure that the king would punish her behavior by withholding the tenure of the land from her father. And because of her, her people would suffer. More personal than that, of course, was her loss of Runnolf. She had called him coward. However could he forgive her? However could she win back his love?

Her hatred for court life grew and grew as she dwelt on all the misfortunes that had befallen her since her arrival. She had lost Firelight. She had been injured. She had seen Runnolf with a slithery female and did not even have the opportunity to try to win him back. She had stood face-to-face with de Witt and was forced to let him live even though he had caused her father's death. She had called Runnolf coward before the entire hall.

"You are allowing grief to speak for you again," Lady Anne said sternly. "Drink your wine and sleep. We will speak of these things again on the morrow."

Lady Anne and Fanchon sat beside Rowena as she cried herself to sleep, and then they went to their own beds to worry over the predicament she had created for herself.

Chapter Twenty-six
✦✦✦✦

WITHOUT REMEMBERING HOW he got there, Runnolf found himself at his tent. Entering, he threw the door covering over the side so he could watch the night sky as he waited for the king's summons.

As the peace of the night settled upon him, he began reviewing the incidents of the evening just past. He had been as surprised as Rowena that de Witt was at court. The man's presence angered, disgusted, and offended him as nothing else had. Not only was de Witt a dishonorable coward, but his carelessness had caused injury to Rowena and Rebecca.

Yet the most important issue in Runnolf's mind was Rowena and the king. Henry's interference disturbed him. What right did the king have to trespass between himself and Rowena? She was his ward! She was his Lady. Henry knew this! What interest did Henry have in Rowena? Jealousy stabbed at his heart and he moaned as if in physical agony. Perhaps Rowena returned Henry's interest. Runnolf knew of more than one woman who had succumbed to the king's charm and suffered for it. Was Rowena destined to be the next? And if she were, what would happen to her then?

"She is uninjured," Corbert reported as he entered Runnolf's tent unannounced.

"In fact," Corbert continued as he seated himself upon a stool, "when I left, Lady de Vere was having trouble holding her own temper while trying to explain matters. Your lady is very stubborn once she has settled her mind on something."

Runnolf's momentary relief at hearing Rowena was well was replaced by a fleeting rise of temper. "What do women know or understand of such matters?" he demanded, the irritation falling heavy in his voice.

"Lady de Vere and Lady Fanchon seem to understand quite well the working of the court," Corbert defended.

The two men sat together in silence. Runnolf used the time to quiet his restless body, to bring his warring emotions under control, and to prepare himself for the meeting with the king.

The majority of the court had long since retired for the night when the summons for Runnolf arrived. It came in the person of a very young page, much in awe of le Geant. He stammered and stuttered, nearly forgetting the formal words of his message. Runnolf took pains to put the youngster at his ease so that he might do the king's bidding with proper decorum.

When the page was calm and secure again in

his duties, Runnolf allowed the youngster to
lead him to the king's presence.

Believing that he had been summoned because
of Rowena's behavior, Runnolf was surprised to
see Sir Aubrey and the king's other barons
present. Once he had been introduced to those
barons he did not know, he realized that this
had nothing to do with Rowena's behavior during the evening meal. He had not been summoned to one of Henry's informal council
meetings since Henry had left the Continent for
his coronation, and he experienced an unexpected surge of pride. The invitation was a sin-
gular honor for a knight of Runnolf's station but
one that had been accorded him often during
Henry's battles for his inheritance. Henry
trusted Runnolf's instinct for battle strategy and
knew le Geant would carry out any duty assigned to him.

Henry paced the floor as his barons helped
themselves to wine and refreshments before settling comfortably in seats scattered around the
fireplace. Runnolf selected a seat in the shadows, away from the majority, yet close enough
to hear everything.

"My lords," Henry began, "Archbishop
Theobald has asked of us a consideration. As
you might not know, the Bishop of Canterbury
held jurisdiction of Dublin, Wexford, Waterford,
Cork, and Limerick until 1140. The Archbishop
wants that jurisdiction returned and he has
asked that we assist him. He is so adamant in the
matter that he has already petitioned Pope
Adrian for his support also."

"One Englishman asking and another granting," de Beaumont murmured smugly under his breath.

De Ilchester was the first to ask the question that was paramount in most of their minds. "How did the Archbishop lose control?" It was hard for them to believe the tenacious man would lose control of anything.

"The people of Ireland are undisciplined and untamed," Thomas à Becket explained. "They rely more heavily upon ancient law than on Church Law, regardless of Christian doctrine taught to them."

"During the rein of my grandfather, King Murchetach O'Brien tried to reform their churches," Henry continued, picking up the explanation. "The pope sent a legate to hold a synod at Kells, but you know the Irish. They promise anything and then do what they want."

"King O'Brien even married his daughter to Arnulf de Montgomery, Lord of Pembroke, hoping to strengthen the ties between the countries," Becket interrupted.

"The Irish have many ancient customs," de Vere offered slowly. "What customs of theirs could the church find so offensive?"

"They recognize eight forms of marriage, as well as divorce!" Becket answered severely.

"Now that is an ancient law I would not want abolished," de Beaumont swore.

There was a general chuckling from all the knights, who had found themselves bound too tightly by the restrictions of the Catholic Church, especially where marriage was concerned.

"Are you considering a full invasion as King William planned for these isles, or are you considering a solution such as the Marcher lords provide?" de Beaumont asked.

"Neither and both." Henry laughed, self-satisfied. His barons were willingly falling in with his plans, and no matter what was decided, he, Henry the King, would be the winner.

On the one hand, he could invade Ireland, claiming all land directly for the crown as King William had done when he conquered England. Then he could reward his barons with land. However, with this plan he would have to finance part of the invasion himself.

On the other hand, he could allow the barons free rein to invade Ireland, with the promise that all land would be theirs as Marcher Barons. He would grant them the privileges of convening their own courts, coining their own money, and continuing to accumulate land by conquest. This way would cost the crown nothing. All expenses would be paid directly by the barons themselves.

"I have also received word that my brother, Geoffrey, is causing trouble on the continent," Henry added.

"Now what is he up to?" de Ilchester asked with concern.

"He has fostered the story that he is the rightful ruler of Anjou," Henry answered boldly. "That I was to hold it only until I had gained the throne of England."

"God's tongue! What gall!" de Vere whispered. Everyone sitting in the room knew the claim was false and that Geoffrey was using it as an excuse to steal his brother's lands.

"Certainly both things cannot be accomplished at the same time!" de Lucy exclaimed. "The land is not yet united enough for that. In a few years, when you have done all that is in your mind to restore the kingdom to its former glory, as it was under your grandfather . . . Then will be soon enough to consider Ireland."

"But you have enough knights sworn to you," de Beaumont argued. "Set them on Irish soil and let them fight and claim the land in your name as the Marcher Barons did for William at the time of the conquest. After that, grant it to them to hold."

His suggestion was greeted with avaricious smiles as the barons envisioned expansion of their fortunes.

"As the kingdom settles into peacefulness, something will have to be done with the restless," de Ilchester added.

"And the best job for the landless is acquiring new land," de Beaumont said, adding fuel to his argument.

Henry looked from face to face seeing agreement in all save one. "What thought have you?" he demanded of Runnolf, who sat quietly as usual, listening to the debate.

"I was thinking of the practical necessities, your majesty," Runnolf answered. And what he said was the literal truth, but the details he considered were not only the transport of the king's equipment and supplies. He was also considering the possibilities of taking Rowena with him.

"I think le Geant is planning necessities involving his ward rather than your troops, my liege," de Lucy teased. Now was a good time to put forth his thought on the lands near Chester, since they could figure prominently in Henry's plans for Ireland.

Runnolf actually blushed from the truth of the councillor's words, but no one noticed. He was grateful for the heavily shadowed corner in which he was sitting.

"I know she is his ward and he is responsible for her, but whyever would he want to saddle himself with that piece of baggage?" Becket demanded. "She is poorly disciplined and in want of a strong hand. He would be better off locking her safely in a convent and leaving her there."

Becket's words angered Runnolf deeply. But then, never before had he held anything as dear as he held Rowena. In his anger he levered himself out of his chair and took a menacing half step forward.

Becket was not a coward, but he did not wish to be challenged by the king's foremost champion. "I do not mean to chastise you, Runnolf," he added hastily in a placating manner. "She has been in your care for a very short time, and you have not had the opportunity to exercise the proper discipline. But once his majesty decides his course of action, you will have even less. It is time you considered a husband for her or some other suitable resolution."

Runnolf's face went pale as he slumped back

into his chair. He clenched his hands into fists, trying to control the panic that had entered his heart. Here was another of Henry's councillors suggesting marriage for Rowena. How was he going to prevent it without betraying their secret?

Thinking he had soothed Runnolf, Becket continued on the subject of a husband for Rowena. "A husband who is not beguiled by a young face and a ripe body," he continued sagaciously. "Yet one who is not too old to beget children upon her."

"Speaking of the Lady Rowena," de Lucy interrupted, "the question of her lands has not yet been settled. The land she claims lies to the west and south of Chester. His majesty holds the wardship of the heir of Chester and of his revenues. The Welsh have yet been quiet, but that is not expected to last. As soon as they feel a weakness, they will again prod and push."

"God's blood!" the king bellowed, striding up to de Lucy's chair and eyeing him suspiciously. "Sir Richard, stop chasing the matter and speak out."

"Grant the disseised lands to Runnolf, or make him castellan in your name. With Sir Runnolf in residence at Fitzgiles Keep, the borders of both lands will want not for care and defense. And if you go to Ireland, you will have a second supply line, through the port of Chester, secure of harassment from the Welsh."

"If you grant him the land, it will be extremely expensive," de Beaumont interjected. "He will have to maintain enough knights to patrol the borders, and he has no family wealth to support such an endeavor."

"But he can claim land and wealth from the Welsh by strength of arms," de Lucy countered.

"If you grant him castellan, then the crown will have to finance his endeavors," de Ilchester added, seeing which way de Lucy was leading. By giving Fitzgiles Keep to Runnolf, the crown would not bear the expense of its defense, nor the defense of Chester's lands, while still receiving the revenues from the wardship of Chester until Hugh de Kevelioc came of age.

Runnolf was at a loss for words. The king offered more than he had ever hoped. More than he had ever admitted to wanting. And yet he felt that if he accepted, he might be remiss in his duty to his king. Runnolf had always fought for Henry, and if the king was going to Ireland or to Normandy to fight, he should be by his side.

"My liege . . . if you grant . . . These things you offer," Runnolf stammered, unable to form one coherent thought. Still he plunged ahead, trying to explain himself. "I will not be free to accompany you to Ireland or to Normandy. Grant instead the tenure of the land to Hugh fitz Giles. Issue the writ in his name."

Runnolf's heart stopped beating for a moment as he waited for Henry's reply. He was so close to having his dreams granted that he doubted his own sanity.

"The Lady Rowena will inherit from her father and the heiress will marry at the king's will," Becket added, bored with the private details of one of Henry's menials. He was more interested in the fate of Ireland and Normandy.

"Or her wardship could be held by the king indefinitely," de Ilchester added. "Along with her revenues."

"I will have Chester's revenues and fitz Giles's," the king whispered, crossing his arms over his chest as he savored the thought of such revenues.

"You will still have need of a castellan you can trust," Sir Aubrey reminded them. "And the defense of the land needs must be paid by the crown."

"De Witt also seeks tenure to his lands," de Lucy added slyly, hoping to provoke Runnolf into accepting the king's offer. All knew the circumstances surrounding fitz Giles's death and de Witt's part in it. "However, his lands are not as far west as Fitzgiles Keep. If Runnolf does not wish the task of defending those lands, it could be granted to de Witt. A suitable marriage could then be arranged for Lady Rowena so Runnolf may accompany your majesty without hindrance."

Runnolf's head snapped up and he glared at de Lucy, causing the other to drop his glance. He had been prodding le Geant in order to gain the advantage for the kingdom, but he had nearly gone too far. Not only had he incurred Runnolf's displeasure but the barons as well. None of them wanted de Witt rewarded for his treachery.

Henry had been watching Runnolf's reactions as the debate progressed. He had seen le Geant's body tense at the mention of the land, a fair indication that he was interested. However, judging from his hostile reaction to choosing a groom for Rowena, this solution to the problem was apparently unacceptable. Mayhap the lady knew her lord's body well, but how well did she know his mind? Better yet, how well did the king know his liege man? The thought of forcing Runnolf to accept was distasteful and he discarded it immediately. If he forced the issue, it would not be the same as if Runnolf willingly accepted it. Once he willingly accepted, Runnolf would give it his all, expending both his own money and energies to benefit the kingdom. Henry needed Runnolf to accept voluntarily.

"I will grant tenure to fitz Giles and his descendants," Henry said, granting Runnolf's request without quibble. "Now, what of the lady herself?"

"All lands revert to the crown on the death of the holder," Becket reminded them as if he were lecturing pages and clerks. "If the crown recognizes the tenure of fitz Giles, since he is dead, the woman becomes the ward of his majesty. Even though Runnolf accepted guardianship for her, he was acting in the king's stead as seneschal. Therefore she is twice over the ward of the crown, and as ward, she must marry whomever the king selects for her."

Runnolf opened his mouth to speak but no sound passed his lips. He had gained what Rowena so dearly desired, yet in so doing he was now in danger of losing her as well as the land for himself.

Henry continued to watch the struggling knight. He knew how Rowena felt about Runnolf. She had told him so with words from her own mouth. Now Henry was fairly certain that in some measure Runnolf returned that affection. If so, this would be an ideal time to reward him for years of loyalty.

"It is not fitting that an heiress and ward of the crown should look beneath her station for a husband," Henry said in all seriousness, yet his eyes were alive with mischief. Of course this was not true; many an heiress had been married to a knight of lesser station to repay loyalty or valor or both.

"We shall have her marry the Lord of Peak Castle," Henry proclaimed merrily.

Runnolf turned pale at the king's pronouncement. He had gained Rowena's desires but he had lost his own. He slumped forward in his chair, his arms resting on his thighs and his shoulders hunched. And then he became confused. William Peverel had been Lord of Peak until his lands had been confiscated for his poisoning the Earl of Chester.

"What say you, my Lord of Peak?" Henry asked smoothly as he placed his arm comfortingly about Runnolf's hunched shoulders. "Are you not satisfied with the arrangements?"

Runnolf was not usually so dense, but he was exhausted from the emotional turmoil of the day and the devious maneuvering of the barons. Strategy plans before a battle were never this complicated. His body ached from the effort to control his emotions. It was as if he were fighting the fiercest battle of his life instead of sitting in a roomful of men. If he had not wanted so badly what the king offered, he would not have been so reluctant to answer.

"Come, come, my Lord of Peak," Henry continued to cajole. "One small maid cannot have given you fear when upon the battlefield all the fiends of hell have not."

"One small maid," Becket snorted derisively. "One small maid whose father never laid the belt of discipline to her back. One small maid who does not know her place. She will cause him more trouble than all the Welsh together."

"We agree with Becket," Henry remarked sagely, enjoying his friend's bemusement. "Maybe le Geant will be too preoccupied with the Welsh to manage her properly."

There was a long silence. All eyes focused on Runnolf while he struggled between duty and desire.

"What say you, my lord?" Henry demanded. The time for teasing was past. Now there was no doubt in Runnolf's mind who was Lord of Peak nor that Henry was determined to have his answer now.

"I have fought for your cause since I was a squire of Lord Avenall when he pledged support to the Empress," Runnolf said, sitting straight in his seat. His eyes, usually so unreadable, were filled with deep emotion as he stared unswervingly into the king's. "This was the first year . . . in many years . . . that I fought for you but not with you."

The emotions that plagued Runnolf were felt

in one way or another by all of the men in the room. Desire for land and loyalty to Henry fitz Empress warred with each other as Runnolf struggled to make his decision and yet feared to make it.

"What of you, sire? Will you not want me beside you in battle?"

Henry swelled with pride and happiness. His judgment of Runnolf's character was once more vindicated. Runnolf's loyalty came before his desire for land! "Want you beside us? God's strength! Verily, we do! Both as man and king," Henry swore, truly overcome with emotion. "But as king, we have need of your services elsewhere. You do desire Fitzgiles Keep, do you not?"

"Yea, my liege, I desire it."

"And the Lady Rowena will not be so burdensome that you would refuse marriage to her, would you?"

"Nay, my lord. I will accept her gladly."

"This will not make de Witt happy," de Ilchester interjected. "Nor the sheriff of Hereford."

"Send de Witt with the king's troops and let him vent his spleen in fighting for the king's cause instead of his own," de Beaumont added firmly.

"Then it is settled," Henry affirmed, smiling triumphantly as he looked around the room for confirmation of his plans. "My friend, I have wanted for some time to reward your loyalty. The land will keep you occupied and happy. From your reports, it is good, rich land with loyal tenants. I do not know if I do you a favor with the lady or not. Only time will tell."

Runnolf slipped to his knees at the king's feet. "My liege," he whispered fervently as he grasped Henry's hand and brought it to his lips. "I am your servant forever."

"Rise up, my Lord of Peak," Henry commanded as he pulled Runnolf to his feet and embraced him warmly. "The night grows old and time is short. With the dawn seek out my clerk, Odo. Have him draft the marriage contract to your wishes. On the day of the ceremony, the two of you will be summoned before the court for the signing of the contract and the granting of the land."

"I must tell Rowena," Runnolf murmured as he started to depart.

"Since we are now guardian for the lady, it will be our pleasure to announce the tidings. Until then, it will be our secret."

"Come, Lord Peak," de Lucy said as he gently led the bemused Runnolf from the king's chamber. "I have witnessed many marriage contracts and have written a few myself. I will help you draft your first."

The two men left. De Lucy was content that the borders between Wales and Chester would be strong with Runnolf in residence at Fitzgiles Keep. And he was fairly certain that Runnolf was satisfied also, with his marriage to Rowena.

The king and his remaining barons watched Runnolf leave, smiling secretly to themselves. It was a rare occasion when all were in agreement on a decision. In this case it was easy. They all respected Runnolf and were happy with his rewards, especially when those rewards were not at cost to themselves or to the kingdom.

"When should the marriage take place?" de Ilchester asked, breaking the silence.

"As soon as possible before that unruly chit causes more problems," Becket opined.

"The court leaves soon for Winchester," Henry said, giving them their first warning of pending departure. "The wedding should be before we depart. At Winchester, there will be too many distractions."

"But the banns . . ." de Ilchester protested.

"The banns will be waived and the king's chaplain will officiate," Becket stated firmly.

"Since I am now her guardian," the king beamed in anticipation, "on the morrow I will tell Lady Rowena our glad tidings. At the same time, I will talk to Lady Anne about the festivities." If something as simple as a horse and some gowns would cause Rowena pleasure, he could hardly imagine what she would do at the announcement of her marriage to Runnolf.

Henry yawned absently as he imagined the pending interview. And seeing the king's preoccupation, the others excused themselves.

Chapter Twenty-seven

✦✦✦✦

THE NEXT MORNING was a nightmare for Rowena. Lady Anne had allowed her to sleep off the wine and emotional exhaustion of the night before. Although Lady Anne had attended the first mass with her servants, she would also attend the last mass of the morning with Fanchon and Rowena.

As they followed Lady Anne to mass, Rowena felt every eye upon her, chastising her for the night before. She tried to dismiss them as being of no concern, but they lurked in the periphery of her mind, making her uneasy. From lowered eyes she searched the church for Runnolf. He was her priority; she must find him to try to apologize. But he was not in attendance.

Returning to the great hall, Rowena broke her fast with a slice of cheese and some watered wine. Her throat was dry and the food hard to swallow, but she forced herself, taking a tiny bite, then a sip of wine, again a tiny bite and a sip of wine.

As she ate, she searched. Again she did not find him. Guilt and fear suffocated her. She could not take a deep breath to stop her trembling without feeling as if great bands of iron were binding her chest.

When Lady Anne signaled that she was ready to return to the solar, Rowena was slightly relieved. At least she would not have to face the accusing eyes of the court, nor would she have to face Runnolf's anger. Yet his anger was pref-

erable to his absence. Wild fancies swirled in her
mind to account for it. He had abandoned her!
The king had banished him! He was with that
woman! And of them all, the one concerning the
woman caused her the most pain. If he was alone
she could search him out, no matter where in the
kingdom he was, and settle what was between
them. But she did not know how to fight the
allure of another woman, even a woman of the
fairs.

Actually Runnolf's absence was innocent. He
had risen early, attended first mass with most of
the servants and clerks, and was now with Odo,
dictating the terms of the marriage contract. At
first he had trouble convincing the clerk that the
terms he had set forth were not in jest. It had
taken de Lucy's presence and calm assertions
that all was correct before Odo would begin writing the document.

However Odo was scandalized by the contract
and refused to let anyone copy it but Andrew,
one of his older assistants whom he knew to
have a severe lock on his tongue. Also there was
a chance that the king, upon seeing it, would
disapprove and issue another. If that were the
case, he did not want Runnolf to suffer the embarrassment of everyone knowing. But beyond
his shock and disapproval, he was a lover of
theatrics and knew that this contract would
cause a sensation when it was read. The more
secret it was kept now, the better.

When that matter was settled to Runnolf's satisfaction, he left Odo to make the required number of copies and went in search of the king, to

gain what information he could concerning the lands of Chester. He found Henry in his chamber, eating sparingly from a plate of broken meats and cheeses while reviewing the documents drawn up by his clerks the previous day. As it always was with Henry, he was not alone; de Ilchester, de Beaumont, and Becket were with him.

"Good day to you, my lord," Runnolf greeted his king, when he was given permission to enter.

Henry greeted him affectionately, offering to share his morning meal with him. Runnolf accepted a small piece of cheese, but he was too excited for food. He was fighting with all of his heart not to make a fool of himself by grinning from ear to ear and shouting out his happiness from the parapets of the castle.

"How may we help you?" Henry asked as he set the plate back on the table.

"I came to discuss your plans for Chester's lands so that I may have some idea—"

"We have no plans as yet," Henry interrupted. "But why are you worried about Chester when you should be worried about the coming nuptials?" he teased.

"You have not yet selected the date, my lord," Runnolf answered.

"Two days hence. Have you selected the proper wedding garments?"

The blank expression on Runnolf's face brought chuckles of delight from the barons.

"We see you have not," Henry said, well pleased to be the font of knowledge for his liege man. "To a knight, clothes are a necessity to keep out the weather. But to a woman, clothes represent her status and importance. Her prime importance is in the whole estate of matrimony. No woman is complete without it. Therefore, your clothes must reflect your stature in my court as well as bring her honor at her wedding."

Henry sent for his own tailors. He had Runnolf measured and the fabric selected before le Geant could protest.

"Now, what bride's gift have you chosen?"

Again the barons laughed at Runnolf's discomfort.

"Surely there is something in the booty you have collected that would suit," de Beaumont asked, trying to be of assistance.

"I left all at Fitzgiles Keep."

"You have brought some gold with you?" de Ilchester demanded incredulously.

"God's brain! Do you think me completely addled?" Runnolf exclaimed, provoked at their condescension. "Needs must I feed and stable the animals and—"

"Take you into the town," Henry interrupted. "Search out some trinket to please the lady."

"Perhaps a solid gold chastity belt," Becket advised wickedly. "One that fits over her errant tongue."

Seldom did Becket allow his wit to travel to the mundane. He was always too concerned with greater things. But this time his barb was well suited. Rowena definitely had not proven herself to be what a proper young woman was expected to be. This ribald jest brought blushes to Runnolf and loud laughter from the others.

"Sir Robert," the king motioned to de Ilchester, "take our friend into town. Help him
search out some trinket or bauble for his lady.
Spare no expense. What he lacks make you up
the difference from my purse. He has the gold to
gift the people. Oh, and be sure that he finds a
gold ring, also."

Henry ushered everyone from his chamber
and then sent a page to summon Rowena and
Lady de Vere. He anticipated great joy in telling
Rowena of her pending marriage, but first he
desired to test her loyalty to his liege man.

The afternoon before, Rowena ardently desired an audience with Henry. Now she was
reluctant to obey the summons. The guilt she felt
over her behavior last night caused her step to
slow. She barely kept pace with Lady Anne as
they made their way to the king's chamber.

"Lady Rowena," Henry greeted her as he
lifted her from her deep curtsy in his usual
friendly manner.

Rowena was surprised at the king's gentleness.
She had expected him to be very angry with her
and severe in his punishment. After all, he had
every right to be angry with her. She had behaved
abominably in front of everyone, and she had
insulted his liege man and champion.

The thought that Henry might be toying with
her before punishment flashed through her
mind. She blushed at so uncharitable a thought,
dismissing it as unworthy of the king who held
Runnolf's loyalty.

"My lord, you sent for me?" she asked timidly. Her guilt would not allow her to look long

into the king's face, and she stared at the floor instead.

"Yea, it gives us great pleasure to inform you that a marriage has been arranged for you . . . to the Lord of Peak."

Rowena stood stunned, unable to breathe, as the enormity of the king's words struck her. Marriage! To the Lord of Peak! What of Runnolf? Was this her punishment? Worse yet, was this a jest? The blood began to race through her temples in such volume that she could not hear the king as he explained the necessity for haste.

"My lord king," Rowena interrupted while he was explaining to Lady Anne when the ceremony would take place. "Sire, you know I cannot marry the Lord of Peak."

"I know," he said, smiling magnanimously while patting her hand reassuringly. "But such things are easily overlooked for the right reasons."

"Does my lord Runnolf know?" she whispered, large tears beginning to collect in her lashes.

"Verily," Henry assured her. So far he was pleased with her behavior. There had been no gleam of greed in her eyes at his disclosure, no self-satisfying smile of victory. "In fact, he spent the morning dictating the marriage contract."

"And he has . . . no objections?" she asked, so softly that Henry had to lean forward to hear her.

"Verily. He wishes only the best for you."

Henry was touched by the deep sorrow mirrored in Rowena's eyes. Her bowed head, in what Henry believed to be acceptance to his will, made him slightly remorseful, and he determined to tell her the identity of her husband before her tears began to fall.

But Rowena's head was not bowed in sorrow and acceptance as the king anticipated. Her sorrow was only that she would have to defy him. She would have preferred otherwise, but she could not in true conscience marry the Lord of Peak. Because of her sheltered innocence, she believed that no woman who was not a virgin, except by widowhood, entered into an honorable marriage. Anyone who deported herself as she had with Runnolf would never be allowed an honorable marriage.

Therefore if the Lord of Peak was willing to accept her, knowing her sins, he was not an honorable man. If he was not an honorable man then he did not merit her obedience and respect. Therefore she would not marry him.

Had this marriage been arranged for her before Runnolf had complicated her life with love and lost virginity, she would have been obedient. She would have married, even if she loved another, and she would have died being faithful to her vows. But her life was not so simple.

Reluctantly Rowena withdrew her hand from the king's grasp and steeled herself. The muscles in her neck began to bulge with the effort it took to defy the king. Nonetheless she must. She raised her head, her soft brown eyes now glittering with determination, her clenched fist betraying her fear.

"My Lord Runnolf told me to speak always truth to you," Rowena began in a voice that vibrated with determination. "I spoke you truth when first I came. But you now choose to ignore it." She paused, mustering her courage to continue.

"I will not marry the Lord of Peak. I have pledged my heart elsewhere. Even if he were willing . . . to overlook . . . some matters . . ." She choked on a stifled sob. "I would not respect him and would not be obedient to him."

Rowena was not able to see the puzzlement on the king's face for the tears that clouded her eyes. And it may have been well she could not, or she would not have been able to finish her explanation.

Henry was incredulous at this turn of events. The only women who ever opposed his will were his mother and his wife. No one else dared! His temper began to rise as his surprise subsided.

Rowena had never been witness to Henry's temper, nor had she heard tales of it. But the servants who came and went unobtrusively were finely attuned to the king's every nuance, his every mood, his every move. His chamber swiftly emptied, no one wishing to feel any part of the wild storm that was building. A few charitable ones whispered a hasty prayer asking the Almighty Father's blessing on the foolish young woman who dared oppose the king.

Once Rowena had embarked on her trail of disaster, she was determined that she should tell the king about the injustices of his court and the people who preyed on others in his name.

"I came here seeking . . . justice for my father . . . and his people," she stammered, still unaware of her danger. Her voice choked in her throat from the effort to suppress her tears, but she stumbled on. "But I was told that I must always stay in your presence lest you forget your duty. I was also told that to hurry your decision . . . I must be willing to grant certain favors to members of your court—"

"Runnolf never—" Henry roared in defense of his friend. He could believe it of some but not of Runnolf.

"If gaining my father's land," she continued as if Henry had not interrupted. ". . . means I must play whore . . . I . . . will not disgrace his memory!

"My lord Runnolf promised that this would be a court of justice. But it is not. It is a . . ." She tried to continue, but she was too distraught, and Henry by now had worked himself into a finely controlled rage.

"How dare you say me nay in my own court!" Henry screamed, his face inches from hers. "In my own castle! In my own chamber! Will you, nill you, you will be married to the Lord of Peak even if you go before the priest bound and gagged. Even if I have to nod your head with my hand in your hair!"

"My lord . . . Runnolf . . . you know . . . I—"

" 'My lord Runnolf! My lord Runnolf!' " Henry mimicked angrily. "Runnolf is not king! I am King of England!"

Rowena stood before the angry king, her knees too weak from fear to obey her desperate desire to flee. She trembled violently from head to foot and her teeth chattered. Her face was as white as the barbette she wore under her chin. Her eyes were so large and her pupils so dilated with fear that Henry was concerned for her. However, his pride as king demanded her total submission.

"Lady de Vere," Henry bellowed with all the theatrics at his command. "Get this viper out of my sight! You will see that she is appropriately dressed for her wedding—tomorrow—between tierce and sext. Spare no expense!"

Lady de Vere curtsied hastily to the king and took Rowena by the hand to lead her out of the king's chamber.

Despite Henry's genuine anger, he had noticed Rowena's resoluteness. It had taken every ounce of her courage to stand before him without cowering. Courage, after all, is not being without fear, but controlling that fear. And courage was a trait that Henry admired, even when it was misplaced in the heart of a woman.

Because Henry knew people, he recognized that for herself, Rowena would defy him. But would she endanger Runnolf? He thought not.

Rowena screamed in fright as the king grabbed her by the arm and spun her around to face him yet again. She muffled any further outburst by biting on her knuckle until she drew blood.

"If you are not present—of your own will—properly attired, Runnolf will be the one to suffer for it," he snarled, his face only inches from hers.

It was a threat that held much meaning, since Runnolf was the bridegroom and she was in love with him. But Rowena was innocent of the knowledge. To her, she must protect the one she loved. She remembered that Lady Anne and

Fanchon had told her that Runnolf had no family
and if the king withdrew his support, he would
stand alone. He would be without his liege lord,
a knight without a shield or cause for which to
fight. Everything Runnolf had was his because
of the respect and esteem he had won in Henry's
heart.

"You will not, in any way, importune Runnolf
to save you from your fate," Henry commanded
and then paused to be sure she was not too frightened to understand his words. "Remember, you
hold his future, his very life in your hands."

When Henry was sure that Rowena understood, he released her arm and waved them both
from his presence.

Not pausing long enough for the formality of
obeisance, Lady Anne hurried Rowena from the
room. Outside, with the door closed, Rowena
nearly collapsed from fright, but Lady de Vere
would not allow her a moment of respite. Keeping up a steady litany of adjectives that blamed
Rowena's parents for their daughter's unnatural
behavior, she half supported, half pulled the distraught young woman to the solar.

Not until they were both safely inside and the
solar door firmly closed to the outside world did
Lady Anne allow Rowena to collapse. Actually
they both collapsed. Lady Anne was every bit as
frightened as Rowena. In fact, she had never
been so frightened in her entire life.

Fanchon rushed to her friend's side and embraced her, murmuring soft words of consolation that held no meaning other than their
soothing sound.

Pulling herself away from the closed door that had offered her support just moments ago, Lady Anne moved slowly and deliberately to the center of the room, allowing the two friends a few more moments of privacy before making the announcement of Rowena's impending marriage.

"The king . . . has arranged a marriage for Rowena," she said between deep gulps of air intended to steady her trembling voice. "Rowena is to marry the Lord of Peak. The ceremony will take place tomorrow between tierce and sext, followed by the wedding banquet. The king has given command that no expense be spared . . . to compensate for the lack of notice."

Her announcement was greeted with stunned silence. None knew the identity of Rowena's intended husband. But Lady Anne did not give them time for commiseration or congratulations. There was a lot to be done before the wedding, and not much time in which to do it.

The women immediately set about turning out more chests of material, searching until they found what they felt would be the proper attire for Rowena.

While Lady Anne and her women discussed the wedding plans, Rowena deliberately dried her eyes on the sleeve of her bliaud and returned to her sewing of Runnolf's clothes.

"Rowena, come. Put that aside," Lady Anne called. "You must help us with your gown. It will take all of our efforts to be finished in time."

"You have my measurements," Rowena answered insolently. "The king commanded you to see that everything be ready. I need only be present . . ." Rowena's defiance was choked by tears clogging her throat. "This will be my last time to sew for my lord and I will not be denied."

Lady Anne detected a core of stubbornness that sparked an alarm in her mind. She was beside herself with frustration at Rowena's incorrigible behavior. The compassion that she had felt for Rowena was fast disappearing. However, she made up her mind to leave Rowena alone, at least for the present. As long as she accepted her fate, that was all that was to be expected for the moment.

Taking one more precaution, Lady Anne allowed Fanchon to stay by Rowena's side, hoping that her presence might be a deterrent in case Rowena decided upon something foolish. Between the two of them, they could sew an entire wardrobe for le Geant, as long as Rowena was present and biddable during the marriage ceremony. Then she would be the responsibility of her new husband.

Chapter Twenty-eight
✦✦✦✦✦

DE WITT PACED his small room in growing agitation. The last of his informants had just left, miserly content with the earnings they had received from imparting a few tidbits of news. Nothing is secret for long in the king's household. However, the news they brought did not lighten his day as it had lightened his purse.

No one carried the tale of the king's late meeting with his councillors, since no squire or servant was permitted within the chamber. The meager glimmerings of news were from the clerks who made the necessary copies of the charter of tenure for Fitzgiles Keep.

"Is it that woman and her unruly tongue again?" a sleepy voice inquired.

De Witt was as always caught off guard by Coleton's catlike ability to move about unobserved and unheard.

"Yea, it is that bitch again," he snarled as he thought of Rowena.

"What has she done now?"

"Naught yet," de Witt admitted bitterly. "It is what she will do!" he added as he continued to pace the confines of his small room.

At any other time, Coleton would have played a waiting game with de Witt, but where this woman was concerned he did not dare. She truly was a threat to them both, and he wanted all the information he could gain on her.

"I hope you did not pay overmuch for old information," Coleton badgered.

"Information! I have gained more information this day, this very morn, than you," de Witt bragged. "Yet I know not what to make of it," he bemoaned in a moment of honesty.

"Mayhap you will share this information with me and I will place it beside my own to make the whole of it," Coleton prompted.

"Fitz Giles's whelp is to be married to the Lord of Peak," de Witt snarled. He was rewarded for this outburst by seeing Coleton's eyes widen. "Le Geant dictated the marriage contract to the king's clerk. The contract is so secret that no one but Odo's most trusted clerk will transcribe the copies."

Coleton was genuinely surprised at the news. He could not remember hearing of a new appointment to the lands of Peak nor had he yet heard of the pending marriage.

"There are some who believe," Coleton volunteered from his store of gossip, "that the king has set his eyes on the woman as his next conquest. If so, it would be a way of ensuring her presence at court. And by selecting the husband, the king would select one who would willingly look another way when necessary."

"She is also to be recognized as heir," de Witt added.

"The king's?"

"Nay, you fool, fitz Giles's!"

In spite of his outrage and anger, de Witt chuckled at the other's startled expression. It was not often, if ever, that he was ahead of his man, and he was enjoying the heady feel of it.

"If it is so," the other added, regaining his aplomb and carefully putting de Witt back in his usual agitated and disjointed state, "she could use her influence to turn the king against you. She could have you expelled from court or she could even contrive to have the king delay his decision on your tenure so that you languish at court, spending great sums of money to effect naught."

His words had the desired effect. De Witt was immediately thrown back to pacing the room and snarling about the injustices of life. There were too many possibilities surrounding the pending marriage for him to know which one to settle upon. But being a man who did not acknowledge his own blame in anything, he settled all his frustration on Rowena.

"Women! It is always women who cause problems!" de Witt raved in frustration. "She has wielded her way into the king's good graces and he has arranged a marriage for her to this mysterious Lord of Peak."

"If the marriage were averted—if the woman were to be eliminated, entirely—would not the lands again be unclaimed as they were under the first Henry?" Coleton asked, prodding for a way out of their dilemma. "Could you then petition the king for the tenure to your own land?"

The gleam of greed began to grow in de Witt's eyes.

"If the king were to claim fitz Giles's land upon the woman's death, you could then petition to be his castellan or even petition that he grant you the entire—"

"But the marriage ceremony will be held on the morrow!" de Witt moaned in frustration.

"With her out of the way," Coleton continued, "you would solve two of your immediate problems. First, there would be no one to remind the king of your association with fitz Giles's death." He paused to see if his words were having their desired effect. "Second, there would be no heirs to fitz Giles's land, and it would lie fallow and unclaimed, or it would revert to the crown. Either of these last two possibilities would open the door for you to possess your own land.

"Even if the land reverted to the crown," he continued, reiterating points that de Witt had already considered, "you would be able to suggest to the king that you well know the land and would make a suitable castellan while caring for your own land."

De Witt focused his full attention on ways to remove Rowena from the king's influence, thereby leaving him an open path to reclaiming his own land. He paced the small space of his room, racking his brain, seeking an excuse for Rowena's death as well as an alibi for himself. Slowly his visage relaxed into a smile of malevolent glee.

"Coleton! Bring me the groom Unwin!" he commanded triumphantly. Not only had he thought of a way but he had thought of it before Coleton.

"But he is near unto death," the other protested. "He is delirious and fevered—"

"What are you babbling about?" de Witt demanded irritably. "Did that bitch injure him as well as cause him disgrace?"

"Nay, the horse stepped on his hand and—" Coleton was given no time to continue his explanation when de Witt waved him to silence.

"Cease your prattle. He will be of no use to us," he muttered, resuming his pacing.

But Coleton did not discourage as easily as de Witt. His mind picked up the clue that de Witt had given him and continued to weave the plot. "Unwin may be close to death, but that does not mean he cannot help us with the woman."

De Witt stopped his pacing and centered his entire attention on Coleton.

"Send a page . . . a young one, too new to the court to recognize you . . . It must be late at night, so we have uninterrupted time . . . Have him tell her that she is needed in the stables . . . Once she arrives, we . . ." Here Coleton's mind lost the thread of his plot, momentarily engrossed in the uniqueness of killing a woman.

"Well, go on. What about our alibi?"

"The groom will be found nearby . . . If he is not already dead they will kill him. If he is dead, he cannot speak against us."

De Witt was excited by the plan. But he was not satisfied with the details. "For what reason would she be summoned to the stables?"

"She sets great store by that mare. And she has a reputation with horses. Would not the groom send for her if the horse were ill or injured?"

"What about the groom?"

"Iwdeal? He is another problem. He sleeps with the mare, trying to curry more favor with the king by impressing him with his loyalty."

"Bah! Loyalty will find him dead," de Witt snarled, more determined than ever to have his way.

"Two deaths will befoul the plan," Coleton protested. He had no qualms about killing Iwdeal, but his death might draw suspicion that Rowena's death was not an accident. "But needs must he be out of the way," Coleton continued as he wrapped and unwrapped a strand of hair about his finger. "We will knock him unconscious . . . then douse him with ale. It will appear he was drunk and . . ."

De Witt nodded his head in delight as their plans fell into place. Neither man could see where they left anything to chance, and both believed the deed as good as accomplished.

Late that night, after everyone else had retired, Rowena remained awake setting the last embroidery stitches on Runnolf's sherte. Fanchon had helped her with the seams of the other shertes, thus sparing Rowena the tediousness of the task.

Tears collected in Rowena's red and aching eyes, but after her incessant weeping there was not enough moisture left to fall. Lady Anne had admonished her several times that she would present a horrible countenance for her bridegroom, but she was past caring. She felt her life was ending, not beginning.

For the thousandth time, she relived the past weeks with Runnolf and thanked the Almighty

Father for allowing her one brief love before she was forced into a loveless duty. She cringed to think how naive she had been when first she met Runnolf, telling him of a brave young knight who would love the land and accept her to wife. How foolish she had been to assume that she could love freely. How foolish she had been to expect respect in return. Life was not at all that simple. Life was practical. Life was expedient. Life was . . . without honor, at least court life was.

And what of Runnolf? Was he truly without honor, or was he able to put it on and take it off whenever the situation suited him? Did his willingness for her to marry mean he no longer loved her? Or did it mean he had never loved her at all?

She had asked these and similar questions of herself many times since coming to court, and she still had no answers. The king said that Runnolf knew and approved of the marriage. That he had even written the marriage contract. That he wanted the best for her.

Even if he did not love her, he was at least trying to help her to a life of honor. And Runnolf would think a marriage, even though a loveless one, was the best thing for her. It was her own fault. If she had not made such an issue of her virginity and its price, and the need for marriage . . .

But what about her father's land and her people? What arrangements had been made for them? She desperately needed to see Runnolf, to ask him, nay, demand from him an explanation. But the king had forbidden her to importune Runnolf about the marriage. Why?

Rowena's tortured thoughts were interrupted by a soft scratch upon the solar door. She hurried across the chamber so that no one would be disturbed and opened the door to admit a sleepy young serving boy.

"Lady Rowena is wanted in the stables," he said, yawning. "One of the horses . . ."

Rowena's mind jumped to conclusions. Runnolf had sent for her! Throwing all caution to the wind, she hurried from the solar, leaving the sleepy boy behind. In her desire to see Runnolf one last time, she did not even pause to find or waken Owain but hurried across the great hall, trying to be careful not to disturb any of the sleepers.

She did not pause at the top of the steps but ran down them at full speed. Sprinting across the bailey, she entered the stable, heart pounding and short of breath. The familiar smell of animals and straw greeted her. The welcoming light from a small lantern was burning over Firelight's stall, adding to the lure of her dreams.

"Runnolf?" she called as she hurried down the line of stalls toward the end where the horses were bedded. "My lord, I am here." Both stallion and mare gently whickered in greeting, but no one else welcomed her.

Mayhap if Rowena had not been so intent upon her summons, she might have wondered why none of the grooms were about. But her mind only registered those things that affirmed her original supposition, that Runnolf wanted to see her one more time before her marriage. Neither of the horses was ill. He had sent the grooms away so they could be alone. Her mind sang and spiraled to new heights of fantasy as she desperately envisioned Runnolf taking her in his strong arms and spiriting her away from the king's control.

So intent was she on her dreams that she never saw the shadowed man who came up behind her and struck her on the back of her head. So swift and so vicious was the blow that the only thing Rowena saw was brilliant flashes of pain before her eyes that engulfed her entire head as she fell into unconsciousness.

As the man struck at Rowena, Leben screamed in rage. He reared in impotent fury and then kicked out with his massive hind legs when the two assailants separated.

"Make haste," de Witt whispered from the shadows by the stable door as he pulled it firmly closed. "She has come alone, but that destrier will wake the entire bailey."

Coleton half lifted and half dragged Rowena's unconscious body toward Leben's stall and propped her upright against the gatepost. Leben would not tolerate their presence near him, and he crowded the gate in an effort to frighten them away.

Taking up a hayfork, de Witt jabbed at the destrier, backing him away from the gate. "Ready? Now!" de Witt panted as he swung the gate wide enough for Coleton to shove Rowena inside.

Leben snorted, then screamed in bewilderment and alarm as Rowena landed on the straw between his legs. He dipped his head to inhale her scent, assuring himself that she was indeed his friend. And then he snorted angrily when she still did not move. He did not like this strange behavior of hers. Again he dipped his enormous head, nudging her inert form. However, this time when he inhaled he was seized with panic as he smelled fresh blood seeping from the wound on the back of her head.

The giant destrier shifted his weight, trying to back away from the confusing smells of friend and blood. He screamed in anger at his inability to gain freedom, rolling his eyes until the whites showed in the dim light of the stall. He was almost past reasoning, yet the smell of friend was stronger than the smell of blood, and the stallion stood frozen with indecision.

"God's wounds!" de Witt swore when the destrier made no move to offer Rowena injury. "Does everything go afoul where this woman is concerned?" Calling down every vengeance that his mind could imagine, de Witt climbed the gate and began jabbing at Leben with the hayfork, hoping to provoke the destrier into trampling Rowena to death.

For some moments Firelight had been snorting and stamping in agitation. She also smelled Rowena and friendship as well as the stink of hate and fear, and in her own confusion she began kicking the side of her stall.

"Haste! The stablemen are beginning to rouse," Coleton panted as he dragged the unconscious Unwin from the shadows and dropped him unceremoniously a few paces from Leben's gate. He blew out the lantern as de Witt took one last vicious jab at Leben.

In the dark, de Witt smiled malignantly as he heard the destrier's scream of pain, his giant hooves thudding into the straw of the floor. He envisioned Rowena being trampled and rejoiced at his accomplishment. Throwing aside the hayfork, he scrambled to safety within the deep shadows to watch the outcome of their deed.

The culprits had barely enough time to hide as the sleepy grooms staggered into the stables to see what had roused the horses. The newly appointed head groom swore mightily as he tripped over the inert form of Unwin lying in the aisle.

"Bring lanterns!" he commanded. "See what ails that black devil! Check all the horses, no telling what is afoul . . ."

"God's love!" shouted one of the grooms. "There's someone in the stall!"

"His master?"

"Nay, 'tis too small."

"Send for le Geant!"

By the time Runnolf and half the population from the castle arrived at the stable, they were greeted by a throng of milling, near-hysterical grooms. Over the din, Runnolf heard the agitated neighs of the horses.

"Silence!" Runnolf bellowed. "Your babbling has affrighted the horses!"

Runnolf's command brought momentary silence. And as if by one accord, the assembly opened a space for him. But the enormity of the situation brought almost instant disobedience as well when the grooms again crowded around him, trying in one jumbled voice to explain his summons.

In the few seconds that the way was open,
Runnolf was given a clear view of the body lying
in the straw before Leben's stall and of Leben's
giant head held high, his ears lying flat.

"My lord!" the new head groom cried, shoving his way forward. "My lord, we were awakened by the screams of the horses and came to
see what was afoul. We found . . ." His voice
cracked and his throat went dry, so that he could
not explain further. Instead, he held the lantern
high and led Runnolf to Leben's stall.

Runnolf's heart stopped beating and his blood
froze in his veins as he beheld the scene before
his eyes. The body of a child or woman lay on
the straw between Leben's hooves.

His mind spun and his throat locked over her
name. "Rowena?" It was but a small gasp coming from his massive body. His eyes took in the
sight, but his heart and mind refused to acknowledge it.

His most trusted friend, his most faithful destrier was standing over the body of his beloved
Rowena. The mighty destrier stood almost perfectly still except for the trembling of his massive
body and the incessant flicking forward of his
ears, desperately listening for the voice of his
master to sound again.

"How will you get her out?"

"He will have to destroy the destrier!"

"But how? There is no way without crushing . . ."

Voices babbled in the background of Runnolf's
benumbed mind as he stared in disbelief. He
was bereft of all feeling. Moments before, he was

the richest of men, possessing both land and lady. Now he was losing the only two beings of importance in his life. He must kill his first friend for killing his first love.

His morbid reverie was broken by a frantic scream from Leben. Runnolf focused his attention on the giant destrier as he dipped his head in agitation and again whinnied shrilly. Runnolf's heart raced in overwhelming fright and disbelief as he watched Rowena begin to stir. He had been so sure that she was dead that he could not, at first, credit his eyesight.

Again the destrier dipped his head, this time baring his teeth, and Runnolf's knees went weak with renewed fear. But the giant did not nip or bite as Runnolf anticipated, but plucked at Rowena's clothes in annoyance.

Runnolf's heartbeat increased to such a pace that the blood pounded alarmingly past his ears. He could not hear the sounds around him as he watched Rowena reach up to Leben, to shakily grasp him around the legs and to hold on to him as she tried to sit up.

"Silence!" Runnolf commanded, again taking control of the situation. "Do not affright him more." His voice was a dry croak, half of its normal force, but he was heard by all save the two in the stall.

A hush fell over the entire stable as all watched Rowena laboriously pull herself to a sitting position by supporting herself on Leben's front legs. Her strange behavior was causing Leben further agitation, and he screamed his displeasure.

"Hush, mighty one," Rowena whispered as she gently held her head in her hands. "Your voice is too loud for my poor ears."

"Everyone climb to safety," Runnolf whispered to those nearest him. "I must release the stallion before he does her more harm."

He needed say no more. Even Henry, King of the English, dressed only in his bed robe, hastily climbed to the rungs of the nearest stall while the grooms climbed inside with their charges. Others scattered for whatever safety was left.

"The doors are open," Owain called softly down the aisle as he and Norbert slowly swung wide the stable doors and then sought shelter behind them.

Slowly and without abrupt movement, Runnolf swung wide the stall gate, but Leben made no move toward freedom.

"Rowena, can you hear me?"

Rowena looked around from her seat on the floor, searching for the owner of the voice that held so much meaning in her life. For the first time Rowena was aware of Runnolf's presence and of the others who were with him.

"Yea, my lord," she answered in a pained whisper.

Runnolf's heart constricted in his chest and his bowels knotted in anxiety as she looked up into his eyes. She looked so small and frail sitting between the legs of the giant destrier. In the lantern light, her face seemed all hollow shadows. He could not tell how badly she was injured, but he could do nothing for her until Leben was out of the way.

"Can you stand?"

"Yea."

"Very carefully, move to the side of the stall. Move away from Leben before he hurts you again."

Runnolf watched in frustration as Rowena obeyed. He wanted to go to her, but he was afraid that any more anxiety would set the stallion on a path of destruction.

However, instead of crawling toward the walls as he had intended her to do, Rowena began to pull herself upright using Leben for support. She moved in half motion, leaning her weight upon the destrier, who whinnied shrilly and tugged at her clothes.

"Please, Leben," she scolded. "You are too loud. Be patient a moment and I will be away."

Once standing, and still using the stallion for support, she hugged Leben's neck and petted his cheek before stepping shakily to the wall as Runnolf had commanded.

Once free of Rowena's presence, the destrier dashed for freedom.

"Rowena!" Runnolf cried out her name as Leben sped past him and out into the bailey. "Rowena!" He nearly wept as he rushed into the stall and crushed her to him. Once she was safe in his arms, he could not control the tears of relief that coursed unashamedly down his cheeks.

Rowena sagged against her lord, her knees weak from her assault, but also weak from the emotions that welled within her. She babbled incoherently into his chest as she burrowed deep within the safety of his embrace. She babbled of her embroidery, her love for him, and her summons to the stable. But her words were too muffled, too disjointed and meaningless to those nearby.

"What were you doing here?" Henry demanded as he climbed down from his perch. "That black devil could have killed you!"

The king's strident voice broke into Rowena's dreams of safety. Without letting go of Runnolf, she turned her face toward Henry to defend her friend.

"Leben did not hurt me," she answered in confusion. She winced in pain as she felt the knot on her head and then stared in disbelief at the blood on her fingers.

"What brought you to the stables?" Henry demanded, suspecting Rowena of some form of deceit. He knew her feelings for Runnolf and would put nothing past her.

At first Rowena was not sure how to answer the king. She had been commanded not to importune Runnolf about the marriage, and yet she had secretly hoped that he would save her from it. She blushed in shame for her secret desires and her intended disobedience. However, she answered the king with the literal truth.

"A page brought me a message. He said something was wrong with one of the horses. I came—"

Runnolf would have interrupted but the king waved him to silence.

"Then what happened?"

"No one was here, not even Iwdeal. There

was a light over Firelight's stall. I came down . . . toward . . . I remember naught else until I was sitting on the straw between Leben's hooves."

"Where is Iwdeal? Does he not sleep with Firelight?" Runnolf asked uncertainly.

The head groom took a lantern and brought it to Firelight's stall. Iwdeal was lying upon a pile of straw used for his bed, with an empty pitcher nearby.

"Is he hurt?" Rowena asked hesitantly.

"Drunk more like," someone slandered.

"Nay, not him," the new head groom countered. "He is a good boy and takes the care of the mare very seriously. Besides, even if he were drunk, the noise of the horses would have awakened him . . . as it did many of us."

"All is not as it seems," Henry remarked as he motioned the groom into the stall to look at Iwdeal. He no longer suspected Rowena of misdeed. She had been in grave danger lying on the floor of Leben's stall. And he believed her claim that she had been knocked unconscious. But so far, he could detect no reason for an attack on her. No one would benefit from her demise.

"He smells like an ale cask," the groom commented as he felt for broken bones. "But I never saw a drunken groom with a knot on his head the size of a goose's egg from falling on a mound of straw."

"And whose body is that?" Henry demanded, pointing to the shadows near the wall.

"Unwin."

"Alive?"

"Nay, Sire. Dead."

The high, shrill sound of a human scream mingled with Leben's shattered the night.

De Witt and Coleton had been hiding in the shadows, waiting for Rowena's death to be discovered. But when she regained consciousness in the stall and still was unharmed, they decided to slip away.

Coleton was more fortunate in that he was able to mingle with the crowd of servants. De Witt, in his frustration and anger, tried to make his way around the bailey to the drawbridge and the safety of the town. But the shadows hid only his body. His scent was upon the air, announcing his presence.

Leben, newly released and with de Witt's scent fresh in his mind, discovered him amid the smells of the bailey. Fury blinded the stallion as he sought out his enemy to take vengeance upon him for his assault with the hayfork. Once detected, the fleeing assailant became as a hare to a hound. The destrier, using his nostrils, centered his attention upon the moving shadows near the bailey wall.

Screams of blood lust again shattered the night. In two or three thunderous strides the destrier overtook his adversary, knocking him to the ground.

"What is happening?" Rowena demanded as she was carried along with everyone rushing to the stable doors. She tried to shove her way past Runnolf, but he would not let her see out into the bailey.

"Some poor fool tried to run across the

bailey," de Lucy sighed, full of sorrow for the hapless individual. What he did not know was that they were witnessing an execution.

Curiosity for the morbid is in the nature of man and woman alike, and Rowena was no different. She tried to see past, but Runnolf pulled her close against him, blocking the sight of the destrier rearing to his greatest height and then falling forward, his massive hooves thudding upon the screaming man beneath him. Again the giant executioner reared, flailing the air, screaming his anger, announcing his vengeance, before falling forward to abruptly silence the agony of his enemy.

"There are too many things amiss in this matter," Henry repeated judiciously when Leben had ceased his vengeance. "We will have it fully looked into."

"Runnolf, see to your destrier before he causes more mischief," Henry commanded as the destrier began galloping about the bailey in search of new targets. "We will escort Rowena back to the solar and return her to Lady de Vere's care," he continued as he slipped his arm supportingly around Rowena's waist. "The night is chilled and we cannot have the bride fevered for her wedding."

Rowena tried to protest, but it was of no use. Leben needed to be caught and returned to his stall before another was injured or killed. And Runnolf was the only one who could accomplish the task. Dejectedly Rowena allowed herself to be led back to the castle. There was to be no time for her and Runnolf this night or any other.

Chapter Twenty-nine

✦✦✦✦✦

THE DAY OF Rowena's wedding dawned bright and blustery. However, the beautiful weather could not penetrate the gloom of the solar or lighten the blackness of Rowena's thoughts.

Henry had delivered Rowena safely into Lady Anne's care with a hazy explanation of the treachery perpetrated against her. Lady Anne and her women were nearly as distraught as Rowena over the attack. They fussed and crooned over their charge as they helped her undress for bed and tried to soothe her injured head with cold compresses. But they could not ease the pain in her heart.

Distraught beyond consolation, Rowena cried the remainder of the night, great wracking sobs that eventually dwindled into pitiful mewling cries like those of an injured animal. Finally she had cried herself to sleep, allowing those around her some semblance of peace before the beginning of the wedding day.

Before first light, Lady Anne called her women together to begin the last-minute preparations. In deference to Rowena's injury and grief, they waited until the last possible moment before awakening her. And then they were forced to wait even longer while she performed her last task of love for Runnolf.

Carefully she repacked the blue velvet material that was yet unsewn into Sir Runnolf's travel basket. On top of that she packed his newly embroidered shertes. She personally gave over the travel basket to Owain's care, with orders that it was to be conveyed into Runnolf's hands as soon as he awoke.

With that task completed, Rowena went to the farthest corner of the solar to pray. She prayed for salvation for her soul, the strength to carry out her responsibilities, the strength to say goodbye forever to Runnolf and to follow her new husband. No matter how much she wished otherwise, her future was sealed with Lord Runnolf's approval.

She desperately wanted confession but she dared not. Confession meant repentance and she was in no way contrite for the sins she committed with Runnolf. Nor did she know if, after her marriage, she would be willing to resist temptation if Runnolf should ask. With these sinful thoughts swirling in her consciousness, how could she be a true penitent? How could she beg forgiveness from the Almighty Father when she was contemplating future sins?

She shuddered, remembering Father Dominic's preachings. "Hell is a place after death," he had said. "A place where souls burn forever for their sins. Hell is a place of eternal flame that sears and scars. Hell is a place of no respite, no reprieve, never a final consummation."

Well, he is wrong, Rowena silently raged. Hell is now! My life is a hell of the living! A hell I have created for myself by allowing lust to govern my life!

"If only I could live these past months over," she sighed more despondently. "If I were to live them again I would not allow . . ." But the truth would not be denied. "If I lived them over, I would not change a day of it," she whimpered in honesty. "I love him almost more than life!"

With this truth admitted to herself, Rowena began her prayers anew. If she could not ask for pardon, she could ask for understanding. She now passionately prayed that the All-Seeing God, the Forgiving Father would look into her heart, see her love for Runnolf and would understand her weakness. She pleaded for Him to find a way for her to redeem herself. She could not ask for pardon, but she could ask for understanding.

Lady Anne watched Rowena at her prayers and her heart ached for her young charge. She was the overseer of this episode in Rowena's life, an episode that would seal her future to her unknown bridegroom. Yet that did not forbid her from sympathizing with Rowena's plight.

She mourned the recent loss of Rowena's father and now the pending loss of Rowena's guardian, le Geant. Too many violent changes in so short a time were bound to make the young woman rebellious. No wonder she fought so against this marriage. No sooner had she adjusted to her new guardian than she was being given to another, only this time in marriage. And there was no one who knew the bridegroom, no one who could reassure Rowena of her future.

Lady Anne wished that Rowena could be married to someone she would readily accept. Someone whom she already knew and respected.

Dreamily, Lady Anne fashioned a relationship between le Geant and Rowena that would have been built upon respect and obedience. Lady Anne perceived a bond of sorts already between them. Had not Fanchon talked Rowena into a new wardrobe by alluding to the fact that her present one would shame Runnolf? Had not the king gained Rowena's compliance to the marriage by threatening Runnolf? Yea, there were the beginnings of a great bond between them, at least on Rowena's side. And if Lady Anne were not mistaken, there was a rough fondness on Runnolf's part. It was a shame that the king had not selected Runnolf for Rowena's husband. That obedience could have grown into a strong marriage.

But now, in England, reality not romanticism held sway. And reality dictated that Rowena be married in a short time to the Lord of Peak. Reluctantly Lady Anne broke into Rowena's meditations.

Rowena allowed herself to be led to her bath, where she was disrobed. Like one in a dream, she obeyed the women, climbing into the tub and settling herself into the warm, deep water. She uttered not a sound as the women washed the dried blood from her wound. In truth, she did not feel the pain. Nor did she offer protest as her hair was rinsed with sweet-smelling herbs and wrapped in a towel. She sat passively as the women bathed her, then stood so Fanchon could wrap her in a towel warmed by the blazing fire.

Both Fanchon and Lady Anne became alarmed when Rowena began to shiver uncontrollably.

Despite her place before the fire, even with more logs added, her shivering did not stop. Her normally translucent white skin was lifeless, and her eyes were dull from her inner misery. The dark amethyst smudges under her eyes became even darker, and there was no trace of color in her cheeks and lips.

"It is fear," Lady Anne told them all as she began chafing Rowena's feet and motioning for the others to assist her. "It is fear of the unknown. It will pass."

Her words were said as much to encourage her women as to reassure Rowena, so that this strange new malady need not throw her deeper into depression. The silence in the chamber was deafening, yet none knew how to break it. None knew words that would console the grieving bride. Eventually warmth was restored to Rowena's nerve-racked body, and Lady Anne continued to supervise the toilet, making sure that no item was considered too minor to be done properly.

First the women put on Rowena's hose of softly spun cream-colored wool and slipped buff-colored shoes on her feet. Then they slipped a kirtle of soft silk the color of sunbeams over her head and tied the laces holding the garment close to her skin. Over her kirtle they placed a bliaud of dark, burnished gold brocade. The material had been the finest that Lady Anne possessed, and her ladies had done a superb job of making it into a magnificent gown. Next, Rowena's hair was carefully combed and draped around her shoulders like a mantle, to hang to her hips in sun-streaked glory.

Fanchon brought the wooden chest that had been delivered earlier and opened it so Lady Anne could remove the chains of gold that lay within. The magnificence of the bridal gifts brought ohs and ahs to break the silence and gave the women a chance to offer Rowena encouragement.

"Lord Peak must think very highly of you to send such precious gifts," Fanchon ventured as Lady Anne removed a circlet of gold and placed it upon Rowena's brow. However, Rowena's mind was too benumbed to comment upon the wealth of the gift.

"Fanchon is right," Lady Anne murmured as she held the double loops of gold to Rowena's shoulder. "Lord Peak places great wealth upon you to show his esteem. But even he could not imagine this to be a neck ornament for a woman."

Perplexed, she studied the chain for a few minutes and then wrapped it loosely around Rowena's slender waist. Once, then twice she wrapped it, and still it fell below Rowena's knees.

"Oh look!" Lady Alyce exclaimed as she held the ends of the chain aloft for all to see. "There is a double gold heart at each end of the chain."

"You are like a golden statue," Lady Anne remarked as she stood back to inspect Rowena's appearance.

There was a slight sob in her voice, which

touched a chord in Rowena as well. However, sympathy was not what Rowena needed now to sustain her through the coming ceremony. Concentrate on the practical, Lady Anne reminded herself silently. Any more kindness will totally unnerve us both.

"A litte powder under her eyes so she will not show her lack of sleep," she suggested aloud to the ladies as they also surveyed their efforts, looking for any detail that would detract from Rowena's beauty or the king's beneficence.

Fanchon hurried for a small case of the finest milled flour and brushed it lightly under Rowena's eyes to lessen the amethyst circles there.

When Lady Anne pronounced all to her satisfaction, each of the ladies came, kissed Rowena with fondness, and murmured some form of encouragement. But it was Lady Clare, whose words came last, that penetrated past Rowena's self-control.

"God grant you a kind and caring man," she whispered from her deepest heart. "If he possesses those two traits, all else will come with time."

Rowena was moved by her words and held her fiercely as if she were her last contact with life. She tried to whisper one last prayer to the Father before descending the stairs, but all she could do was babble incoherently.

Almighty Father . . . forgive my cowardice . . . grant . . . courage . . . grant . . . Lady Clare's wish . . . kind . . . caring . . . loving . . . Runnolf . . . Father help me! she screamed silently in her heart.

Lady Anne watched Rowena in her struggle for control. She saw her eyes cloud, threatening to send torrents of new tears to wash away the powder from under her eyes. Remembering how King Henry had used Runnolf's name to assure compliance, Lady Anne now invoked Runnolf's name to instill obedience and control.

"You do not wish to shame Sir Runnolf by your behavior," she stated firmly. "Pinch some color into your cheeks and bite your lips a little. At the bottom of the steps, pause, search out the king, and go to him, since he is now your guardian," Lady Anne instructed. "Concentrate on everything—anything—but what is upsetting you," Lady Anne cautioned as she kissed Rowena gently. "It will help . . . now and later."

In the grip of blind obedience that would not allow her to cause Runnolf shame for her misconduct, Rowena did as she was bid and then followed the women down the solar steps.

The throng of guests parted to allow the women passage through their midst. From the base of the steps, Rowena saw Runnolf's massive frame towering over those around him. She forced herself to ignore him. She could not look in his direction or even think about his presence lest she run to him, begging him to free her from her fate.

The quiet murmuring of the waiting assembly grew to gasps of awe at Rowena's golden appearance. Their approval gave her assurance that she was not failing Sir Runnolf. And that assurance gave her courage to walk slowly, deliberately, with head held high, toward the dais where Henry, King of England, waited for her with her future husband.

She was pale yet composed in her dignity. Her step was slow yet firm. Only those who knew her story recognized the strength it took for her to behave so. Her arms were still at her sides, and her small hands were clenched into fists, the skin drawn tight about her knuckles. Her face, usually a canvas of her emotions, was expressionless.

Following Lady Anne's instructions, Rowena noticed everything, beginning with the organization of the hall. It was arranged as if the king were sitting in justice instead of prepared for a wedding feast. The discrepancy held her attention for only a moment before it slipped away to the future, the unknown. For a moment she felt a raging stab of panic before she was able to force herself back to the present.

She looked for the king's councillors and immediately recognized Becket in his magnificent court attire. She saw de Beaumont and de Lucy, de Ilchester and de Vere along with some others. It took her befuddled brain a time to realize that Becket was not standing upon the dais with the king, but standing across from him amid the others.

Her glance strayed to Runnolf, who also stood across from the king but a little apart, a solitary figure who captured her attention. She experienced a deep pain, almost physical, reminiscent of those pains of warning she had experienced when first they met. She whispered a short prayer of thanksgiving for the warning and forced herself to glance away, to slowly search over those assembled near the dais, seeking out an elegant stranger who was to become her husband, one rich enough to afford her wedding gifts.

But all around her were familiar faces. Rowena began to cherish the hope that the king had changed his mind about the marriage. Mayhap Runnolf had persuaded him to cancel his plans. Self-deluded, she allowed a ray of hope to lighten her misery.

She tried to center her attention upon the king, but no matter how hard she tried, she could not keep her attention from drifting to Runnolf. The closer she moved in his direction, the more difficult it became, until finally she yielded to the temptation and turned her full attention upon him.

"Heavenly Father, do not let me shame him," she pleaded. "Forgive . . . Understand . . . No shame to him . . ."

She looked into Runnolf's eyes and saw his gray glitter of approval. Her heart fluttered, her blood raced, and color returned full force to her face. Encouraged by his approval, she continued her approach.

As self-assured as she felt in his approval, she nonetheless felt tremors of anxiety course through her body. She would not spoil things now with a major breach of conduct. She fought for control, trying to pull her glance from him, but she could not. In desperation she focused on his magnificent clothes.

He stood tall and proud, resplendent in a dark,

rich green knee-length wool tunic, under which
Rowena could see a sherte with dark embroidery
along the neckline. The tunic was belted with
new leather and elegantly buckled with the rearing stallion she had purchased for him on their
journey. His black chausses were held with black
cross garters, and he wore a pair of soft new
leather shoes. His look was subdued yet elegant
in its simplicity. Rowena's heart beat frantically
with gratitude. Everything about Runnolf's appearance gave her honor and approval.

From intimate knowledge that made her blush
crimson to the roots of her hair and the depth of
her throat, she knew that he had not possessed
those clothes before their arrival at Oxford. They
must have been made especially for her wedding! He could not have borrowed them, because they fit too well. A lump of sadness filled
her throat, blocking her breath, but the discomfort did not distract her from glorying in his
splendid attire.

One final act of defiance Rowena allowed herself as she came to stand silently before the king.
Instead of curtsying low to him as was expected,
she stood before him, her jaw tightly clenched
and slightly jutting forward.

The entire assembly was surprised by Rowena's behavior and murmured in consternation. Lady Anne's knees began to shake as she
vividly remembered the last time Rowena had
defied the king. Runnolf scowled. He did not
understand her. He had gained everything Rowena had wanted. He could not think of anything he had forgotten. Slowly he turned fitz

Giles's ring upon his finger, wondering what was amiss. He had thought of everything, even to giving her the ring that once belonged to her father, after repeating their vows.

But Rowena knew none of these things. Her entire energy was focused on controlling her fear and maintaining this act of dissent.

Instead of reacting with irritation and anger as she had hoped, the king smiled broadly. He recognized her courage and defiance in the face of futility. He took no offense at her disrespect. He understood her completely. She was truly a match for Runnolf's courage and loyalty. She was everything Runnolf needed to begin a dynasty on the Marches.

"You are well come to us, daughter of Hugh fitz Giles," Henry said, smiling. His smile was friendly, even congenial, lacking any sign of gloating or animosity. "May this day be the most memorable of your life."

Rowena's throat was locked by her effort of rebellion, and she could not respond to his greeting. Knowing her fear and sensing her predicament, Henry ignored her lack of response. He cleared his throat while shifting his attention to the gathering. An immediate hush descended upon the assembly.

"There has been an inquiry into last night's events," he rasped. "The man killed was Rolf de Witt . . ."

There was a murmur of confusion at de Witt's name. What had he been doing in the bailey? He had no business there. He lived in a small room over one of the local taverns. Even the noise from the destrier would not have summoned him so far.

"A man is now in our custody and is being questioned," the king continued. "So far we have discovered that de Witt planned the death of Lady Rowena. He is the one who attacked her, who shoved her into the destrier's stall and tried to blame Unwin."

For a moment Rowena forgot her fright in the mystery of her attack. Her own confusion was mirrored in the muttering of those about her. Why would de Witt wish her death?

"But why?"

Rowena felt rather than heard the deep tones of Runnolf's voice vibrate through her as he directly questioned his king. His anger and concern for her safety gave her heart reason to sing. She would cherish his continued concern for her in her heart of hearts forever.

"Why?" the king repeated after Runnolf. "Why is hard to fathom, but it seems that he wanted the Lady Rowena out of the way so he could have claim to his land and hers as well."

There was silent consternation at the king's explanation. It was incomplete.

"We will know more as the interrogation continues," Henry added. "What we do know is that he tried to influence our decision by conspiracy and sedition against our loyal subject." Henry's voice grew cold with contempt and warning. "No one influences us in such manner without punishment!"

The king paused, looking from one baron to the next, from one ranking knight to the next, allowing the import of his warning to sink into each and every mind.

"De Witt has been punished," Henry added. "Verily, his punishment fitted his crime."

The king held out his hand to accept a large piece of parchment handed to him by Odo. Carefully he opened it, allowing the tension to mount as he deliberately played upon the expectations of the assembly.

"I, Henry, by the grace of God, King of England, Duke of Normandie and Aquitaine, and Count of Anjou, make it known that Hugh fitz Giles is granted the honor of Fitzgiles Keep in total . . ."

Rowena's ears roared as the purport of the king's announcement struck home. Her father had at last been granted tenure to his land! She fervently thanked God for answering one of her most ardent prayers.

". . . and that Rowena, his daughter, is his recognized heir."

Rowena swayed as her legs became unsteady beneath her. She would have collapsed upon the floor if Fanchon had not stepped to her side to support her. ". . . his recognized heir." The words rolled about in her mind. Heir! What new, terrible implication did that word hold for her?

She watched in mesmerized agony as a young clerk of the king's household held a portable desk upon which Henry signed his name.

"Accept your charter," Odo called to her after he had hung the document with the doublesided seal of the King of England.

Her arm felt leaden as she raised it to accept

the parchment. The parchment itself felt like hot coals in her hand, and she stared at it, waiting for it to burst into flame. She had to fight the urge to throw it upon the floor at the king's feet.

"We are also here today," King Henry continued, calling her attention to himself and forestalling any impetuous acts on her part. "We are here to witness the signing of the marriage contract of the heiress of Fitzgiles Keep to the Lord of Peak."

Rowena's heart fell, along with her outrageous hope that Henry had changed his mind about the marriage.

"Odo, read the contract."

Odo stepped forward, and imitating his sovereign, cleared his throat to gain everyone's attention.

"Be it known that Rowena, heiress to Fitzgiles Keep, will retain all right and give justice to the land. The land and honor will be heritable by legitimate children conceived upon her body or failing any living issue of her marriage, that said lands and honors be heritable by whomsoever she chooses."

Rowena heard the words of the contract with disbelief. She had never heard a marriage contract read before, but it did not sound like anything she had ever heard her father or mother speak of.

There was a low murmur of protest from the gathering. Rowena, daughter of Hugh fitz Giles, was to control her own land independent of her husband. She could, by her own choice, select her heir. True, this was an old custom of the Saxons. There was also a Welsh custom that women held and inherited land independent from or jointly with their brothers. However, neither custom was generally sanctioned by the Normans.

Rowena looked over her shoulder at Runnolf and saw him nod slightly to her. This was his doing! He was still protecting her! He was also protecting her people against her husband! His kindness and generosity was not lost to her. She wanted to run to him, to thank him, to . . .

But Odo's voice called her attention again to the contract.

"And be it known that the Lands of Peak, Hadden Hall, and Glassop, that I hold in my name will be mine alone, free of any claim by my wife."

Again there was a murmuring of discontent, until the king's voice rang out to quiet them. He too was surprised by the terms of the marriage contract, but when he considered the two involved, he decided he should not be. After all, Runnolf was an honorable man, and he had brought Rowena to court to secure the tenure of the land in her father's name. Once this was accomplished, he would want none to think that he had profited by it.

Smiling and full of goodwill toward his two loyal subjects, Henry determined to stem the controversy he knew was brewing. With his public approval of the contract no man dared contest it.

"As guardian of Rowena fitz Hugh, I affix my signature to the marriage contract. And pass it to the witnesses."

The murmuring continued as the king, Runnolf, and all the barons present signed the copies of the contract. It took a considerable amount of time to sign the marriage document, since there were an unusual number of barons present who wished to show their support to the king even in so mundane a matter. Rowena used the time to whisper prayers of repentance to the Almighty Father. She had asked for and received everything for which she had ever prayed, everything except Runnolf. The king had granted the tenure of the land to her father. The king had arranged a marriage for her to a great lord. Runnolf had been able, through that marriage contract, to entrust her people to her care. And her new lord had been willing to accept the unusual conditions of the contract. She had so much, and she was ashamed that she was not satisfied.

She swallowed her pain and bowed her head in final acceptance. She must fully acquiesce to the inevitable. She would marry this great lord. She would be obedient . . . respectful . . . biddable . . . loyal . . . and faithful. She would give up her dreams of Runnolf and a life with him. She would seek confession, do her penance, on her knees in the snow if necessary, to become worthy of the honors that had been bestowed upon her.

This morning's events were the most unusual any had ever witnessed, and it appeared there would be more. Again the hall fell silent as Odo passed another document to the king. Henry, ever conscious of his people, waited for their complete attention before continuing.

"I, Henry, by the grace of God, King of England, Duke of Normandie and Aquitaine, and Count of Anjou, make it known that Runnolf le Geant holds from us the hereditary concession of Peak Castle, Hadden Hall, and Glassop. And likewise his heirs."

Rowena's eyes opened wide in surprise. Runnolf . . . Lord of Peak . . . her bridegroom! The room spun about her. Tears formed in her eyes and the king blurred in her sight.

"Merciful Father," she rejoiced. "You have heard my prayers." Her prayers were interrupted as Odo called Runnolf forward to do homage for his land.

Pride swelled in Rowena's heart threatening to burst the confines of her chest as Runnolf, in one great stride, came forward and knelt to Henry, his liege lord. In sober dignity he placed his hands between those of the king.

Becket also came forward and held above them the king's own sword, the hilt forming a cross, calling God as immediate witness to the homage about to be pledged. The gem-studded hilt twinkled in the torchlight, throwing glitters of color over the two men.

"Sire, I, Runnolf le Geant, pledge that from this day forward, as in every day past, I will be thy most faithful man. I will be so in all sincerity and without deceit."

Runnolf's voice, which was usually so modulated as to be devoid of emotion, now vibrated with sincerity.

Fast on Runnolf's words came the king's reply. "We do pledge to you, Runnolf, Lord of Peak, that we and our heirs will guarantee to you and your heirs, the lands held by us against every enemy with all our might."

Henry bent forward and kissed Runnolf upon the lips, giving him the sign of peace. Then he lifted his liege man to his feet. Taking his own sword from Becket, he belted it about Runnolf's waist.

"You are a great boon to us," he whispered huskily as the two embraced. "May your loins be fertile and your arm forever strong."

Rowena's voice was hoarse as she joined the assembly in crying "Fiat! Fiat! Fiat!" The sound, reverberating through the rafters and carrying to the bailey, was echoed by all those who held Runnolf in high regard.

When the cries had subsided, Henry clapped Runnolf soundly upon the back. "As the new Lord of Peak, have you considered an appropriate device for your escutcheon?"

Runnolf looked toward Rowena, his features softening slightly. "Yea, my liege, I have," he answered without hesitation. "I have chosen the rearing black stallion on a field of purest white."

Rowena's happiness knew no bounds. Her heart was swollen with unsurpassed pride. He had taken her design as his own!

"Well chosen, Runnolf!" the king exclaimed.

There were more cries of *Fiat!* as the assembly also gave their approval to Runnolf's choice.

"We still have to wed them and bed them," Henry bellowed over the noise. "My lords, if you will conduct the groom, I will conduct my ward to the church for the exchange of vows."

The king stepped down from the dais and waited while Rowena dipped into a deep, graceful curtsy. Henry smiled as much to her as to himself. He had won her obedience, and she would be happily obedient to her new husband.

"Are you not pleasantly surprised?" Henry whispered as he placed her arm on his and led her from the great hall.

"Verily, your majesty. Surprised and pleased," Rowena managed to answer quietly in spite of her excitement. She wanted to shout her happiness, to dance in ecstasy. But then she sobered. "But why . . . You knew who . . . how I . . . That I never would have opposed . . ." The audacity of her questions left her breathless waiting for Henry's response.

"What is hard won is more dearly cherished," he responded as he patted her hand reassuringly. "Besides, the whims of kings are best left unquestioned."

At the top of the bailey steps, Henry paused. "You have received much from Henry the King," he said jovially. "Now receive from the man, Henry fitz Empress."

Henry signaled to someone on the fringes of the crowd. Within a heartbeat, Iwdeal led Firelight forward. The mare was prancing and nervous with the closeness of the crowd, but she allowed her groom to lead her.

Rowena could see that she had been meticulously groomed. Ribbons of white had been laced into her tail and mane. She pranced and pulled at the end of her lead, showing her dislike of the crowd, but she did not bolt or rear.

Rowena's heart skipped a beat as the mare whinnied in greeting to her, and then Iwdeal led her back to the stables.

"I give her to your care," Henry said. "Train her properly, ride her as if she were your own. One colt in every three will be yours."

"Oh! My lord! Oh!" Tears flooded Rowena's eyes and spilled down her cheeks.

Henry grinned happily. So small a gift and yet so great a pleasure! Again he marveled at her as he led her across the bailey to the porch of the church.

Henry paused at the foot of the steps while they waited for Runnolf to join them. The gathering was anything but solemn as the bridesmen jostled and joked Runnolf along, then ushered him up the steps to stand beside the king's chaplain.

Rowena could not hear all that was being said to him but he was almost smiling. If her heartbeat was fast before, it was now erratic. She could tell Runnolf was pleased, truly pleased, at his king's command that he marry. And she was as pleased that she was to be the bride.

Runnolf held Rowena's sole attention, but if she had looked out amongst the assembly she would have been pleased that all her friends were present, as well as the barons of the land, to bear witness to her wedding. Norbert and Owain stood bursting with pride, ready to pledge their loyalty to their beloved Rowena and the new lord of Fitzgiles Keep. Blythe, Rebecca, and Mannfrith, as well as all the merchants of his guild, were also in attendance, as were Ferrand and Runnolf's other servants.

But Rowena did not see, nor in that moment did she care. God, the Almighty Father, the Doer of all good things for His people, had granted her most ardent prayers. She was to be Runnolf's wife! The mother of his children! The lawful Lady of his keep! No woman ever prepared to repeat her vows more humbly, more happily than she. No woman ever intended to be more chaste, more loving, more obedient than Rowena.

"Let him who is to give away the bride come forward," the chaplain's voice rang out over the merrymakers.

A hush began to fall as King Henry, in all the splendor of the realm, led a radiant Rowena up the steps to the porch.

"Let him give her to the man as his lawful wife," the voice intoned as Henry placed Rowena's hand in Runnolf's.

The world receded even farther as Runnolf accepted Rowena's tiny hand in his. The king stepped aside and returned to a place in the bailey before the porch, leaving only the two of them and the disembodied voice of the priest who spoke God's words on earth.

The chaplain's voice rang out over the hushed

gathering. "Does any person here now present know any reason that this couple may not be lawfully joined together in marriage?"

The hush deepened over the hundreds of people who thronged the bailey to witness the blessing of the bridal couple. Everyone strained to listen for a protest. There was none!

Dutifully, obediently, humbly, happily, Rowena knelt at Runnolf's feet. Her destiny was now to be his! Her happiness to be his! A wave of pride coursed over Rowena as Runnolf's voice rang out clearly for all to hear.

"As dower gift, I give to Rowena, my beloved, Fitzgiles Keep and all its demesne lands . . . to give justice in her name."

There was a gasp of awe at Runnolf's announcement that he, a knight of the realm, would grant so much honor to a woman, but then those that knew them smiled. Sir Runnolf was an unusual man and Rowena was an unusual woman and in that context it was not surprising at all.

The chaplain's voice again intruded, leading the ceremony on toward its conclusion. "Do you Runnolf and do you Rowena, consent to this marriage?"

"We do," they answered in unison.

Without prompting, Runnolf continued, "I, Runnolf le Geant, take thee Rowena, daughter of Hugh fitz Giles, as my wife."

They had been bound before by love in the privacy of their hearts, and with every word, with every act of the ceremony, Rowena and Runnolf were binding themselves more tightly, one to the other, in the eyes of the witnesses.

The priest blessed the ring that Runnolf removed from his hand. Very gently, Runnolf slipped the ring on and off three successive fingers of Rowena's right hand before placing it on the third finger of that hand.

Roewna felt the weight of the ring and for the first time she glanced away from Runnolf. It was her father's signet ring! Tears of happiness and joy mingled and splashed down Rowena's cheeks as she looked up into Runnolf's purposeful gray eyes.

And then he handed her a heavy sack of coins to distribute amongst the poor, and solemnly intoned, "With this ring I thee wed, and with this gold I thee honor, and with this dowry I thee endow.

"I receive thee as mine," Runnolf continued, his voice filled with emotion. "You are my wife and I am your husband!"

The assembly greeted his words with resounding cheers, drowning out those echoed by Rowena. But Runnolf heard and his heart swelled with love.

The chaplain turned and opened the doors to the church. They had been wedded on the church steps, in the sight of the people who would bear witness to their union for a lifetime. Now the chaplain led the way into the church.

Rowena slipped her hand into the large one of her husband. Feelings of security and safety engulfed her as his calloused palm gently cradled her soft fingers. Rowena was dramatically aware of the differences between man and woman, lady and knight, she and Runnolf, and she gloried in the feelings his towering strength engendered. She was totally committed to this giant of a man, totally aware of her responsibilities, and totally determined to be all things for him until the end of their days together on earth.

For the first time she could remember, Runnolf smiled, and that smile was meant only for Rowena, as hand in hand they walked to the foot of the altar where they knelt to celebrate the special wedding mass.

About the Author

✦ ✦ ✦ ✦ ✦

Joan Balser began to write short stories as a young adult. Although she was born in Washington, D.C., she and her family moved to Orlando, Florida. While raising three children and holding down a full-time job as a police dispatcher, Joan wrote her first novel. In *Passions of the Realm*, Joan has created a sweeping love story set in Medieval England during the first year of the reign of Henry II. Joan and her husband, Larry, also a history buff, travel extensively and are inveterate collectors of rare books.

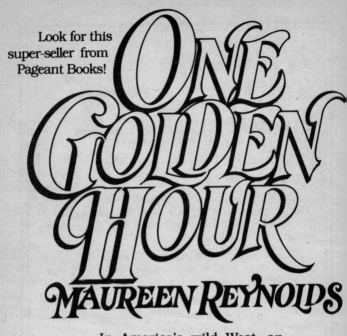

THIS SUPER-SELLER FROM
PAGEANT BOOKS WILL
CAPTURE YOUR
HEART!

Forever Yesterday

JAN LESOING

Annie Ellis is a lady's maid in her mistress's clothing,
but the outfit is a wedding gown! Coerced into a
marriage meant for her mistress, Annie leaves
Chicago for the sandhills of Nebraska with her new
husband. Their hardworking days and sensuous
nights soon evolve into grand passion—but can
Annie shield the dangerous truth of her identity? Or will her new husband forsake her to shield
his wounded heart?

ISBN: 0-517-00623-5   Price: $3.95

AVAILABLE AT BOOKSTORES NOW!